Children in the Night

CHILDREN
IN THE
NIGHT

BY HAROLD MYRA

ZondervanPublishingHouse
Grand Rapids, Michigan
A Division of HarperCollins*Publishers*

Children in the Night
Copyright © 1991 by Harold Myra

Requests for information should be addressed to:
Zondervan Publishing House
1415 Lake Drive, S.E.
Grand Rapids, Michigan 49506

Library of Congress Cataloging-in-Publication Data

Myra, Harold Lawrence, 1939–
Children in the night / Harold Myra.
p.   cm.
ISBN 0-310-57251-7
I. Title.
PS3563.Y7C48
813'.54—dc20   1991
91-10636
CIP

Edited by Harold Fickett
Interior Design by Ann Cherryman
Cover Design by The Puckett Group, Inc.
Cover Illustration by Marilyn King

Printed in the United States of America

91 92 93 94 95 /   / 10 9 8 7 6 5 4 3 2 1

CONTENTS

In our dark world,
is not each of us like a groping child?
Are we not all children in the night?

—ATTRIBUTED TO RESLINN,
FOUNDER OF THE ASKIRIT NATION

Children in the Night

Part One

Can a man live in darkness?
Can he hunt and make war?
In darkness, can a woman carve weapons?
Can she nurture her children?

The determined do so every day.

But in darkness, can men and women dream?
Will they sing visions
to nourish their people?
Will they whisper hope
to children born in the dark?

Will they laugh?
How will they laugh?

—QUESTIONS FROM THE ASKIRIT SAGES

Chapter 1.

—— The Child ——

The small boy hunched down, the sea lapping against his ankles. Reaching forward, he found a stone worn smooth and flat; he rubbed it back and forth on his fingertips. He brought it to his lips, then to the sensitive folds of his eyelids, moving it gently, as if the stone were a tiny, soft animal. In the total darkness of Aliare, smooth felt beautiful.

After savoring its texture, he stood and walked back to a circle of smooth stones he had placed with great care. He put his new prize in the one place remaining, then stepped with satisfaction into the circle's center.

Once again he squatted down in the blackness, safe in his circle of smooth, beautiful stones. He listened to the cries of birds, the buzz of insects, his father's voice in the midst of the talkative fishermen sorting the day's catch in their nets.

The strong, spicy scent of a bilkens root entered his nostrils. Carefully, he stepped out of his secure little circle and ran to his father. "Me some?" he asked.

The father laughed, holding a big piece of root found in the net. "So you smelled it way over there, did you?" He bit off a long piece and handed it to the boy. Yosha bit into it; the strong scent made his nose tingle and his eyes water. He walked to the sea's edge with its end sticking from his mouth; the root jiggled up and down as he chewed. He stood with his feet in the waves, staring at the sea, hoping to see a flash of luminescence from an eel or some fabled creature. But he saw nothing.

He bit down hard on the root, concentrating on a slight squiggling sound he was hearing in the waves. He leaned toward it; his hand darted out and captured a wriggling snake as thick as his wrist. It thrashed around his arm and across his chest, its tail slapping angrily against his belly. "Daddy!" he called out. "Come see! Come see!"

"What is it?" his father called back, his hands pulling oysters from a pile of small flopping fish.

"Snake!" the little boy cried.

"Throw it back!" the father shouted in alarmed, harsh tones the boy had never heard before. But Yosha did not throw it back; instead he clutched the coiling mass the harder as he heard his father's feet rushing toward him. "Yosha, throw it back!" he heard again and felt the snake being yanked from his hands and then heard its body hit out in the waters. His father's big hands slid down his arms as he asked, "Did it bite you?"

The child did not answer. The father said, "Snakes can be poisonous! I've told you that!" He hugged the boy as his hands ran over his body in search of broken skin. "Stay away from snakes. Some are smaller than your finger and others bigger than you are, but any of them could hurt a little boy like you."

"You held a snake once, Daddy."

"But it wasn't poisonous. That kind only spits."

"Was mine poisonous?"

"Maybe."

The boy touched his father's belt, his fingers traveling over the ridges of the pouches sewn all along its length. "Are the keitr in your belt poisonous?"

"You know they are."

"Are the eels that glow poisonous?"

"No. Nothing with light is poisonous. But watch out for their teeth!"

The child pulled at his father's belt. "Daddy, I want to go to the light above—right now. Let's go see it."

His father sighed. "Some day we will. It is promised."

"No, now!" he insisted. "Let's go see the light now!"

The father hugged the boy again. "The light is coming. Some day we will find the way to it. But now we have the sparks from flints and the sounds of the sea. We have the soft little choi to hold and the music of the birds to awaken us." Yosha felt his father's fingers at his lips, lifting the corners into the shape of a smile. He reached up to his father's face with both bands and found the deep creases his broad smile.

"Some day, we'll see the light," his father promised.

The Boy

Yosha swam down deep beneath the surface of the sea. He was to receive absolution this day, and he was trying to ready his spirit for the Rite of Purification. He grasped a familiar boulder and propelled himself yet deeper, eyes open, searching for luminescents. A few luminous minnows punctuated the blackness, but he longed for a greater light to nourish his eyes. He needed to rise for air; still, he peered into the depths, straining to see more. He was as deep as he'd ever gone.

He gave up and kicked off from an encrusted boulder. Just then a band of light caused him to jerk his head toward it. His body continued to rise as he passed a motionless fish the size of his leg, glowing yellow-green and motionless. He pushed his hands up against the water to stop his ascent, but at his movements, the fish darted away.

As Yosha resumed his rise to the surface, he tried to retain the impression of light, squeezing his eyes to mix it with colors.

He rose dripping from the shore to stand in Aliare's familiar darkness. Far above him was the roof of his world, sealing Aliare from the light. Behind him was the vast sea. Under his feet was aceyn, the thick, fibrous sea plant that through the aeons had extended its thick carpet over the barren rocks. Into it had come sea nutrients, and then earthworms and insects—all manner of food for birds and burrowing mammals and, therefore, the Askirit peoples. On these shores villagers labored over the day's catch, fashioned clothing, bought and sold goods. But each night the great storms of sierent swept away anything left on the shores. The people of his village of Wellen retreated to their caverns above the shore where, in countless tunnels and grottoes, they made their homes and workshops. The aceyn had entered even the caverns, bringing its pleasant scent and its foods and life.

Except for sparks from flints and the glow of luminous creatures, no one in Aliare had ever seen light. But the Askirit believed in it and sang of it. They believed their Creator lived in light and, indeed, was light. They used their ancestors' words, "day" and "night." But day had no light. Day was when the sea was calm; night was the time of violent storms, which made their world too damp for fire.

Yosha began climbing toward the caverns, his feet edging forward in gentle arcs, soles tipped slightly inward so they would not stub but graze the trail. He sniffed the sea and village odors and listened to the sounds of people, birds and small animals. His hands, feet, and sides touched the configurations of water-shaped stone all about him.

He entered the caverns, feeling his way past numerous workshops and tunnels leading to personal dwellings; then he descended a wide passageway to its depth. The other boys were already standing in front of an apprentice priest, who said as Yosha entered, "Geln, lead the prayer of supplication."

One of the boys prayed, "We seek your light, Maker of worlds. Purify us."

"Yosha," he heard, "recite 'Creation.'"

The sacred liturgy of his people came easily to Yosha's lips. He recited:

"In the beginning, the world above was bathed in light. But Eshtel brought judgment. A great sphere struck the planet, breaking apart continents, shattering civilizations.

"The world became void; a thick dust covered the surface.

"Eshtel moved again, creating a new world. Waters rushed into deep fissures in the planet's crust, gouging out canyons and peaks, shaping a new land in the hollows beneath the surface.

"This new world he called 'Aliare.'

"As the planet moved on its axis, torrents from the sea plummeted deep into the chasms. This he called 'ute.'

"As the planet turned, the waters reversed direction, exploding up and out. This he called 'kelerai.'

"The reversal of ute and kelerai caused violent storms to engulf all of Aliare. This he called 'sierent.'"

Yosha finished his part, but his mind remained on that last word. Why had Eshtel created sierent? Villagers had been swept away by it to certain destruction. Yet Yosha also loved sierent. How marvelous it was to huddle in the caverns, safe, listening to its furious pounding and roaring all through the night. He thought of another statement from the ritual: "Eshtel's doings mystify even the wise."

The apprentice priest gave another command. "Bles," he said, "recite 'Judgment and Mercy.'"

Bles recited:

"When judgment rent the world, Eshtel saw that many fell into the darkness below. On them he had pity, and he gave them water, and in it the creatures of the sea for their needs. The water he called 'esseh.'

"Eshtel saw their despair and gave them flint for sparks. He said to those filled with longing and hope, 'Out of the wreckage comes life. Seek the way to the light.' And those who obeyed he called 'Askirit,' and their land he called Tarn.

"Open your ears, then. Declare the ancient promises. Carry

the light throughout Aliare. Let every Askirit in the kingdom of Tarn seek mercy and purity and light."

The boys then responded, "We seek mercy and purity and light."

Yosha thought it ironic Bles had been chosen to recite, for Bles sought none of these things, particularly mercy.

The apprentice priest canted the final phrases: "Praise the Maker. Praise him for Aliare, our world. For Tarn, our nation. For our people, the Askirit; may he make each of us holy."

Then the boys lined up in front of the inner sanctuary. When the leather curtains parted, Yosha's nostrils flared at the smell of dried blood. He stepped forward with a holy expectancy.

They formed a semi-circle; the priest asked, "What evil have you done?"

The boys responded in unison, "We have not sought the light."

"The requirement is blood," the priest announced. He stepped to Yosha, gripped his wrist firmly and pressed the boy's hand against the face of a small animal called a choi. Yosha felt its cold nose on his palm; with his fingertips he traced the fur on the bony ridges around its eyes, then felt the fluttering lashes. His fingers moved in the required circular motion on the beast's eyelids.

"Where is the light?" the priest asked.

Yosha clenched the choi so tightly that the startled priest eased his grip on the boy's wrist.

Yosha exclaimed fervently, "I seek the light, but I fail to see it!"

His loud exclamation startled the priest; the man hesitated, then moved on to the other boys. Each now responded with the same words as Yosha had, but in a perfunctory way.

After they had all touched the animal's eyes and confessed their guilt, the priest killed the choi with a knife. Then he scattered a handful of blood across the width of the cave.

Yosha set his face, anticipating the droplets. They hit his cheeks like the warm spray of waves at midday.

"The guiltless animal dies," the priest intoned. "Only in purity can you live to face the terrors of darkness." The priest's coarse beard rubbed Yosha's cheek as the old man bent close and recited the ancient words: "When broken and ravaged, set your face like a rock. Seek the light. Break the teeth of your enemies."

The priest moved to each boy in turn. Yosha felt impatient to put these ritual words to the test. Set my face like a rock, he thought. Yes!

Yosha was again aware of the warm breath and beard of the priest before he heard him pronounce, "Eshtel's light nourishes your eyes." The priest then instructed him solemnly, "Lift up your strong arms. Never flinch, not from the jaws of leviathan himself!"

The priest stepped to the choi and began cutting the carcass. After a moment he rose, and Yosha felt the old man's fingers pushing a small portion of the warm flesh between his teeth. He did this with each boy, then pronounced them absolved of their impurities.

As Yosha emerged from the cavern, he heard the other boys hurry off. Yosha stood, still chewing on the raw flesh. He enjoyed feeling the holy energies coursing through him as he stood on the trail.

A man bumped into the boy. Yosha tried to edge away, for he avoided adults. But the man asked, "Kret?"

The name meant "the wild." Yosha had earned it by his frenzied attacking style in the game of bokk when trying to capture the slippery leather ball. Playing in the darkness, the boys could try anything short of detectable violence like biting, clawing, or choking. Yosha prized the nickname, but he refused to answer to it.

The villager, annoyed, snapped his fingers at him and said, "Kret, speak up when you're spoken to!" Then, not waiting for an answer, the man stalked off.

Some adults, remembering how his father's death had changed him, spoke more kindly to Yosha. But most believed the children's nasty tales about the orphan; he was used to hearing his nickname spat out like a bad piece of fish. Kret!

—— War Games ——

The boys went from their monthly Rite of Purification directly into their war games. Yosha, eager to begin, arrived first at the intersection of trails in the hills above Wellen. He checked again each seam of the ten pouches on his belt. Generations ago, the Askirit had devised a method to teach the boys to handle these pouches with great respect. Their pouches did not hold deadly keitr like those on a man's belt, but each was filled with a foul-smelling liquid drawn from the glands of a deep-water crustacean. A leak on a boy's clothes made him a laughing-stock.

During their war games, the boys attempted to inflict this ignominy on opponents. Hearing a foe in the darkness, a boy would launch the bag of odious liquid with his sling, much as a man launched a keitr. Splattering widely, the stink marked an opponent as "dead."

Yosha sat on the aceyn, his snug leather clothing bending easily with his body. He adjusted, just above his ankle and therefore far from the pouches, the sheath of his malc. The one real weapon the boys carried, the malc was actually two blades, its handle identical to its second blade. In the darkness, the malc was sent end over end so that however it hit, the blade would slash. Today, however, it would stay in its double sheath.

Other boys arrived and Yosha stood as Kark, the man charged with the orphans' care, strode up and ordered them to stand for inspection. Kark took great pride in the boys and drove them hard. Daily he drilled them, barking orders as they traversed obstacle courses. He instructed them constantly on the use of voice and whistles as signals and as diversions. He taught them echo-location clicks and yelps, but emphasized how their enemies could turn those tactics against them. "Cast a stone to get the echo," he would say, "but watch the swish of your clothes, and don't think when it strikes they can't figure out where it came from." He told them stories of barbarians waiting half a day for an Askirit soldier to make the first move.

Kark inspected their weapons and gear, then stopped in front of Yosha. "Describe the trails," he ordered.

Yosha was pleased to be chosen. The word map lay embedded in his memory; he described every turn of every trail and formation ahead.

Kark then reviewed tactics and the pace he would set. From many villages, squads of boys would climb swiftly, trying to beat the others to their objective: a caged pencray. The large bird was the Askirit nation's symbol, a predator with a great wingspan, which soared above the crags of Tarn. The several hundred boys and young men would attempt to free it and let the pencray soar again—but they must do so without being splattered by an opponent's projectile.

"Never fire unless you're sure of a target," Kark said. "You're listening for clues, for reverberations of feet, for a shoulder rubbing against an outcropping—so don't give clues yourself. Absolute silence! And no scents on this sortie; I'll break open mine only to signal a regrouping. But don't expect it. Silent speed. Silent speed. Listen. Listen."

At Kark's whistle, they moved quickly up their assigned trails.

Alone, Yosha rapidly gained altitude. He loved the crags as he loved the sea, feeling the brisk breezes and the sounds of different birds from those near the waters. Hugging the cliffs, he made himself as small a target as possible. He gripped his sling tightly, the pouch secured, but he was less interested in using it to score on someone else than in freeing the bird. Yet he couldn't rush ahead—he had to follow Kark's assigned pace. He wished he were out here on his own, fighting real enemies, for death did not seem to him so ominous with the ritual promises ringing in his ears.

His trail opened into a wide valley with no protection on either side. Here opponents could cross from any number of other trails, or criss-cross trails to intercept opponents. He bent low and kept moving briskly until in mid-stride he heard something off to his right, the swish of someone's arm flinging something.

He stopped instantly and crouched into a tight little ball. A projectile splattered on the trail ahead, the stink filling the air. He remained tightly crouched, dismayed. The stuff had been flung from a location where a member of his squad should have been. He waited a long time before he moved forward again, giving the stink on the trail a wide berth.

From a point above him and ahead, an exultant cry went up. Almost immediately came shouts of triumph from a squad from another village; they must have moved a bit more recklessly, on trails a bit more exposed. Now many shouts went up and he thought he heard the cry of the bird as it was freed, but perhaps it was the boys imitating the pencray's thrilling cry. He moved quickly now, the sortie over, anxious to join the others at the empty cage.

To the triumphant squad was given a pencray carved from stone. Then the boys competed in endurance tests, climbed knotted ropes, and finally sang patriotic songs. All the while, Yosha wondered who had thrown the projectile at him. Kark often warned them about friendly fire, saying, "It's too easy to hit your friends by mistake." But who could have made that "mistake"?

At evening in the village, Kark insisted the boys finish off the day with a game of bokk. Most of the boys were weary and played without vigor. But Yosha again earned his nickname of "Kret." He played fiercely, throwing his body at the ball and at all obstacles, lashing out when it slipped from his arms, retrieving it in a frenzy, and carrying it off like a mother protecting its young. He was sweating profusely when they were dismissed, and alone he ran into the sea and started swimming with abandon out to the large waves.

—— The Dream ——

Yosha was six again, and his father was holding his hand, their fingers intertwined as they groped their way through the darkness along the edge of the sea. They were singing softly, hunting game birds with their nets, but mostly enjoying the sounds of the water and the sea air.

Suddenly his father squeezed Yosha's hand painfully hard. The small boy was yanked forward. The father quickened the pace, hurting Yosha's fingers. "Quickly," his father said. "Be bold, Yosha!"

Then Yosha heard the thunderous Whap! of a gigantic body crashing at their feet, and his father crying, "Help me! Yosha, help me—now!"

What! Whap! Whap! The mountainous body shook the ground, shook Yosha's bones, but Yosha could not move to help his father. Then gigantic teeth smashed upon their intertwined hands and took Yosha's fingers and all of his father into the massive, repugnant maw.

Yosha swung with his other hand at the wall of teeth, the pain of his severed fingers pulsating up his arm. The great teeth opened again, rose above him, and he screamed aloud.

He awoke and jammed the scream back down his throat. But it was too late; the other boys were sure to have heard. The dream still vivid in his mind, he pulled his trapped arm from under his body and lifted it. No feeling, no movement—it was like handling the severed tentacle of an octopus. Blood rushed into the freed arm; pinpricks of pain slowly brought it alive again. Yosha flushed. He knew the humiliation would begin once more, as it always did after a nightmare when he cried out.

When his father had been taken by Kjotik, Yosha had been on the other side of the village. But he had heard the terrifying whaps that had shaken the rock beneath him. Always in the nightmares that awful mouth and those teeth took his father from him. Always he lacked the power to save him.

The five other boys in the room with him were also orphans. He knew they, too, had their dreams and nightmares, but he was the only one unlucky enough to cry aloud.

They kept quiet. Maybe this time he would escape their teasing.

The silence was finally broken by a forced burp. After another long silence came a suppressed giggle. Then another burp ... and another ... then more silence, a series of burps, and finally all five boys burping like croaking frogs, burping to imitate Kjotik swallowing his father.

Yosha pursed his lips tightly, then bit them. He would not react this time, as he always did. He fought the urge to throw himself at them and claw at their throats. His attacks always ended with their wrenching him to the rock floor and slamming his head against it. It was not the memory of those five pounding on him that kept him from attacking just now. New thoughts had been growing in his mind. He stifled his rage, letting it fuel his new determinations.

The boys were belching loudly now, taunting him, and starting in on their cruel ditty that never failed to enrage him.

Burp, burp, gulp, slurp
he's down, down, down,
BURP
Burp, burp, slurp, slurp

he's down, down, down,
BURP

Yosha grimaced at their buffoonery. He clenched his fists
with all his strength. He willed himself motionless even as he
longed to choke their throats.

"Itchworm, don't sob!" Bles taunted.

The boys never called him Yosha or Kret, only Itchworm—
for a parasite that had once caused itchy scabs all over his body.
The scabs were gone, but not the name. "Itchy," Bles said with
mock concern, leading the other boys to his bed, "tell us about
your nightmare." They all hovered over him, clucking, "An
orphan! Poor child! Poor terrified child!"

"What did you do in your nightmare?" Bles demanded.
"Did you run like an insect? Did you grovel?"

Yosha hated the way the nightmares alerted them to his
fears. Voices in his mind clamored at him. Some said, "Dig your
fingernails into Bles's eyes! Quickly! Quickly! Maim him before
they can knock you away." These voices also said, "Hate Kjotik!
Hate those who laugh! Their obscenity is a stench to your father.
Gouge their eyes!"

Quieter voices said, "Get power within. Grasp the Holy like
a rope in the sea."

Yosha lay still as a stone while the voices within clashed and
the boys taunted. He clenched his teeth, seeking the flickers of
light in his dreams. He forced himself to listen to the quieter
voices, knowing that striking back would mean only greater
humiliation. He forced his body to lie quietly and his mind to seek
the light.

In these moments of restraint—of choosing the quieter
voices—the legend of Yosha began. The taunts of the boys forced
him to choose. He could let the chaotic voices within take control,
or he could resist and embrace the promises. Long after the other
boys had finally returned to their sleep, he was still wide awake,
sensing new shapes within his inner chaos.

—— Bones ——

Yosha moved with his usual agility, feet probing the darkness ahead and to the sides, arms flowing forward like a swimmer to touch obstacles and locate his position. Yosha knew exactly where he walked by the path's grade and its curves, by the ridges and depressions under his feet. He could even mark his progress by the scents and sounds from the nearby water.

The crags and cliffs of Tarn had been shaped by the pounding waters of sierent: water blasted through shafts, sprayed through fissures, swirled through gulleys. All of Tarn was a wonder of bizarre configurations; cones, washboard ovals, thin crenellations. Most important to the Askirit, deep caverns twisted into the depths of Aliare. The mountains of Tarn were honeycombed as well with places to hide, build, and dwell.

Ute, that great cascade into their world, and kelerai, when the waters exploded back up, generated not only ventilation and life but wonder and songs. An Askirit poet said that surely on the surface, where the waters roared out of the planet's depths, one could view the most awesome sight in creation.

Through the night, everyone sought caverns for shelter from sierent. Even sea creatures would migrate to the depths. It was the time, people said, for the lords of death to be about, seeking in the storms their own, sucking them from their shelters and taking them to the abyss.

Water was not only esseh—"lifegiver"—but also constant companion. The Askirit passionately described the motions, tastes, and dangers of water against rock, water under their boats, water providing their food, their clothing, their nets, and their prey. Water also carried the seasons from above. They could sense it in the water temperature and changes in the taste of the fish. They felt quickened by the warmer waters and the smells of spring above.

During the day the villagers of Wellen fished and conducted

commerce at sea's edge. But during sierent, the sea rose twenty times the height of a man, so they chose work grottoes and dwellings far above the water, and woe to the person left on shore when the winds grew too strong. But high in the crags, one could ride out sierent in a shallow shelter, listening to the winds and water beating against the peaks.

Yosha lowered himself into the familiar odors of Liriko's workshop, which was shaped like a pregnant archerfish. The shape of every dwelling and work grotto was the unique, often bizarre result of erosion. In contrast, in every bone-cutting grotto in Tarn, and wherever Askirit had dispersed, chairs and equipment formed the same wedge in the center. The workshop's tools and benches interlocked like a three-dimensional puzzle that every Askirit could assemble.

He recognized the festive morning scent his mentor wore and grunted his greeting, gripping the wedge and pulling a bench from it. He tried to shake his preoccupation with last night's humiliation and grabbed a rasp made of hundreds of tiny fish teeth. He continued on with shaping a huge jawbone into a boat prow, his strokes much harder than necessary.

"You're energetic this morning," said Liriko. "Remember— smooth, careful strokes."

Yosha ignored the advice and started whistling. He knew Liriko would be placated by the tune, for it was the children's learning song, taught to those apprenticed to the bone cutters. Yosha never sang it now, for it was too childish a song for a boy on the edge of manhood, but the words flowed through his mind as he whistled.

> *Would you be a master craftsman?*
> *Come and work.*
> *Your fingers must be clever,*
> *to form the blades of Tarn,*
> *the spears and tools and wheels.*

Bones, bones, bones,
a thousand bones;
each becomes a perfect shape
beneath your fingers.

Come and work.
Your hands must grow strong,
to split the bones of sark,
the bones of sark for spears,
and mattet bones for hammers.

Bones, bones, bones,
a thousand bones;
each becomes a perfect shape
beneath your fingers.

Work and work and work.
Become a master craftsman.
But first now, learn your bones.
Niroc bones for tiny nails,
Osk bones for benches.
Bones of a peshua to pick your teeth!
Ah, what would you do without bones?

Yosha rasped the boat prow for a time, wishing he had Liriko's strength to cut through the larger bones. The smell of sawed bone at first bothered him, but now it had become familiar and even pleasant. The odors of fermenting sea vegetation in vats—used to set the sharp edges of weapons—mingled with the smell of bones and brought back a long-ago memory of his father.

The two had been sitting at supper and his father had surprised Yosha by placing a sharp dirk in his hand. It smelled like weapons just dipped in the vats. "Spear your supper," his father said. The little boy stabbed at the chunks of meat. "I got one!" Yosha declared, then felt his hand being guided, the dagger's point turned around toward his mouth.

He remembered also his father's leading him in the crags, listening for birds. "That's a kestle striking prey," his father would say, or "That cry means fear."

He had a third memory: his father wearing a leather jacket, his chest bare, holding Yosha on his lap. He was rubbing Yosha's hair, and the man's arm with the tough, smooth leather had rubbed against Yosha's shoulder. He had let Yosha explore the pouches of poisonous keitr on his belt. The pouches, also made of noirim leather, had been pungent, musky, and strong. Yosha was awed even now as he thought of his having touched a pouch with keitr.

His present ambitions mixed with these memories. Somehow, he wanted to avenge his father's death. Yet he knew that launching hundreds of keitr against leviathan would accomplish nothing. Leviathan was impervious. But why then, Yosha wondered, did the holy ritual command: "Do not flinch at the jaws of leviathan!" And the priests in the ceremonies chanted, "The righteous shall chase leviathan back to the sea!" Was his father not righteous?

Villagers called leviathan Kjotik, Marauder. Far from not flinching, the stoutest men would scream with fear at the repellent odor and slap of Kjotik's bulk on the shore. The creature thundered upon villages in bizarre feeding frenzies. No one understood what brought Kjotik, but everyone speculated. Some said it was forced from the sea by hunger; others that it preferred human flesh. Its visitations were capricious. A village could fish and hunt and sing for fifty years and never experience the jarring thud of Marauder's body.

"Liriko!" Yosha said, "let us sing a song, the one you taught me." And Yosha began:

> *A wee little boy named Taipse*
> *knew nothing of the sea.*

He only knew his spears were sharp
and promises were true.

A wee little boy named Taipse
heard Kjotik shake the land.
The screams of people made him mad.
He grabbed his little spears.

A wee little boy named Taipse
ran straight to Kjotik's mouth.
He squirmed between the giant teeth—
He faced the ghastly breath!

A wee little boy named Taipse
jabbed his spear up high.
He stuck it in Marauder's mouth
and Kjotik coughed him out.

A wee little boy named Taipse
had chased leviathan.
It sank beneath the boats
and never came again!

Never, no never,
no never came again!
Never, no never,
no never came again!

When they finished the song, Yosha said, "I love that little song. And I hate it."

Liriko, who did not want Yosha to resume his agonized complaining, said, "It's just a silly nursery song—like all those rhymes of children who ride great fish into the air or find unknown treasures from the world above."

Yosha snorted. "The sacred words say we are not to fear leviathan's teeth! Yet we run like frightened birds."

"No man has ever stopped Kjotik!" Liriko stepped away from his work, agitated. "Men have set boulders to crash upon him. They've flung hundreds of spears at him. But he spits out poisoned arrows like pebbles. And keitr cannot chew through his hide. He is a whole world come above you." Liriko was standing, shaking his fists. "You cannot beat back a whirlpool with your hands; you cannot stop leviathan with weapons."

When he finished speaking, he stood breathing quickly. Finally he added, "You know the saying among the barbarians: 'Three deaths a man cannot avenge. The water's rage, the fever's chill, and leviathan.'"

"Yes, I know the saying," Yosha said. He was holding one of the spears that were ready for the vats, turning it in his palm. "But the priests chant, 'Fear not the teeth of leviathan!'"

"Fear not! But they do not say to attack—"

"Fear not the teeth!" Yosha interrupted, gripping the spear shaft tightly. "'The righteous shall chase leviathan back to the sea!' Are holy words for nothing? The Askirit are to break the teeth of the unrighteous!"

"It does not say that! 'The righteous one shall break the teeth of the enemy.'"

"My father was righteous!"

"Ah!" Liriko declared, and sat down heavily on his bench. He hated these arguments with Yosha—no wonder everyone called him Kret. "Your father was a good man," Liriko said simply.

"Holy promises!" Yosha said. "Does no one hear them? Does no one take them for what they are?"

—— The Maniac ——

In the evening, during the calm before sierent, villagers congregated at the sea's edge. Yosha sniffed the ocean scents as he crossed the long, gentle slope of aceyn. He avoided the crowds and stepped into the water, listening to the waves breaking around him and the earnest voices of adults mixing with the babble of children.

Downshore, where a formation of cliffs rose from the sea, he heard shouts from the boys his age: "They're coming! Move over! Not yet!" The big, flat mycea were floating in to affix themselves to the faces of the cliffs, and the boys jostled for position, each with toes stretched out to touch the edge of one and then leap upon it.

The Askirit thought of the mycea as a plant, for they cut the thin giants into strips and ate them with fish or meat. It had a fibrous texture and crunched pleasantly under the teeth. Yet at dawn the oval creatures peeled themselves off the cliffs and rippled purposefully forward on top of the sea, sides curled high, catching the little eddies that moved them out to stronger currents. At eve they came by the hundreds to ride out sierent by flattening themselves against the cliff face. Once affixed, a mycea was almost impossible to pry loose.

The big ovals, twice Yosha's length, were now crowding against the cliffs, edges curled high, groping for the hard vertical surfaces. The high curl formed a tilted saddle for the boys to ride. But they had to leap on the mycea gently, for if they landed too hard or pushed down an edge, water rushed in and the mycea sank—thus the origin of the saying, "You're on a wet mycea," which meant someone's argument was sinking.

The boys shoved each other, shouting loudly when someone jumped forward and hit too hard, sinking the thin raft. They began jumping from one mycea to the other, yelling for others to follow if they could.

Yosha turned from the sounds and walked to the cavern's farthest opening. Behind him were the seaside slopes of his village; to his right, within the vast mountain, were the thousands of caverns, alcoves, and tunnels in which his people lived and worked. But to his left was a gigantic vault, a high open space within the mountain, which never failed to lift his spirits. It was called Aeries. Within it, massive pillars rose from the floor, and—high above—thousands of dangerous and unexplored configurations made him feel free and heroic. Here he could be alone, and here were the skipes, the little birds of magic and light.

The birds were what had brought men through the centuries to this place of sheer ascents and inhospitable heights, for skipe eggs were considered a delicacy. Yet no one could climb unaided these soaring, dripping configurations of stone. They descended like slabs of vertical, windswept seas. Yosha's ancestors had built pylons, bridges, and platforms of aceyn rope, and had dangled thick sea vines from the heights, but now they were old and treacherous. Yosha hated the season when men and boys would come noisily to climb and to gather eggs, clambering over the ancient ropes and vines, calling with bravado from the scaffolding. Each year some fell to their deaths, and in Yosha's opinion, always foolishly, for they jabbered among themselves, thinking too little about the rotting vines.

The adults constantly warned the boys against coming here. To insure their admonitions would be heeded, they placed the cage of Belstin the maniac at the point of ascent.

Previously, the maniac had been in a cage near the dwellings and shops. Those who felt sorry for him would lift him in his cage during the day and carry him to the sea's edge, placing him far down the shore where his imprecations could not be heard. But twice Belstin had broken out and terrorized the villagers. Therefore they bound his hands so he could not break loose, and over time his hands became clenched claws. Not long before this, however, he had broken out yet again, shattering his cage so that people said he had done it in the power of the furies. Now his cage rested high above the cave's floor, just near enough for villagers to lift water and food to him on a tall pole.

Yosha moved as silently as fog toward the dangling vines. He nimbly pulled himself up hand over hand, not even attempting to gain leverage with his feet on the slippery formations until he came to a rickety, ancient bridge. He distributed his weight among his feet and hands, leaning forward to grasp a fragile trellis lashed to the vertical face. He got his feet on a narrow niche in the stone folds, gripped the trellis, and pulled his way up the face of the massive stalactites, their thick half-circles smooth and wet, yet gritty against his legs and hands. For a moment he released a hand to feel the smooth, wet formations, taking pleasure in the odd whorls and irregularities.

"Fiends! Fiends blue as death!"

The shout in his ear jolted Yosha, making him grab the vines with his free hand and grip them tighter with the other. Was the maniac's cage right next to his ear? Was the maniac grabbing at him?

"Fiends!" The voice blasted at him so forcefully the echoes in that vast expanse came back like shouts and rocked down the distant tunnels. "Watch out! They'll chew your soul and spit out your guts!"

Yosha heard a terrific crashing in the cage and then a shout of triumph. "Hah! Got one!" the maniac yelled. "The slobbering gheial's a stench in my fist. Smell it!" He heard the maniac stomping on the floor of his cage, leaping up and crashing down with his full weight so that Yosha thought he must surely break the cage into pieces. "That one's gone," he yelled. "I've smashed his brains into the pit!"

Yosha found himself shaking, but he began again to move upward. He labored up the face till he reached a cluster of thick vines dangling from above.

When he was far above Belstin, he rested a moment on an ancient platform, carefully judging its strength. After swatting an insect on his leg, he climbed a rickety pylon to a yet higher level.

It creaked and groaned as he scaled it. At its top, he squirmed through a long, snake-shaped hole, getting his shoulders up on a rounded formation that faced a great chasm. Here he had to cross a last rickety trellis, this one extended from one bulging formation to another, with no nearby vines and no niche or ledge to leap at should it start to give way. He had traversed it many times before, but he always wondered if the rot might suddenly prevail. He made it safely across, to the high configurations beyond ropes and vines, much of it unexplored, all of it fantastic with shapes and surprises.

His hands were no longer shaking from the jolt of the maniac's screams, but he could still hear Belstin far below shouting imprecations. He shook off the sounds and listened instead for the twittering of the little birds. He stood upright and after a time heard rapid, loud clicks behind him, then the sound of wingbeats and the impact of a little body thunking against his knee. The echo-location system of the skipes sped them with remarkable ease through the most convoluted tunnels, but it did not keep them from bumping into people. Yosha stared in the direction of the departing wing beats, probing the darkness for the sparkles in its tail. Some said the sparkles were totally imaginary, little glints of white that were tricks of the eyes. But legend said that blisks—tiny, magical beings with wings smaller and softer than the down on a skipe's chest—delighted in laughing the sparks into the birds' tails. Yosha was convinced he had seen the sparkles many times, but he admitted to himself that he would squeeze his eyes often while staring at the sounds of skipes winging by.

Finally he reached his destination. Birds twittered noisily in a vast vault below him. Water had collected in a small pool nearby and he could hear the birds now and then splashing in it.

But what drew him to this place was an odd formation. It was a rift in the outer wall, like a great lower jaw jutting into the air. Within this rift, tall, pointed stalagmites rose like giant teeth. He crawled between them. At the mouth's edge, he hung on to one shaped like an incisor, larger than his body, and leaned his head and chest out over the sea. He envisioned himself in the mouth of Kjotik. His body halfway out from the mountain's rock face, Yosha braced himself as breezes brushed his face and the sounds of villagers rose from below.

Behind him, something startled the birds and they exploded into the air with a loud beating of wings. A little covey winged by, twittering loudly. People said that wind whistling through apertures was really blisks playing one-stringed instruments. Faster than his heart was beating, wings and winds and the drumming of his fingers on stone became music calling Yosha to exploits. The great beast's jaw embraced air and sea and the unexplored wildness of high caverns. From this jaw, all was possible, even the challenging of leviathan.

Beneath his feet radiated several tunnels. Yosha had explored them all, crawling into a deep one to hide his great and only treasure. He crawled into the tight space now, through the gritty surfaces. At tunnel's end his fingers touched his carving, and he squirmed his way back out. He leaned against one of the big teeth so he could touch it and dream his dreams and feel his past and future.

Others might have said the carving was unremarkable. As a wedding gift, the motif of the shoulders and heads of a couple leaning over a game was not unusual. But the sculpture presented likenesses of his father and his mother!

The man's elbow was thrust out upon the rough limestone slab, his other arm outstretched with his fingers on one of the twenty game depressions. His expression was one of perplexity. The woman's hands rested under her chin, one grasping five smoothly rounded pebbles, and her expression was whimsical. Both had thick shocks of hair and youthful faces.

Yosha's fingers moved over the smoothness of their expressions, over the ridges of their hair, over the arm of his father extended in play. When his hands touched the baby carved on the far side of the game slab—a tiny baby barely out of the womb—

his eyes filled with tears. It was the custom in such wedding sculptures to include the probable fruit of the couple's union. The babe's features were barely distinguishable, for it was covered by skins, with only its nose and forehead sticking out. It wasn't Yosha, yet it was, for he had been their only child.

The baby's presence with them made him long to touch them and speak to them. Yet it also filled him with courage and determination to reveal what the babe might do in their memory.

Tracing the expression on his mother's mouth, he heard an unexpected sound. It was not the fluttering of birds nor even the calm movement of a snake or scratching of a reptile. It sounded like a foot scraping against the surface.

He listened and heard it again, the unmistakable sound of cautious feet and then the sound of breathing as someone negotiated a difficult rise. He felt invaded, violated, and he grasped his carving tightly. Should he rush it back to its hiding place or keep it in his hands?

The intruder began humming a tune, one Yosha recognized. The song went:

> *Open, open, open your gift.*
> *Aliare is yours.*
> *Touch, touch, touch,*
> *the scaly skins of esks.*
> *Taste, taste, taste,*
> *the mellow flesh of rewns.*
> *Drink, drink, drink,*
> *the bubbling Askal nectars.*
> *Sniff, sniff, sniff,*
> *the freshened scents of sierent.*
> *Leap and laugh and sing,*
> *sing, sing, sing,*
> *for Eshtel gave a gift.*
> *Aliare is yours,*

Touch and sing and laugh and taste,
For Aliare is yours. . . .

The voice broke into words, singing "scaly skins of esks," but began improvising, laughing as he sang, "rub the pesky scaly esks, laugh at blisks and skipes—"

"Mosen!" Yosha called out. He recognized the voice of a boy slightly older than himself, not an orphan but a different kind of outcast. "Did you follow me here?" he asked accusingly.

"And have you been lying in ambush?" Mosen shot back, but not unpleasantly. "I explore here all the time." Mosen navigated closer to Yosha, who thrust his carving into a hollow behind him.

"Oh? How do you slip past Belstin the maniac?" Yosha asked.

Mosen whistled. "He does rather wake you up if you're sluggish!" Then he clucked his tongue in disapproval and said, "Why do they cage that tormented man like a beast?"

Yosha had seldom talked to Mosen, but he remembered similar complaints from him. Mosen and his parents had a reputation for criticizing everything. They went so far as to prophesy doom on their village and on the nation. No one took them seriously. Yosha said, "If they didn't cage him, maybe all those fiends would get loose and get us!"

He meant it as a light remark, but Mosen shot back such a sharp retort that Yosha sensed why the older boy was avoided. Mosen said, "So you don't believe in fiends and furies? He who doesn't believe, they say, is a latrine ready to be filled."

Yosha decided to laugh instead of taking offense. "Who knows what are fiends and furies and gheials, and what are self-tauntings of the soul?"

"You think they don't exist?" Mosen asked. He made a derisive popping sound by expelling air from his cheeks. "We know the ritual speaks of them."

"Yes," Yosha agreed, "but not much. Not much."

"Are they wisps of air, conjured from children's frights?" Mosen moved past Yosha and lay against one of the largest stalagmites. "We know little of evil, and we know much," he said. "The fiends are pent up and enraged. That's why so many call them the furies. They have been roused by what's coming. They're infuriated, for they know they'll soon be mocked by hope."

"If they are so enraged, where are they?"

"Ah, you would be devastated to know how much of Tarn's heart they have. Yet they're not flesh and blood—they're mere specters and wraiths, with no power over us except as we give it."

Yosha ran his hand over the carving behind him, assuring himself it was still there. "You are talking like a priest," he said. "Do you plan to be one?"

"What else?"

"Then I have a question. The ritual says nothing about how to discern the voices from the pit from our own inner thoughts."

Mosen slapped his knee, a sound indicating the answer was obvious. "Does it matter?" he asked. "Always resist evil. Think! Evil urges self destruction in a hundred forms. It goads toward cruel conquests. It whispers love for Askirit triumphs more than for Eshtel himself. We hear little spoken against this."

Mosen's last remarks made Yosha uncomfortable. Who was he to criticize the priests?

"We must accept all the truth," the older boy was saying, "even the smallest command."

"And we must trust all the promises!" Yosha quickly added.

"Exactly!" Mosen exclaimed with enthusiasm. "And obey all the commands! Like showing mercy and worshiping Eshtel and giving even a helpless pagan justice!"

Yosha said, "We are commanded not to fear leviathan. Do you fear leviathan?"

"I fear idolatry more. But I'd run for my life if Kjotik hit this village."

Yosha grunted his disapproval of this last remark, but he

loved Mosen's spirit. He knew he had found someone as passionate as he about the great forces that drove their souls. "We must believe the promises," he insisted to Mosen. "And we must act on them."

Chapter 2.

—— Enre ——

Standing behind her, Asel's mother combed her hair in quick, agitated strokes. "After today, I may never touch your hair again," she said in lament.

The young woman reached up and grasped both her mother's hands. "Perhaps you won't," Asel admitted. "Once I take the vows, my choices are few."

"Yes," her mother said, "as mine have been ever since the Enre came to us."

On the day Asel turned two years old, like all girls born to the Askirit, she had been visited by a woman of the Enre. Asel remembered nothing of that day, but her mother had often told her every detail. She started again with her favorite story: "Without a word of greeting, that frail old woman darted into the house," she said. "The Enre inspected you right away, like the stitching on a doll. She insisted on feeding you, but you decided you didn't want to eat. She sang to you and asked you what stories you liked best. She put you on her lap and held her fingers to her temples. She started to chant; on and on she went while you sat quiet."

"What did you think?" Asel asked, as she always did.

"Nothing at all. Why should this time be different from the times she had visited your sisters? Not one in a thousand girls is selected. Why should I think something remarkable would happen?"

"But it did," Asel said.

"Yes, everyone says so. She lifted you above her and announced, 'You are Enre.' That was a jolt. But the old woman had barely said it when she gave one little cry—just a faint sound I could have missed entirely—and dropped stone dead under you. She just collapsed, and you fell on top of her. But you didn't cry. You just got up and walked away—wandered off like a bird."

"What did it mean?" Asel asked.

"That's what everyone wondered. Maybe she picked the wrong girl and was struck dead. Maybe she was just old. Maybe she had selected the new Varial, and the specters from the pit were so infuriated they rushed at her and killed her."

"And that's how all the talk about me began?"

"That's how it began."

At first Asel had loved the whispers about her, the awe of other children and even adults. To be selected was an honor; she had been taken for months at a time by the women of the Enre to be taught their mysteries. But to be, perhaps, the next Varial! As a small child, it had made her feel extraordinary. But as she grew in understanding, the speculations of others about her became a burden. She began insisting that the small village was simply starved for talk and was making something out of nothing.

The burden, however, settled upon her. She embraced it and fed on it because it made her unique; yet she hated it. She felt compelled to do everything to make it possible, yet she wanted to flee the pressure and live like other girls.

The burden defined her. To be Enre, she must stand in the ritual more pure than the priests. She must respond to Enre questions with the wisdom she was ever learning. She must love the water and master it, navigating currents, diving from great heights, stalking ocean prey. She must master defense and offense with the weapons of her hands and feet. To be Enre was to be trained precisely and committed whole-heartedly. But to be Varial was to lead all the Enre of the nation.

She remembered nothing of the old woman collapsing dead

beneath her. But images from that event haunted her. The old woman had declared her Enre, then, with the words barely out of her mouth, was stricken dead. Killed by the gheials that now terrify me, Asel often thought. She believed she must pursue her Enre destiny with more intensity than any woman ever had before, if only to be strong enough to escape being dragged into the abyss.

"One day, if you become Varial, you will have many choices," her mother was saying.

Asel always discouraged such comments. "I would have far fewer choices," she replied sharply.

To be thought of as a future Varial not only set her apart. Asel felt it also marked her as spiritual prey. She had once heard a fish caught by a hook and thrashing in the water, which was then caught in its gut by a second hook. Suddenly the fish was still, quivering and nearly torn apart by the two taut lines. She thought of herself as that fish: the holy ones, the priests and Enre were yanking her forward with a hook in her mouth; the furies and specters kept dragging her away with a hook in her belly. She could not thrash about; she obeyed in every particular the Enre discipline. Yet she longed for freedom.

"I remember it was not four years ago when you were talking wistfully of marriage," her mother was saying, "of maybe leaving the Enre, but I never tried to persuade you either way."

Yes, she thought, she could have chosen to leave the Enre. At twelve, each girl was given the choice. Asel had longed to return home, to marry like the other girls, to escape the hooks pulling at her. She had thought often that both the holy ones and the unholy might leave her alone if she tried to reclaim the normal life of an Askirit woman.

But a short time before her decision would have to be made, she saw something that forever shaped her life. She was sitting by a pool, small children playing around her. They were her regular charges, and she loved to play games with them. She swam and danced with them, laughed and teased them, fell with them into roughhouse piles of thrashing little arms and legs. As she sat with one of them, who was playfully pulling at her hair, she heard a little splash. It was a frog in the pool, a pembra, one of the small luminous frogs rare in Tarn and highly prized. It was among the most luminous of Aliare's creatures, so much so that many said they could see colors around its bulging eyes and puffed-out, thumping throat. Asel held it high above her so the children could see its diffused glow, and she called out, "Look!"

She heard squeals of delight and the rushing of their feet toward her. "Asel! Let me touch!" cried one. Suddenly they were all upon her in a crowd.

That is when it happened. She lowered the frog toward the children. As she did, she saw their faces alight with joy and wonder. They seemed as luminous as the creature in her hand. The faces she had so often lovingly explored with her fingers were now curved cheeks and glowing eyes and soft, smiling lips. Incredulous, she laughed, staring at a little boy, bursting out with words like light itself: "Child! Your face pulls tears of joy from my eyes." And she lifted the boy and put the glowing frog next to his cheek.

She pulled a little girl to her. "Child!" she exclaimed, kneeling beside her. "You are glory and light!" Her tears fell in the girl's hair, then touched the child's cheeks, each drop holding and reflecting another world of light.

"Child," she said in quiet awe, handing the little frog to the smallest boy. "You cannot be so beautiful!" She let him explore the slippery little creature with his fingers, and she helped him bring its glow close to his face. She exclaimed loudly,

"Child! Child! Child!
What love is escaped into this dark world!"

For the rest of her life, Asel felt awe when she remembered those moments. She had seen their faces as living traceries of diffused and moving light. She did not believe the glow from the frog had simply lighted their faces and her spirit. She believed she had been visited by holy creatures.

——— The Island ———

Asel sat on a cliff jutting over the sea. Beside her were a score of other girls, chosen from among thousands of initiates in the far-flung Askirit kingdom. The past four years, these girls had trained in the lethal movements, the healing touches, the wisdom and mysteries of the Enre, the holy women. Now they could become Enre, if they could survive The Initiation.

The girls faced their mentors, who sat across from them. One asked the first question: "Why have you been chosen?"

A girl replied, "To penetrate Nor."

The island of Nor. Asel felt a thrill pass through her body at the sound of the word. In moments she would actually be swimming toward that alien place. From childhood, she carried images of vast, natural halls of stone in which the Enre held their holy rites, challenging the evil so close to its cliffs. Nor was Tarn's farthest bastion, standing against Dorte, the region of the damned. Dorte's inhabitants were believed to be pawns of the dark powers, forced to perform unspeakable abominations upon their children, upon each other, and upon any who dared venture there.

Smooth as a tooth, round and craggy at the top, Nor rose impervious to the currents smashing against its rocky shore. No one could scale it, but a deep current could carry a swimmer to an interior lake, for Nor—like so much of Tarn—was a labyrinth of volcanic tubes and caverns. The underwater passage to the lake was known only to the Enre, for they alone had mastered the water, and they took great risks as an exercise of faith.

The Enre believed Nor was a citadel against evil powers

ready to spew forth against the Askirit kingdom of Tarn. They believed the only reason they could hold Nor against the powers was their songs and their prayers and their shouts of righteous triumph from the peak, where they faced the damned and called blessings upon them.

"How came we here?" a mentor asked.

An initiate responded: "The woman who fell from the light has given us hope."

"Tell, then, her story," the girl was instructed. Asel's lips moved silently with the familiar words as she told the tale.

"It was the beginning of darkness, before Aliare, before the Askirit, before Kjotik and keitr and sierent. All the peoples and all the nations lived in light. But they desired darkness. They sought evil's power; they trafficked with the specters of the pit.

"The Maker called them to the light, but they turned away. He sent a thousand voices to invite them from the shadows, but they went deeper into darkness.

"The Maker grew angry. He shook the world like prey. Quakes split the lands. All the peoples from all the world above plunged into death and darkness.

"The woman, Nor, awoke. She felt wet rock beneath. She felt blood on her face and sides. In her right hand, gripped tight as death, was the wrist of her granddaughter. Nor reached for the little child with her other hand. She drew her upon her body. The child lay limp, bloody. Nor pleaded, 'Awaken, Varial.' But her pleading did not rouse her. Nor prayed with a loud wail, prayed till she had no breath left. She lay back to die.

"But the child, Varial, whimpered. The sounds aroused the old woman. She kissed Varial's lips and whispered love into her ear. She told her the pain would not be forever.

"On hands and knees the old woman and the little girl probed the darkness. They felt water. They drank. They washed their wounds.

"They found worms to eat. Their wounds began to heal. But

the child kept weeping. 'Where is the light?' she wailed. 'Where is the light? I am smothered. When will we climb to the light?'

" 'When we are better,' the old woman said. She held the child for hours upon hours, singing songs of the light, for Nor had always loved the light and hated the rituals of darkness.

"They climbed. They returned to the water and found better food. They rested. They climbed and climbed but could find no way out. The child wept and said, 'We must go up!'

" 'Yes. We will seek the light. But until then, we have water, do we not?'

" 'Yes,' said the child.

" 'We have food.'

"The child made a gagging sound.

" 'We have breath and strength. We have the songs. We have hope. We must look everywhere for the light.'

"They searched. For years they searched. And always the grandmother gave Varial hope and taught her all the truths from above.

"Years passed. The day Varial found a band of Askirit warriors, she was alone, her grandmother long dead. But Nor's songs and tales were ever with her. Varial kept them all, and the powers of the Enre."

"Why do we tell the story?" a mentor asked.

A different girl gave the required answer: "We are Nor and Varial. We continue their search for the light."

Asel was glad she had not been assigned a response. She was concentrating on the challenges ahead, visualizing the currents and undertows into the island named Nor, until the leader asked:

"Are you worthy to enter Nor?"

"We are not worthy," all the girls said in unison.

"What will make you worthy?"

"Seeking the light."

"What is your mission?"

"To reach the scent of Nor and Varial."

"When did an initiate last get through and claim the scent?"

"Three generations past."

"But this night," the Enre master said, "you may succeed. This may be the night spoken of by new generations. This night, one of you may reach the scent and be sung of by all the Enre of Tarn."

Asel knew the woman was determined to keep that from happening. The harsh discipline that made Asel and her companions so skilled and toughened was only a beginning to what these leaders of the Enre had learned and endured. Their honor was at stake to keep the initiates from finding the scent, for it would mean they had failed.

"Go to Nor," a mentor said.

The young women responded in unison, "If we reach the scent, the light will have led us."

The Enre mentors stood, the ceremony over, and said in a more familiar tone, "You will all find much cause for humility this night. Tomorrow may you be both humble and alive."

—— Nor and Varial ——

Asel plunged in a precise arc from the cliff's edge to the sea below. When she surfaced, she started swimming with strong, confident strokes. It was spring above. She could smell the freshness and feel the beginning warmth in the water.

How she loved the water. The Enre constantly trained in it, mastering maneuvers, learning capricious currents. Esseh was water's name. Esseh hissing on rocks, roaring at sierent, flowing over hands. Esseh, in all its shapes and forms, all its force and nurturing power.

Esseh also meant woman.

Water had scores of other names among the Askirit. Metrel,

when it showered off cliffs and descended in a fine mist. Roisep, when it fumed into a hole in a rock and made a clapping sound. Roist, when it would strike a deeper hole and make a loud bang. Eler, when it dripped from the roofs of caverns in hundreds of little drops. Ardeddd, when it broke through openings in rocks and beat like drums against the floor. Temel, when it pierced a narrow gorge, spraying over the top with a swishing sound. Melg, when water and algae mixed to become a slippery danger in the crags. Storge, when the mountainous waves of sierent rose from the sea and struck the shore. Puenner, when a shallow wave rushed over a flat stretch and smashed against a cliff.

"Today I may be puenner myself," Asel thought, "if I do not catch the currents right. I could be either swept past the island or knocked senseless on its rocks."

She swam silently now, cautious, her head slightly out of the water to listen, her left arm extended for touch, her right arm stroking. She felt the whirling current on her fingertips and turned into it. Letting it carry her forward till it quickened and sucked at her, she took a deep breath and plunged into it, stroking down, down as quickly as she could.

Deeply submerged and propelled by the current, she stroked for more and more speed, getting desperate for air. She started wondering if she had entered at the wrong place.

She broke through the lake's surface at the edge of panic, drew a great breath, submerged again and came up very quietly for more air. She wondered about all the girls who hadn't made it through alive. Once in the lake, however, she feared little; she suspected its fiercest inhabitants were the fish the Enre on Nor lived on. No, the challenge now was not survival but stealth for the very serious game with her mentors. She twisted her body crossways from the current, kicked gently forward, then let herself drift.

Asel listened. With one ear out of the water, she heard only the waves washing against the shore a distance away. With her ear in the water she picked up the faint sounds of a file-fish, grating and ripping like the tearing of dry leather. She drifted toward it, listening, listening, planning, rehearsing. Her outstretched fingers grazed a stone, and she gave a silent kick toward it, then floated with the waves into the shore. She allowed the waves to wash her in like a bit of flotsam, in and out, in and out, a little closer each time. An Enre master would be searching the shore nearby, or might be very close, listening for changes in the waves.

She quietly grasped a big rock to halt her being pulled back out again. Slowly she pulled herself up on the rock, lodged her right foot securely ahead and began to crouch forward, in the classic defensive posture, glad for the noisy slaps of the water covering her movements. She steadied her feet. Still crouched, she stepped forward, listening, sniffing the air.

Despite her mastery of the water, she trembled. For most of her sixteen years, the women of the Enre had swum with her, teaching her how to use the water's resistance to build strength, how to interpret the sounds, scents and tastes of the sea. On both water and land, they taught her the disciplines of grace, agility, speed, balance, buoyancy. They sparred with her, instructed her, cavorted with her. Now the best of them stalked her.

The rock formations suddenly grew sharp. She climbed with sure strength, but when her footholds grew precarious, the rocks' slippery edges were too sharp for her to trust her weight to her handholds. Frequently, she had to step down and try another ledge. She was angry at herself every time she slipped and made a noise, angry at herself for breathing too loudly.

As she gained somewhat higher ground, she still heard and smelled nothing. Better to crouch silent than to move in the wrong direction, she told herself. Better to stay till sierent threatens than to give herself away. Yet her waiting availed nothing, and finally she started moving forward, her fingers probing ahead like a nervous insect's antennae. She concentrated on the power of the inner light and of Enre beliefs, powers more important by far than sure movements of nerve and muscle.

Then, come and gone like the briefest touch of a sea anemone, the scent of Varial teased her nostrils. The scent! She had dreamed of it since she had first been told of the island. It was herb-like, tart, yet with a richness like the clean, pungent smell of sparks. It startled her, made her pulse run, but was instantly gone on the wind. From which direction? To the left? She thought so and waited a long time to sense it again. But she smelled nothing and started to move to the left.

She had barely turned her body when a woman leaped on her from the side, crushing her to the ground. At the impact, Asel twisted with all her strength in the evasive move she had often found effective. But the woman clasped her wrists in a painful twist, and with a shudder, Asel's body lay under the Enre like a netted fish.

Could it be over that suddenly? She had thought at least she would block a move by her captor, at least spin out from her grasp once or twice.

"You did well," the woman said, pulling Asel up, still grasping her wrists painfully. "You got close enough to catch the scent."

Asel blinked away tears. She was surprised at them, surprised at the intensity of her disappointment. Smelling the scent had raised her hopes higher than she had realized. She swallowed and found she could say nothing as the woman started putting the tight lashes on her left wrist, very carefully exploring her arm and hand for hidden blades or abrasives. The Enre were especially well known for the kist, their device to secure a captive. Every struggle tightened the bonds of the thin but extraordinarily tough lizard skin.

After thoroughly searching her fingers, the woman placed the kist on Asel, then grasped her right hand to begin searching it. Asel wanted to try a maneuver as the woman shifted her weight, but she knew this, too, would be futile, for the procedure for applying the kist was precise and allowed for no action against it, unless the captive was of far superior strength. The woman ran her hand down each finger, then started at the top of the thumb.

When she was halfway down, Asel muffled a cry. The woman stopped and felt the fresh wound and the loose skin on her thumb where she had applied a bandage. It was common for the Askirit to bind wounds with thin membranes, rolling one several times around an appendage. The Enre who was now trussing her up had no way of knowing that Asel had purposely gouged her thumb severely with a sharp rock the day before. Under two layers of membrane, she had inserted one layer of the spiny skin of a pek, a type of pricklefish.

In checking her thumb, the woman pulled down twice, checking the bandage, but she did not remove it. If the Enre master had run her fingers up, instead of down, she would have felt the sharp abrasive underneath—but Asel knew the search procedure meant running the fingers down. She was carried to the shore, then tossed almost on top of several other girls, laid out like the day's catch.

Asel lay silent, like the others, but she was rubbing the knuckle of her thumb against her other thumb, rubbing up so the skin of the pricklefish could cut through the membranes. It took a long time to free first one thumb, then the other. All the time she worked, she was listening to the stalking Enre masters, where they were stationed, what they said as they brought more girls down and dropped them unceremoniously with the others.

Once both thumbs were free, she used the abrasive to start splitting the membrane on her left hand, then her feet. When she was free, she moved cautiously, listening to hear if anyone noticed her movements.

Two women were talking as they brought new captives to the shore. Their voices covered the sounds of Asel's stealing away. She went only a short distance and stationed herself in the direction she thought the scent might be. She crouched there, studying the Enres' voices, movements, and positions as they sought the remaining initiates. She sniffed for the scent again, but detected nothing.

Finally she heard what she had hoped for: a woman called out a number. It meant everyone had made it alive to the lake, and that each had been captured. It also meant the Enre masters would reassemble.

As soon as she decided the last group of Enre had gone past her to the shore, she climbed silently in the direction she had come, figuring the last to come down must have been guarding the scent. She heard them starting a ceremony below, lecturing the humbled captives about how The Initiation began the process of becoming an Enre master. Asel was desperately hoping they were not counting the girls as they spoke to them.

She climbed a long distance, thinking she had surely lost the scent, before she got another whiff of it. She stopped, sniffed, tried to ascertain its direction. She didn't move, but grew anxious, knowing her time now was very limited. Any instant there could be a cry and they would be upon her. "This is the time I could fail," she thought, "when I am so close." She sniffed in every direction, caught the scent again, and moved toward it. She moved as silently as she could, impatient for greater speed. The scent was becoming stronger and stronger and seemed to her regal, magnificent.

Her heart pounded as she climbed up a steep slope of rock, the scent strong in the air. Her outstretched fingers hit something. She explored its curved edges. It was sculpted. She sniffed and felt higher. Her fingers probed, until she grasped the open basket of scent. Her hands were actually touching it!

She stretched up, put her fingers down into the liquid. She pressed her thumb against the edge, then lifted the basket. As she did, she realized the basket was hanging from the fingertips of a sculpted hand. After splashing the scent over her face, she reached up to touch the strange hand above her. It was much like her own, young fingers splayed out, beseeching. She had to stand on tiptoe to feel the top of the hand, then followed its arm down and forward to the shoulder. She felt the neck, then, slowly, as if savoring a delicacy, she touched the chin and lips and cheeks. She read with her fingers the exquisite sense of yearning on the young woman's face. Yearning! Asel felt around the girl's body and came to another figure, this one of an old woman whose arms were also lifted, whose face was also carved to express her yearning. This woman's whole body stretched toward the light.

Asel had often heard about the statue called The Yearning, which was an ancient likeness of Nor and Varial. But she had never thought she might some day touch it, for her teachers had pretended it had been destroyed hundreds of years ago. It was said that the figures of the statue yearned so for the light that anyone who touched them would be filled with the same longing. That is precisely how Asel felt. Her fingers moved slowly on their flowing garments, pausing on the wonderfully shaped arms and shoulders. She felt she could never stop exploring the fine detail of their faces. She found herself stretching up with her arms like Nor and Varial, yearning for the light above.

She spread the scent on the young forehead of Varial and the wrinkled one of Nor. Then she started singing softly, the image of their faces forming ever more clearly in her mind.

As she sang the words rushing into her mind, she became so lost in her yearning and joy that she did not even know the others had all come upon her. She stayed transfixed in wonder. She did not stop her singing even when the Enre took each girl and dripped scent on their foreheads and said the sacred words. She moved gently aside as each girl was allowed to touch the faces of Varial and Nor, but the words kept flowing through her. Asel heard their voices and felt their presence, but the yearning had come so alive in her from touching these ancient women of stone that she was aware of nothing else.

The Listener

Asel awoke next morning to the voice of Varial. "The scent becomes you," the leader of all Enre said. "May you always give it the honor you gave it last night."

"I opened myself to the light," Asel said in the traditional reply.

"You needn't be formal," Varial said. "You hardly noticed us last night. That was adequate humility—you were oblivious to your triumph. That stood you in good stead, for some of the Enre were angry you found the scent after you were caught."

Asel was alarmed by this statement. She tried to sound assured but not cocky as she said, "The command was to find it before sierent."

"So it was," Varial said. She reached down for Asel's hand. "Come with me. I want to take you to the top of Nor." She pulled her up, then turned and started walking briskly.

Asel followed, and when they started the long and steep ascent, she wondered how old the woman was. She knew that the leader of the Enre must always be able to swim into the island. Some would try no matter what their years, and many over the centuries had died in the attempt. But it was no dishonor to declare one's time was past and to set in motion the process for a new selection. Varial's voice and manner seemed old, but her gait and easy breathing indicated reserves of strength.

Varial reached the peak of Nor, high above the sea, and stood facing Dorte. Asel stepped beside her, refreshed by the moist winds against her perspiring body, and sniffed for scents. Behind them was Tarn; before them, the regions of the damned.

She stared at the darkness, listening—wondering what truly lived in Dorte. "Are the tales true?" Asel asked.

"Too many of them," Varial said. "Stand and let the wind blow on your face and through your hair. Listen to the currents.

Look at the shades of darkness. Some say they can distinguish between Tarn and Dorte."

Asel raised her face to the winds and savored the smell of the sea. "Will we stay on Nor long enough to distinguish such things?"

"You will, Asel." Varial handed her a rod of flint. "I am appointing you The Listener."

Asel cocked her head, astonished. The Listener was a role for only the most experienced. She could not imagine a novice being given such a task. For a full season, The Listener stayed alone on Nor, her senses trained on Dorte, poised to warn Tarn should strange events begin on that threatening shore. No one knew just what The Listener waited for, and it was said only a Listener could hear what might be coming, for such warfare was spiritually discerned.

Asel, not at all certain she was ready for this honor, asked, "Did you select me because I found the scent?"

"No," Varial said. "I chose you because of the way you sang of your yearning."

"But everyone sings," Asel said, taken aback. "One sings in Aliare, or one dies."

The Enre leader lightly touched Asel's face. The girl took a breath and found herself inhaling Varial's perfume. "You sang new words," she said. "You sang from the inner light. The Listener is not just a sentry. She must be chosen, for only she will hear in time if the eruption begins."

"Is it true," Asel asked, "that The Listener is completely alone for a full season?"

Varial put both her hands on Asel's cheeks and held them firmly. Her perfume was strong in the younger woman's nostrils. "Yes," Varial said, "the Enre have always posted The Listener alone. Through the millennia she has communed only with the light. Thus, wondrous things may happen. The Listener is at the convergence of the shaping forces of Aliare." Varial paused, then warned, "In such a place, in such a fulcrum, The Listener may be greatly changed. But not always for the better."

Asel knew it had been known to break a woman. But she said compliantly, "May it be so." She tightened her eyes, putting her fists to them, creating colors that appeared to her as swirls of red and blue in blackness.

"Nor is yours," Varial said. "When you desire to climb to the top, do so. Listen. Watch. You will be surprised at what you can see. You will find yourself praying much, and that will fill you with the desire to sing the songs of praise. Do so! Turn to Tarn and sing, and then turn and sing the Enre songs to release the damned. Sing of light and joy. Raise up your arms, as you did with Varial and Nor. And when you feel the exuberance from above, use this rod."

Varial took the rod from Asel's hand and lifted it above her head to slabs of flint. She spun and slashed with it, spraying sparks in all directions, singing a martial song of triumph. She sang in exulting, ringing tones that did not stop until all the words of the anthem were done, and then she sang it a second time.

"Do this as often as you wish, or as little. All who look up from Dorte will see the light spraying out from the peak and will hear the triumph in your voice and they will wonder and will fear the Enre. The light-hungry peoples of Tarn will see your sparks atop the island and will be nourished. The damned will fear the light, and the Askirit will rejoice."

Asel took the rod and struck the slabs of flint. The sparks flew in wide showers, some falling halfway down the cliffside before burning out. Asel laughed, delighted at the spectacle, and said, "I may wear out the flint if you leave me here!"

"Sing and send sparks all the season, if you wish. Do as you please, so long as you are pleased in the light. But if you sense from Dorte that Tarn may be in danger, leave at once to give us warning.

—— Temptations ——

For all the spring season, Asel listened, alone. She sometimes felt the exuberance Varial had spoken of and struck sparks in wider and wider sprays until she sensed their brightness as a blur of light. She would sing, raising her arms in that insatiable yearning, raining the sparks down upon the sea below. She would descend from the peak and walk the lake shore; she swam for pleasure and to find food. Always she wondered what might transpire, and whether she was adequate to deal with the forces that might arise against her, or, perhaps, within her.

Eventually, she felt the loneliness begin to dampen her buoyancy. The furies began whispering obscenities and all the expected accusations. She took refuge in the rituals and chants, and sang the hundreds of psalms she knew and made up her own in praise of the light.

One night she felt ill from something she had eaten. "You have seen our shores," the specters seemed to be saying. "We are closer to you than Tarn. You are alone. You hear the waves striking the rocks of Nor. Don't you sense boats on those waves? Haven't you heard odd noises?"

Asel clenched her teeth. She stood, wobbly and uncertain, and walked to the lake. She splashed water on her face, and she forced herself to chant a ritual of hope. But the furies said, "Even now something is starting to scale the cliffs. But you are sick and trapped here. You will fail to warn Tarn."

Asel stepped into the water of the lake and walked in up to her waist. She lowered her body until it was submerged, rubbed her arms and face under the water, then stood again. The voices became garbled, as if a hundred people were all shouting for her attention. She tried to shut the voices out, but they were raucous and insistent. Her body seemed to move deeper and deeper into the center of the lake, where pressure from the depths increased. The garbled voices became tentacles, reaching for her throat and head, choking off her air. "Why were you so intent on getting to Varial's scent?" a voice came through distinctly. "Why fulfill all those prophecies when you have so often longed to escape them?"

She felt herself fall forward into the water. She kicked her legs out behind her and tried to turn around toward the shore. She'd swallowed water as she fell and began coughing. Suddenly, she experienced a surge of anger. What was happening here? With her full arm, she struck the water in a hard stroke. She swam as hard as she could in her illness toward shore. She stroked furiously until, dismayed, she became convinced she was heading in the wrong direction. She stopped, floated, listened for the lapping of the waves on the shore, thought she sensed its direction and began a slow, sure stroke toward it. Finally she reached the shallows and let the breakers roll her body back and forth so she could gather energy to drag herself out of the water.

She lay on the shore and slept. When she awoke hours later, she felt the fever had broken. She remained very weak. She ate some oysters, rested awhile, then started climbing. It took her much longer than usual to reach the top, where she sat down on the highest ledge, breathing heavily, listening. The waves striking the rocks far below seemed normal. Yet how could she know if some of those movements were more than water? Were things coming onto the island? Varial said that The Listener would know. But she did not know.

She saw a firefly by her feet. It was no bigger than a spark. "Yes," she thought, "it is the season for them." She caught it, held it in her hand and stared at the pinprick of light turning on and off. She fed her spirit on its light. It was said that in Dorte the darkness swallowed all light, even the light of a tiny firefly. She looked down at those threatening regions and wondered if it were true. She heard occasional faint calls and screams from there— nearly inaudible sounds, but ones that made her cringe.

She grabbed for the rod, grasped it firmly and struck the flint as hard as she could, again and again. She searched for movements or sounds in the threatening waters below as she created showers of light.

As she called out and sang and kept striking sparks into moments of life, a vision appeared, brighter sparks than she was creating with the rod, sparks forming themselves into faces. The faces were young. They were children, but whose children? They nodded and grimaced, frightened faces, thin and ready to flee. These were not the joyous faces from her vision of her beloved children that had so powerfully shaped her life. This vision shimmered ominously, distorting the expressions of bewildered, seeking children.

One child's face emerged from the others. It came close to her and she could see it clearly. It was a girl, looking directly at her, but backing away from something, eyes wide, about to cry out. She seemed to be pleading for something, pleading that Asel do something, as if she knew Asel and was waiting for her. The sparks that made up the girl's face kept moving, then grew brighter and brighter until they were suddenly flash-white and gone.

When Varial returned on the day appointed, Asel told her of the vision. Her response was, "So it sometimes is with The Listener."

"The child is with the damned," Asel said. "It is a sign to me. When I swim away from Nor, it must not be toward Tarn."

"You would swim to Dorte?" Varial asked. "That could put all of us at risk."

"A season of listening makes risks the natural path," Asel said.

"Even your voice is changed from when I left you," Varial said. "The Listener, and all who invade the depths, can also betray us catastrophically. The furies long to destroy the Enre and all of Tarn. Who better to help them than you?"

Asel breathed deeply and was quiet. Varial said, "You should not go."

"Does that mean I may go—under your protest?"

"Other Listeners have had such visions, but none have gone to Dorte. Why should I let you be the first? Why should I let you put us all in danger?"

"But I see her face!" Asel exclaimed. "The child trembles in my eyes. She begs me for something. Years ago, children came to me in a vision that still fills me with hope. Now children have come in terror and have filled me with purpose."

"But what purpose?" Varial asked. "If the child is with the damned, she fulfills the desires of the damned. She is luring you to our destruction."

"No! The vision is light! It inspires songs and psalms in me. My soul lifts high in holy purpose!"

The older woman was silent. Then she said dryly, "Holy purpose is often difficult to assess."

Asel resisted a quick answer. She swallowed, waited, then said, "I know the purpose within me." She paused again. "What is in that land that I should fear it so? Why do we call it the region of the damned?"

"I do not know, Asel. It has always been forbidden—as I should forbid you now. You have heard the sounds. The Enre have always held Nor as a fortress against them—"

"But we took this island!" Asel exclaimed. "The ancients said the Enre took Nor when it was in darkness. They found their way in and claimed it!"

Chapter 3.

—— Young Women ——

Under his right arm, Yosha carried a bundle of twenty spears fresh from the setting vats. In his left hand, which he held before him to warn of obstructions, he carried five new double blades for malcs. His bare toes touched the edge of the weapons grotto, and he carefully balanced his way down the familiar steps.

The Askirit built four types of triangular tool-and-bench stations. Men traditionally worked the bone-cutting and tanning grottoes; women made the weapons and boats. In addition, each had one other station exclusively male or female: the intricate cabinets for making scents and perfumes. Men and women sometimes worked together on other tasks, but the mysteries of scents remained exclusive to each sex.

Distinct aromas defined their lives. Scents identified, aroused, challenged. Children wore designated scents at specific ages. For festivals, people would release scents they had recently concocted. No man going to his wedding night had previously experienced the seductive aromas awaiting him. No woman tried to replicate the musky odors men used in courting, nor the male initiation scents.

As Yosha entered the weapons grotto, he noticed the tangy scent the apprentice wore. A year older than Yosha, Aleta had just reached the age when she could wear an adult perfume.

She took the rough-hewn weapons from his hands, and the touch of her fingers gave him a slight thrill of awakening manhood. He listened to her stack the spear shafts and expertly drop the blades into a bin. The Askirit described their women as "clever" and their work on weapons as acts of love. But Yosha wished men did this work. Contrasted with cutting bones in Liriko's shop, he vastly preferred this grotto where skilled women put final touches to the perfectly balanced weapons.

"Do you know that Bles has plans for you?" Aleta asked abruptly.

He grimaced. He was startled by the statement and had no idea how to respond. Why was she saying this to him? Had she been put up to something by Bles? Aleta had always been cordial to Yosha, but never friendly, for none of the girls were. They took their cues from the boys. Yosha was the Wild, the Itchworm, the Outsider. Addressing him in a normal tone of voice was like handling the stink-fish; one could become ostracized.

Had she chanced on some information and felt she needed to help him? Or had she been put up to this by the boys? Either way, what sort of trap awaited him?

After his long silence she said, "Forget I mentioned it."

"You make a wonderful malc," he said, touching the top of the weapon on his calf. "It can slice the palm at the slightest touch."

Aleta did not respond. He left the workshop awkwardly and made his way toward the sea, listening for the slightest sound. At water's edge, he sat anxiously for a long time on a secluded outcropping. So many dangers, he thought. Vague threats. Hostility. Sierent and slippery crags. Poisonous creatures.

He thought of the pectre villagers had recently trapped. A deadly insect no bigger than his thumbnail, the pectre was rare, scuttling deep in fissures—but able to spring like a flea, instantly cutting into a man's flesh.

No one could ever explain how they sometimes found their way into fishermen's nets. Because they did, before emptying them, men poked their nets with long poles to reveal the telltale spitting. Not one net in a thousand contained a pectre, but when one did, a great cry went up.

Three times in his life, Yosha had heard the sound. Each time brave villagers rushed to the net with thin, tough sacks dangling open from long poles. A rope extended from each man's hand to a draw-string on the sack, which could be tightly closed a pole length away. The men dangled the sacks' open mouths before the pectre, shaking the sacks, trying to make it strike. When it did, everyone immediately tightened each bag. Then they shook the bags, listening to sense if it was captured, patiently listening, poking, backing away, shaking the bags. The danger each faced was that the pectre might light on the sack instead of in it, and work its way up the pole.

Several years ago—the second time Yosha had heard the cry—he had grown bored with the interminable process when the silence was broken by a man's scream.

Yosha shuddered at the memory. When the more recent pectre had been captured, he and all the village had sighed in relief.

But it was leviathan, not pectres and snakes, that stirred Yosha's blood; the rituals spoke of mighty deeds against the sea monster. As he listened to the winds drive the waters, he imagined its great bulk mastering the depths, surging toward the shore at his feet.

"Waiting for leviathan?" a girl's voice asked.

Yosha whipped around. He was chagrined she had gotten this close. What if it had been Bles? "I always think of Kjotik when I come here," he answered. Jemm was the daughter of his father's cousin, and aside from Liriko, the only one he felt tolerated him. He was never certain if it was the blood-tie obligation or that she simply wanted to be with a boy—any boy. She always teased him, bantering, giggling; she allowed herself to touch his face and hands in ways that raced his blood.

"Kjotik won't come tonight," Jemm announced, rubbing his bare shoulder. "You have scared him off again."

She led him to the pools where others were looking at three luminous eels that had been caught during the day. They were stripes of faint light that would suddenly wriggle and dive, then emerge at another edge of the pool.

He stared at them, drinking in the diffuse light.

"Let's go," Jemm said, and they turned toward the sound of the villagers singing and the sight of sparks rhythmically striking on and off with the music. The pinpricks, produced by dancers striking flints together, enlivened the blackness. They stuck the flints above their heads, then sideways so the sparks sprayed in each direction—white embers with traces of reds and blues.

What power in light! he thought. The Askirit sought it in every possible form. How good the portent of a firefly landing on one's body! In contrast, barbarian tribes feared it. To them, a firefly alighting on one's arm was a frightening omen. If barbarians caught anything luminous from the sea, they cast it back.

Yosha and Jemm sat with the other villagers of Wellen, eating a simple meal. When they were finished, Jemm started tapping a hollow bone. Others shook small bladders filled with pebbles and started singing and moving with the music. They started telling stories, each memorized from childhood.

Yosha stood. "Out of the wreckage, flint," he said to the group, striking sparks from two fat flints in his hands.

"Out of the wreckage, light," came the expected response all around him.

Yosha then told the story of Sember, a little boy who had danced on the skin of the world above, but then fell into darkness. In the mud, the boy played with rocks and made a spark with flint. He shouted exuberantly that he had found light, but others mocked Sember. The little boy made more sparks, for they filled him with hope, and he kept shouting "Light!" as he struck his flints again and again.

Yosha then called out the refrain: "Sember found a piece of flint."

The others sang in response, "He found a piece of flint."

Yosha stopped for the long pause, then sang again, "Out of the wreckage, flint."

The others sang, "Out of wreckage, light."

Yosha kept leading the chant, fervently calling out the lines, striking his flints with all his strength and seeing the sparks from a hundred others shower about them in the darkness. Then he dropped his hands to his sides, and his chin to his chest, his eyes full of tears.

Jemm's fingers tapped out a message on his palm. "You always tell the same stories. No wonder you are Kret. You want to be a hero, and all heroes are crazy."

His hand playfully snapped shut, trapping her fingers, then releasing them with a sliding motion—a message of affection with a touch of intimacy. "You're much wilder than I am," he tapped out on her palm.

The Askirit communicated as rapidly by hand signals as speech. Called Yette, their tactile language was in some ways more expressive. As the voice communicates more through tone and accent than the words themselves, so the fingertips, the edge of the nails, the knuckles, the flat of the hand, even the elbow and shoulder conveyed wide ranges of meaning.

Yette, used softly and gently, was a language of intimacy. It could be romantic and poetic, or earthy, conveying the most explicit terms of endearment. Used brusquely and precisely, Yette was the silent language of the battlefield; with elaborate courtesy, it became the language of intrigue in the king's court.

A child at the far edge of the crowd burst out laughing; the sound reminded Yosha of a time his father had told him a story in Yette, his fingers racing across his palm and up his arm like flapping wings, causing him to giggle and then laugh aloud.

Jemm danced her fingertips on his collarbone. It was an innocent message: "Let's go back to the shore." But her touches had been awakening his body, and he thought of the saying that certain messages on the wrist by a bride were more erotic than the scents of the wedding night. He flushed, wondering at her effect on him. She did not even wear an adult scent yet. He wanted to touch her face, to feel its curves and hollows, to see if she was beautiful. At the water's edge, she put her forehead on his, touched noses, then laughed. With three fingers running across his forearm, she asked in Yette, "Why are you always so morbid, talking about war and keitr and Kjotik? Why not talk about pleasant things?"

"But Kjotik is a worthy enemy!" he signaled back earnestly, his fingers racing on her palm. "It's wonderful to plan—"

"Wonderful?" she interrupted aloud, pulling her hand away as if he'd jabbed it. "Kjotik's disgusting!"

"No, *planning* is wonderful. It's wonderful that maybe Kjotik could be stopped."

Jemm laughed again, much more loudly than the first time, and boldly put both her hands on his face, squeezing his cheeks and then exploring the hollows around his eyes. "Yosha, maybe you will also break open the roof to heaven some fine day, and we'll all dance in the light. Stories are stories. Don't be so serious! You'll miss everything that's going on around you."

He reached out to Jemm with both hands and tried to control the slight trembling in his fingers as he moved them timidly over her face. She continued to caress his eyes and cheeks, then abruptly gave him a playful pinch and stood up.

Yes, he decided, her face was beautiful. He hardly knew what she was saying as she bid him good night and he started walking home.

Halfway there he remembered Aleta's warning about Bles. He began to listen cautiously again, but he sensed nothing unusual until he was almost through his doorway. There his nose detected Kark's presence; he always wore the same biting, military scent. "Yosha, you are late," he said.

"Sierent has not yet—," Yosha began apologetically.

"Late is last-minute. You know that! And why didn't you eat with the other boys tonight? They tell me—"

"They tell you lies all the time. They—"

"All five are lying to me?" he interrupted angrily. Kark stood ramrod stiff before him. He took a step closer to the boy and said, "You antagonize everybody, including me. You'd better settle down and shape up, Kret! Any more fighting and you'll be hanging out there for sierent." He spun his body in a military motion and stalked off.

By the time Yosha was prone on his bed, he could hear Kark already into his ritual prayers for the night, repeating the holy words. Of all the boys, Yosha most fiercely believed every word of the ritual and sought the light with all his strength. Yet Kark had no confidence in him. Yosha listened to him repeating the words and felt his spirits lift as he silently mouthed the cadences with him. He marveled that he and Kark could be at such odds when they believed and tried to act upon the same truths.

Long after Kark had gone to sleep, Yosha was still repeating sections of the ritual. He pondered the ones that warned him to trust no man. He thought about the warning by the apprentice.

—— Pectre ——

The first sound Yosha heard next morning was the quiet shuffle of feet around his bed. He heard a sniff, then Bles's voice quoting the holy words:

"The powers cannot keep you from the jaws of death."

The other boys chanted the repetition:

"... the jaws of death."

Bles chanted the next line:

"You are his son, but death is near."

"... death is near."

Yosha's mind raced to understand what was happening. Were they trying to enrage him again? Frighten him?

"Do not pity yourself," Bles said.

". . . pity yourself," the others intoned.

"Perform wonders! Break the jaws of death!"

". . . the jaws of death!"

Yosha stood, and as he did, he heard something move at his feet. He thought he heard the creature spitting. Instantly, he thought of the pectre that had been caught in the nets just days before. Terror spread through him. How had they gotten it in here? A waist-high wall enclosed his bed; he was trapped with it. Once it struck him, the flat pectre would slice its way so fast into his flesh that nothing could stop its wriggling body.

"Fiend," people called the pectre, for its gruesome life cycle and its spitting warnings. To die from a pectre took several days. The mind went first, causing hallucinations and wild gyrations. The body began wasting away. Then came the horror. Pectre by the hundreds suddenly began slicing and rippling out of the emaciated body, squirming everywhere in search of new hosts.

For this reason, a man bitten by a pectre was quarantined. As soon as he began hallucinating and lost touch with reality, he would be taken to one of the "snakeholes" found deep in the caverns. Some said these perfectly round holes had been made by gigantic serpents; everyone believed they were bottomless. After suitable prayers, the delirious victim was cast in.

All this and the memory of the fisherman's scream and desperate slap at the pectre slicing into his chest pulsed through Yosha. Bles! The pectre caught the day before! Kark had chosen Bles to cast the thing in its sack into a snakehole, into the bowels of Aliare. But Bles must have kept it somehow, Yosha thought, he must have kept the thing!

Yosha stood motionless. The other boys were silent now, just like the long silences of the fishermen years before when he had heard the pectre strike. Should he make a move? What kind of move?

"Let not the demons smell your fear," Bles quoted.

". . . smell your fear," the others repeated.

Before they had finished the words, he heard a thud at his feet that made the creature spit. The noise made Yosha's skin prickle, the smell of his fear spreading into the air. They chanted more taunts. What had they thrown in? Did they really hate him this much? he wondered, sucking at his dry mouth.

Yosha moved his arm as slow as time, reaching for his leather shirt. His fingers touched it, and he ran his fingers up the seam. Then he slowly, slowly lifted the shirt, raising his hand waist-high, and let the garment hang down in front of him.

No reaction. He slowly stepped onto his bed, which was ankle high. Not enough height, yet maybe . . . His mind weighed whether he should stand here forever or try to leap the wall, holding the shirt before him. He lowered himself almost to a squat, measuring his chances, feeling the trembling in his body and knowing he would weaken the longer he stood.

He sprang, with all his body straining for height, the shirt in his left hand to block the pectre, his right hand reaching for the top of the wall. He stumbled over the shirt and fell heavily. A sharp pain bit into his thigh and he screamed, smashing his open hand against his leg.

He lay gasping, wondering how fast a pectre gets to the brain and how it would start taking over his mind. He wondered if he would know when they threw him over the edge. Would he die on the way down, plummeting toward gheials? He wondered if his father would be waiting for him in that next world, or if he would enter it alone to meet terrible beings.

Silence. A terrifyingly long silence in which he felt he was already becoming delirious.

Then he heard laughter. It was loud, coarse laughter. He squeezed his eyes, fighting to grasp what had happened. The boys were now laughing derisively, in triumph. It was all just a practical joke! It must have been some other insect or spitting reptile thrown in with him, but they knew his mind would be on the pectre just captured.

Oh, how they must hate me! Yosha thought, and how he hated them! The voices in his mind demanded he leap the little wall and kill them. Oh, how he longed to strangle Bles! Their laughter went on and on, becoming strained and false.

Then he realized that outside the door, girls were laughing too. He listened intently, picking out voices. To his astonishment, he detected Jemm's. He heard her say something about Kjotik, then she burst out laughing with the others.

He leapt suddenly from the bed and over the wall, stormed through the boys before they knew he was upon them, and crashed past the crowd of girls to the air outside. Behind him he heard excited voices, exclaiming at his humiliation.

He raged to the sea's edge. Jemm's betrayal had jolted him into moaning helplessly to all that was holy. He stood rigid. Was everything just a gruesome practical joke? Was his life nothing, like the empty promises of the rituals?

Slowly, slowly—from his desperation and emptiness—came a strange lightness. He felt as if this calm collecting in him was like the quiet pools formed on top of a cliff by the spray of waves battering its face. This strange calm was powerful, transforming. He slowly sat down, placing his bare feet in the sea, letting the hatred leech out, and letting his resolution build. The violence that remained in him he directed toward Kjotik. His wild nature sketched out scenario after scenario, which blurred the line between temptation and resolve.

He tried not to think about Jemm. Had she really seen this as merely a practical joke? Was this part of Yosha's needing to simply see "the fun in life?" How would she respond to a pectre in her bed? The girl in the weapons shop—Aleta—was she his only real friend? At least she had tried to warn him.

He longed to leave this village. Now, he would never wholly trust a man again, or a woman.

—— Zeskret ——

Yosha hunched on a crag far above Wellen, silently listening to the birds. In the months since his humiliation, the birds had become as important to his soul as the sparks and the songs at festivals. He would roam for hours, listening for their calls, hearing them greeting the morning, scolding each other, scratching for food.

He could identify most of the birds by their calls. He loved the stories of the mountain birds of prey and the sea birds with wing-spans as wide as two tall men.

The bird he thought of most, however, was no bigger than a child's fist. At the flint gatherings, tales were told about its mad ferocity. Yosha felt a kinship with this bird, because it took up any challenge larger than itself, and especially because its name was zeskret. The word "kret" meant wild, but "zes" meant a military-like discipline, so the bird's name paradoxically meant "a disciplined wildness."

Yosha's nickname "kret" carried no respect. But men would speak of the zeskret in tones of wonder.

Thus what happened in the next moments there in the crags high above his village became a personal omen. He was startled by a sharp cry of alarm from a clestra, a large bird with a hooked beak. It cried out again and flapped hurriedly away toward the sea. Then came the sound that thrilled Yosha. He had heard a zeskret many times before, but only its songs as it fed on insects or called to its mate. This cry was terrible and wonderful, tingling his nerves. He had heard the sound described in stories about zeskrets attacking snakes, lizards, and birds many times their size. He guessed the clestra had gotten too close to the little warrior's nest.

The zeskret hit the clestra with a rat-tat-tat-tat-tat; the larger bird cried out and flapped frantically to gain height. The zeskret was much faster, striking again, almost immediately, at its underside with another rat-tat-tat-tat-tat. He heard it again, rat-tat-tat-tat-tat, so fast Yosha could not imitate it with his tongue. The clestra became a panicked flurry of wings and piercing calls. Three more staccato bursts from the zeskret amid the clestra's cries of outrage, and the fighting sounds began plummeting until he heard the nearly inaudible splash of the clestra's body.

Yosha stayed motionless, savoring the incident. He compared the little bird, so small it could fit in his hand, with his own size against Bles and the others, and his own frenzied but ineffective wildness against them. He relived the zeskret's cry again and again, trying to regain the thrill of first hearing it.

Several nights later, as he was sitting at water's edge during the singing, he thought he heard a woman in the crowd use the word "Kret." He walked toward the voice and heard her telling the story of a time he had attacked the other boys. She was saying nothing of their cruel provocations but described Yosha's reactions and how the boys had beaten him, and how Kark had then disciplined him for starting a fight.

Yosha let her finish the story, then said to her, "But I am not Kret. I am Zeskret! Mark it. Know that I am Zeskret and Yosha and no other."

He determined, starting that moment, to act immediately in the spirit of his self-declared nickname. Instead of drinking the allotted skin full of kek—a mineral water flavored by clams and herbs—he saved it and drank plain water instead. As usual he sat by himself, listening especially to Bles and the boys, thinking, imagining, planning. He waited patiently until it was late and an elder had started telling a story. Sidling over in the press of the crowd, he put his bottle of kek into Bles's hand. Bles's own supply would soon be gone, and he knew it was unlikely his antagonist would wonder who had handed it to him.

Late that night, his theory proved correct. He had been lying awake for several hours before he got up and walked to Bles's bed. He carefully held a bottle next to the boy's ear and trickled water into a cup. Bles moved. Yosha poured a little more water, then stepped away. The other boy rolled over and took a deep breath. Yosha was dismayed for a moment that he seemed to be going back to sleep, but then Bles jerked his leg over the edge of the bed, stood up, and walked toward the corridor.

Yosha followed Bles as quietly as possible, stopping only to pick up a long pole. He stayed far behind, knowing Bles's destination, yet close enough for his purposes.

Outside he heard the loud winds of sierent tearing at the far entrances of the caverns. When he emerged into partially open air at a split in the cavern wall, the winds tore at him and he could no longer hear Bles. He kept following, more quickly now. He walked a narrow ledge overlooking a deep rock basin that served as one of the village's several latrines.

As Bles began relieving his bladder, Yosha propped himself sturdily against the rock wall and extended his long pole until he felt it touch his enemy's back. "Don't move!" Yosha whispered. "One sound, one twitch, and I'll shove you over!" Yosha's voice trembled. He had thought at this moment he would sound fierce as a zeskret, but he thought he sounded as terrified as Bles must be.

"Take one step back—slowly," Yosha ordered. "Don't turn!" Yosha eased the pole back, keeping the tension between Bles's shoulders. Bles said nothing, but Yosha sensed his fear. "I have thought about every move you could make," he warned. "Your footing is narrow and this is a stout pole. Try anything, and you're gone."

Yosha dropped one knee and changed his position. "But why

should I warn you? Why not shove you over? You've beaten me unconscious. You call my father a hunk of meat! You're odious! Why shouldn't I cleanse Aliare of you? My father is probably watching, chuckling, saying, 'Give him a shove, boy. Do it for me. It's about time.'"

Bles moved his foot slightly, bracing against the wind, and Yosha nudged the pole forward. "But I don't hate you, Bles. Aren't you lucky? We are told not to hate."

Yosha paused a long while, then said, "But we must be very clever in war. It says that, you know. And you have declared war on me. Right?"

He was running through the script he had rehearsed so many times. He was too tense to enjoy it; he kept thinking of all the ways the situation could be reversed and how Bles might not hesitate to push him over. He had to get this done quickly. "Bles, tell me about your father," he said.

Bles said nothing but emitted a groan. "I mean it," Yosha insisted, "You were nine when your father died. You have to long for him, to want his shoulder under you." He snarled the next words: "What did you love about him?"

Bles's voice croaked, "Everything! Everything! He hunted with me. I loved that. He told me I was the best at singing, just like him."

"And he said you were like your mother, didn't he, Bles?"

"What do you mean?"

"Didn't he!" Yosha demanded.

"He said I sounded like her, and my hair was thick like hers." Bles's voice choked on the last word, and he pleaded, "I'm slipping. My legs are wobbly, and I've got to hold on to something!"

"You'll hold air!" Yosha ordered. "Do you remember your mother's hair?"

"I was only two when—"

"What do you remember?"

"Her voice."

"Did your father ever cry about her?"

"Yes."

"Did you? Don't lie!"

"Yes."

"Do you cry about her at night?"

"Yes."

Yosha paused, allowing a long silence. Then he asked, "Tell me how you dream about your mother and your father."

"I don't dream about them."

"Thinking or dreaming about them, tell me! Now!"

Yosha pressed him for detail after detail, knowing his only means of survival after this night would be what Yosha knew about Bles—and proof that he had groveled.

"Beg me now not to push you over!"

"No," Bles said.

"No?" Yosha roared. "You will beg, or die, right now. Beg!"

Bles pled for his life, sobbing and shaking.

"Slowly step back," Yosha said. "You'll live tonight. But if you tell anyone of this—anyone—you'll wish I had pushed you over."

—— Maachah ——

Yosha shouted back at the furies taunting his mind as he approached the small city of Rens. The moment he had turned his back on his village three days before, determined to visit Maachah the priest, the furies had assaulted him.

"You're a runaway now," they taunted. "Kark will beat you bloody. He'll give you to Bles as a slave. Why run when you're winning? When they're starting to fear you!"

But Yosha knew the boys hated him more than ever. He

tormented himself that his assault on Bles may have been stupid. It hadn't solved anything—he was more ostracized than ever.

He had told Liriko moments before he had left Wellen, "Tell Kark I am going to see a priest."

"Tell him yourself," Liriko said. "You can't run off—we have a priest right here."

"Pagh! He hasn't helped me a bit!" Yosha retorted. "And everyone's convinced I need a lot of help! Tell Kark I have to have a priest, and it's got to be Maachah."

But even as he spoke those words, the furies had whispered that Maachah was the last person to see. Yosha thought of a statement by King Rycal: "Maachah the priest is either holy or insane. I'd rather face leviathan than go into the ritual with him."

The tormentors of his thoughts whispered, "If your own king would rather face leviathan than a ritual with Maachah, what do you think will happen to you? Maachah will know you for what you are. He'll pierce to your rotten core."

All along the journey they had tried to stop him. "Your father and mother are waiting for you. They're longing to hold you and love you. The trail's edge is slippery. Twice you almost fell. Why not slip again, fall free like the birds you hear calling, join your parents who love you. They are the only ones who love you."

As he entered the city, they whispered, "You are wasting yourself here. Kark and the others will grab you by the neck and drag you back with a rope. Escape to the crags. Gather keitr and become a man. You're already the Wild. Become wild like the mountain outcasts. They live as they please, like the zeskret. Escape the trap."

But he walked on. He heard the voice of a young girl and asked her where Maachah was to be found. She gave him directions. He slowly felt his way in the strange city, clicking his tongue for echoes, feeling the walls, carefully extending one foot after another, until he came to a line of supplicants.

There proved to be only four people in the line, all chattering as easily as if they were queued up for fresh fish.

Yosha listened to their domestic talk for a time before he asked, "What is Maachah like?"

A man replied, "Maachah's crazy. Scary crazy. And weird crazy. That's why we're all here."

The others laughed, as if they reveled in Maachah's bizarre reputation. "He's fierce," a woman said. "Everyone's afraid to answer his questions."

"You mean the impure are afraid!" the first man said, and everyone snorted loudly at this obvious reference to Rycal's statement, which rankled the people of Rens.

Another said, "Maachah's crazy and he's fierce, but he's like a child, too. He can talk like a child, sing like a child. In the pools, he'll drape an eel over his neck as children do and wriggle its tail so it shimmers on his shoulders."

Yosha said, "I've heard he sees to your very core. But others say he sees nothing, that he simply scares people."

"Listen," a woman said, "He sees. The fact is, he's not just a holy man. He really *is* holy. And the proof is this—you know it when you're with him. If you've got lots to hide—like Rycal," she paused meaningfully and laughed, ". . . then you are sure to know it. But if you're seeking the light, you know it, too!"

As one of the four ahead of him stepped forward and the others resumed their talking, Yosha felt more apprehensive than ever. In the Rite of Purification, a priest could ask you anything—anything at all. And if you didn't answer honestly, the good priests knew you were lying. And they could refuse you absolution.

The three ahead of him filed in one at a time for their moments alone with the priest.

Then it was Yosha's turn.

"What is your name?" Maachah asked, as soon as Yosha had parted the thick skins hanging at the entrance.

"Yosha. But many call me Zeskret."

He was instantly angry with himself for making his first words a lie.

But the priest simply walked to the water and cupped a little in his right hand. "May your eyes be cleansed," he said, touching Yosha's eyes with the dripping fingertips of his left hand. "And your lips. And your ears. And your hands." The priest poured the rest of the water in his hand over Yosha's head. "He cleanses only those who know they are impure," he said, "only those who desire light more than life, for light cannot be soiled."

Yosha blinked the water away from his eyes. "Sit down," Maachah told him.

As he obeyed, Yosha realized the furies no longer taunted; the oppression had lifted. He thought the woman must be right about Maachah. But if Maachah was holy, it made Yosha even more afraid.

"Do you believe in the light?" Maachah asked.

"I believe."

"Do you see the light?"

"I see it in the holy words," Yosha said, drawing from the ritual phrases.

"No, not in words. Do you *see*?"

"Only sparks and—"

"Now! See the light!" Maachah commanded. "Believe it! Wash the sleep from your eyes!"

"But how can I see it? Where should I look?" Yosha asked, suddenly desperate.

"Look around you! The whole planet is shot through with light!" Maachah exclaimed. "Open your eyes, child! Can't you see the holy ones standing beside you? Their light is gleaming off your face!"

Yosha turned right and left. "I don't see it!" he cried out. "My eyes are open, yet I can't see anything at all. But please, Eshtel above, I want to!" Even as he said this, Yosha began feeling something urging him to leap up and shout out in praise, to grasp the light with his hands, to pry his eyes open. But he saw nothing, and he fell to his knees in supplication.

Maachah said, "Don't bow to me. Get up." Yosha obeyed. "To see the light," Maachah said, "one must have a great longing."

He led the boy to a corner of the room. In a basin swam several small, luminous fish. "Why do we stare at the light?" Maachah asked. "Because we are blind, wretched men, deposed from glory."

"I have a great longing!" Yosha said. "A terrible longing for the light. A longing wonderful and ravenous. It devours ..."

"Ah," said Maachah, "your longing devours you. That is because you are in exile. But the Spirit of Light probes the darkness. A day is coming when light will shoot into every crevice of Aliare and through all the worlds, and all will see it. He will indeed devour you, and light will overwhelm you."

"But I see no light! I see only men who hate me!" Yosha exclaimed in his impetuous manner. "My father is dead. The elders despise my questions. The boys lie about me, though I try in every way to do right. Even the women speak of me with contempt, though I am an orphan and still but a child."

Maachah touched his hand. "Splendid! Splendid!" he said heartily. "That is wonderful in a hundred ways!"

Yosha shut his mouth. He sat down and held his head in his hands and then harrumphed loudly. "Splendid? Wonderful? When a girl betrays me? When I am beaten for no cause and laughed at by the whole village?"

Maachah sat down opposite Yosha. "You have heard of honest Hést, who was thrown into the dungeons for supposed bribery. The king's men hated him, and he rotted there for years. But when he came out, he exclaimed, 'The dungeons have freed me! They released me from greed. I now need nothing and have everything.'

"Yosha, you have heard from childhood how you must suffer. How suffering is the path to purity. It toughens and readies you for battle. Each of us must suffer. 'Much suffering, much power.'" Maachah touched the boy's face. "Tell me, then, Yosha, how would you like to suffer?"

Yosha had no response to this odd question. He finally replied, "I do not know what you mean."

"Would you like to suffer in a great battle, doing exploits to be sung about? Would you like your suffering to be heroic? At the hands of barbarians? Ah, that is not suffering, that is adventure! But what you have described is glorious suffering, precisely the sort extolled in the liturgies. See for yourself. Your suffering brought you here. Your suffering is driving you to the light, purging, humbling you."

"But my suffering brings me close to death!" Yosha exclaimed. "It is full of fiends' voices! They are driving me mad, taunting me at every turn."

Maachah dropped his hand from Yosha's face to his shoulder and gripped it firmly. "We live in the kingdoms of death. The hunger of the furies is insatiable. You must yearn for the light."

"I do! I try to reject them, to control them, to ride the furies—"

"You cannot ride the furies!" Maachah interrupted sharply. "Who ever said you could? That is their own lie! They blind you, mock you. They want you to ride them, dance with them, argue with them. You are mortal. You are mere mud and clay."

"But they are always at me! I cannot shut them out of my mind."

"Of course you cannot. Seek the light! Dream of exploits, but only in the power of the light!"

Maachah led Yosha to a small basin of scented oil. He dipped his fingers into the basin and touched the distinctive scent to Yosha's eyelids. "You are absolved of your sins," he said.

Yosha stood there awkwardly, still raging with questions. But he had been absolved and was dismissed. He stepped slowly away, drawing into his nostrils the familiar scent of absolution.

As he touched the skins at the entrance, Maachah said

quietly to him, "You wretched little boy. You are the hope of the nation." And Maachah chuckled, like a man amused at a mysterious and deeply satisfying wonder.

—— Beld ——

"You'll find Beld repairing weapons," the man told Yosha. "Make right turns till you hit the entrance."

Yosha had left Rens and spent nearly a week finding this little hamlet far up the coast. Long ago he had heard a remarkable tale about a man named Beld: that he had been swallowed by leviathan but then spat out upon the shore. The tale had captured his imagination.

He was oddly nervous when his foot touched the entrance. He felt, somehow, he was about to meet his father.

"Have you come to help?" a man's voice asked.

"I have little skill at weapons," Yosha replied, entering the small space.

"If you mean this is woman's work, you're right. I'd gladly trade you for a woman! We've lost three to childbirth this year. If I don't get this belt fixed, I'll have keitrs chewing my hand."

Yosha walked further in. "I've always wanted to work on weapons," he said. "I'd like to help."

The man grunted noncommittally. "Why have you come here?"

"If you are Beld, I'm here to learn if the tales—"

"Yes, the tales are true!" the man interrupted impatiently, shoving a keitr pouch into Yosha's hand. "There's nothing more to say. Now sew in the old holes—don't make any new ones."

Yosha reached for the awl and fingered the worn seam. "My

father was also taken by leviathan," Yosha said, fingering the empty holes.

"I'm not your father."

"I know. I just—"

"Two others came here like you. A girl hoped I was her long-dead father, and a woman absolutely knew I was her husband." He grunted and flipped the keitr belt he was working on over his shoulder so that, in the close quarters, Yosha felt it breeze by his head.

Yosha began working on the pouch, carefully pulling the rawhide through the holes. He stifled his questions for a while, but finally asked, "How long were you inside Kjotik?"

"A day. At least a day."

"What do you remember?"

"Gagging. And smothering. I was coughing up gunk, and my eyes burned as if they were dissolving. Even after I was out of the beast and they soaked me in water, my eyes burned. My skin still seems puckery."

"Why did he spit you out?"

"Obviously, I'm bad meat!" the man said, sniffing at his well-worn joke.

"Maybe we could all become bad meat!" Yosha exclaimed. "Maybe you wore a scent Kjotik hates, or your keitr belt poisoned him. Maybe there's something—"

"I'm not the first to be spat out. I really don't care why. I'm just—"

"But we all sing the promises. We're not to fear leviathan, but everyone panics when Kjotik hits the shore. We make liars of ourselves and of all that's holy if we cringe at Kjotik."

"Cringe? I've never cringed! But I've sure as death run like a launched keitr. The marauder wriggles at you like a maddened snake! It's like a mountain of waves, and its wriggling gives it momentum to thrust itself into the air and then come down on you like a hammer on a flea. I know what you're thinking," Beld said. "You can't revenge your father, boy!"

"What about the promises?" Yosha asked.

Beld ignored him. He wrestled with the thin membrane of the inner keitr pouch as he stitched it with a fine bone needle.

Yosha leaned toward his host and emphasized his words: "I know Kjotik's hide cannot be pierced. But leviathan has a mouth! And he spat you out. We are not to fear him. He is not spirit! He is not sierent. He is a brute to be hunted, a mountain of flesh to be outwitted."

Beld snorted lightly at the boy's breathless run of words. "So Kjotik has a mouth. How many keitr can you shoot into it before you're swallowed?"

Yosha finished the pouch. Beld handed him the inner sleeve he had repaired and let him carefully tuck it into the tough leather. "When you put the keitr in," Beld said, "you make sure he's been gathered properly, head into the sack, wings folded back and not bent crooked. They can't fly right if they hibernate in there all bent like that. Be precise. The launcher fits into this groove in the pouch, hooking the triple threads of the inside sleeve."

Yosha, who had heard this many times before, plied Beld with questions about every possible weapon that could be used against leviathan. The man tolerated his questions for several days only because the boy kept his fingers working.

—— Kjotik's Jaw ——

Yosha returned to Wellen and went directly to the Aeries, where he immediately started pulling himself up past the dangling cage of the maniac. He traversed the trellises without hearing any lunatic outbursts.

On his knees in the formation he called Kjotik's Jaw, he

gripped the giant tooth of stone and leaned out over the sea. Even here, in this place of power, he still felt vulnerable. Had Maachah really helped him? He'd been absolved of his sins by priests before. Away from Maachah's presence, he realized why they called him "weird crazy." Who were these glowing creatures Yosha couldn't see? What did his exclamations about lights shooting through worlds mean? Maybe lights in Maachah's mind, like psalms that spoke of light you were commanded to see but couldn't . . . and sea monsters you were commanded to confront, but got bitten in half if you did.

Maachah's parting words taunted him. What did the priest mean that he was the hope of the nation? Was Maachah laughing at his intensity, laughing like everyone else? He shuddered—maybe laughter would be preferable to what Kark would do when he got back.

Abruptly, something brushed against his knee. He convulsed his body backward, jerking his knees around and thrusting his right arm defensively across his face. A blast of foul breath and the shout, "Gheials!" assaulted him. Something touched his shoulder.

The maniac! How could he be up here? Yosha couldn't fend him off on these slippery heights—they'd both fall to their deaths.

The maniac shouted again, "Gheials scrabbling all over you! Tentacles, suckers, bleeding your neck!"

Panicked, Yosha twisted away from him and crawled toward the largest tunnel nearby. The maniac kept shouting as he crawled close behind him.

"Belstin!" a voice commanded. "The birds! The music! Come listen!" It was Mosen's voice, commanding, authoritative. The maniac kept shouting and crawling after Yosha. Mosen kept ordering him back, saying, "Belstin, something greater is here. Come. Come."

Yosha stopped in the narrowing tunnel, flipped onto his back and braced his legs against his pursuer. "Gheials!" the maniac shouted at him one last time, then backed away toward Mosen's voice. Yosha reluctantly followed at a distance until he heard Mosen talking of light and wings and the food that he must have been handing Belstin.

The maniac began eating quietly.

It was a long time before Yosha said to Mosen, his body crouched defensively in the tunnel's mouth, "How did he get loose?"

"I helped him out," Mosen said. "Everyone thinks he's still in there, since I rattle his cage when they bring him food. He can live and eat up here, free and harmful to no one."

"No one but me!"

"Belstin will hurt nothing but your ears," Mosen said.

"How can you do this, Mosen?"

"How could you go to Rens? Sometimes we must seek the light despite what the keepers of the light say."

"But you cannot violate—"

"Violations made Belstin a maniac!" Mosen interrupted. "Violations of our own laws." He sat down heavily and said, "I've been listening to him. Everyone knows he went crazy in the wars. But why? In his sleep, he keeps mumbling the same story.

"He and the other soldiers had to round up an entire village, men, women, children. The villagers were accused of sabotage. He had to help force those families out on the shore. They made not a sound—even the children were quiet and brave. But then, as it grew later and later and sierent came on, he heard their cries as the winds started sucking at them. Belstin had to listen to those cries till the last one was swept away."

Yosha grimaced. "But no Askirit troops would do that!"

"Or admit they did. We occupy barbarian lands—to bring them light." He said this last contemptuously. "But in war, they say, 'niceties' are forgotten. Yet Belstin can never forget those cries."

Yosha knew little of what transpired beyond Tarn's shores. He had never much thought about it.

"Should we lead barbarians to the light?" Mosen asked.

"Of course," Yosha said reflexively.

Mosen waited for a moment, then confessed, "My parents were born barbarians."

Yosha was astounded. "I didn't know that," he said, wondering if he was stumbling over his tongue. How could Mosen's parents be barbarians?

"They were initiated in another village," Mosen supplied. "And now they love the light more than most Askirit do. But we had to leave that first village."

Belstin stopped eating and suddenly shouted at something.

"All he yells at are foul creatures from the pit," Mosen said. "His mind is obsessed with them."

"And possessed as well?" Yosha asked.

Mosen patted Belstin's shoulder reassuringly and made a little vibrating sound with the tip of his tongue. "He's not possessed by them. He fights his furies. They leered at him full in the face when his nerves were too taut and his conscience too tender. He looked among his fellow soldiers for the pity our rituals require, and he found none."

Yosha said, "Perhaps he resists evil more than us all."

"And perhaps he is more holy. He hates evil—yet he senses gheials squatting around him all the time, like birds in a rookery. Belstin's not possessed. He's daft. Excruciatingly daft. He is my great, Holy Wreck."

⸺ Leviathan ⸺

Yosha did not receive a beating from Kark as he had feared. He humbly told the man about his desperate need for a priest to help him straighten out, and how he had found the light, and what a believing and godly priest Maachah was. Kark laid upon

Yosha many extra duties and restrictions, but these he welcomed since they helped him avoid the other boys.

His obsession remained leviathan. When he asked Kark if he could somehow have access to keitr in the event Kjotik were to attack their village, the man was dumbfounded.

"I need only four," Yosha explained in great earnestness. "Just four keitr and four launchers. They could stay right here, but when Kjotik hits—"

"You'll come running to get my keitr when Kjotik hits? You got this idea from Maachah? He must be as crazy as they say. When Kjotik comes, we're all scrambling out of there! You know you can't shoot leviathan."

"But the mouth! It's vulnerable."

"The mouth? The only way you're in position is under it. You're going to stand there under its mouth and shoot it? Shoot a hungry mountain falling on you?"

Yosha never brought up the subject with Kark again. For two years, he humbled himself under him and tried to totally avoid the other boys.

He did this by working most of the time. When the furies began whispering to him, he sang psalms, and with gritty resolve, memorized the longest sections of the chants and the wisdom of the sages.

At the same time, his mind was always at work on plans to combat leviathan. He worked at his obsession so much that at times he couldn't help spilling out to others his ideas and hopes.

People jokingly called him Zeskret-Kjotik. "Get the little bird to attack leviathan," people said to him. "Get it under Kjotik's flukes. The zeskret will hammer at it until it's so tickled it will giggle itself back to the sea."

Yosha tried hard to laugh with the villagers as they ridiculed him, but he never could. What was funny about this? Why couldn't they see they were the faithless ones who should have been helping?

Liriko was the only person naturally kind to him, but even

he said, "Work all you want. But the Askirit peoples have wept and prayed and labored at this for thousands of years and have accomplished nothing. One boy is not going to stop leviathan with dreams and bones."

Yet Liriko let him go on dreaming and working. Yosha wheedled supplies from Aleta, the weapons apprentice, by doing errands for her and thanking her for the warning about Bles.

He gave up hopes of getting keitr, so he gathered hundreds of selcrit instead. Tiny crab-like creatures, selcrit had both sharp pincers and nasty little teeth. When frightened, they pinched and slashed in a panicked, erratic pattern. It was almost impossible to shake them off and many of them, working together, could quickly strip the largest fish to the bone.

He made pouch liners of fine mesh, so that after catching the selcrit, he could keep them netted in the pool. Daily he fed them bits of fish. He found if selcrit were trapped in the mesh net for more than a day, they started dying, so he would release four batches of selcrit from his four pouches, then replace them with others from another pool.

It was the beginning of the third year when leviathan struck Yosha's village. Kjotik always came in the evenings when everyone was on shore instead of safe in their caverns. The villagers were eating and singing, working on projects and planning the next day.

Yosha felt shaking under his feet and the deep boom of Kjotik's impact on the shallows close to shore. Even before he heard the first screams, Yosha started running toward his pool. He had fashioned the launchers end to end so each would release in opposite directions. They lay crossed and lashed together in the pool, four mesh liners filled with selcrit dangling from the four ends. He yanked the contraption from the water and put his thumb next to the trigger. It would propel all the bags at once. Hopefully, four bags, four directions. He also grabbed a standard launcher he had fitted with a heavy dart and hook. He secured it to his shoulder harness and ran.

He could smell the beast as he plunged toward the reverberations and the villagers' screams. He ran recklessly, the hundreds of selcrit in the mesh bags whipping against his legs, clicking angrily. Kjotik made no sound but the WHAP! WHAP! WHAP! of its body as it wriggled and rippled forward, lifted, crashed down, lifted and crashed down. The smell of its fetid breath filled the air, and a wave of dread rushed through Yosha's vitals—not a sharp, clean fear, energizing him, but a horror at the thought of becoming a morsel of the beast's rotting cud. How he longed at this instant to have found a way to place the selcrit in a trap Kjotik would crash into. Despite his revulsion, he ran toward the sea monster, his body acting in accord with the thousands of times he had imagined every motion of this strange attack.

WHAP! The beast crashed down near him. He ran to it and collided against its rippling sides. He was spun violently onto the ground. Almost instantly, Kjotik rose above him and the next instant crashed down. The wind knocked out of his lungs, Yosha desperately gripped the launchers. The cavernous mouth enclosed him and then a wet mass covered him as he was sucked up by the creature's moist, hot breath. His body kept getting pulled up, up, up.

Desperate, terrified, he pushed with his thumb on the crossed launchers. The selcrit spattered off in four directions. He jabbed at the trigger at his shoulder and his little harpoon sped off and hooked itself in Kjotik's mouth. The line jerked Yosha to a stop, keeping him from being inhaled more deeply down the creature's throat.

He felt selcrit ricochet off his body; several clung to his legs, chewing at them. He shook at them wildly as he spun in the flow of secretions and sea water.

Then he felt everything moving upward. Yosha realized Kjotik was lifting himself again. As quickly as this thought came to him, Kjotik WHAPPED down, and he felt as if every bone in his whole body had been snapped in two. The wide lashing of his shoulder harness cut into his flesh, and he fought to get his breath in the nauseous soup.

WHAP! WHAP! Twice more leviathan moved forward, and Yosha knew he could not survive many more such cataclysms. But then the creature stopped and quivered. It suddenly shook and lifted itself again. As it crashed down, its shaking became a frenzied shudder. Yosha was nearly unconscious. He knew it was now or never, and slashed with his blade at the rope connecting his harness.

His body instantly spun off in one direction and then quickly swirled in another. His head went under again, and as he lost consciousness, he had no idea if he were being spat out or swallowed.

Kark found him, a glob in the slimy vomit spread widely upon the rocks. At first he could not determine if it was a body, let alone something alive. He felt the arms, realized what it was, and rushed his fingers to Yosha's face. He pried open his mouth, reaching in to pull out debris. Breath? Did he sense breath on his fingers? Kark dragged him quickly to the water and washed his face, touching the pulse on his neck.

Kark caught himself from crying out in wonder. The villagers ran to him when he called out that Yosha was alive. Kark washed him in the sea, carried him home, and anointed his body with healing and pleasant scents. "This marvelous child," he murmured. "This marvelous child."

The villagers in their astonishment asked if ever before leviathan had come upon a crowded shore and left no one crushed and no one dead. It did not even swallow the boy who had entered its mouth.

"If this could happen—if Yosha could make this promise come true," said Kark, "perhaps we truly will find the light in our generation." He spoke in a sort of daze, with no sense of vision, but the people made his words a prophecy wherever the story was told. And on hearing the tale, people would be quick to quote the dark side of the prophecies: "When the Askirit find the way to the light, evil will invade with all of its fury."

Chapter 4.

—— Dorte ——

Asel stood on Nor's cliff far above the sea. Varial stood beside her, full of misgivings. Asel pressed her toes in a tight curl against the stone surface, eager to descend and to enter the waters she loved and to penetrate the mysteries that beckoned her.

Varial tossed down the long rope and Asel began rappelling. On and on she descended, the sound of waves against the shore growing louder. Spray started wetting her legs, and she was relieved when her toes finally touched rocks. She explored the ground with her feet before releasing the rope, worrying that she might be on a low ledge instead of the shore. Convinced, she gave three strong pulls on the rope, and almost immediately it slid briskly up through her hands. She heard it flapping above her, and then she was alone with the loud sounds of water rushing by. Other than her dagger and clothing she had nothing with her but two fireflies she had caught. "What will happen?" she wondered, "when I release them into the darkness of Dorte?"

She maneuvered over the slimy tumble of angular boulders that descended into the angry currents. Asel knew she had to move far out on the rocks, grasping them with fingers and toes, then catch an outward current before she was dragged under. More quickly than she had hoped, the water battered away her grip and she was swept into the currents.

She stroked vigorously, the churning waters rolling her sideways. Her body picked up speed and she thrust out her hands to protect herself. Her shoulder and side slid hard against a slippery bulk just as she was sucked under. She was spun and tumbled forward with no control over her body until her head surfaced. Gasping for air, she was rushed forward in the current, beyond the confluence of boulders and water.

To establish direction, she extended her arms forward in the flow. Tarn would be on her right, Dorte on her left. She stroked left, pulling out of the current's control and before long was comfortably swimming toward shore. She found its gravelly edge and cautiously pulled herself up.

So—she was on Dorte, land of the damned. For a long time she sat listening, wondering what might attack her. She heard nothing extraordinary, only a lizard's scuttling on a ledge and the distant cawing of a carrion bird. She finally moved in a defensive crouch until she found a boulder, then knelt beneath its overhang, listening, alert for any sound. She heard birds, insects, and amphibians, but nothing more.

She reached for the caulked case at her side. The tiny mesh bag within was dry. She put her finger at its mouth and let one of the fireflies crawl onto it. When she lifted her finger from the bag, the intermittent glow moved up her finger toward her knuckles. She blew on it. It battened down instead of flying off. She blew more gently, under it. She smiled at the little creature and spoke to it. Finally her breath lifted it from her finger, and she watched the dot of yellow light float into the air and rise higher. Then it dipped down a bit and moved slowly away. It alighted on something, a blinking speck in the distance.

"That answers that," she thought. "At least fireflies keep glowing in this land of the damned." Asel had also wondered if she would feel a spiritual oppression when she came here, but she felt the same here as in Tarn. She was tempted to let the other firefly loose, but thought better of it. She explored the shore, slowly, ready to defend herself or escape to the sea. As she climbed, she heard occasional screams in the distance, but the steep ascents and crags were like those of Tarn, except for the lack of trail markings. She memorized distinctive rocks to guide her return.

When she had climbed so far inland she could no longer hear the sounds of the sea, she grew more apprehensive. Even barbarians considered Dorte's abominations unspeakable. How would she defend herself against unknown enemies?

She searched out a shelter for sierent; not too far into the cavern, her toes felt the edge of a snakehole, the sort into which pectres and their victims were cast. She gave it wide berth; yet she slept unharmed and awakened to a dawn like any other.

The second day she found strange formations: spikes tall and swirling, and wide holes like whirlpools in stone. Her spirit became increasingly oppressed. All I've heard in this cursed land, she thought, are strange screams, rodents, lizards, and the cries of birds. Even the air feels weighted with evil.

She heard voices far off. Drawing as close as she dared, she stopped and listened. They were boys—several years younger than she. Asel was surprised to hear words she understood. They spoke a language laden with strangely pronounced Askirit words.

The boys were arguing about fish and complaining about sweat and hunger. They were dragging something behind them, and she surmised it must be the morning's catch. She followed their voices and the sound of the dragging sack until they suddenly turned silent and she heard adults talking. Then came shouts and men speaking roughly to the boys. The men grabbed the sack and started distributing the fish. Except for the shrillness and frequent insults, the voices and sounds seemed like those of an Askirit village.

The boys walked away and she followed them into a cave in which she found a network of dwellings. After feeling her way deep into the labyrinth, she heard the voices of the boys again mixed with those of men and women, chattering and whimpering and accusing. Asel went deeper into the caves, found a low cavity in the wall and crawled in.

As she listened to men demanding and women threatening,

she refused to think of what they might do to her if they caught her. The people seemed afraid, not so much of each other, but of something without. She heard a man refer to "the sledge," and she sensed dread in his voice. Later she heard a woman say something about "the sledge of the dead."

She lost the conversation and was wondering about its meaning when she heard footsteps coming toward her. It was a child, probably about ten years old, and by her movements, Asel guessed she was carrying a baby on her hip. Asel shrank back into the corner. The girl kept coming, walking with the confidence of knowing exactly where she was going. She stopped and reached down to the floor, brushing against Asel's shoulder. The child gasped, then sniffed to catch her scent.

Asel wondered if she should reach out to assure the child. But that might be more risky than not moving at all. She decided to risk something else. Despite the fact a firefly in this place might frighten her, she opened the sack and tried to get it on her finger. As she succeeded, she whispered, "Light. Don't fear. Don't fear. Light feeds us. Don't fear."

She heard the child's feet move. Then she felt the little hand touch her finger next to the firefly. She watched the insect move in one direction then another, and finally the little light climbed on the child's finger. It progressed across the knuckles, lifted itself and flew off—but Asel reached out and caught it. She held it out so the girl's fingers could make a bridge to recapture the prick of light.

Asel patted the baby on the child's hip as they watched the firefly. Then the child's other hand started tracing the outline of Asel's face. Her slightly shaking fingers explored the hills and valleys of Asel's eyes and mouth and jaw. Asel smiled and kept smiling, and touched her lips to the little fingers and patted the baby again. "Light. No fear," she repeated. Then, as gentle as feathers floating on air, her fingers touched the girl's cheek. Asel felt fear in her face, but she kept caressing her with a feathery touch. As she did, the face of the little girl became the terrified child of the vision that had brought her here. Asel wondered, Am I letting my mind connect that vision with this child's face? Yet as she felt the high curves of the cheeks, the tiny nose, the wide eyes, she thought, It *is* the child! Why should I doubt it?

She eased the girl and baby into a comfortable position and whispered, "I am here to give you light. I will not hurt you." She rubbed the girl's shoulder and let the firefly crawl up her arm. She asked, "Is the baby your brother or sister?"

She did not answer. "Do you have a mother, a father?" Still silence, so she said, "My name is Asel. Do you have a name?"

"Breea," the girl said.

"Wonderful! It's a name as full of light as this glowing firefly. It's a name as wonderful as Cerca, Dee, Pars—my little friends at home who are just about your size. And what is the baby's name?"

"He is Nen," she said.

Asel described to Breea many beautiful things in Tarn before she asked her, "What is the sledge of the dead?"

Without hesitation Breea said, "It comes tonight."

"Yes," Asel said. "But why does it come?"

"It comes for us," Breea said, a tremor stealing into the hand that touched Asel's. "It comes tonight."

Asel could learn nothing more from her about the sledge, but when she asked, "How does it come here?" the girl said, "It is dragged. The Tremblers drag it."

"The Tremblers? What are they?"

The child did not answer, but sat hugging the baby. Asel touched her face reassuringly and felt tears. "Why do the Tremblers make you so afraid?" she asked.

Breea said something about her father.

"Did the Tremblers hurt your father?"

"He is dead. Maybe he is a Trembler."

Asel asked more questions, but Breea simply repeated herself. "Is your mother here?"

"She was taken."

Asel coaxed Breea to her lap and held the child and baby lightly, smoothing her long, dirty hair and whispering stories and fables. Her ear stayed cocked for changes in the voices of the others as they came and went. The more time passed, the more shrill the voices became. It was clear their minds were on the sledge.

—— The Sledge ——

The moans and whistles of sierent make even an Askirit shudder as he prepares for shelter. The barbarian trembles far more, his mind clothing the wind with gheials and specters. In Dorte, as Asel heard the very early gusts of sierent, she shuddered despite her resolve and faith, sensing the fear of all those around her huddling at the cave entrances.

Finally, mixing with the wind, came the sound of distant grinding. The child and babe were beside her. Breea would breathe rapidly, then take a deep breath, sigh, and lean against Asel; then she would tense and begin breathing rapidly again.

The grinding grew louder, joined by rasping sounds, as if something were being dragged over uneven terrain. Asel thought she heard a distant grunt, then a barely audible moan. A rhythm of bare feet thudding against stone, and leather straining against flesh blended with the scraping and grinding of what Asel assumed was the sledge. Breea's hand gripped Asel's wrist. The sledge's movement toward them was long and laborious. Several times it stopped abruptly; she could hear quiet grunts as the Tremblers strained to get it over some obstruction, until it moved again with a jerk.

When the sledge stopped, Asel could hear the Tremblers' heavy breathing. She grimaced. Surely they are men, she thought.

The villagers sat motionless. Asel heard leather straps drop from shoulders. She judged a score of them stood in place and wondered at the weight of the sledge.

Then a quavering male voice, one of the Tremblers she judged, said: "Tonight it will be a child."

She heard air expelled from adult lungs all around her. But Breea's hand, fingers intertwined with hers, tightened painfully on her knuckles.

Then came the long silence. No sounds whatever. This lasted so long, Asel wondered if the evil forces were feeding on the terror of each child.

Finally the same voice quavered again: "Tonight it shall be a child of the third."

The third. Asel knew this included children in the years before puberty. It would probably include Breea.

More silence, as long as before. Then the voice again: "Walk forward."

Breea stood. She handed the baby to Asel. Other children rose and starting walking forward. No mother wailed. No child shrieked. Just the shallow, short breaths of the children as their many feet shuffled very, very slowly toward the sledge. Asel found herself walking forward with Breea, their fingers tightly intertwined, the baby nestled in Asel's right arm.

She tried to make her footsteps sound light and childlike. They moved forward until they were standing by the Tremblers. Whatever they were, they smelled of things even worse than fear. She wanted to put a cloth over her nose, but she breathed through her mouth instead. The children all stood in the long silence, sensing only the indistinct moans of the Tremblers. Asel was praying for the light, reciting Enre chants of praise and glory, pleading for light to penetrate the darkness.

A great many children stood with her. Why hadn't they fled? But each, she supposed, thought someone else would be chosen. Each hoped against hope it would be another. And that in itself was part of the evil.

That is when the rage pumped through Asel's body. She snarled from deep in her throat and ground her teeth. Breea turned toward her. Asel reached down and felt the tears on her face. She handed little Nen to her, remembering the vision of Breea's face with eyes and lips shimmering in terror. She felt at the same time the evil power smothering her. Asel's scream split the air. She shouted at the Tremblers, "Get out!" as she let go of Breea's hand and stepped toward them. She let the rage take her and called out, "Lord of light! Eshtel! See these abominations!"

She called for light, but no light came, only the silence and the eerie, almost imperceptible moans of the Tremblers close before her shivering in their places. Asel suddenly attacked, her fingers out, using the disciplined strategy she had practiced thousands of times. Her knee caught a man's body on the side, and he fell with a whoosh of air from his lungs. Another she clipped with her hand on the side of his head. She heard him topple and lie flat, still wailing softly. She turned to rush through them again, then thought better of it and stepped toward the sledge instead.

But she hesitated. Should she touch it? She cautiously moved closer, then reached out her hand and explored its edges. The sledge was covered with leather, supported by high hoops. Asel pulled out her dagger and slashed the leather with her blade. Unopposed, she yanked and pulled it away, first on one side and then the other, expressing her rage in a frenzy of ripping and tearing.

Then it was done and she stood with her arms at her side. The lack of resistance mystified Asel. She explored the outer edges of the sledge. It felt like the rim of a coffin. She walked around it, tracing the shapes with her hand. She decided it was not one but two waist-high coffins. She listened in the direction of the villagers; she could not tell if they were still there. The Tremblers stood or lay where she had crashed among them, breathing in eerie, faint wails.

Had she cleared away the furies with her cries for the light?

The Askirit rituals promised just such consequences to faith and righteousness. Could she thus liberate the damned? It seemed nothing opposed her, but the oppression of the night blanketed her like a sick man's delirium. Her anger mixed with fear and the taste of dread. She hated this place. The smell around the sledge sickened her. She forced herself to reach into the coffin closest to her.

Empty.

She stretched and reached to all corners.

Nothing was in it.

She walked around the sledge and put her hand into the other coffin. A third of the way down she felt a bony shoulder. With shaking fingers she traced the thin shape of an old woman's shoulder. The arm was like a skeleton with moldering, thin leather wrapped loosely around it. The skin was flaky and deeply wrinkled. Asel cautiously slid her hand along the back of the neck, feeling flaccid skin that barely held the bones together. She felt the old woman's throat, her chin, and then her mouth, which had no teeth, but only sagging gums. What was this smell? Not just decay, dryness, filth or fear, but something else—an acrid stench. She felt as if it were eating into her hands.

She felt the woman's eyes. They were sunken halfway into the sockets, but they were moist, sticky, and as she touched an eyeball, she thought she sensed movement. She jerked her fingers away, then held her palm to the woman's mouth. Asel waited for long moments, but she felt no breath on her hand.

Was the movement her imagination? But then, was she also imagining a voice? She thought she heard a high, querulous voice. She studied the Tremblers, listening, using all of her senses. No, it was not they. She heard a voice babbling somewhere.

Then she clearly—very clearly—heard a gargling rattle of a voice. Asel's mouth went dry. Did that voice come from this pile of bones, this jumble of putrefaction?

She leaned far down, close to the woman's face, listening. "Girl, what are you doing?"

Was it speaking to her? Asel's eyes stared with such intensity she felt she nearly pulled its features out of the darkness. How could it speak? If so, she would answer! "What do *you* do?" Asel demanded. "Terrify children?"

The gasping, rattling sound asked, "Why are you here?"

Were the bones speaking? She leaned closer to the corpse's face, listening hard, trying to sense if that bitter smell came from its mouth.

"You will do," the high, querulous voice said, this time distinctly audible. Before Asel could raise her head, she felt the bony hand clench its fingers into her hair and her scalp and yank her forward. She fell full into the coffin, jammed against one side, immobilized. The hand pulled Asel's face closer to the sunken mouth and its stench. Asel gagged.

"You will do," the flat, inhuman voice said again, then erupted into a shrieking laugh.

Asel strained to cry out but could not. She was dizzy and disoriented. She felt herself being sucked into a whirlpool. "You have come to us," something was saying. "You are ours now. But you will enjoy it. You will have the power you have always wanted. Isn't that why you came?"

But all Asel felt was a horrible dread.

She sensed she was standing on a ledge above an abyss. Reptiles slithered over her bare feet. No, not reptiles, a phlegm-like ooze. It was something alive, caressing her, voracious, hungering not for her body but with desperate intent to seep far deeper than flesh, mixing spirit with spirit. The ooze rose to her ankles. She felt enormous energy invade her feet, energy to run, to leap across the abyss.

"You need never fear a barbarian again," a voice said. "You will fear no one. But you must fear the abyss. It is close, very close. Do not fall into it." The living ooze rose up her body, caressing and gripping her, moving her feet closer to the edge. It rose to her waist, alive and penetrating. The ooze filled her with an explosive energy, even as her feet kept stepping closer to the abyss.

"You were right to come here," the voice said. "This is where you can use your power." Asel tried to recapture her muddled thoughts, but all she was aware of was the ledge on which she stood, the abyss below, the ooze that was now coiling about her, rising toward her neck—warm, alluring, pulsating, consuming yet desirable. "The light," Asel tried to say, "the light." It was not even a clear thought, but she kept struggling to bring her mind back, to concentrate on something other than the ooze and the abyss.

A phrase appeared in her mind like a spark. "The light is greater." She grabbed at it. She tried to concentrate on it. "The light is greater than the darkness," she thought, repeating the line from the ritual. "The light is greater. The light is greater." The words cleared her mind just enough to remember another promise—that no power can take the soul if it cries out for mercy. "Mercy!" she cried out with all the force of her lungs, "Mercy!"

She wept. "You cannot have my soul unless I give it!" she declared loudly. She cried out for light to invade her, even though at the same time she did not want to release this powerful new energy in her body and spirit.

——— Waifs ———

Asel sensed as she awoke an intense pain in her neck and shoulder. All night long she had been soaked and battered by the night storms, surviving sierent only because she was high in the crags. She forced herself to shift her elbow. Then she carefully moved the weight of her upper body, which was wedged against the arm of the corpse and the edge of the coffin. As she raised her shoulder, the arm fell away into a jumble of half-connected, flesh-wrapped bones.

She started upright, remembering. Nausea spread up from her stomach as she lifted her body from the bones on which she had been lying for so many hours. As she pulled herself from the sledge, she fought a spell of dizziness and wrinkled her nose at the stench on her body. She desperately wanted water to wash herself, but she feared what she might find searching for it. She listened intently. No one seemed to be near; not Tremblers, villagers, nor children. Crouching defensively, she moved toward the lake she knew was nearby.

As soon as she sniffed its clean scent she strode briskly into it, then tucked down and plunged underwater, seeking a sandy bottom. After searching she finally found a narrow stretch of coarse sand. She scooped up a handful and rubbed it against her arms and legs, trying to expunge the stench and cloying presence of the night before. Again and again she rose for air, then descended to rub the sand through her hair and over every part of her body.

Each time she surfaced, she listened closely for sounds of life. She heard none. What had happened last night? She remembered the arrival of the sledge and the sadistic call for the children. She vividly remembered her rage and the horrible moment when she felt herself pressed against that gruesome frame of the sledge. Had she simply been overwrought and clumsy, falling against that body and foolishly thinking it alive? Had she begun hallucinating? Perhaps she'd merely broken up some cheap shaman's tricks to control the villagers. Or, she wondered as she rubbed at her skin and briskly pumped her arms and legs against the clean water, had she crashed into evil's heart?

Clean at last, she could not escape the feeling of defilement. She left the water and went directly toward the sledge, wondering if it would still be there. Her foot grazed its edge and she reached out to touch its sides. Holding on to one of the coffins, she ran her hand down its length, then across the foot and up to the head. She hated the feel of it, and the remaining mustiness in the air. Her palm caught repeatedly on the slashed leather from her attack last night. Yet as she forced herself to carefully explore first the one coffin, then the other, she found nothing that indicated something else had been there in the night.

Finally, she splayed out her fingers and moved them toward the place where the old woman's face had been. She felt nothing and probed all the way to the coffin's bottom. Her fingernails scraped across the sledge bottom. Yet as she moved her hand to the side, she felt rotted cloth. She forced her fingers over it and felt the bones beneath the clothing.

Was that a cough behind her? She listened intently and thought she heard a movement. Were the keepers of the sledge back to claim their own?

"Who are you?" she demanded.

Silence. But then a scuffling sound and a little sneeze that sounded as if it had been made by a child. "Are you still so afraid?" she asked, thinking it must be the villagers.

A man's doleful voice said quietly, "When they return for the sledge, perhaps you will learn to fear."

"Do they need this cursed sledge?" she asked, surprised by the sharpness in her own voice. Instead of fear she felt her gorge rise. She found herself almost involuntarily stooping to grasp a large rock. Lifting it above her head, almost teetering with the weight, she crashed it down on the sledge. The splintering sounds inflamed her more, and she reached into the wreckage with both arms to grasp the great stone again. She lifted it once more above her head. Again and again she smashed it into the sledge and the coffins, flattening them into the ground.

She stood sweating and breathing heavily. She turned toward the silence behind her. For long moments she waited, but the villagers said nothing.

"Are you so fearful?" she asked them all. Her voice still sounded bold but she was losing some of the indignation that had driven out the fear.

No one answered. No one moved.

"You can fight the fear!" Asel declared loudly. "You can call on the light. You can banish fear from your chests and breathe in courage. The light is greater than the darkness!"

A woman's voice said, "I see no light."

"If you believe, you will see! Do you not hear my voice? Did I not cry out for the light in the midst of death? Am I not standing here alive?"

No one answered until finally a man said, "They will get their revenge."

Another added, "They will return."

"Who will return?" Asel demanded.

But at that question, the villagers went quiet again. Asel asked and even pleaded for answers but got none. She said, "Come with me to the light! Leave this darkness and this evil!" But they began to disperse.

She called out, "Breea!" She waited a moment but heard nothing, only the continuing movements of feet as the villagers walked away.

"Breea!" she called out again.

She felt a light touch on the side of her left hand. Quickly, Asel turned her fingers and clasped the little hand. Breea gripped her fingers tightly and shifted the weight of little Nen on her hip so that they both leaned into Asel. As she felt the children under her arm, she vowed never to desert them.

To whom did they belong. Anyone? Asel thought of asking the villagers in a loud voice if anyone had a claim to these children, but then she thought better of it. "Breea," she whispered, "do you want to go with me to the light?"

The child did not hesitate. "Yes."

"What would your mother say?"

"I have no mother."

"But little Nen, your brother ..."

"We found each other," she said fiercely. "He's mine! I'm all he has."

Nen had plopped himself on the ground and was playing with stones. Asel sat beside him. Breea lowered herself tight against Asel, who gripped her shoulder gently and tried to imagine what the girl was feeling. She hated to keep asking her questions, but after a time she said, "Where do the Tremblers come from? Who are they?"

"Those taken from us," Breea said.

Asel hugged the girl with her right arm and put her left hand on Nen's head. "Do you think you will ever know your father again, Breea?"

"I would never want to meet him!" she declared with finality.

A flicker of light in the direction of the devastated sledge caught her eye. She looked closely, then blinked several times in dismay. Golden eyes of light seemed to be staring at her, moving slightly as if evaluating her. She gripped the children and felt fear for them rather than for herself. The luminous movements taunted her in the blackness. Then one started moving away from the other in a bizarre effect that widened the eyes.

She stood, leaving the children where they were, and walked toward the glow. As she was almost upon it, the eyes rose from the ground, still staring at her, but suddenly jerked in midair as a laugh split the silence. "Here," a high-pitched voice said, "you can have her," and the eyes came flying at her. She put up her hands to protect her face as the little glows flew past at the same time as something hard struck her hands, then fell with a thud.

The golden spots were now on the ground, starting to move again, slowly, like insects. She knelt and touched the object near them. It was a skull. The missing skull from the coffin.

The laughter erupted again, followed by a taunting young voice: "Smash the skull like you did the sledge."

She stood, the skull in her hand. Breea came up behind her and said, "Luminous carrion beetles."

The brash young voice declared, "Beetles in the eye sockets!" He laughed again. "Made the old hag come alive, didn't I?"

"Delin!" Breea said in a firm, impatient voice. "Don't mess with skulls and carrion beetles."

"But carrion beetles love skulls!" the boy insisted petulantly. Asel judged he was probably about six. So, she thought, children are children, even here. Just a boy teasing her with the skull.

Suddenly she felt ashamed of how she had treated the body of this old woman. If evil forces had used it, she should not desecrate it further. Instead, she should consecrate it to the powers of light.

"Breea, help me gather the bones," she said. She placed the skull by a rock and started gathering the bones from among the broken pieces of the sledge, holding her breath against the lingering stench. Delin taunted them, but Asel kept talking to him about the light. "Come with us," she invited. "Come on a journey with us."

Breea found an old sack into which they placed the remains. Asel said, "We will give them proper prayers and consign the old woman to sierent to bear her to the light." She once more called out to the villagers to join her, but she received no response.

"Carrying bones around!" Delin taunted. "Why would anyone want to go with you to do that?" But as Asel led Breea toward the sea, little Nen between them, Delin could not resist following them, calling out to them and joking about the burden they carried.

As they walked, a determination took shape within Asel. "Take the light to all of Aliare." That was a command she had repeated in the liturgy hundreds of times. She had always thought of taking light to the barbarians, but now it became a command to push back the darkness in this place of the damned. To rescue children, to attack the unspeakable.

At the same time, she was mystified. All the promises assured the Askirit that Eshtel wanted all people to live in the light. If so, why didn't he flood them with light? She had confronted evil and cried out for the light, and was sucked instead into nightmares of darkness. If light was greater than the darkness, why could she not liberate this village? Why was she skulking off, fearful of the furies catching her before she could make off with Breea and Nen to the sea? Why were the people still cowering, waiting for the keepers of the sledge?

She must not only bring the light to the damned, she thought, but she must find the way above, that its light would search out every corner of Dorte.

Chapter 5.

—— DawnBreaker ——

Yosha and the other initiates waited tensely for their friend Taeres to return. Six days before, they had all followed Kark to the peaks to gather keitr. They camped in a great canyon beneath the caves in which, one by one, each would fill his belt—or feel the keitr's teeth.

At dawn each day, one boy had set out full of hopes and fears. Bles had been first; the other boys had resented the choice, for waiting one's turn, supposedly memorizing liturgy and lore, intensified their nervousness.

All that first day, Yosha had forced back his feelings of wishing Bles would stumble in the caves. He prayed against the voices luring him to feed his feelings of animosity, and when he had heard Bles's voice call out from the distance in triumph, "A full belt!" Yosha had genuinely felt relief and joy.

Day after day a boy would go out in the morning, and the others would wait. Yosha fretted, anxious to take his turn. He thought constantly about keitr, about their caves and poison and their strange life cycle.

The keitr Yosha sought hung by the millions in their caves, sleeping, birthing their young, flying off with babies clinging to their fur, foraging by their echo system. They inhabited caves throughout the high crags of Tarn. Many wondered why the keitr, among all the creatures in Aliare, had been given a poison strong enough to kill a man in a score of heartbeats. Some thought the answers lay in ancient stories that told of flesh-eating keitr on the planet's skin, flocking from their caves at night to seek prey larger than man. But in Aliare, the keitr's largest natural prey were small rodents, and seldom did it attack even these.

Its primary food was insects; in great numbers the keitr burst out of their caves and hunted in Aliare's darkness during the hours just before sierent, snapping up with infallible accuracy countless winged insects. Chief among their prey was the chibdys. Winged but grub-like, the size of a boy's thumb, the fat chibdys fluttered its thick, soft wings so rapidly it created unique sounds that attracted predators. It was almost as if the chibdys prided itself on being a ubiquitous, substantial meal, and therefore announced its presence. But for the keitr, the fluttering meal was also its only natural enemy. The two creatures were interdependent, for the chibdys could lay its eggs in only one host—the body of a mature keitr.

At the time of year when ute fell with greatest force and bits of vegetation from above would be so thick children would shout excitedly at the nets as they found sweet-smelling fragments, millions of female chibdys would instinctively begin to release pheromones to attract the males. After mating and gestation, females would begin a migration toward the caves of the keitr. Though the females were now fat with eggs, they would release far more of the pheromones than during the mating period. Waves of males joined the migration, but the females dipped and soared away from them, flapping against the winds toward their goal.

The keitr, instead of confidently winging out of their habitat into the clouds of advancing chibdys to eat their prey, became extremely restless. The pheromones made them scream and claw the air. Men a half-day's journey away would wince at the sounds of keitr reacting to the migration approaching them. Knowing the chibdys would soon flap into their caves, the keitr would suddenly explode into the air to attack their now deadly prey. A seemingly endless torrent of maddened keitr would strike the vast, soft cloud of chibdys with a desperate snapping of teeth and with darting, twisting wings.

The sluggish female chibdys, which all through the year and even to this moment had placidly offered herself as a meal, was transformed in one respect. Her stinger, never previously used, was also an ovipositor. At the slightest touch of a keitr, she would thrust viciously against her predator, and if she penetrated keitr flesh, injected her eggs. Even if the chibdys were swallowed— even if bitten in half—the stinger struck reflexively, whether in the keitr's mouth, its throat, even its stomach.

The unsuspecting male chibdys had his role too. In the thick cloud of food the keitr was unable to distinguish between male and female. As it snatched a male and gulped it down, a female might simultaneously penetrate its enemy. In the melee of frantically stabbing ovipositors and rushing wings, the keitr eventually ate most of the chibdys. But a significant number had deposited their eggs, and as the well-fed keitr flew back to their caves, some experienced small sensations of numbness. By the time an infected keitr clung to its own niche, it was already tiring. Within days, it would be a paralyzed host to the chibdys eggs, a mountain of food for the emerging grubs. Before thirty sierents, they would emerge from the empty, hanging skin and fly away.

Yosha smiled when he thought of how the Askirit spoke of this cycle as the Maker's irony—that the invulnerable keitr, which alone could "see" by its echoes and was at home in the darkness, should be penetrated in its lair by the chubby chibdys.

A jubilant shout from the sixth boy interrupted his thoughts. Another back safe, with a full belt. Soon it would be his turn.

On the eighth day, however, they waited for the return of the designated initiate far beyond the expected time. By afternoon, dread had crept into the camp. Kark broke the morbid silence by declaring an inspection. As the boys lined up, he began a meticulous survey of those with keitr in their belts, examining each of the pouches again, and all the while instructing them on the details of their care. He stretched the inspection on and on, but still the eighth boy did not return.

He started talking about their coming initiation in the capital city of Aris. "Soon you will be at the temple entrances," Kark said, "you who will be men. And how will you enter the temple?"

"In most wonderful silence," Yosha answered.

"And what will you hear?" Kark asked.

A village boy said, "Strings and voices sounding glory throughout the temple. We will dance and strike flint and hear music never heard in Wellen. We will be at Tarn's heart!"

"Eshtel celebrates!" Yosha declared. "He celebrates with his people!"

But dread remained. Kark had the boys practice military signals, some made by voice, others with whistles and the cracking of stones and striking of bones. The voices and even the whistles of those who had not yet gone to the caves revealed their nervousness.

Finally, Kark stood, holding his own noirim protection. "If I do not return," he said, "Yosha, you are in charge."

The unexpected declaration caused Yosha to sit bolt upright. Why had Kark said that? The tough military man's new respect for the boy who had astounded him, combined with their mutual religious intensity, had created a bond between them. But Yosha wondered if Kark understood the position his declaration put him in.

Kark moved heavily out of the camp and toward the caves.

Yosha shifted the weight of his back against the wall of rock, thinking of Bles who was sitting across from him. Should he say something? He could explain that he hadn't been playing up to Kark. Yet anything he said to Bles would come off as weak and apologetic.

Time dragged slowly. Yosha stood and began walking toward the latrine. When he was well past the boys, he heard Bles say, just loudly enough for Yosha to hear, "Itchworm hasn't left us any orders. Now who's in charge?" He was clearly angling for support. Geln, one of the village boys who had joined in the singing, angrily retorted, "Shut up, Bles! When you go up against Kjotik, we'll listen to you!"

"Yosha hasn't even gathered keitr yet," Bles spat back instantly.

"Kark decides who's in charge!" Geln declared emphatically.

Much later they heard Kark's heavy breathing, and they knew he was carrying Taeres. He stepped into the middle of the camp and laid down his burden. "He lives in the light now," Kark said.

Long before dawn the next morning, while the moisture-laden winds of sierent were still gusting, Kark roused the boys from their shelters to start their duties. He had gotten them up as early as possible, which meant when the storm had become only wet, stinging rain, instead of winds that could pull handholds loose. The brusque commands from Kark contrasted with the sober tasks of securing Taeres' body. Yosha grimaced as he unfolded Taeres' pack; spread out and wrapped around his body, it would serve as his coffin. He helped the other boys secure the straps around him; then he and three others each grasped a thong at a corner and lifted Taeres for his last journey.

They marched into the final winds of sierent and began climbing against them. Yosha knew that to honor Taeres, they had to start this before sierent ceased; but the wind against his face and ears, and the slippery rocks, made for slow, unpleasant going. Yet Kark urged greater speed as they climbed, and Yosha was relieved when four other boys took over the carrying of the weight.

At last they gained a crag at a high point overlooking the sea. The winds were moist breezes now, and Kark told them to remove their jackets and headgear. He helped them place the body on the ledge jutting out beyond the trail, then sat with them facing the sea.

"We begin before the dawn," Kark said, "so we can give hope from the night." He held up a piece of flint and struck it, creating a small spray of sparks. After reciting the required liturgy, he said, "Geln, tell the tale of the DawnBreaker."

It was an improbable old myth, but often used at funerals. The boy cleared his throat and recited:

The first man was made in the night,
for the Maker wished to surprise him.
He wished to wake him with the glories of the dawn.
The first man lay sleeping in the night,
the Maker's breath fresh in his mouth,
the Maker's life pulsing through his body,
the Maker's touch on both his eyes.

The dawn began.
The dawn lightened.
Colors soft as down shone above.
The first man looked up.
Rays of light, glorious, sprayed the sky,
wider and wider,
Crimson streaks in the pale blue,
brighter and brighter.
A great rim of light appeared.
The beauty lifted him,
lifted the man to his feet.

"Look!" he cried. "Look!"
The dawn lifted his spirits to the light.
He had to tell someone.
Before him was the majesty of dawn,
behind him, darkness.
"Look!" he cried out,
and ran to the darkness,
ran to announce the coming glory.

"Look and see!" he cried out,
running as swiftly as dawn itself.
"Light is coming," he called out,
"Dawn is coming!"

The first man ran swiftly, swiftly,
just ahead of the light.
"The dawn is coming!
The dawn is coming!"
He ran with the Maker's fresh life
in his lungs and legs.
He ran exuberant into the darkness,
announcing light.
He ran ahead of the dawn,
crossing the place where he was made,
but still he ran,
on and on,
announcing dawn,
until the Maker said,
"Fly, then! Announce the dawn forever!"
And the Maker transformed him into a bird.
The auret,
the DawnBreaker,
who never stops announcing,
"Dawn is coming,
Light is coming!"

DawnBreaker lightened the world,
announcing the dawn forever.

The Maker formed another man,
and he also made a woman.
When the dawn broke,
the man was filled with wonder.
He was lifted to his feet.

He exclaimed, "Look. Light! The dawn!"
The woman said, "Yes! Brighter than stars!"
They praised the Maker together,
for the man could announce the dawn;
he could tell the woman.

The Maker was pleased.
He brought them dawn each morning.
And with it he brought auret,
DawnBreaker, announcing the world.

Everyone knew why they had ended these rites with the DawnBreaker tale. The rugged winds of sierent were gone; the air was fresh with morning breezes. Far below, where the waves of the sea struck the shore, they could already hear the first cries of the aurets. It was the bird people called dawnbreaker, for each morning, the entire coast of Tarn was alive with them and their sharp cries. The birds would begin at sea's edge, then rise on the winds, carrying their announcement of a new day to the crags.

The boys sat solemn and silent with the wind in their hair, hearing the aurets in the distance. They concluded the ritual by each placing a drop of scent on Taeres' face. Then they started the laborious descent, which would take most of the day.

At midday, they passed a waterfall that they had heard far in the distance. By evening, the flow would be a comparative trickle, for sierent lifted the waters and stormed all through the night, but when it was over, the rocky cliffs quickly rushed the waters back to the seas. The little funeral cortege had been following a wide, heavy stream, which by the time they reached the sea was so small they leaped it easily.

Kark himself snugged the leather tightly around Taeres' body. They waited until nearly sierent, then placed him in the water and walked the floating body out waist-high, each boy holding a ridge of the leather seams. "Sierent will carry his body above," Kark said. They gave a push so that the body floated out, then made haste to find shelter before sierent could suck them with Taeres into the sea.

—— Keitr ——

At dawn on Yosha's day, Kark ordered the boys to form a circle. Yosha was placed in its center, and Kark stepped through the circle to face him. He quoted passages about Askirit courage. "Throughout Aliare, carry the light. Even where darkness reigns, carry the light." Then Kark chanted,

> *This day,*
> *you become a man.*
>
> *Yet the keitr may strike.*
>
> *This day,*
> *you may see and be seen*
> *in the world of light.*

With his right hand, Kark touched Yosha's eyes and said, "We will soon shout at your return. Or we will envy your entry into light."

Then the boys, one by one, moved in front of Yosha and touched his eyes. He smiled grimly at Kark's ritual statement. Envy his entry into light? Everyone here was terrified at getting killed up in those caves. Of course, to *see,* to actually *live* in the light! But what might that mean?

Kark intertwined his fingers with Yosha's and said, "The man with keitr empowers the Askirit kingdom." Then he fitted between Yosha's shoulders the precisely square pack of noirim leather. The reptile's thick skin provided the toughest covering the Askirit could make. In fact, workers said shaping it was like cutting bones; yet it was not impenetrable to an alarmed keitr chewing repeatedly at one spot.

The ceremony over, Kark whispered to Yosha, "Between keitr and Kjotik, I'd risk keitr any day. You'll do well." Then he slapped the pack to motion him away.

As Yosha started climbing, Kark's words made him wonder how he had once run without hesitation into the mouth of Kjotik. Now he felt anxious, worrying about his clumsiness. All the waiting has done it, he said to himself, all the interminable waiting and sending Taeres into sierent. His mind kept rehearsing every motion he would soon make to gather keitr. The little mammals would soon be captives on his hips, or they would send him to the light.

The climb, though strenuous, eased Yosha's nervousness. He grasped the moist rock projections firmly, testing each foot and hand position as he ascended the shafts of rock. In climbing, Yosha felt a sweet nostalgia for every stimulus: sounds of the sea far below, scents left from the storms of sierent, the slippery feel of the scored, rippled, and pitted rocks. He leaned into a wide depression in the cliff wall and rested. The mountains were unforgiving; although the Askirit were nimble and cautious, more than once a fatigued hand had caused a man to fall.

Yosha was sweating and trembling when he reached the caves. He rested long enough to steady his fingers, smelling already the keitr guano. He dropped his pack and started putting on the thick reptilian leather. Its weight made him feel clumsy; only his nose, ears, and hands stuck out. Over both the leather and his exposed skin he smeared thick tallow with a scent known to be the least upsetting to keitr.

For years he had practiced incessantly how his feet were to tread the cave floor, how his hand was to creep up, holding the open leather pouch with the food—crushed insects—at the bottom. As soon as a keitr nosed down into it, he must, with a swooping motion that would not disturb the other keitr, clasp it shut at the top and ram the creature in. The difficulty was not so much in trapping the one, but in not alerting the others. Ever since he was a little boy, he would practice in caverns from which hung little model keitr, carved of bone. All the boys of his village would do it by the hour; it was said anyone who did not grow up in the crags practicing from his earliest youth could never acquire the skill.

Yosha felt confident about his fingers, but the keitr were unpredictable. No matter how great the skill, one alarmed keitr could create hundreds of agitated movements around it. The motion of the wrist in yanking the creature away had to be precise, and most of all, it must not touch another in the darkness.

He shoved his leather-clad feet before him, welcoming the barrier between his skin and the cave floor, which he knew would be alive with hard-backed carrion beetles feeding on the droppings.

His motions were interrupted by squeaking within the cave. The sound pumped acid into his stomach. Keitr seldom were that noisy. Was something wrong? He stood motionless, listening. He did not even swallow, standing still until he felt he might tip over from dizziness.

When he decided to edge forward again, he thought, I feel fear; perhaps my scent glands are especially strong and the smell of my fear annoys them. He wished he'd spread the tallow thicker and scented it heavier. He wondered, Can they hear my breathing?

He raised his hand slightly above his head and leaned forward, the pouch open. If his hand grazed a keitr, he must instantly judge where it was. He must grab and plunge it into his pouch quickly, the left hand ready to rush the open pouch to the keitr's head, then close it up, trapping it inside. If the keitr were caught, within a few heartbeats it would stop struggling.

He felt something soft graze his thumb, and his hands moved in an instant reflex. A keitr was in the pouch, squirming against his left hand. As he secured it with his right, he realized his hand was a little wet from the droplets of condensation that form on the keitrs' bodies as they hang head down. He secured the bands carefully, knowing they must release properly when flung toward an enemy.

Yosha held out the open pouch where he heard another movement. At the slightest nudge on the pouch's edge, his hands again moved more quickly than his thoughts. "Mustn't think this is so easy," he warned himself, tying up his second catch. He advanced along the wall, placing his feet first, then moving his hand forward, each motion practiced thousands of times.

On his seventh keitr, the little creature grazed his hand with its claw before it was thrust into the pouch. Yosha smiled. He knew it would mean a slight fever for him and some pain, but the claws were never fatal. He would now forever bear the mark of gathering keitr.

Finally, his belt full, he felt relief even as he remembered the warnings: after gathering, one can become overconfident and stumble. With great care, he began threading his way out, retracing his path along the wall.

He was still in the cave when he heard restless movements above his head. These grew quickly to jerky scratchings. Before he could clear the entrance, the keitr began screaming. Thousands above him started flapping and clawing, and he fell flat, face in the muck, pulling the noirim flaps over his ears, then burrowing his bare hands under his chest.

The cries shattered his strength, his coherence, his resolve. Could this be happening? It was long after the migration of chibdys. The cacophony of outrage above him occurred once, and only once, each year. There was only one possible explanation. It was said to be a simple thing to capture some female chibdys and keep them tightly wrapped. Kept months beyond their mating time, unwrapped and set free, they would immediately release trillions of pheromones, as if frantically late for their appointment. The keitr would be enraged, whatever the season.

A small body struck Yosha's right shoulder; fangs bit the thick leather. He heard other keitr wildly flap at the cave walls and out into the dark air, their maddened cries chilling Yosha's spine. He became furious as keitr after keitr hit his body. Who had released those chibdys? Had it been Bles?

Many keitr attacked him, but none stayed at it, for the pheromones drew them away. At one point he realized that eight keitr were clawing and biting at his back and neck, but finally he felt nothing for several moments, and after that, only an occasional impact.

His mind raced as fast as he wished his body were. But until sierent, the frenzied keitr made escape impossible. Kark and the others would be tightly dug into their shelters to escape the maddened keitr. He blanched at the thought of staying in the cave under the keitr all night. He had to get out. Yet he dared not move before sierent began, for the keitr were winging every-where.

Through the long, long day, Yosha arched his neck so he could breathe the dank air beneath him. The humiliation of lying there was mixed with the terrible revelation that an Askirit wanted him to die and that all his longing to be righteous and grasp the promises might be the very reason someone detested him.

He refused to even think about Bles. He recited long sections of the liturgy. Then he tried to concentrate on a story he had been creating. Besides the rituals and ancient myths that were taught word for word, the Askirit made up their own stories to share at gatherings. To craft a good one required many mental revisions before telling it aloud, for a well-crafted story was appreciated as thoroughly as a well-sculpted face in stone. Yosha tried to concentrate on the process, but the sour air and discomfort numbed his mind.

By the time keitr began returning, the winds of sierent had begun. He moved his cramped body forward, his lungs desperate for clean air. The winds gusted into his face, refreshing him; he moved more quickly, trying to keep the noirim tight over his back. He knew he could not try the steep, tricky descent to the camp; the winds would blow him off the cliff wall. But high in the crags, sierent was not fatal if one could find a crevice.

He wondered if Kark would have told him to crawl deeper into the cave beneath the keitr and to ride out sierent there. But to Yosha, that was inconceivable. He fought the increasingly strong winds but failed to find a shelter. Totally inept in the thick noirim leather, a gust from a different direction knocked him flat. Eventually he simply huddled into a deep depression in a gorge near the trail. With the winds pummeling and tearing at him, he told himself as he breathed fully of the moist, clean air that he was in a much better place than he had been most of the day.

That night, he never slept; sierent kept buffeting and rolling his body in the little gully, first one way, then the other. But finally the worst was over, and moving into the weaker winds, he attempted the slippery descent.

Partway down, he heard someone below. He immediately thought of Bles. No, he told himself, don't assume it was Bles who released the chibdys. Hundreds of recruits are gathering keitr. It could have been anyone for any sick reason. Yet he stopped descending and crouched off the trail.

Before the climber was much closer, he recognized Kark's characteristic cough. "A full belt!!" Yosha called out. He resumed his descent as the older man yelled out in exhilaration. As they met, Kark reached out and touched his face. "Only a claw mark on the hand," Yosha said, grasping the older man's shoulder.

Kark then held out his hand as Yosha unfastened his belt and handed it to him. The experienced soldier's fingers traced down each of the keitr pouches to make sure they were filled, and filled properly. Then his hand descended across Yosha's face in a sign of camaraderie, and he tapped in Yette on the boy's hand, "I tried to come." Neither said anything more, for both knew someone had tried to kill the gatherers of keitr on Yosha's day.

When they entered the camp, the other boys mobbed Yosha

with the traditional roughhousing congratulations, the tone of their voices expressing a giddy relief. Yosha wearily joined in the fracas as they smeared a triumphal scent all over his face and neck and hair.

—— The Temple ——

Aris, capital of Tarn, was a city of two levels: a myriad of interlocking caverns below; a maze of deep-cut trails and caves above. Both levels led to a large bay. An hour's climb above Aris stood the great King's House, with many vast rooms housing treasures and the king's court. Askirit history chronicled the nation's kings who built Aris and the temple and who fought and died for them.

Sounds of birds and the sea and the smell of the port city's commerce greeted Kark and the initiates as they descended a steep, difficult route from the crags. They made their way immediately toward the great temple and found as they got closer that the trails were filling up with people heading toward the sanctuary. As they neared its entrances and were jostled forward, they had trouble staying together. People were speaking loudly, and Yosha had been listening to fragments of their conversations when he realized he had become separated from the others.

Inside the temple, still listening for familiar voices, he groped with his left hand for the wall. When his fingertips touched it, he felt the carved face of a young man looking up, eyebrows raised, head thrown back. But Yosha was swept along, his fingers pulled from that face. His fingers kept probing the wall and finding exquisite carvings of men and women and children. All had their eyes upward, expressions of worship carved onto their faces.

When he came to a stairway, his toes grazed a riser. He bent down, sideways against the wall to avoid being pushed forward, and felt the carved images of shells and birds. As he ascended he continued to trace on the wall scores of carved faces of worshipers until he reached the level of the sanctuary itself. There he encountered the life-size figures of a man and a woman. He pressed himself next to them and felt the ridges of their clothes, their faces, and their arms, which were stretched high toward the inner temple.

He left them reluctantly and moved with the thousands of congregants into the sanctuary. As he did so, the sounds coming from within lifted his spirits. Yosha had all his life heard the phrase "maidens with stringed instruments," but now he heard hundreds of them playing and singing around the perimeter of the inner temple. Coming at him with the music was a new scent, one used only in the temple. He inhaled it, a rich, full fragrance.

He moved forward toward the center, as close as the press of bodies allowed. Male singers, shaking pevas and striking percussion instruments, harmonized with the women's voices and strings. As they increased the tempo, the worshipers began singing; Yosha joined in, relishing every word, his voice lifting with all the others.

A priest announced the recitations. Other priests recited them, then exhorted the worshipers to faithfulness.

Yosha was startled and pleased to recognize the voice of one of the exhorters. It was Maachah. "We stand here before Eshtel," the priest was saying, "but why do we pray to him? Not—I say not—because he needs us to be here!"

Yosha thought the old man from Rens, in contrast to the other priests, sounded brusque and perhaps too informal for this magnificent temple. Yet the energy in his voice gripped his listeners. "Eshtel lives in the light. He lives in glory, with magnificent creatures of glory. They, too, sing with us today. They, too, rejoice—right now!—with the Almighty and with us. But these magnificent creatures also listen. They listen with Eshtel to our prayers, for they know the great conflict in Aliare. They see the evil and the good. As our prayers ascend, they will waft into the nostrils of Eshtel. For even Eshtel himself has been weeping for us. He and all the beings of light will weep with us as we go to our prayers.

"But they do not weep in despair," Maachah continued. "Eshtel and the glorious ones weep in hope. They savor the scent of our tears. They gather our tears and prayers and transform them into something new. Eshtel himself fills them with holy energy and hurls them back into our darkness as blazing shocks of hope!"

Maachah's voice had grown louder, resounding throughout the sanctuary. "He mixes our prayers with fire and spirit!" Maachah declared. "They are hurled into Aliare, and the beings of light rejoice!"

Maachah paused and let his words echo in the massive vault. Then he said, more quietly but with equal fervor, "Yet many an Askirit dreads their return. Are you ready to pray for such a terrible thing as the return of our prayers?"

He ceased his exhortation and began instructing the people to pray. Yosha heard the uneven murmur of voices around him pouring out troubles and pleadings.

Another priest began to speak, reciting:

> *Hope will come,*
> *The Hope of Aliare.*
> *He will invade the world.*
> *He will afflict his enemies with light;*
> *He will nourish his friends with light.*

> *He transcends Aliare.*
> *He hurls fire from world to world.*

> *Hope will come,*
> *The Hope of Aliare.*

The priest concluded his recitation, then another stepped forward to perform the final ritual. "Who is the most holy person in the temple?" the priest asked.

"The person beside us," the congregants responded.

"Why is that one holy?"

"Because of the holy light within."

Yosha had participated in this ritual many times before in the little sanctuary in Wellen. He turned to the person next to him and said the expected words: "Holy is the one who seeks and loves the light. Holy are you." He reached out to where he judged the person's face to be; he was shorter than Yosha had expected, and his fingers encountered a thick shock of hair. The other worshiper's fingers had already reached out and were touching Yosha's chin.

As he moved his hand down the forehead, Yosha decided it was a boy about his own age. Yet as they began reciting with the congregation, the voice he heard beside him was a guttural rasp. Yosha's fingers were moving across the young man's eyes as he felt the other's fingers on his cheek.

As the sacrament continued and they spoke to each other of their bodies being repositories of glory, Yosha's fingers jerked a trifle as his hand encountered the boy's left cheek. It was indented—wounded somehow, and slightly wet. What was this he felt? Was it blood? Yosha traced his fingers lower and realized the whole side of the young man's face was caved in and misshapen. He moved his hand lower to escape the distortion, but the jawbone must have at one time also been crushed, for it felt rumpled.

Yosha stopped reciting, something he had never done before. He awkwardly touched the other side of the young man's face as the shorter congregant's fingers traced across Yosha's eyes. The other side of the face was normal except for a slight depression in the jaw. As they completed the sacrament, Yosha awkwardly resumed reciting the words, yet he felt tongue-tied. The young man's face was the most disfigured he had ever touched. He wondered how anyone could have survived the damage from those deep gulleys in his flesh.

The sacrament was over when Yosha heard a voice breaking into his thoughts. "Do not be shocked," the strange voice was saying, and he realized it was the young man. "As you have touched the glory, I have touched the glory."

He didn't know how to reply. He noticed his fingers were a little sticky, as if the wetness on the other's face had indeed been blood. If he has a wound, why doesn't he bind it up? Yosha wondered. He felt mesmerized by the young man's face. Voices swirled around him and people pressed him toward the entrances.

He decided not to say anything, and the stranger disappeared into the crowd.

—— An Odd Tale ——

Yosha descended the stairs and wide causeways, again listening for familiar voices. Outside the temple, he finally heard Geln's voice and called out to him. Pednol was with him, and the three talked excitedly about their experiences in the temple and their longing to find the way to the light.

Yosha mentioned the young man with whom he had just shared the sacrament, describing the face he had touched.

An older man nearby overheard him and said, "You're talking about the cripple. Battered to pulp by sierent, he was." The man spoke rapidly, as if he had much to say. "Comes from Martt. That's my town. The boy's face is still awful battered up, don't you think?"

As the man continued talking, Yosha's embarrassment at being overheard was quickly replaced by discomfort at the old man's garrulousness. In a rush of details, the stranger spoke with happy authority, as if knowing all about this hometown phenomenon, this oddity, gave him distinction. "What they fished out of the water that morning you wouldn't have recognized as human. Just a pulverized thing, like meat you'd softened with a hammer. But it was breathing. Yes, breathing! Turned out to be a boy, just a few years old. Who knows where it came from. Might have been Askirit from down the coast or a barbarian from anywhere at all—some boy that wandered off and fell into the sea. I've heard people say he'd come from above and survived ute, but that's impossible! They're just thinking of the old story of the boy from above. You've heard it many times—"

The old man gave no opportunity for them to say that, yes, they had heard it many times. "It's the one about the boy who found a hole and crawled in," he said, "calling for his father to come with him. But the hole was too small for the father, and the boy heard calls from below. He pushed further in and then the boy slid into ute and into the sea of Aliare and ended up on the shores of Tarn. He's still trying to get back to his father, and when he does, they say, the light will come to Aliare."

The man paused and chuckled. "Just a tall tale," he said, "but they named the boy after the story, named him Ute, as if he really came from above. But no one could survive sierent, let alone ute. It couldn't be true, but it was! He was breathing. That's what no one could figure. So they took him to Chaisdyl—a little stick of a woman—to watch him till he stopped breathing. They figured to give him a decent burial and send him back to sierent that night with a proper covering and prayers for his soul.

But Chaisdyl took that boy and bound up his wounds and kept him breathing that day. They say she wept over him and put so many tears all over his body that they soaked in and started the healing. But that's just talk. She kept him breathing, talking to him and all, but she didn't hold him, of course, he was just this mashed up thing, all gory and battered. The slightest touch would make him moan."

Yosha finally was able to interrupt by saying, "So is more than his face affected?"

"Oh, have no doubt! Both his legs are all caterwauled, like broken sticks. Not just broken in one place, broke all over. So he's all twisted when he stands, and he has to lean on a cane in each hand. His right arm and hand are reasonably close to normal, but his left just hangs there like a dead eel. And you heard his voice, didn't you? Like a dying frog. Throat must have been crushed. Seems sometimes he can hardly get air through it let alone speak. Yet I've also heard him make speeches. That he's alive at all is because of Chaisdyl. She's not Enre, but she's holier than many of them I've met. She's given the boy her every waking hour."

Yosha said, "I felt something sticky on the side of—"

"Blood," the man interrupted. "Strange, huh? They put a couple of bones in to hold his skull together—niroc bones, I think—and they did the job, held it together, filled in the cavity, but something didn't take. It's like a fresh wound all the time. Nobody can explain it. Weird, if you ask me. Always a little blood on his face. But he won't cover it up. Says he can't, but won't explain why. Strange, strange boy." The man's tone had taken a critical edge.

"What do you mean?" Yosha asked.

"Says weird things. Won't bandage his head—kind of disgusting, that blood on his face. Hobbles around on canes, but on the trails has to drag himself up and down, his mother tagging along everywhere."

Yosha had heard enough; he thanked the man and suggested to Geln and Pednol that they return to camp. They started back slowly, moving with the far thinner crowd now coming and going from the temple. A wide, level terrain by the main bay extended a long distance before the trail back to their shelters. As they traversed it, listening to the calls and shouts and hubbub of the busy port, they slowed a little to breathe in the scents. They walked past the stone docks and balanced themselves on the thick ridges leading down to the water. They reveled in their being in the capital city, and Yosha soon forgot the bizarre tale of the crippled young man.

—— Shadows and Light ——

In warrens above the sanctuary, the priests of Aris prepared scents and sacrifices for the ceremonies. Here they also performed the Rites of Inclusion.

Yosha stood in the line awaiting Maachah, much as he had in Rens. The young man in front of him, a burly but nervous youth, cursed and said, "Of all the priests in Tarn, why'd we have to get stuck with Maachah? They say his questions are darts to the belly."

Yosha felt different; he welcomed the edge of fear expanding in his body. He wouldn't want the young man in front of him to know that he was perhaps the reason Maachah was here. He had sent a message to Rens, saying he would consider it a great honor if Maachah could prepare him for initiation. Since sending that message he had hoped, but had little expected, the priest would come. When he had heard Maachah's voice in the sanctuary, he had been overjoyed. But this morning he was also apprehensive, wondering what their second confrontation might be like.

He probed the wall's side ridges with his toe. All the temple was precisely crafted, and he couldn't get enough of touching its ridges and columns, even in the corridors like this where there were no carvings. The young men were lined up not far above the sanctuary, waiting to ascend yet another level.

Through the long morning, one after another of the boys was led by a temple page up the corridor. Finally he came for the young man just ahead of him and told him to follow up the long stairs. As their footsteps receded above him, Yosha stood alone, having waited half the day, anxious to complete the process.

In the distance, at the temple's entrances, he heard strange clattering sounds in an unnatural, jerky rhythm. Click, pause. Click, click, pause. Click, pause. Click, click, pause—the noise of sticks sounding in the empty corridors. The scuffling of twisted feet accompanied the rhythm of what must be canes coming in his direction across the temple floor. As the odd shuffle laboriously came closer and closer, aiming right for him, he realized it had to be the cripple. He kept coming until he was standing close behind him.

What was he doing here? Had he come to say something? The situation was awkward, even preposterous. Did Yosha have an obligation to greet him? If the other boys had still been ahead of him, he could have talked to them. But here he stood alone with this strange young man. He felt so awkward he became aware of the sound of his own breathing in the silence.

"Yosha?" the voice croaked behind him. He felt the young man's gnarled fingers grip his shoulder. It was a fraternal touch, perhaps too familiar. He felt mildly threatened by the encounter.

"Yosha," the voice insisted.

"Yes?" Yosha caught a whiff of the scent he wore, a man's scent—in fact, an old man's scent, one worn by the sages. "Yosha," the quavery yet purposeful voice said, "you must not give up." The cripple squeezed his shoulder, then released his grip.

Yosha did not respond. He stood awkwardly waiting, rapping his fingers against the wall, trying to figure out a reason for this invalid to be here at the purification rites. For him to have gathered keitr was physically impossible; he wouldn't even make it up the steep ascent to the priests' rooms.

At last the page came for him, and the two began to ascend the long, narrow stairs. They climbed higher and higher into the honeycombed mountain, along the channel erosion had created long ago. Yosha's arms were both out wide, fingers stretching to touch the walls for balance. The page moved quickly on familiar territory, and Yosha wished he would slow down. All he needed now was to stumble, crash into the page and feel like a fool.

Suddenly the page slowed a little and asked, "Are you the Yosha who entered the mouth of Kjotik?" Yosha said that he was, and the page said, his tone deferential, "We have a song we sing about that."

"I think I have heard it," Yosha said, a little embarrassed.

They stopped at an entrance to one of the priests' caves directly above the temple, and the page said, "This is it." Then he walked away.

Yosha reached for the curtain and pulled it back. Immediately he heard Maachah's voice demand, "What is your name?"

"Yosha."

"What evil have you done?"

Yosha was taken aback more than he had anticipated. It was common to invite a confession, but Maachah's request sounded abrupt and harsh. "I have sought my own desires instead of the light," Yosha said. "I have—"

"In what ways specifically?" Maachah interrupted.

"I have desired power for myself. I have drunk the praises of women and boys. The glory seems like mine, though I know it belongs to the light."

"You have not been choosing humiliation, then." Maachah stepped away, walked to the water basin, and scooped some up in his hand. He anointed him in the usual way with the usual warnings and promises.

The echoes of Maachah's voice told Yosha they were in a large room with wall coverings. The priest told him to sit on a bench that he would find along the wall, and Yosha groped his way toward it.

He located it and seated himself, his hands hanging down to the sides of the bench, on which he felt carvings of wings and eyes. The priest remained standing.

"Are you seeing the light?" Maachah asked. "Have you

opened your eyes? Or are you too busy listening to songs about Yosha?"

Why had Yosha ever asked for this priest? Any other would have chatted amiably and given him absolution. He wished Kark could be here to speak up for how he had ignored so much of the praise. Yet he hungered for something Maachah had and was willing to pay the price. "It is not hard to forget the songs when someone tries to kill you," Yosha blurted out, trying to sound strong but not disrespectful.

"You're changing the subject. I told you once, the benefits of adversity are incalculable."

"The benefits are difficult to appreciate when you're lying face-down in a keitr cave," Yosha said, but immediately wished he hadn't.

Maachah asked why Yosha had been forced into that position, and he told him about Bles. "What haunts me is wondering why the voices so badly want me dead," Yosha said. "On the way to Rens they were at me constantly, and I see now if I had obeyed any of their suggestions, I would be dead. Now they must be talking to Bles about me."

"Do the voices still come to you?" Maachah asked.

"Yes. But I plead for the inner light, and I fill my head with all the psalms and promises I can remember. When I hear the voices, I'm filled with fear."

"A reasonable fear. Some do not fear, and they converse with troubling spirits like old friends. But think about this. They may start using more subtle tactics on you. They can lead you to do evil because you love the good."

Maachah paused, letting the words sink in. "You can smell naked evil," he explained, "but how about getting good things done in evil ways? Watch out for your passion for truth." He pressed a small pencray intaglio into Yosha's hands. "The truth is, we claim to love the light, but we flee it. Yosha, you must be more than good. You must be holy!"

Maachah's words confused Yosha. He sat silently, with no

answer to all these statements. "Yosha, I have told you a great good is coming. Remember, out of wreckage, hope." He dropped his voice to nearly a whisper. "Eshtel is not a spectator. He does not snigger at our obscenities. He does not gasp at our perfidy. He is Eshtel. He makes of misery a new good. But only for the lovers of light do the scattered confusions cohere. Now—right now— seek the way. You and I must not miss the great good that's coming."

Yosha tried to decipher the flow of words. Finally he asked, "Why do you think we may miss it?"

"Because my own evil is a terror to me," Maachah said immediately, taking a deep and baleful breath.

"What terror?" Yosha asked.

"Shadows block the light," Maachah said. "But you'll find the light where you least expect it."

Maachah's tone had shifted from interrogator to earnest prophet and counselor. As they talked, he confided that he had been harsh with Yosha because he was afraid his exploits with Kjotik might have ruined him. He gave Yosha absolution, smeared scent on his eyelids, and said as he left, "Open your eyes. Eshtel is never obvious. His light is in the secret places—where you'd never think to look."

—— Ute ——

Yosha stepped outside the room and was met by the page, who asked him to follow him down to a different exit. As he turned and started walking behind him, he noticed the scent on his own shoulder where the cripple had touched him. He wondered if Ute was still waiting and stopped mid-stride, asking, "Are you going to get that crippled boy and bring him up here?"

The page stopped and said that, yes, he supposed so.

"But how will he make it up those stairs?" Yosha asked.

"I don't know," the page said. "But he's the last one to be brought. I have to get him."

Yosha found it inexplicable. "Look, I'll find my own way out. It's going to take you forever to get him up here. Go ahead," he urged, and put his hand on his shoulder, taking advantage of the fact the boy had sung songs about him. The page hesitated, then agreed and stepped off in the opposite direction.

Yosha could not resist the temptation to eavesdrop on what would go on in that room, though he knew that if caught he would be severely censured. He tiptoed back near the entrance of the room and positioned himself along the wall where he thought the page would be least likely to bump into him. Then he waited. And waited. It took a very long time before he heard the distinctive clack of the canes, and the wheezing and flip-flop motion of the cripple's body as it endlessly, painfully ascended the stairs. He shuffled almost beside Yosha, then turned to push open the curtain with his shoulder.

"What is your name?"

"Ute."

As Maachah proceeded through the ceremony, nothing unusual was said. The priest accepted the standard responses to his questions. Yosha wondered if he was simply trying to be kind to a cripple. Before dipping his fingers in the scent to absolve him, the priest asked, "Why did you make all this effort to be cleansed?"

"It is required," the young man said. "Tomorrow is the initiation."

"But that is for those who have gathered keitr," Maachah said, in tones far kinder than Yosha had heard him use before.

"I have gathered keitr," the cripple said.

"How could you? How could you climb to the caves? It is forbidden to be helped by someone. How could you reach high enough to capture a keitr? You haven't been trained, nor would they take you."

"No, they wouldn't take me."

When Maachah mentioned the training, Yosha realized the priest had, indeed, been assigned to deal with this young man with aspirations higher than his body could realize. Obviously, of all the priests, they would choose to dump this problem on Maachah—an outsider with a controversial reputation. No one could bend Maachah or intimidate him.

Yosha heard the cripple's canes click, then a buckle released. "Here," he said, "examine my keitr belt. It is a full belt."

"That's not the point," Maachah said. "Do you mean to tell me you gathered these yourself?"

"I gathered them myself."

Maachah did not reply. Yosha heard him sit down, and nothing was said for a long time. Then the priest said, "I cannot accept that. I don't want to harass you. Perhaps you know my reputation. I can ask very uncomfortable questions. But I don't want to do that to you."

"You may do it to me."

"Why are you lying?"

Yosha heard the young man retrieve the belt from Maachah and flip it across his lap in the military manner. He then opened the pouch, pulled out a keitr in its protective inner sleeve and held it in his hand. "I have gathered this keitr and each of the others. I will release it and then show you how I did it."

Maachah actually spluttered in a manner totally uncharacteristic of the boisterous priest. "What kind of stunt is this?" he demanded. "Trying to intimidate a priest by threatening him with a keitr?"

"I'm ready to return to the light," said Ute. "Don't you long for it too?"

"Committing suicide does not take you to the light!" Maachah exclaimed.

"I was speaking to your fear," he said, in a level, assured tone. "I have no intention of being bitten."

Yosha decided that the boy was both arrogant and crazy, that when his skull had been crushed long before, his brains must have been ruined as well. He hoped for Maachah and himself that the deranged young man wouldn't let that keitr loose.

But Maachah wasn't trying to soothe the boy. Instead, he challenged him in a steady, accusing voice: "You have no more intention of releasing that keitr than you had of gathering him."

"My intentions are not known to you," the cripple said.

Yosha then heard a flapping of wings and a scream from Maachah at the same instant that something large crashed about in the room. Yosha's blood raced, not knowing whether to flee or fall flat, for he could do nothing against an enraged keitr. The noises in the room suddenly stopped and Yosha envisioned both Maachah and Ute dying on the floor, the keitr searching for an escape route right past his own cowering body.

But then he heard the cripple saying, "The keitr is back in the pouch, Maachah. But still you do not know my intentions."

Yosha heard nothing from Maachah, and there was a long silence. Then the cripple said, "The rituals of the Askirit reveal the light. They nourish the eye and soul. But the priests of the Askirit are like keitr who have been stung by chibdys. They carry death in their flesh. They hang with their heads toward the decay. They are empty skins full of worms about to emerge."

Yosha, still recovering from his own terror, was now astounded at Ute's harsh statement.

He was not surprised at Maachah's angry demand: "Then why are you here before me?"

"Because you love the light. Because you are not one who sings of the light and then casts men into the abyss. Because you are not full of worms, but full of hope."

The cripple had been seated on the bench and now rose laboriously. "Why do you think," he asked, "that we speak of

Aliare's hope as both water and light? How can it be esseh and Eshtel? Woman and Maker?

"Because both give life," the priest said immediately.

"Yes. Now tell me where it is written that a man must gather keitr before he can enter the most holy."

"It is written that only the able may enter the Tolas."

"Spirit and body. Esseh and Eshtel. Life and light. When one lives in light, he is able! He enters the most holy. It is his home."

Maachah paused and was silent for a time. Then he said, "It is not up to me, but I'll give you absolution," and he walked across the room to dip his fingers in the scent.

"No, it is not up to you," the crippled young man agreed.

Maachah applied the scent to his eyelids, absolved him, then said, "You have a lot of pluck."

Ute's voice was barely loud enough for Yosha to hear, but he sensed the uncanny certainty in it: "I see shafts of glory lighting your face. Light that is alive, clean, passing in majesty into the chasms beneath us."

When Maachah finally responded, his voice was changed. "Is it light I see on your face and in your wounds?" he asked. "My old eyes have had many tricks played on them."

Yosha heard movements in the room and realized Ute was moving toward the doorway. He flattened himself against the wall as the page appeared to escort the cripple down. As the two of them passed him, he stared intently at Ute, but he saw no light—no light at all..Yosha followed the two for a time, staying far behind, hearing the canes and the twisted body working its way slowly down to the temple entrances.

—— Laughter ——

On and on Yosha had been climbing with the other initiates to the very highest levels of the vast temple complex. They sweated profusely under the ceremonial robes, even though these were made of loosely woven sea fiber and human hair—a double symbolism appropriate for their entry into the holiest, the Tolas. All during the long climb, temple guards had required passwords, for only selected Askirit were allowed entry to the most solemn rituals of all.

Finally, they stood at the corridor leading to the Tolas itself. Yosha's bare feet evaluated each ridge and pebble as the young men waited to step forward. A slight breeze touched his face even as his feelings of shameful unworthiness warmed it. As he was led to his assigned place in the Tolas and stood with hands stretched high above his head, he sensed an unspeakable presence, like a fragrance wafting into his senses. Far above him, at the peak of this holy mountain, was an opening to the outside air. He heard the distant cries of birds and felt the freshness of midday.

Through the opening above him was the roof of Aliare, remarkably close from this mountain's peak. He stared up into the darkness, the deep yearning upon him. Sparks from the ceremony caught his eyes and he lowered them, hungrily staring at these signs from above. He began singing with the others; tears wet his lashes. The assembly sang softly until the high priest began the Rite of Inclusion by saying to the novitiates, "The Tolas is holy. Here, you are received into righteousness. Bring no impurity. Here, you cannot hide your thoughts from the light."

He went on to recite long sections of the rituals, then had the initiates repeat pledges of fealty to Eshtel and to the Askirit kingdom. After all the recitations and exhortations had been completed, the priest declared in a loud voice, "Askirit, receive the light! Young men, let your joy ring out to all the peaks of Tarn!"

At his words, the initiates' sweet longings and composure

were suddenly shattered by an astounding peal of strange, ecstatic laughter. A voice among them had erupted joyously, splitting the silence. With a chill, Yosha recognized the unmistakable voice of Ute, the cripple. Outrageous! he thought. How could that deranged young man possibly have gotten himself up to the Tolas? It would have taken him all morning to have made the climb.

The same laughter rang out again, eerily echoing off the rounded walls. The crazily joyous, raucous sound was amplified by the echoes, as if many voices were laughing in that most holy place, and all of them sending that laughter up through the open peak and out to all of Tarn.

"Stop!" the high priest demanded.

Instantly, the laughter stopped.

Not a movement disturbed the hush in the Tolas. All remained standing in terrible silence, waiting. Yosha's heart was pounding. The cripple had desecrated the Tolas! The silence went on and on, as if the abomination had immobilized all who stood there.

Finally the high priest, his voice hesitant, concluded the rites by pronouncing a blessing on the new men of the Askirit. Yosha did not know if guards had taken the cripple away or not, but for him, the strange young man had broken the sense of presence and the beauty he had always longed to find in this place.

Yosha felt relieved when he was finally out of the robe and in the fresh air outside the temple. Kark and his fellow initiates were celebrating the rite in a subdued way, talking mostly about the bizarre event. The day before, after Yosha had eavesdropped on the exchange between the cripple and Maachah, he had sensed a strange power in Ute. But now Yosha fully shared his companions' anger. The rumor was that no one could find the young man, though all Aris was buzzing with talk about him.

"How could they let a crazed cripple into the Tolas?" Geln

asked. "You heard the old man from his hometown—he's probably not even Askirit."

Kark let out a blast of air. "What priest could call him *able* enough to enter the Tolas?" he asked. "He's not able in mind or body."

Yosha said, "All our lives we have longed for that day in the Tolas. But then, laughter and desecration!"

"You needn't worry," a pleasant voice nearby assured him. "They're taking care of it!"

"The priests have already decided," another added. "He goes back to the sea where he came from!"

The word had spread far beyond those who had been in the ceremony. "The Tolas has been desecrated!" someone cried out in a loud voice. "The foreigner has desecrated the Tolas!" Before long, Yosha and the others were pressed tightly in the growing crowd.

"We've got to hurry!" several people started shouting. "We've got to hurry!" The crowd was pressing toward the trails that led down the steep inclines toward the bay of Aris.

"Why are we hurrying?" he asked the figures ahead of him.

"The foreigner is hiding in the caves."

The broad trail broke into numerous sharp descents, and as everyone surged into them, they concentrated on their hand-holds and footings. Yosha was unfamiliar with the trail, and he found himself pressed by the people behind. Once a man's foot struck his hand, and he cried out, but people surged past him as he stopped to recover. He had to flatten himself against the edge since he couldn't move quickly on these slippery drops. Soon the crowd was far ahead of him. He followed their shouts, taking a trail that seemed to lead toward the sounds. After committing himself to the trail, however, he found it ambled to the left in an easy descent, widely circling instead of leading directly down.

With the sounds of the crowd receding ever farther below, his passion for helping capture the strange young man began to cool. How many hundreds does it take to find one cripple? he thought. It's the priests' job anyway. Likely they'll put him in a little boat and let sierent suck him up to finish the job it almost did the first time.

Yosha was walking now, feet easily probing the slight descent of the trail, listening to shouts far below him. He rested, spinning his staff between his palms. Then he heard far ahead a slight click, then another, and another. He stopped and listened. What might that be? The sound continued until he recognized the distinctive shuffling of the cripple's body and the clicking of his canes.

He wondered what trail Ute might be on. As the sounds slowly grew closer, he realized he was coming up the very trail Yosha was sitting on. The click, pause, click, click, pause advanced at an excruciatingly slow pace toward him. Accompanying the sounds were the patient steps of a woman.

As they came closer and he looked below at the sounds, he thought he saw for an instant a shifting, bobbing luminescence. But when they drew closer, he decided he had seen nothing. The cripple was breathing heavily, his canes skittering as they struck unfamiliar rough spots. Yosha had not the slightest idea of what to do. He could cry out and attract the mobs who would take this out of his hands. He could simply drag the young miscreant down to the priests. But when they were so near to him they were almost touching his legs, it was the woman he thought of, the woman who had taken from the sea this drenched, crushed child and had nursed him back to life. Before doing anything else, he felt compelled to say something to her, something before others came and wrenched away her son.

"Chaisdyl, I am sorry this day had to come," he said.

The two stopped abruptly. "We are weary," Chaisdyl said, and helped Ute sit down on a boulder at the trail's edge. "Thank you," she added, in a tone that accepted Yosha as having already helped them.

This alarmed him; he was no accomplice to these two. "Ute, you should not have laughed in the sanctuary!" He spoke as if to reprimand a child. "It wrecked the rite for all of us. You desecrated the Tolas!" He felt his gorge rising again and was about to say much more but then decided the young man wouldn't understand any of it anyway.

"What does the ritual say?" the cripple asked. "Does it not declare, 'The joy of the holy makes me a child!' And does it not say that the Hope of Aliare will shout for joy from the temple? Why did we not all shout for joy?"

"What?" Yosha asked. He had no idea what the young man was talking about.

"When I was with Maachah, you were there by the door, listening," Ute said. "I knew you would be."

Yosha flushed. He had thought he had not been noticed by anyone. But he had no intention of apologizing. "And you saw Maachah glow!" Yosha said derisively. "And who knows what *he* saw." But when he had said this, he felt unworthy, having ridiculed Maachah.

Ute said, "The wound bleeds. It must be open to the air."

Yosha looked closely at him, trying to see even the faintest luminescence, but he saw only darkness. "Do I hate the light?" Yosha asked. "If I throw you to the priests, if I throw you into sierent, do I hate the light?"

"Do you wish to kill me?"

"Why shouldn't I?" Yosha's fingers of both hands were drumming on the keitr pouches on his belt.

"Because I am pursuing you," he said. The cripple's confident tone seemed misplaced in the frail, thick voice. "It is time to wash your eyes."

His presumption affronted Yosha. "What about *your* eyes?" he asked angrily.

"I see your yearning," Ute said, ignoring his question. "I see your drive toward the light. But it is impure. I have chosen you because you are Zeskret."

Yosha was startled at the use of his nickname. He felt he was losing ground and turned to Ute's mother. She dabbed at the cripple's wounds with a cloth and said to Yosha, "The wound must be open to the air, but the blood must be carefully wiped away."

Yosha said to her, "Can you help him to see how he hurts himself talking like this? He makes no sense."

The woman stood up and said, "We must go. We have rested enough."

"Yes," Yosha said awkwardly, wondering if he would be considered an accomplice if he let them walk off.

"You are Zeskret? The fierce bird?" Chaisdyl asked, placing the wet cloth into a pocket in her garments. "They named him Ute. Most people call him Kecha, the cripple. But I use a different name. I call him Auret—DawnBreaker. He is always like those heralds of the dawn, always giving me hope."

Chaisdyl and Auret then positioned themselves on the trail and began their slow procession upward, laboriously passing him. He listened to them move by, then said, "Chaisdyl, if you escape, you will both always be on the run. Can you help him understand? Is there nothing you can do for him?"

She did not stop, but she turned her head and said, "You know the story about the boy who came from above? How they say he was always trying to keep the miracles from leaking out?" She laughed quietly but with surprising heartiness. "Auret is always that way. I am grateful simply to wash his wounds and to listen—just listen ..."

Part Two

Can't sleep?
Something hiss from the abyss?
Don't worry.
Don't worry.

Noises in the night?
Gheials gonna bite?
Don't worry.
Don't worry.

Something creeping close?
Open wide; it's inside.
Don't worry.
Don't worry.

Go to sleep. Not a peep.
Don't worry.

—MOCK NURSERY SONG, SUNG BY OLDER CHILDREN

Chapter 6.

—— Shrieks ——

Asel felt her way through an opening into the main cavern of Gendt, once a prosperous city. But that was long ago, when the kingdom was young and before Aris, her rival not far down the coast, had been made Tarn's capital. Asel gave a short yelp and listened for the echoes. The vault was as large as reputed, high and wide, with many corridors echoing back.

Several years had passed since she had returned from Dorte. Beside her stood Bralin, an intense, short man of extraordinary tenacity, who shared Asel's dreams of spiritual conquests. "This is vast enough for a temple," he said. "But the people of Gendt are few. You could house all of them here and still get lost."

An old Enre with them, Tersa, said, "Then let us make it a cathedral. That takes but one worshiper."

From the cavern's center came sounds of many feet approaching. Military men began forming a half circle around them as an authoritative voice announced, "I am Pelck, the raka of Gendt. Welcome."

Asel greeted the city's military commander with a thump of her hands indicating respect. "I am Asel."

The man sounded annoyed at her words. "Yes, I know. And he is Bralin, and you speak for him."

The raka knew how to create dissension, she thought. Ignoring his provocation, she said, "We have a mission to carry out."

"With mostly women?" Pelck asked, cracking his knuckles.

"Enre," Asel retorted. "Fourteen of them. And six men. All righteous and unafraid to carry the light to Dorte."

"And children also, I understand." Pelck clucked his tongue. "Sierent is not far off," he said. "Have you found shelter?"

"Yes," Bralin said. "We are looking for others to join us."

"But why search for volunteers in Gendt?" a man beside the raka said. "We have only a few men and many widows facing the barbarians across the water. Go to Aris! They can give you hundreds."

Asel would not admit that Aris and other cities had been unresponsive. Instead she asked boldly, "How can you swear season after season to take the light throughout Aliare, but never leave Tarn?"

Pelck gave a mighty sigh and said, "This city can barely protect itself. When the barbarians attack, the light here goes out!"

The man beside Pelck said, "And why take the light to the living dead?"

"They are not dead!" Asel instantly retorted.

"Oh?" Pelck asked. "Are they barbarians? Dupes of the dead? You're raising these children you brought back as Askirit, but who knows what they are?" He made a quick slapping sound, forefingers against palm, meaning Asel should consider the consequences.

His words and the sound made Asel furious. She found it difficult to control her voice as she said slowly and intensely, "Say nothing like that again."

"Perhaps," he said, his own tone matching hers, "you have not thought of the true cost. Your forays to Dorte could release on all Tarn the horrors of the waking dead."

Bralin stood up and rapped his staff against the rock floor. "We will go to Dorte. Is there not one fearless man here?" he asked. "Not one man righteous enough to penetrate the darkness?"

The response was silence. They said abrupt farewells, and once out of earshot, Tersa said, "Doubt nothing! You have been given the vision, Asel. And we, too, see the children of Dorte waiting for us."

They retraced their way down the trails toward caverns near the sea, where they had left the others.

Dangerous heights required patience and care. Asel, having dropped to the next ledge, was waiting for Tersa to let herself down, when she heard a sound of terror a distance away. It was a woman's scream, a shriek of astonishment that lasted just a few heartbeats, then was instantly cut off.

"That was a woman's voice," Asel said. She did not wait for Tersa to drop. She called up to her, then darted off in the direction of the sound, off the trail and probing with her hands outstretched over the rocks and boulders until she felt a different trail under her feet. Voices came from near the scream, and she moved toward them, wary of what might be coming in her direction.

Then she noticed the slight whiff of a strange odor. She crouched defensively, feet inching forward.

Her foot touched something soft. She stopped, not changing her stance, and carefully explored with her toes what they had touched. It felt like the back of a person inert on the trail.

The voices came closer. She knelt; it was a woman. The foreign odor was clearly discernible, especially near the woman's head. She felt her face, then her fingers probed beneath her chin and touched a wet mass of ripped flesh. Her throat had been savaged by something.

The voices were near and she called out, "The woman is dead. Be careful." She heard them stop, then advance slowly. Asel patted over the body of the woman, but she found nothing unusual except for the ripped throat. She started feeling the ground beside the woman, meticulously tracing further out, feeling the surface of the aceyn to understand what had happened.

The villagers were standing apart from her, listening to her movements.

"What killed her?" a man asked.

"Something unknown," Asel said. "Her throat is ripped away. Must have happened in an instant. We all heard her scream."

Asel's fingers were still exploring the ground when she felt crumbling roughness and a hole in the aceyn the size of her wrist. With her dagger, she jabbed into it, probed as deeply as the blade could go in, and with the blade still in the hole, knelt to sniff. The smell was strongest there. "Do you smell something foreign?" she asked.

The man who had spoken before came forward. "Definitely. Something never on these shores, I'd say." The man himself smelled of the fish he had been cleaning and scaling, but the strange odor was stronger.

"There's a hole here," she said. "I've probed it with a dagger. See what you make of it."

"I'm not going to touch it!" the man said quickly. Like all Askirit men, he wore a keitr belt and had his hand on a pouch. "I can't send a keitr after it. It would just fly back out of the hole at us." He stood nervously, scuffing his feet.

A boy said, "Maybe it's not in the hole at all."

Asel replaced her dagger, then stood and rubbed her fingers on her jacket to wipe off the blood.

"They're from the pit," the man said quietly. "I've said all along we shouldn't be using the deep caverns in Gendt. For generations, no one's had the guts to explore all the way down in them, and there's good reason. I tell you, they've been invaded by specters. That's why so many people have left Gendt. The caverns are deep and deadly; what else but creatures of the abyss come up from the ground like this?"

More villagers arrived, but before explanations could begin, they all heard first one, then two, and before long, three more screams, each from different parts of the village, all within a hundred heartbeats, and all the same: a horrible shriek, cut off suddenly. Everyone stood stunned, motionless. Asel wondered why Bralin and the others hadn't gotten here by now, but perhaps those other screams explained it.

Quickly, with all four limbs, she started retracing her path as best she could remember back to the trail where she had left them. She angled in the wrong direction once, but finally located the trail just above the place where she had heard the scream. She lowered herself on the same rock configuration and let herself drop. As her feet hit the ground, she smelled the foreign odor again. She grabbed her dagger and put her foot out warily, crouched again, and after a time again located the body of a woman.

She knelt and felt her face. It was Tersa.

She touched as little as she could beneath Tersa's chin, only enough to be sure that her throat, too, had been ripped out. With her blade first, this time, she probed until she found the same sort of hole with the same odor.

Another scream rent the air, this time in the direction they had left Breea, Nen, and Delin.

She scrambled down the trail, nearly falling several times, trying not to think about the words of the man who insisted these were creatures from the pit. His statements disturbingly matched Pelck's accusations that she'd bring Dorte's forces upon them. And Pelck's despicable insinuations about Breea tore at her. She tried to purge her mind of Askirit tales describing wicked girls possessed by gheials, tales mixing with images of Breea calling to the creatures of the abyss, opening her arms to the gheials, turning into something unnatural herself, then setting out on a macabre rampage.

Such vivid tales she thought improbable, but she did think the horrors had come to take back Breea and Nen and Delin; that first they were seeking her, killing all these women in their search.

She ran even more quickly, hearing another shriek before

she reached the shelter. She burst past the open, leather hangings at the entrance and called, "Breea!"

"We are all here," Onnt, one of the Enre women, said. Breea ran to Asel and clung to her, Nen and Delin beside them.

"Where are Bralin and the others?"

"They are bringing their weapons into this cave. They were with Tersa when she was attacked, but they could do nothing and fled to us."

When Bralin and the others entered with their spears and long blades, he said, "What use are these weapons? We have no idea what's at us."

Asel said, "Every one of you, get a dagger in your hand. It comes from below. It rushes straight for the throat. Hold your dagger at your chin and be ready to thrust the thing through!" They did so and stood, listening, holding their daggers awkwardly, absurdly, like stalagmites, with the daggers held so tightly the muscles in their hands began to cramp. They heard another scream outside, and the tension drained their strength.

As suddenly as a blow to the head, something erupted near Asel's feet. Then she heard claws scurrying frantically up on someone behind her. A young man's scream was barely out of his mouth before she heard the savage attack at his throat. Whether or not the man was able to stab at the creature before it hit she couldn't tell, but he fell forward on her even as she smelled the odor and felt the alien creature in frenzied motion between his chest and her back. She tried to whip around with her dagger, but the man's body had knocked her sideways so that she fell to the ground.

She bounded up, reaching for the children, but she couldn't tell where they were. As suddenly as it had hit, the thing was gone. She reached down to where the young man had fallen; he was lying dead like the others.

"Why are we standing here?" a young woman demanded. "We're no more safe in here than outside. He was holding a dagger, but it got him!"

Asel heard other voices, too—villagers who had crowded into the cavern, seeking the protection of Enre and armed men. But they found no protection. "We've got to get *someplace*!" a woman exclaimed. "Shouldn't we run to the sea? Or to the crags?"

Asel said, "They come up from the ground. We must go where there is no aceyn—deep into the caves where the aceyn does not reach."

"That's insane!" a villager said. "The caverns are where they're coming from! You'll kill us all. They'll come at us in packs if we go down there."

"That's where we go!" Asel said fiercely. "It's certain death here. And the high crags are too far away."

"Grab your stuff and move!" Bralin ordered, and they began running deep into a cavern none of them had ever explored. They ran at a reckless pace for a long distance until finally the aceyn gave out, and they were on solid rock.

Standing in fearful, sweaty clumps of three or four, they listened in relief to the silence, for here they heard no more shrieks. Bralin approached Asel and said to her, "One of the villagers was at the outskirts of the city, down by the sea, not long before this began. She heard some men talking. They were speaking a language she'd never heard before."

—— Chaos ——

Yosha knelt beside a man he had heard shriek from not more than fifty paces away. It was the third person he had found with his throat ravaged. This one had just taken his last breath and still twitched with life. All Aris was in chaos, the screams coming from every area of the city.

Yosha, now a page assigned to the temple, had been walking toward it when he had heard the first screams. He had quickened his pace, his mind rushing through possible explanations but coming to none. He had smelled the strange odor and had found the hole from which the thing had erupted. But none of that told him a thing except that it was lethal and totally foreign to his experience. He rushed up the now familiar, winding trail to the temple entrances, bumping into people as he hurried forward. Might it be safe within the temple? he wondered. Soon he was part of a mass of shouting, weeping, screaming men and women who pressed through the entrances toward the causeway.

Then came a shriek within the temple, near the center of the sanctuary. A startled cry went up, a cry such as had never before been heard in Aris. Another shriek rent the sanctity of the temple a second time. The people began storming toward the entrances to escape from the place in which they had sought safety.

Yosha sensed the danger of being trampled and ran along the inside wall to the ramps leading up to the priests' rooms. Someone smashed into him and he fell. Others fell over him, pressing the breath out of him as he crawled to the wall. He wrenched his body along the floor so it was parallel to the wall, seeking space, wriggling forward, gulping for air but feeling smothered by the bodies stumbling and falling. He fought forward, his left hand groping frantically for the doorway he knew should be there. Desperately, he rammed himself ahead. When his fingertips touched the doorway, he lunged and got his fingers on the edge. He yanked forward, just enough to get a firm grip. A knee hit his forehead, stunning him for an instant, but then he forced his right hand over to his left to pull himself forward a bit more. Finally he got his head into the air of the stairwell. He took in deep gulps of air as his body continued to be jammed against the wall. He yanked himself bit by bit into the opening, then lay breathing deeply, trying to ease his bruised body into a position that lessened the pain.

He crawled up the ramp a short way, concluding as he

moved that he had no broken bones. But surely, he thought, a great many people behind him did, as their panicked cries pursued him. He crawled up the ascent, hearing others moving above him, and wondered if it might be safer above or even more hazardous in that smaller place.

He finally reached the aperture of the priests' room where he had met Maachah. Far beneath he could still hear the shouting and wails as an undifferentiated din. Within the room, he heard animated, demanding voices. He stood as straight as he could and entered, sidling with his back tight against the wall. He heard Maachah's voice and moved in its direction.

Someone said, "Judgment is here! Our ancestors in the light once felt the world crack under their feet. We in the darkness hear the ground erupt with the teeth of judgment!"

Another said, "The pit has belched up its furies. The things from the abyss are loosed!"

Yosha recognized Maachah's voice as he shouted in a chiding tone, "We know nothing about what is happening, and we know nothing about which prophecies are upon us. Shut up about furies and the abyss!"

"But what else?" a different voice demanded. Yosha recognized it as Hrusc's, one of the most powerful priests in Aris, the man many expected to become high priest one day. "We tempt the abyss by letting pagan converts wheedle themselves into the nation," Hrusc said. "They claim they seek the light, but they're impure. They were born barbarian, and they remain barbarian. Their oafish bodies no more seek light than a fish seeks land!"

"What are you talking about?" Maachah asked hotly. Everyone in the room bit his fists, ground his heels against the rock floor or his teeth against teeth. "Let's talk about what to do!"

"Do?" Hrusc said in outrage. "We have failed to keep the Askirit pure. We have brought so many pagans into Tarn, the furies can claim the land."

Maachah was equally angry. "Hrusc, they're *our* barbarians—and barbarians no more. We're commanded to convert them. Only pagans hungry for righteousness make it through the rituals."

Hrusc slammed his palms on his hips. "Maachah, the abyss hears you with glee. Apostates have cracked the kingdom! Converts have polluted Tarn and opened the pit!"

His words were cut short by a shriek close beside him. In that small room they heard the sound of the frenzied claws racing to the throat, and several felt blood spatter on them as a man's hands jerked futilely to protect himself. His body toppled over into Maachah, who grabbed it boldly and lowered it to the floor.

Yosha awoke. He tried unsuccessfully to recall the dreams from which he had just emerged. He thought of the shrieks. All night long he had feared sleep.

"Sierent is over," Maachah said. "We will soon see if this terror returns."

Yosha sensed others lying and sitting in the room and the priests talking at the other end. He moved closer to where Maachah sat with his back against the wall. "If these are gheials of the night," Yosha said, "it is strange they attack only by day."

"Strange indeed," Maachah said. His words were cut off by a shriek from a priest's room some distance away. Someone bolted to his feet. "No!" the man shouted angrily. "No!"

Maachah grabbed Yosha by the arm and pulled him toward the entrance. "Come with me," he said. "I can't stand to wait like a bird for sacrifice." They walked along a level corridor, Maachah moving briskly and Yosha following his lead. "Let's take the tunnel that leads to the prison," Maachah said. "I suppose you've heard that the cripple—Auret—is there."

Yosha had heard about that. It had been years since he had met the fugitives on the trail, yet he still felt uneasy about them. The strange young man had acted as if he had some special claim on Yosha. Was that because they had met in worship, hands and faces expressing the glory? Had that triggered something in Ute's troubled mind?

"I heard they put Chaisdyl in prison with him," Yosha said. "That she's kept him hidden all these years."

"Hidden. Or perhaps something else," Maachah said. "But with Aris in chaos, now's the time to set them loose! If he's crazy, he's one of Eshtel's crazies!"

Yosha had no intention of getting involved with breaking loose a prisoner, but he kept walking with Maachah. Prisons in Tarn were simply huge caverns in which the authorities housed both men and women. Being thrown into one meant being cast into anarchy. Yosha thought the prisoners hardly needed this new terror. To try to stop thinking of the screams and to hear the sound of his own voice, he said, "His name is Ute. Why do you call him Auret."

"Because Chaisdyl named him that, and who knows— maybe the tale fits him."

Yosha snorted in a way that attempted humor. "Whoever heard of the Maker changing his mind and turning a man into a bird!"

Maachah snorted back with equal lightness. "I don't think Chaisdyl cares about such questions."

As they moved through the long tunnel, aceyn under their feet, they heard occasional screams, shouts, and shrieks, sometimes close, sometimes in the distance as the second day of the terror began. At the prison entrance, a sentry's voice barked out, "Password!" He spoke with a military confidence that contrasted sharply with others' terrified voices.

They identified themselves and gave the day's password. The sentry let them pass to the guards at the prison entrance. Again they were met by men who demanded they follow military procedures. When Yosha complimented them on their discipline, the guard said, "I'd as soon get my throat ripped out as get torn apart by the refta. He promised to do it slowly and painfully if I panicked." The refta was a prison warden, often with a reputation as rough as that of the inmates.

They entered the massive cavern. No one was near the entrance and Yosha wondered where the prisoners were hiding. His weapons were with the guards, which made him feel vulnerable. Stories of prison murder and rape were the expected and even desired result of being a king's prisoner. As they walked unprotected further and further into the prison, he began to doubt they would find Chaisdyl and Ute alive. It was unlikely a cripple and a woman could survive prison for long. "Maachah, why are we venturing so far in? They could jump us easily, and the guards won't help us."

"I've come here many times," Maachah said. "They won't kill a priest, not the ones willing to walk in."

"That's a chancy attitude and you know it. And I'm not a priest."

In response, Maachah shouted into the depths of the cavern, "Where are you? You know me—Maachah!"

A voice called out, echoing in the high chamber. They headed toward it and soon heard talking and movements. Yosha soon sensed hundreds of people were sitting and lying on the cavern's floor. Maachah asked, "Where are Auret and Chaisdyl?"

"Here," said the woman.

"She has bound up everyone's injuries," Auret said. Yosha could hear his strange voice as he slowly got to his feet, adjusted his canes and slowly walked over to them. "She has barely slept since we arrived here, caring for them."

An old woman's voice from among the prisoners said, "I'd be dead now if she hadn't come." Several other voices piped up in agreement. As the prisoners continued talking, Yosha noticed how greatly their restrained tones contrasted with the panic in the priests' rooms. There was even hearty laughter off in a corner, echoing back at him and around the cavern.

"Has there been none of the terror here?" Yosha asked. He wondered if this might be the one safe place in Aris.

"We lost seven—two women and five men," Auret said calmly. "From the sounds in the distance, we may expect to lose more."

"We've known death of all sorts here," a man with a deep voice said. "But since Auret and Chaisdyl came, we've found reasons to keep each other alive!" The man laughed then, as if he had made a great joke.

Yosha didn't follow the humor, but he said, "The king's prison is not where I would expect benevolence."

"Do you think the king has ever been in this prison?" Auret asked him sharply.

Yosha thought it an odd question. The king lived in the King's House above Aris. He worshiped in the temple and in the Tolas. Why should he come to this place? "No," Yosha answered, "I doubt he ever has."

"Perhaps if he came here," Auret said, "the terror would not now be upon us."

Yosha had no idea what he meant, but he heard Maachah repeat an ancient proverb from the ritual. "Many a king loves violence. But the king who loves justice will have peace."

Auret said, "The priests and the lords of the Askirit repeat many words and perform many liturgies. In them can be found light and healing." He then stepped closer to Yosha and said directly to him, "But they forget the warning: 'Lift a rock. Beneath it you will find all manner of crawling things.'"

Maachah grunted assent. "We came," he said, "to see if, in all this chaos, we might secure your release."

Auret propped his canes against the wall, braced himself against it and sat down. "I will stay here now," he said. "What is coming makes it better for me to remain."

Yosha wanted to question him about that statement, but Auret began talking to some of the prisoners, and soon Chaisdyl and he were in a group of them, listening to a man's story about how he had been put into prison. But before he was able to finish, they heard a shriek from further in among the prisoners. Chaisdyl rose instantly and started toward the sound.

Yosha stood, blood racing and ears tingling, feeling all the panic of yesterday. "How long can this go on?" he asked, trying to control his voice so Maachah wouldn't hear the tightening in his throat. He stood with the priest, who was helping Auret with his canes, and then forced himself to move with them toward the sound of Chaisdyl's voice.

They were blocked by the crowd of prisoners until someone said, "It's the cripple. Let him through," and immediately the crowd gave way for them.

"It's Beluis," Chaisdyl said, "the woman you were speaking with yesterday."

"She now runs and sings in the light," Auret said, and Yosha sensed a wave of peace here that seemed almost physical. Auret knelt beside the dead woman and performed parts of the ritual of hope as the prisoners listened and joined in at the prayers. Chaisdyl told the traditional tale of the DawnBreaker.

Maachah simply listened to them and did not offer to perform the priestly duties. When Auret was finished, the cripple stood and said, "The Askirit who have terrorized the world now feel the teeth of terror themselves." He said it like a man holding a broken son in his arms and consigning him to sierent.

"But," Yosha dared to say softly, not in argument but almost as a plea, "You are Askirit! Chaisdyl is Askirit. We are all seekers of the light. Whatever is at us is darkness and evil."

"Yes, that also is true," Auret said. "Yosha, you seek the light. But don't think you've found it when you still stumble in the darkness. Open your eyes wider. Look for the promised secrets."

—— Boats ——

All night long, as Asel and her companions fled to higher ground through the tunnels, she dreaded the thought that she might have unleashed these horrors. "Are they from the pit?" she asked Bralin as they fled. "What else would strike so randomly, so hideously, then be gone?" She made a popping sound with her tongue that indicated disgust. Then she almost whispered: "Could it be, Bralin, that I brought them? Could they be after all of us who plan to penetrate Dorte?"

Bralin repeated the popping sound Asel had made. "That's only the foolish speculation of Pelck. He was trying to unnerve you." Asel waited for him to say more, to reassure her with additional arguments. He took a long time before adding, "There are many deadly things in Aliare. This is some natural creature. If they were from the pit, believe me, they could find you!"

"On the other hand," Asel said, "they may be horrifying us, playing with us, enjoying their meal. I have known them to lick their lips over the terror of children."

They finally reached a great cavern high above the aceyn. The raka's soldiers were there and immediately summoned them to join several hundred others. "Whatever is happening," Asel said to Breea beside her, "we must remember, the light never changes. It is stronger than darkness."

Pelck's voice boomed out in front of the assembly. "We have learned the source of the terrors," he announced confidently. "We have found a man, their prisoner for ten years, who escaped from them yesterday by sacrificing his hand. His name is Solket. Listen to his story, but be patient. He speaks weakly, for he lost much blood."

Then came a dry voice, barely discernible in the damp cave. "In my youth, I stood sentry duty on a barren coast far from Tarn. Suddenly, I heard the familiar shrieks. I stood at my post as

I heard my fellow soldiers being killed. Then, suddenly, I was struck by a hard object and dragged away.

"I awoke on a ship, a prisoner of the Laij. I soon learned they are a warlike people, absolutely determined to conquer the whole world." Solket took a slow drink of water; they could hear him breathing hard. Then he resumed. "The Laij use natural beasts. Merrets, they're called. As natural as keitr—and as terrifying."

At this statement, something snapped in Asel and she felt enormous relief. Natural beasts! That meant they had nothing to do with Dorte!

Solket was saying, "You think animals don't explode out of the ground to rip out throats? The merrets do. It happens because the Laij use the scents of its enemy, the traek—a large, nasty reptile. Its smell drives the little merret crazy, for the traek loves to eat its flesh."

He paused again, sounding as if it took an effort to speak; everyone waited respectfully until he resumed. "You have to understand the merret. It lives entirely below ground, burrowing in the aceyn and eating worms and slugs and insects. It's all nose and mouth and ugly teeth, a rodent the size of your fist. The nose is bulbous and detects everything.

"The traek also has a phenomenal sense of smell. Once a traek smells a merret, the little rodent had better go for the reptile's throat. So the merret goes crazy as soon as it smells a traek, knowing it's kill or be eaten.

"Properly trained, merrets erupt from the ground to find a throat . . . any throat."

Solket made a snapping sound with his fingers. "Training. The Laij have perfected it. They're safe themselves because they've trained the merrets to respect a special scent on their own feet and hands."

He stopped then, and Asel longed to ask him questions, but she and all the rest sat patiently. Finally Solket said with deep emotion, "The great passion of the Laij is to take Tarn, to destroy the Askirit." Asel heard mutterings throughout the crowd in response to this revelation.

Solket added, "For ten years, I've lived to escape, to warn the nation. Only if we understand their tactics do we stand even a small chance against them."

After Solket was gently carried off in a litter, Pelck stood again. "We've learned much," he said. "The Laij use terror strategically. Total secrecy until the merrets strike. One day of terror, then a second day. Even now you can hear the shrieks in the city, but we have now told everyone to flee to the crags. The third day, invasion of all Tarn. That's tomorrow. They'll attack our cities simultaneously, and they'll come not only with their merrets but with thousands upon thousands of spearmen."

Asel spoke up: "But if we flee to the crags, they'll have all our cities! Then they can hunt us down!"

"But in the crags the merrets are useless," Pelck answered, sounding annoyed at her again. "We'll loose keitr at them—"

"But we'll have no supplies up there," she interrupted, "and if they have thousands upon thousands of spearmen in our cities—"

"Would you take the people of Gendt and throw them against this invasion? We'd all be dead tomorrow. I'd rather flee to the crags and gather vast numbers of keitr."

Asel was crouched by Solket's litter, trying to get new scraps of information. "You told us the Laij know everything about us," she said. "Help us learn everything about *them*!"

"For ten years, that's what I've lived to do," he said slowly, still fighting his weakness. "When they interrogated me, they didn't realize how much I was listening. And they didn't think I would sacrifice my hand to escape."

"How did you do that?"

He didn't answer her.

"I am Askirit and Enre," Asel said testily. "You don't have

to protect me from blood." Then her tone softened. "Can we get some of the protective scent? That would change everything!"

"They carry it in a flat pouch strapped to their calves. But you'd have to fight through spearmen to get to the Laij who carry the merrets. And without the scent on you in the first place—"

"But how do the Laij transport—"

"Each soldier carries two of the beasts, with loose shrouds over them so the animals think they're safe. A merret is solitary and too ornery to walk above ground; females are the most ferocious, and the males often get killed as a result of mating. But male or female, they hate company. So naturally the Laij keep two merrets together, making them edgier and nastier."

Asel kept Solket talking as much as he was able. She learned that the Laij had achieved remarkable things. Always the Askirit had believed no one could sail beyond a half-day's range, for lack of shelters. But the Laij had. Their ancestors had taken great risks, many being swept away by sierent as they searched for island caves. They found just enough to establish routes through the seas.

She thought about the islands to the south that had always marked the end of the world for the Askirit. They jutted up like big molars, sometimes scores of them, sometimes in small scatterings, but most often single islands widely dispersed. There were few bays or coves, let alone shelters.

"It's their sea power, their thousands upon thousands of boats, that make their dreams possible. And their conscripts. They've used the terror of the merret to conquer nations and indoctrinate young men."

"But we have done nothing to the Laij!" Asel exclaimed.

"Except block their conquest. They are obsessed with Tarn. They say they don't believe in gheials or specters or light above, only what they can touch or hear or smell. Hah! They fear the pit! I've talked to them when sierent howls. They stare at luminous fish. A strange lot. . . . They are religious—deeply religious—but they don't believe a thing!"

Asel made a clucking sound. "But they believe in themselves well enough," she said.

When Asel heard the first slap of wave against boat, she smiled even as she swam toward the sound. She and the twenty other Enre in Gendt were all in the bay waiting, knives ready. "I wish all the Enre were in every bay of Tarn right now!" she thought, knowing the invasion was starting everywhere.

The slaps grew louder, and then she could distinguish the sounds of what must have been hundreds of boats. Far outnumbered, the Enre still might achieve not only the sinking of some boats, but their primary objective: securing the protective scent.

Clearly, any counterattack on land would likely fail to get the scent. Through many wars, the Laij had perfected their defenses. But perhaps they were unprepared for the range and skill of an Enre swimmer. The Laij boats, relatively light and portable, carried up to fifty men, but they were reinforced only at strategic places. Solket thought at the very back, underneath, was a section with only a double layer of skin. A swimmer with a knife might cut a hole.

She felt the wash of the nearest boat approaching and dove beneath it, then raised her left hand to feel its surface moving past. "Feels like a great fish," she thought, kicking after it and trying to match its speed. Then the rear slipped over her and the boat was gone.

As she kicked toward another, she evaluated what she had learned. The boat had been shorter than she had thought. This time as she dove under the moving craft, she stretched her left hand far toward the rear and her right hand with the knife toward the front. Then, as soon as she felt its rear edge go past, she thrust up with the blade.

It cut through, but it was almost wrenched out of her hand by the forward motion of the boat. With all her strength she held on. Then, with both hands she tried to slice up and down. She used a frenzied energy to saw at the skins as the force of the water pulled her body along. She finally succeeded in creating a circle; suddenly the round flap disappeared and the knife was almost jerked out of her hand and sucked into the boat as water rushed up into it.

She let the craft pass over her and then surfaced. Immediately she heard yelling. The boat was no longer moving speedily away from her, but slowing and, she thought, listing. Instead of waiting, she went after another boat that was closing on her position. This time, she struck more surely, but the physical exertion was numbing. As the flap tore away, letting a geyser into the second boat, she swam back toward the first. She would not go after a third boat, knowing she must save herself for the next mission.

The first boat had capsized, leaving its passengers struggling in the water. She smiled as she thought of the Laij elite trying to hold on to their merrets; they were probably swimming away from them in panic. She hoped she wouldn't come across one of the rodents in the water; hopefully they were poor swimmers and would drown.

In the melee she swam among the flailing survivors, grazing her hand across shoulders and arms, searching for the telltale welts on the clothing of the merret keepers. At last she found one, and she swam silently beside him as he stroked toward shore. This one seemed like a strong swimmer. She wondered if she should find another. But then he stopped to tread water for a moment, and she struck suddenly, one hand thrusting him under, the other dispatching him with the blade.

She found it an easy thing to locate the pouches strapped to his lower leg. She unfastened them and tied them to her own in the same manner. Then she set out to find another, wanting to gather as much of the scent as possible.

—— Invasion ——

Yosha again woke from dreams, but this time into a reality that matched his nightmares: a shriek in the distance ... Maachah's voice arguing with other men ... the realization that any instant a shriek could be heard in this room, from his lips. He was in the largest cavern above the inner temple, where the priests and military officers had spent a difficult night.

"We should have evacuated the city yesterday—order or no order!" the raka of Aris said. "We've sent six messages to Rycal and not a word back. There's no aceyn up where he is, and I'll bet no terror. Half the people have fled to the crags already, but all the fighting men and priests here are getting slaughtered!"

"We agreed to get out yesterday," Hrusc said. "So give the order."

"Without word from Rycal," said the raka, "I'd be a dead man!"

"And you can't leave the Tolas unprotected," said a priest. "That's the heart of the kingdom."

"We can take it again," said the raka, but his voice was an agony of indecision. If he gave up the temple of Aris without express orders from the king, he would be thrown with his sons into the pit, his name a stench in Tarn forever.

Yosha suddenly exclaimed loudly, "What do I hear?"

"People screaming," Hrusc said in an ugly tone, sounding perturbed at the page's apparent stupidity.

"No!" Yosha shouted. "Something else. I can hear the word 'spears,' and the sounds are different!" He fled from the room and began racing down the long stairs to the temple proper. He thought of the guards in the prison who had done their duty and of the cripple who didn't panic, and he set his teeth to face whatever had changed.

As he drew closer to the entrances, he sensed the crowds were as terrified as ever, for shrieks could still be heard but also cries of "barbarians" and of "spears." Instead of making Yosha fearful, this news energized him. He said to a temple guard, "We're being invaded. This enemy we can fight! Set your keitr!"

He moved quickly out the entrances into the panicked crowd and grabbed man after man and said, "We have enemies—real ones—to fight!" Half the people in the city were soldiers, and he rallied a group of them. As he moved with them toward the sea, he realized other men had reacted the same way he had and were also moving toward the advancing troops. "Get ready to fight," he yelled out.

Toward the great bay of Aris, he could hear the moans of the wounded. But the barbarians advancing toward them made no sounds. This would be a battle of silence except for the shrieks and the cries of those hit. A sheaf of bone spears struck and clattered to the right of him, and he heard several men go down. Thousands of spears swarmed in the air like insects. He fired keitr, wondering how there could possibly be so many attackers coming up from the sea.

The bundles of bone were thrown by atlatals, slings that propelled them in high apogees so they came almost straight down in lethal sprays. Yosha communicated to his companions in Yette. All the Askirit were well trained in the nerve-racking warfare of silent spears and keitr, except that always before the odds had been in their favor.

He crouched under a fat ridge of rock, making his body as small as possible, holding his launcher ready. Because of the atlatals, the spears had great range; they were killing and wounding men all around him.

His enemies were now close enough to hear their movements. He released another keitr, heard it hit and break loose, then the scream of the keitr and the man. In previous battles, as keitr were launched, the enemy would quickly shift positions, but he now could hear the pounding of feet, thousands of them, storming toward him with no hesitation.

In desperation, as quickly as their fingers could move, he and the others launched their keitr at the silent waves of spearmen. Scores of keitr struck, but these Laij-trained battalions kept rushing forward.

His keitr depleted, Yosha fled back toward the temple, pausing only to grab a keitr belt from a fallen soldier. He turned, settled into a new position, and quickly launched several. Everywhere, keitr were finding their marks, yet still the Laij conscripts came, with the Askirit forced back rapidly as spears clattered all around them.

Yosha gathered belts and scurried toward the temple, firing keitr as quickly as he could. He marveled at the discipline of the invading troops, for no pagan force had ever fought like this before.

His back was against the temple entrances now, and he backed in. Hundreds of other men crouched there as well. "Crowd at the entrances," he said, not loudly enough for the attackers to hear. "Hold the temple."

"That's what we're doing," a sarcastic voice hissed as he heard keitr released beside him. Volley after volley of the little winged assassins crashed among the Laij troops and took man after man, but it was like throwing stones against storge—the waves kept rushing forward.

Then the Laij changed tactics. Fifty paces away, they stopped throwing their spears in high apogees and cast them straight forward. Many hit the crouching defenders, and Yosha realized that someone must have given them explicit details about the terrain. Spears were now flying into the temple itself.

The defenders were forced to leave the entrances, and Yosha, with several others, sprinted to the ramp. They crouched together there, firing keitr across the expanse of the temple at the waves of invaders pouring through the entrances. Spears clattered around Yosha and the other defenders. He reached for another belt of keitr, but he had used them all.

He raced up the ramp, and at its top, by the statues of the man and woman, he turned onto the next corridor up, climbing as quickly as he could move to the next level. He burst, winded, into the room where he had left Maachah and the others. No one was there.

He hesitated, then ran up the long, long ascent to the Tolas. He encountered no one on the way and arrived bathed in sweat and breathing in great gulps. Many hundreds of men were packed there, some praying, some cursing, some asking, "Where is the raka? Where are the king's troops?"

Yosha stood at the top of the long ramp, trying to get his breath, poised to ambush the barbarians who would be coming up, barbarians intent on invading this place in which no pagan had ever walked before. He held his dagger tight, feeling along the wall for the ideal ambush site. Perhaps he could take several as they came up.

Then he heard Hrusc's voice. "This leads up and out on the rim of the aperture high above us. It is steep, and there are no trails once we emerge from the Tolas. We may end up trapped there, or we may find our way to the crags."

Yosha heard Maachah's voice not far from Hrusc's, and he moved quickly toward them. Everyone was pressing to get to the trail, and the progress forward was very slow.

When he finally had his right foot on the ascent, he realized the reason: its narrowness required single file. Tight against the person ahead, pressed by someone behind, he climbed until he was sweating again. Eventually he started feeling a breeze, and then he emerged in a wind that cooled him. When he was fully outside, he started thinking that perhaps the king's troops could yet be rallied. He determined to find his way to the King's House.

It was long past midday before he was close enough to hear a sentry's challenge. The man let him pass. Two more sentries, and he stood at the causeway leading to the vast grounds of the royal complex. An officer challenged him, and he said in a rush of words, "I've come from Aris. The city is fallen and we must alert the king and assemble the men."

The sentry's voice sounded odd as he said, "Rycal is not here. He took his troops and set off toward the coast."

"To Aris?"

"No. The trail north."

"But he must know everyone will come here, that we will all be looking for orders. Why would he leave?"

"That is the question everyone is asking," the soldier said. "Perhaps he considered the royal grounds indefensible. Perhaps he will attack from another direction."

Neither man said anything about less savory possibilities. As more men came from Aris and ground their teeth at Rycal's absence, Yosha began to think very dark thoughts about his king. By the time Hrusc and a large contingent of priests and soldiers arrived, men were openly expressing disgust. Yosha proposed taking a contingent of men and racing after the king, to put an end to the speculation and to bring his troops back to the defense. But Hrusc said, "Let him go for now. We cannot spare a man."

The early winds of sierent were ruffling their hair when Yosha heard the closest sentry challenge someone. "I have news for the king," a woman's voice rang out.

The sentry let her pass and Yosha asked, "Where have you come from?"

"Gendt," she said impatiently. "I must see Rycal. Who are you?"

Her intensity and confidence marked her as Enre. He said, "My name is Yosha. I have just escaped from Aris—it is fallen. I, too, came to warn the king."

She breathed deeply and said, "It need not have fallen! The terror is a mere beast! The enemy boats can be sunk. Where is the king? I have the scents right here with me that can change everything!"

Yosha's heart leaped at these revelations, and he said, "We are but a handful left! The king is gone. But tell us what can be done, and we will do it!"

"We must alert all of Tarn," Asel said. "We have to find the king and his troops!"

"You will not find him!" Hrusc's voice boomed out from the direction of the king's house. "Not only has the king fled, but it is clear to all of us that Rycal is a traitor."

Chapter 7.

—— The Holy Three ——

For three years Yosha had fought under Hrusc against the Laij. But he had deserted the Askirit forces and fled to his home village, even though it was occupied by the Laij. Now he sat in Kjotik's Jaw, propped against a giant tooth, touching the carved faces of his father and mother. He wondered what they would think of his being hunted down by Askirit troops. He bit down on a bilkens root and felt the sharp tingle through his nostrils. "I seek the light," he whispered. "But it's gone."

He heard a voice below him. Gripping the carving in his left hand, he maneuvered over the grotesque and wondrous configurations toward the sound. The man was quoting the liturgy to a stately rhythm. "The wonders of this world," the voice recited, "and wonders of worlds unseen. Give praise! Glory! Light swallows darkness."

Suddenly the voice exclaimed in a jarring shout, "It's on you! The tail is whipping death at your eyes!" Yosha heard a crash. Then came Mosen's voice, loud and commanding, reciting the liturgy where the other voice had broken off: "Light swallows darkness. Evil withers at hope."

"Mosen!" Yosha called out.

A whistling sound acknowledged his greeting. They maneuvered to each other and embraced. The other voice went back to reciting the liturgy, keeping the stately rhythm by shaking little shells.

"Can this be Belstin?" Yosha asked.

"The words of light transform him. But he still sees fiends everywhere."

"What do the Laij think of this?"

"I tell them I'm feeding a maniac up here and invite them to come with me, to climb the pylons and trellises and see for themselves. 'The vines are ancient,' I tell them, 'but the Laij are superior and nimble.'" Mosen laughed heartily. "They back off. They respect the insane, but to keep things neat and tidy, they like all deviants put in hidden places."

They talked of Belstin's relapses and sporadic agitations. "But his hands," Mosen said, "I have rubbed and pried and oiled them back to nearly normal!" He reached out and pulled Belstin's hands toward Yosha. "Feel them," he said. "Claws no longer."

Mosen joined Belstin's recitations again for a moment, then said, "When he's not saying the liturgy or shouting at fiends, he sits quietly weeping like a child."

"These days, we all want to weep," Yosha said, his voice betraying his despair.

"Yes," Mosen agreed simply.

"I've fought under Hrusc, with thousands of other Askirit," Yosha said. "We've defended the crags—"

Mosen gripped Yosha's shoulders tightly. "We are grateful—despite Laij retaliations. Our village has suffered. Innocent young men have been executed."

Yosha stiffened. He was sitting elbow against knee, the heel of his hand jammed tight against his jaw. "Who can find mercy in Tarn?" he said. "Hrusc shows no pity. He blames pagan converts for subverting the nation. How easy it is to stir up hatreds! Hrusc has betrayed us—Maachah left him long ago." Yosha was surprised at his own outburst. A mere two days before, desperate to restore the Askirit nation, he had defended Hrusc to another soldier.

Mosen said, "My parents and I fear Hrusc as much as the

Laij, for he and his men still consider us barbarians. I've heard he's a magnificent orator—"

"He's 'Tarn's only hope,'" Yosha said dryly.

"How ironic," Mosen said, "that he fed everyone's hatred of Rycal, but now in his 'purity' he's more ruthless than Rycal ever was."

"It drives me mad!" Yosha exclaimed. "Hrusc says the harsh world of Aliare demands crushing all opposition. But in the Tolas we pledged to use keitr and blades for justice—not revenge."

Mosen sounded a vibrating assent with his tongue.

Yosha and Mosen descended toward the village, Belstin's chants and imprecations echoing behind them. They walked the familiar shores, avoiding Laij patrols, listening to the restrained talk of adults and subdued antics of children. Yosha nearly stumbled over a receptacle the Laij had placed for bones and other debris. To the Laij, everything should be saved for possible use. In contrast, the Askirit let sierent wash away most of the day's discoveries so they could start afresh at dawn.

They left the shore and entered the great cavern, silently walking to the formation for which the village was named. Wellen meant "net hauler," connoting a very large, stocky man who could lift full and heavy nets. When the cavern was first settled, the formation in this largest vault was declared Wellen, for it reminded the settlers of a big man holding up the roof.

Yosha and Mosen walked up to the free-standing stalagmite and touched its thick ridges. It was as big around as five men; somewhere above their heads was a branching upward that vaguely resembled two thick arms. Before the Laij invasion, villagers had constantly congregated here. Elders had held court and people played games, sipping kek and chewing on a variety of roots. But when the Laij had come, they forced the villagers to build two pools beside the beloved formation.

"The nearest pool's luminescents are from everywhere in the

world," Mosen said in Yette. The glowing, alien movements fascinated Yosha, but they felt ominous here in the heart of his village. The other pool was dark, with vigorous splashings.

"What's in the other one?" he asked with his fingers.

"Abominations." Mosen replied.

Yosha flicked four fingers hard against Mosen's shoulder, an expression of dismay.

"The pectre you know well," Mosen said. "They deserve their name—gheials. The Laij have brought something equally heinous. They are eels. We call them gheial eels."

"But eels cannot enter the body like the pectre," Yosha said.

"These can. Writhing masses of them spread slime over a victim, then wriggle into body orifices so they can eat their victims from the inside. The body becomes a mass of frenzied, feeding eels, which consume everything, then burst through the shredding skin, leaving only bones and pieces of skin for the fish."

Yosha was horrified by Mosen's description. He leaned back against the chest of Wellen, wanting to stop his ears against the splashings in the pool.

"Twice a day the Laij feed them," Mosen said. "They bring in large lizards trapped on the islands and throw them in alive."

"But why this pool in the heart of our village?"

Mosen snapped his knuckles together. "The pool is a lesson and a terror," he said. "They force all villagers to stand here when an Askirit is thrown in. Then they lecture us," he said with a sarcastic spin of his palm, "about the other pool's symbolizing a wise and civilized culture."

"Insane!" Yosha said. He laughed sarcastically and said, "Belstin is obviously right about *everything*!" Yosha had always loved luminous eels and the quick water snakes, but now he didn't know if he could ever touch one again. How he hated the Laij for this barbarity! He felt naked and vulnerable, knowing the Laij would quickly throw him into the pool if they detected his identity.

Yosha tried to ignore the splashings of the eels and stared at the luminescents. Oblong shapes, round, little points—all sorts of images nourished his eyes. He got up and moved closer, staring. Alien ... but still light.

He sat beside Mosen again, the one pool assaulting his ears and the other feeding his eyes. He thought of Hrusc's apostasy. He thought of the Askirit kingdom's demise. How little different it was from the stories told about his earliest ancestors. Centuries ago, these had had nothing. They faced known and unknown terrors. Powerful oppressors dominated them. Yet they had formed the kingdom, this handful of men.

Just a few. Then came the memory of the Holy Three. The Holy Three by which the Askirit culture had begun.

The Askirit said it all began with one man, a man who held precious all the sacred truths. He had determined to love the light and to seek the way above. Filled with passion, he sought out others. After many years, he found two. They memorized all the truths and the wisdom as well. After a time, another three were recruited; they, too, sought the light. Then three more. And many threes, and hundreds of threes, all determined to do more than survive, but to embrace the remnants of glory.

Yosha grieved at what little was left of all that. Yet were the odds now worse than those that once faced the Holy Three? Here was Mosen. And Maachah's passion for the light was as vigorous as ever. What more was needed?

Suddenly he felt a thoroughly new enthusiasm. Was he the only one in all Aliare to whom the light was pouring out images of the Holy Three?

His eyes feasted on the light in the pool, the beauty of Eshtel's luminous creatures lifting his heart. He thought of a phrase Belstin kept repeating from the liturgy:

"Darkness flees from light."

Mosen had recited the phrase to soothe Belstin, and then Belstin had repeated it. Now Yosha thought about it again and again: "Darkness flees from light."

Years before, all the force of Yosha's being had been focused by one phrase from the ritual: "Fear not the teeth." Now this familiar but somehow new holy phrase filled his senses the same way, driving out fear and bewilderment. Just as he had run to the mouth of leviathan, he would run toward the light, dispersing the darkness eating at his soul.

He reached over, gripped Mosen's wrist, and vigorously tapped out several times: "Darkness flees from light."

The Skull

Yosha's vision and passion soon became Maachah's and Mosen's. The next year, they sought the light together, wandering in secrecy. Belstin chanted and shouted beside them, unable to converse but crying out for the light. They recited, memorized, and praised, alert to danger or opportunities to help the captives of their devastated land. With everyone, they shared their urgent enthusiasms and visions of light soon to come.

They never sought recruits. Although the Three were hunted by both Laij and Hrusc troops; although food was sparse in the crags high above the aceyn, their spirits were high.

After more than a year, another man, Hean, followed them. He persuaded Passicul to join them as well. In Wellen, Kark heard of this resurgence of the Three, and later he learned with amazement that it was Yosha, Mosen, and Maachah. He risked capture by seeking them out and became the third with Hean and his friend.

Yosha welcomed his former mentor. These were the first. Then, before another year was over, came scores and eventually, hundreds of men. They were drawn by the new legend of the Holy Three. Each yearned for holiness.

Word of the Askirit rebirth spread everywhere, till nearly a thousand men were with them. They were sent out three by three, for they were all fugitives, avoiding patrols, moving from cave to cave, lightly organized, scattered in far villages or remote crags.

In the third year Kark sought out the Three in a deep shelter with many escape tunnels. He asked, "Have you heard that Hrusc has captured some of our men?"

"It has happened before," Yosha said. He did not say what they all knew: that they would be executed.

"We are told," Kark said, "they will be forced to walk the Bridge."

"The Bridge?" Maachah said. "Sacrilege!" Yosha and Mosen also expressed indignation. Only by choice did an Askirit walk the Bridge. In a formation called the Skull, the narrow stone Bridge jutted out over the abyss, then curved back and rejoined the lip of the precipice. Extraordinarily bold men seeking purity had from ancient times chosen to walk that narrow band above the pit. Despite their courage, it was widely thought those who fell had proven their unworthiness.

"So Hrusc forces them to prove their purity," Mosen said.

"Purity!" Maachah spat out the word. "Hrusc is corrupt. The test is a mockery!"

"But very clever," Yosha said. "This ridicules our demands for purity. "He'll force man after man to walk that Bridge. If anyone falls, he's apostate."

"Not *if* anyone falls," Kark said, striking knuckles on knuckles. "Hrusc secretly broke off a section in the middle of the Bridge. Not one can get across."

Maachah made a gruff, guttural sound of disgust. "So everyone who walks the Bridge proves Hrusc's point," he said, "and anyone who claims a section is missing gets laughed at as a coward. Fiendish!"

"And the man on the Bridge who backs away from the gap," Kark said, "proves he's impure. They'll push him off with a pole."

Maachah repeated the guttural sound. "I once knew Hrusc as a man of depth and subtle reasoning. I had high hopes for him.

But he was once humiliated by a pagan, and that filled him with hate. He's determined never to be humiliated again." He let out a loud blast of air. "These atrocities will be judged by greater than ourselves," Maachah said. "But I cannot stand the thought of our men walking the Bridge."

Next day, seven groups of three sat listening to Kark describe Hrusc's treachery once again.

Yosha said, "We will not allow it."

Mosen stood. "When Yosha and I were boys," he said, "I listened to the priests and obeyed the commands. But then I learned how brutal our armies and even our king could be. I then cried out in my prayers, 'Purify Tarn! Hear the moans of the weak!' I wanted Tarn purified. Instead, it was devastated. The Laij sent their terrors.

"Hear my lament. But hear also the hope—the absurd hope, the firefly blown in the wind. For though we are scattered in the crags—though we have no homes—though the temple has been desecrated and we are hunted like birds—still we rejoice! For we have light, and dawn is coming!"

Maachah jumped up and exclaimed with his usual buoyancy, "The light to come is more than glimmers! We'll find the way to the light itself!"

Yosha had often heard Maachah make such predictions, but they stirred him more deeply this time.

"When we were children," Maachah said, "we were taught this truth: to find the light, look in the least likely places!"

Yosha stood beneath the massive formations from which came the world's nightmares. Standing above the kingdoms of Aliare like a grim specter, this peak had over the centuries mixed with tales of keitr and the abyss to make its name inevitable: the Skull.

The Askirit knew it was a distorted image, for the cave openings made a surreal configuration, a twisted, misshapen skull leering with mis-matched eyes. The largest cavern's opening was ten times the height of a man; next to it was an elliptical entrance half its size. Aeons of sierent's storms had cut a rippling, swirling effect across its face. Below the openings, scores of small caves of various shapes and heights ran beneath them like an interminable mouth, a mouth filled with millions of keitr.

The two large openings that formed the eye sockets of the Skull did not connect with the smaller caves below. The eyes led to a gigantic vault; above, the vault was open to the roof of their world; below, it opened into the pit. Into the eyes of the Skull and across a short plateau to its edge, the Askirit over the centuries had dragged barbarians and traitors and cast them headlong into the abyss.

Thousands of Hrusc's soldiers were moving up the trails and toward the Skull. Yosha joined them; he moved easily into their line, knowing their codes. He listened for a signal indicating his comrades had located the prisoners. He worried they'd be herded into the Skull before the men could reach them and was relieved when he heard a zeskret call. Smiling broadly, he let out an agonized shriek, cutting it off suddenly, like that of a man attacked by merrets.

Quickly but silently he moved a hundred paces down another trail, even as he heard shrieks elsewhere. He shrieked once more and again quickly moved away. Authentic, he thought with a grimace, remembering the actual sounds much too well.

Yosha's men knew that in the years of fighting the Laij, Hrusc's forces had never experienced an attack by merrets on the barren crags. But the screams would surely horrify them for a moment at least, enough time, perhaps, for their company to subdue the guards and to spirit the prisoners down one of the many trails.

Hundreds of men ran past Yosha, exclaiming that it couldn't be happening in the crags. "What's going on?" they demanded.

Shortly, in the direction he had heard the zeskret signal, he heard someone call out, "It's a trick! The prisoners are escaping!"

Yosha then yelled it out himself, "Prisoners escaping. They're getting away on trails to the west and north!" He ran with the men, milling with them, creating more and more confusion until he was satisfied that the others had escaped.

Eventually the troops once more began ascending toward the Skull. As they topped the trails, they fanned out in the great valley that was level with the smaller caves. Yosha moved with the men and heard the voice of Hrusc above him. He realized Hrusc was standing at the edge of the opening that framed the larger eye of the Skull.

When the assembly stood quietly before him, Hrusc shouted out, "Intolerable! Traitors have struck here at the heart of the nation. Traitors, not Laij! Askirit who say they are pure. But do they support us? Do they attack the Laij with us? No. They shriek like Laij victims. They defile the Skull!

"But you," Hrusc shouted, his voice changing from outrage to grand resolve, "you are the true Askirit! You have survived the horrors. You will restore the glory!"

Hrusc stopped his rapid delivery, creating a dramatic pause. Then he said more quietly, "You know the serpent, resta, how when it is attacked and injured it lies motionless but coiled. Then, suddenly, stuugkt! A counterattack. A strike that staggers its enemy." Hrusc hissed like an alarmed resta. "Askirit survivors, Stuugkt is your new name! Stuugkt! Stalkers from the Skull who counterattack. Like resta, you will strike with deadly force! You will kill the Laij with keitr, with blades, with thousands of ingenious traps. You will show all Aliare that the Askirit rule. We will cast traitors into the abyss. We will conquer the Laij, and we will find Rycal in their camps. Rycal—yes, Rycal—shall walk the Bridge!"

Hrusc paused again, and Yosha sensed his power over the

crowd, which murmured its assent to every line. "How shall we deal with the Laij?" Hrusc shouted. All around him, Yosha heard men loudly imitating the attack sound of an infuriated keitr. Every Askirit man was adept at the imitation, but Yosha had never heard a throng snarl with it, spontaneously, from the depths of their throats.

"What shall we do with Rycal?" Hrusc cried out. The keitr sounds around him were even louder than before as they gave their answer. Some yelled out, "The Bridge! The Bridge!" but could barely be heard above the angry keitr cries.

"The Laij have Rycal," Hrusc shouted. "We will smash the Laij and we will take Rycal. And what shall we do with the traitors who have attacked us tonight? What shall we do with those who refuse to let us test the defilers?"

Roars of keitr cries and calls for the Bridge washed over Yosha. He had planned to plant among the men standing around him the truth about the section missing from the Bridge. Now he realized these Askirit would not care. They would believe anyone Hrusc sent to the Bridge should fall to the abyss. Yosha marveled at how his own people, who had always worshiped the light, could so quickly embrace hatreds.

Hrusc said, "The traitors tonight have proven we must act. No longer will we hesitate to purge those who sabotage us. We will act decisively. And we will build an empire greater than the Askirit have ever known."

Then Hrusc spoke so softly Yosha nearly missed his words. "But who should lead you?" he asked.

The response was immediate. "Hrusc! Hrusc! Hrusc!"

"But I am not a king," he said. "If I am to lead, I must be more than a priest."

Someone not far from Hrusc shouted, "King and priest! King and priest!" Yosha thought it might be Bles. The chant quickly arose, "King and priest. King and priest." It swelled to a crescendo until Hrusc shouted, "So be it. Thirty sierents from now, we will hold the coronation here. Until we take Aris back from the Laij, the Skull will become both palace and temple."

—— A Troubling Proposal ——

The hideout of the Three deep beneath the surface was named the Spider. Its shape was that of a very fat spider with interminably long, slender legs—the many narrow tunnels leading to it. Yosha sat just within one of these legs, listening to the men in the Spider celebrating. They were exuberant at spiriting away the three prisoners from under Hrusc's nose. It had been years since they had had anything at all to celebrate, and the little victory had them singing and making a festival of carving a mural on the wall of three men leaping forward in freedom.

The sounds were pleasant to Yosha, but he did not join in. He alone had remained to hear Hrusc's harangue. He had been sobered by its power and by the responses of throngs who expressed such hatred for this little band so joyously singing and carving nearby. He knew that now they would be hunted passionately by all those disciplined Askirit with the keitr on their belts and the keitr scream in their throats.

"Yosha." It was Maachah's voice. "I heard you'd gotten back. Our adventure has become a remarkable exploit!"

"Yes. These three, at least, will not walk the Bridge."

Maachah made a triumphal sound by popping the air out of his cheeks by simultaneously slapping them. "Come and celebrate with us," the priest said.

"I do celebrate. But I also think of Hrusc's threats at the Skull. We tweaked his nose, but we also inflamed him, and we gave him an excuse to hunt us down." Yosha described all he had heard, including the coming coronation of Hrusc.

Yosha concluded, "For a time we should go to the far reaches of Tarn where neither Laij nor Askirit patrol."

"We would do little for the nation that way," Maachah said.

"We will do less from the abyss," Yosha replied. "The Three are called not to wage war but to seek holiness, to seek the light—"

"And you remind *me* of that?" Maachah said. "But the light is here. Remarkable things are happening. Listen to the spirit of the men!"

They paused a moment and listened to the singing nearby. "Yet thousands of Askirit soldiers," Yosha said, "want nothing more in life than to smother those sounds."

Maachah reached for the keitr belt around Yosha's waist, unfastened it and held it in front of him. "Hold this belt in your hands," he said. "Think back to the time as a boy when you said over and over, 'Fear not the teeth! Fear not the teeth!' You asked deep in your soul, 'Don't the promises tell us to fear not the teeth?' What did you have in your hands then to face the teeth of leviathan? Now you have no more and no less—you have the same promises. Fear not the teeth—even Hrusc's teeth!"

Yosha fingered the pouches of the belt. "Maachah, I do not want to be a fool. I do not want to waste our lives. We are like pebbles about to be swept away by ute."

The priest refastened Yosha's belt. "Yes, but we have the greater power," he said. "We have the righteous throughout Tarn who long for the Three to liberate them."

Next morning the Three met outside the caverns to greet the dawn together, to meditate, and to listen to Belstin sing the psalms of the morning liturgy. When the dawn winds ceased, Kark joined them and Maachah said, "It's time to act. Once crowned, all Tarn may follow Hrusc."

"But what can we do short of assassination?" Mosen asked.

Kark clucked his tongue. "Yosha, you were close enough at the Skull to wing a keitr at him."

"It's unlikely I would have hit him."

The four strategized half the morning but failed to produce a plan.

Maachah said, "Hrusc's being king would add enormously to his power. Symbols inspire—we've seen the vision of the Holy Three bring men from all over Tarn. What we must have is a legitimate king!"

"But who?" Mosen demanded. "Rycal's line is disgraced."

"We need a new line," Maachah said, a rise in his voice. "We have the high priest in hiding, and he always anoints the king."

"But who?" Mosen insisted sharply.

Maachah waited a long moment before he said slowly and distinctly, "Yosha."

The use of his name startled Yosha. Was Maachah being his usual ironic self, or was he serious? He almost snorted at him but instead let someone else ask the obvious questions.

"Anoint him on what basis?" Kark asked. "The nation would laugh."

"And think us not only fools, but desperate," Mosen said.

Maachah then spoke like a man making a well-considered move in a game. "Yosha, you would become king," he said, slowly and deliberately. "And as you received the pectoral, you would also take a queen."

Yosha laughed.

"Yes, laugh," Maachah said earnestly but lightly, "for it would be a great festivity of laughter and hope! It would be remarkable, a new thing in Aliare. For Yosha, one of the Holy Three, the boy who faced leviathan but fights now as a man, this Yosha would marry Varial!"

Varial? This time Yosha did snort. Then he chortled and said, "All that you have always said about the light and opening our eyes—all that I believe, Maachah. I have always believed you.

But your dreams have become preposterous. Varial does not wed. You are casting hooks into the air."

Maachah took no offense, but he changed his tone and said rather sternly, "We have a thousand men. It is something. It may be enough for what Eshtel means to do. And Varial? Enre everywhere have been tracked down and killed, but more than two thousand still live, and every one would give her life for Varial."

"Granted," Yosha said. "But why are we talking about this? Every Varial is a virgin. No Varial has ever wed!"

"Maybe . . . ," Maachah said, chuckling a little roguishly and slowly drawing out his words, ". . . maybe she's never been asked."

Kark took up Maachah's light tone and said, "But who would ask Varial? She's thousands of years old!"

Yosha led the laughter, then sighed in mock exasperation. "She's a very old woman," he said lightly. "You can't ask a young man like me—"

But Maachah interrupted him, saying sternly, "You know better than that! The new Varial is Asel—a young woman. You met her in the King's House."

Yosha admitted that was true. "But she can't destroy centuries of tradition!" he insisted. "She can't dishonor her vows!"

"Tradition, yes. Vows, no," Maachah said. "Varial pledges chastity, but that does not preclude matrimony!"

"You're spinning cobwebs to catch birds," Yosha said. "And what do we have to offer Varial?"

"Hope," Kark said instantly, with conviction. "We have none. She has none. But together, perhaps, we can find hope!"

"Each of us has great hope," Mosen corrected. "Even if the Askirit nation falls, we have the light."

Kark clapped his hand against his thigh. "Mosen, that's not enough! We need hope for the nation!" Kark's voice rose in his excitement. "Varial needs that hope. We need that hope. Maachah is right. If the people heard the high priest had crowned Yosha and Varial king and queen—and that we and all the Enre followed them—the effect could be astounding!"

Yosha felt like a man swimming in an alien sea with unknown creatures nudging his body. Were these prey he should hook? Or predators he should flee? Would nets soon drag all of them to the bottom?

Chapter 8.

—— Varial's Journey ——

Asel maneuvered carefully through the high crags with twenty Enre, including Breea, who had just completed her initiation. Laij scouts never ventured this high, but she and her elite twenty stayed alert for Hrusc's patrols.

As she passed the sentries guarding the open encampment of the Three, she judged them few in number but skilled in deployment and discipline. That pleased her, for she wondered about these men and their urgent request to meet. Maachah she knew as a staunch friend of the Enre, but Yosha—despite meeting him briefly at the King's House—she knew mostly by reputation. She had heard his visions had brought the Three together, and she knew the folklore of his exploit with leviathan. Kjotik Killer, they called him, in typical Askirit exaggeration. She viewed that as the act of the boy, but what kind of man was he?

"We have come at the request of the Three," she told the last sentry. "What is it they want of me?" She realized he would not tell her, but perhaps he would drop a clue.

He simply said, "They are not a hundred paces further up the trail."

When Yosha heard the signals that Varial was near the camp, he felt snared. How had he gotten into this position? He had always thought he would have wed long before this. But without peace, how could a man marry?

How could he conceive of Varial as his wife? She was legend. She had a spiritual intensity that could make even Maachah uneasy! All Askirit women experienced tough training for survival, but Varial was Enre, and the best of the Enre.

In the distance, he heard her give the day's password, announce herself, and then start speaking to Maachah, who had gone further down the path to greet her. Then he heard not only Varial and Maachah walking toward him, but others with her. Had she come in force to this ragtag troop of exiles?

After formal statements and introductions, and after they had discussed the dilemma Hrusc had forced upon them, Asel decided her instinct to trust Maachah had been well founded. She liked his boisterous enthusiasm and thoughtful optimism. She liked Mosen, Kark, and the other men as well, for all the Enre who had come with her found in such terrible times a buoyancy from finding strong allies.

But Asel wondered about Yosha. He had greeted and welcomed them, and he had spoken vigorously at times, expressing indignation at Hrusc's and Rycal's treachery. His indignation resonated with her own, and she sensed deep spiritual currents within him. But she also thought he seemed at times diffident.

As the day turned into evening, she wondered if Maachah and the others were the real power here. Perhaps they had used Yosha's renown as a boyhood hero to hold the group together. Was the Kjotik story one more of those overblown events? Had he simply gotten himself swallowed and spat out—and became a hero just by happening to have been on the shore at the time?

Yosha fidgeted as he sat with his legs crossed at a sharp angle, his fingers drumming on his knee. How could he possibly have gotten talked into this? Maachah had insisted he ask Varial in the proper way. Yet not only was Yosha appalled at the idea of asking Varial to marry him, he was sure she would be equally appalled. She would think it a joke, just as he had when Maachah first advocated the idea. She would laugh. Then she would apologize for laughing, not knowing what the true intent was.

How had he let the others convince him that he must ask her? They could sit there quietly, grinning to themselves, while he winced at every comment. Something like this should be negotiated, he thought angrily. Maachah should have gotten Varial aside and done the same with her as he had with them — introduce the subject and get the logic of it into her head.

Then Maachah's voice interrupted his thoughts. He was saying to Varial, "With Hrusc about to be proclaimed king and high priest, it is imperative that we act first. We have talked a great deal about all the possibilities, and we all find ourselves in a very weak position. Except for one possibility . . ." He paused just long enough for effect. "Yosha has something to say about a bold move that we have concluded could change everything."

Yosha realized with dread that Maachah had given him his opening. He sat like a stone, his face flushed, until in the silence, the anticipation of Varial and everyone else forced him to start talking. "We are so few," Yosha said, "and the brutal policies of the Stuugkt are making the Askirit more pagan than the barbarians. We need to bring together all our forces, to capture the hearts of the Askirit by banding together in common purpose." He said much more about their predicament and the fact that they were greatly outnumbered.

Varial said, "I agree. We are feathers blown toward the sea."

Yosha wondered how to introduce the topic without blundering. He knew all his comrades were waiting for him to clearly state his intentions. Finally he blurted out, "Maachah's idea was for me to ask you to wed." He paused, the last word hanging in the air like a bird menacingly aloft above his head.

"It would be an affair of state," he explained, his tongue

thick in his mouth, "done only so there might be a king and a queen in Tarn. A king and a queen who could rally all the people."

He stopped again, fearful of her laughter or her pity, but then said clearly. "Therefore, in front of these witnesses, I make my plea that you consider my offer to wed—for the sake of the kingdom."

Varial did not laugh. She said nothing, sitting as quietly as Yosha had when Maachah had forced him to speak. Yosha waited, then felt obligated to say something more. "It's a matter of survival," he explained. "We all have to be ready to make any sacrifice." As soon as he said it, he flushed again. How might she take that statement?

Varial still said nothing. Was she flabbergasted? Angry? Amused? Maachah rescued Yosha by saying, "Varial, we have the high priest in hiding. We can herald the new king and queen throughout Aliare before Hrusc knows it's happened—and before his own ceremony at the Skull. The whole of Tarn's imagination can be captured! We can draw the Askirit who love the truth out from their slavery to the Laij. When this nation hears that Yosha and Varial are king and queen, they will have something to believe! Now, we have no king. We have no hope. But we will soon have a priest-king if we do not act. It will be Hrusc, and he will rule from the Skull."

Maachah continued with his vision of the marvelous impact should she agree. Mosen and Kark and several others spoke up as well, but Yosha said nothing more.

Finally they heard Asel say, "Varial never weds."

"Until now!" Maachah said instantly in his high-spirited, slightly humorous way. "When has Varial been hunted in the crags by Askirit troops? When have the cities of the Askirit been enslaved? When has Tarn had no king?"

Yosha said. "Varial, I hold you in the highest esteem. As is the custom, you have whatever time you need to consider what has been proposed. Be assured, if you should reject this, I would still view you as no less than Varial, and no less than a queen."

—— A Light Caress ——

Asel slept not at all through the night. She had been stunned at Yosha's proposal and had not known how to respond. Hundreds of times she had walked to the depths of the cave that sheltered her and then back again, pondering all the implications. After leaving Yosha and the others, she had discussed the proposal at great length with her advisors—who had thrown it right back into her lap. If she sensed the inner light guiding her, they had said, she should wed Yosha. If not, they would support her refusal.

She felt no leading one way or the other. She felt uneasy about this male intruder who would challenge her way of life. How could she violate millennia of tradition in which Varial never wed? And how could she allow a man to make love to her? "No," she said forcefully in a whisper, tramping the cave floor. "Not now!"

Asel had long ago suppressed the nascent desires she had felt years before, and when they appeared occasionally, disciplined herself against them. "To put a man into my bed for the good of the state," she said to herself, "seems unholy, a dissipation of my call. I am Varial, not a piece of political strategy!"

But she could not reject the logic she had heard from so many, and she could not quiet her vague desires. "Yosha may turn out to be the worst possible husband for a woman who is Varial," she defiantly muttered aloud. "He could demand all sorts of things Varial could not accept!" She thought of his awkwardness this past day and how little she knew about him. Was he the sort of man she could respect? Could she live with him, wage war with him?

She concluded she had no answers to these questions, so with this thought, she determined her course of action. Before the dawn winds of sierent had quieted, with strong gusts still blowing, she strode to the entrance of her shelter, jerked the leather covering away with one hand and pulled herself through the opening with the other.

It was a lengthy walk to Yosha's shelter, but she covered the distance quickly, despite the winds blowing against her. Only the sentries were already up as she called at the entrance, "Yosha!"

The time she stood waiting for him to come out was longer than she was accustomed to, and when he did appear, she sounded irritable as she gave him the greeting of early dawn and asked him to step down the trail with her.

He came with her, without comment, and when they reached the area between the shelters and the sentries, she said, "I have talked to my counselors, and I have talked to myself. But how can I make a decision? You have asked me to wed, but I know nothing about you. We haven't had one day of courtship. You have given me nothing but a night of pacing!"

Yosha lost all of his sleepiness at her spirited complaint. He took it as a personal attack, for he felt as much a victim of the circumstances as she. "If I have offended you, just give me your answer!" he said brusquely. "I'm as much trapped in all this as you are."

She liked the spirit she heard in his voice, and she felt relief at having been able to air her complaint so forcefully. She said, less stridently, "I am sorry to have awakened you at the break of dawn. But if you were asleep, you were less agitated than I."

He made a popping sound with his tongue, indicating empathy. "Remember, I've had days of wrestling with this," he said. "Running to the mouth of Kjotik was a clear and simple duty compared to asking you that question!" But then he thought, Oh, no, perhaps I've offended her again.

"If we have so little time to make a decision," she said, "we have much to discuss. Let's find a trail away from the others."

He chose one that was a wide circle ambling below the camp. As they walked along it, each probed the thoughts of the other as if they were disinterested diplomats. They questioned each other about what they loved and what they hated. They spoke formally about the meaning of rituals and the urgencies of seeking the light. Both felt strong emotion when they lamented Askirit dreams now in rubble and how they must restore the glory. The day wore on, and Varial did not bring up the subject of marriage but asked, and sorted, and pondered. Though hungry, they did not go back to the camp for food but kept walking. Yosha wondered what more could possibly be said, but Asel remained undecided.

They were seated on a ledge above what was in late evening a trickle of a waterfall when she said, "It is customary and even necessary in courtship to touch." She said it in a stilted way, as if she had difficulty admitting the necessity. "I do not know your face, or even your hands."

"It is hard to complete a courtship in a day," he said wryly. "Our words dance around each other like a small child's feet on slippery rocks." But he reached for her hand, touched her fingers, and explored her palm. Then he drew it to his cheek.

She moved her hand to his chin and gently tracked up the curves of his face to the eyes and nose and mouth, her fingers shaping the form and the texture of his skin. Her palm gently planed around the side of his jaw, then moved to his lips. She touched his hair and ran her fingers down to his neck.

He waited for her to finish, then he placed his hand on her chin and moved his palm down over her throat and then back to the side of her face. He touched her lips with his fingertips and moved his palm over her cheeks to her eyes and felt her lashes flicking against his fingers. He shifted his weight and lifted his arm so he could put it around her and touch her face from the other side. As he did so, he felt a little shiver across her shoulders.

He reached over and boldly felt her pulse, just above the collarbone, catching its rhythm.

They had often explored the faces of others with their hands, but never with such intensity as this, and never with so much depending on the necessity of blending feelings and logic. Both were surprised at their reactions to this simple touching, and they were embarrassed that these light intimacies of adolescent courtship could awaken their sensuous natures. They sat close beside each other, listening to the evening cries of the birds.

The expected conclusion of their touching—if they had any intentions at all of continuing the relationship—was a light grazing of the woman's lips across the man's, a sign of the beginnings of affection. In one sense it was inevitable; not to do the traditional kiss would have been nearly a repudiation. Yet might it say more than she meant?

She hesitated, her hand still on his neck. Then she moved her face next to his. She raised her hand to his cheek and let her lips graze his, like tiny waves kissing the edge of a brook.

—— Ceremony ——

It had been a hard five days for Yosha. The turn of events made him uncomfortable for many reasons, including the uneasy feeling that his call was to be one of the Three, not a barely legitimate king. He wanted to get out and climb the trails, but the others had begged him not to endanger the plans, to stay put for a few days while the high priest and the others made their way to the camp, and everyone worked on the preparations.

He felt trapped and more than a little resentful. Asel had never said yes to his plea. There had been only that light graze of her lips on his, which was far from a declaration of commitment.

"A sign of emerging affection," he muttered to himself. "She never did say anything to me, never did accept."

Yet the morning after their day together, Asel had assembled her people and said to him in front of them, "We will need five days." She then commenced to review the details of the ceremonies as if they were waging a military campaign. She did not usurp control, but she assumed her own responsibilities in a no-nonsense, even hasty way. Then, by mid-morning, she and half her Enre were gone. In leaving, she had extended the clenched-fingers handshake to Maachah, Mosen, Kark, and to him equally, as if he were merely one more factor among many details and one man among many comrades.

Through all this, he had tried to position himself with equal force, asking questions, making instant decisions, and objecting to proposals that seemed unnecessary. When she and her retinue had left the camp, he had turned immediately to discussing the day's necessities with Kark. No one seemed aware of his discomfort. Instead, they conjured up all sorts of visions for the new Tarn and the new kingdom. Even Mosen seemed excited, and the entire time Varial was gone, the camp was abuzz with new hope for a new kingdom, plans for draining Askirit troops away from Hrusc and eventually expelling the Laij from their borders.

Now Varial was back in camp with her Enre and several hundred men, making final preparations on the far side of the valley. Yosha was not to see her this day, but her counselor, Bralin, told him she had brought the children from Dorte with her, a fact that amazed Yosha.

"*Here?*" Yosha asked. "Don't you—don't all of us—take an awful risk with the dark powers?"

Bralin took a deep breath and expelled the air slowly. "Isn't that the risk we are always taking?" he asked.

Yosha turned from Bralin and walked to the entrance of his own shelter. He preferred to judge for himself what dangers should be brought here. He entered and found the high priest of all the Askirit in the depths of the cave, busily giving instructions to a score of priests who had come with him bearing bulging packs. He was an intense little man who seemed to Yosha all rite and ritual. Yosha asked him some questions about the ceremony, and the man kindly but firmly refused to divulge the details. "I have already told you all you need to know," he said.

The next morning, after the ritual bath and the donning of the required woven clothing, with its rustling, ridged sleeves, Yosha walked in front of Maachah and Mosen to the chosen site. Men and women from all parts of the camp were also walking toward it, and he couldn't help contrasting this day with ceremonies at Aris and the King's House, with their thousands of celebrants and their splendid accoutrements of sacred and regal significance. Here, no more than a few hundred would gather in this place far from Aris and the Skull. It was as if they were playing a children's game in the crags, a pretend coronation and even a pretend wedding.

He walked with the others over the rising gullies and ridges toward the rock shelf that jutted out like a natural platform above the valley. They were not in formal procession but casually talking among themselves. "Few of the king's insignias are available," Kark said. "Rycal took the intaglios, the belts with carved balances, the clothes, the headdress—all but the pectoral, which the high priest rescued before he escaped from the Laij."

"The high priest's men have been making new vestments," Maachah said, "and a new pectoral for the queen. She is to wear one like yours, for a new reality has arisen—Varial as queen." Maachah said this with a spirit of having just announced a great boon. But Yosha clenched his teeth and wondered what Varial the queen—given all this power—might say and do as his wife and co-regent.

They walked between several hundred who already were seated on the ground; they heard numerous Enre approaching and the two groups blended informally on the wide ledge below the celebrants.

The high priest fussily positioned himself with several of his assistants, then finally called out, "Yosha and Varial."

As Yosha stepped forward, he heard someone moving on his left, and at the same moment he caught a whiff of ele, the bride scent. He had experienced it before at other weddings, but as Varial moved beside him the airy perfume affected him differently this time. How odd, he thought, a bride scent for receiving the regal vestments and pectorals, and the groom scent, which he could smell strong on his own neck.

Asel caught a whiff of melne, the scent of the groom, just as the musicians from the high priest's retinue began singing and playing their instruments. The music was both sacred and patriotic, majestic and worshipful—not far different, she thought, from the ceremony in which she had been named Varial. In many ways, that moment was more impressive and "real" than this ceremony about which she had so many misgivings. The bold, astringent scent of the groom seemed like another intrusion into her focused, disciplined life.

When the music had finished, the high priest spoke at length of the Askirits' unchanging quest to find the way to the light above. He praised the loyalty of generations of kings who had ruled Tarn. He spoke with surprising brevity, Asel thought. Before she realized the priest was through, he was instructing them to kneel.

She knelt beside Yosha and felt the priest place a loop over her head, with a pendant hanging from it. He then moved to Yosha, and she heard the ribbed sleeves rustle as the priest put the pectoral in place.

"Touch the emblem, each of you," the priest said. Asel moved her hand to the intricate pectoral hanging below her collarbone, fingering the carvings of serrated wings cut into intricate rising shapes, a cameo of a circle of light at the top, rays rising in an arc. "This is the symbol of your regal responsibilities.

Your privileges will be few contrasted with your responsibilities. You will feel their weight at every dawning and every wind of night. Touch its sharp edges, which rise with the sharpness of light."

She gingerly touched the many edges of the emblem, stroking out with her fingers, realizing she had never felt anything sharper.

"You are sworn to uphold the cutting edges of Tarn's law, even when it divides your own flesh. Even when it destroys those you love."

He paused a moment, then said, "Touch the many wings. These are not the wings of keitr, which spell death. They are the wings of many birds of sea and crag that fly in hope in Aliare, birds that fly toward the light above, wings of the kees, of zeskrets and eslens and aurets and mescidees . . ."

The priest stepped back, and his assistants took his place. She felt them putting vestments over her shoulders, which rustled oddly as the men draped their fullness to the ground. She touched the thick ridges and ran her forefinger down one of the deep, woven ribbings, purposefully made stiff so that her slightest movement would announce her royal presence. She heard Yosha's clothes rustling beside her.

Then the priest's hand was on her head, and she heard him ask, "Do each of you embrace these sacred duties and these sacred symbols as more vital than life itself?"

"Yes," she said, with Yosha's response nearly in unison with hers.

They rose, the ribbing rustling so ostentatiously she felt foolish. The priest then put into their hands a stout staff, inlaid with many faces. "As the faces of your scepters all look up toward the light above, so you will lead the people to find the way."

Maachah then took the high priest's place. In each hand he carried a little rewn. Asel had heard one of the little birds flutter in his hands during the high priest's charge to them. Now in silence, Maachah slit the throat of each and let their blood flow on his hands. "Do you mingle your blood and your love?" he asked. When they assented, he placed the female rewn in her hand, the male in Yosha's.

He led them to some stones that had been arranged as an altar. She knelt silently with Yosha and handed the female rewn to him; he gave the male to her. After the exchange of the sacrifices, they placed both rewns on the altar, their hands outstretched. She then felt Maachah's bloody hands on hers, binding them to Yosha's. "The sacrifice of purity and of blood make you one. Do you pledge your holy word forever?"

The weight of the word "forever" made the "yes" that came from her mouth little more than a whisper; Yosha's was not much louder.

A priest washed her hands in a bowl of water. When finished, she shook off the excess water and stood beside Yosha. "We now have both a king and a queen in Tarn!" the high priest announced. "Yosha and Varial. May you wage war, but soon reign in peace."

The people below the promontory on which they stood shouted the traditional acclamations, with the wedding party quickly joining in with equal exuberance.

Since the royal trappings were so few, the wedding festivities soon began. Asel felt herself being pulled by several Enre to a group that had begun singing and opening packages of food. It was the custom for the bride and groom after the wedding ceremony to move separately among the people, responding to their jests and well-wishes.

She removed the rustling robe from her shoulders and accepted the fealty and well-wishes of those she had led during Tarn's devastation. She found her fingers tapping and fluttering lightly on the faces and arms of her friends, even tracing smiles on Solket's face, doing all the things she had been taught were the expected bridal responses. She moved gracefully to the shaking of shells and bones and percussion pettetels.

Wedding scents mixed with the dancing and flint sparks and

shouts. They talked and sang joyously, filled with more hope for their nation than had seemed possible. They felt nostalgia for weddings past, in which they had celebrated without care. But these veterans of battles danced and sang as if they had already won the battles ahead.

Asel had already touched hundreds of hands and faces when she came upon the children. Breea had brought several from a nearby village to join Delin and Nen, and now she was teaching them songs, urging them to join in. But Asel realized they were hesitant and abashed, for all she could hear were weak attempts at phrases and a bit of banging on pettetels along with the shaking of their little anklets.

Asel grabbed their hands and danced with them, singing and trying to lead them into the rhythm, pulling their small bodies into motion. Oh, she thought, she would make singers and dancers of them all some day! She whirled them around and around and fell down among them, laughing. She pulled little Nen to her and started singing him a nursery tune:

> *Soykk the stubborn was a silly beast.*
> *He stuck his nose in Mama's feast.*
> *Mama gave that beast a smack.*
> *But Soykk the stubborn came right back!*

> *Soykk, the beast,*
> *Soykk, the beast.*
> *Who of you is Soykk, the beast?*
> *Stubborn Soykk!*
> *Stubborn Soykk!*

She finally got some of the children joining in and rhythmically shaking small bladders filled with pebbles. She had the feeling, as she moved from the group of children to the adults, that she was hardly acting like a queen. But she decided not to bother looking for the robe of office she had put aside. She was both queen and Varial, and she was determined to shape her own role.

A woman not far from her began the wedding dance with the traditional anklets of lestel teeth clicking rhythmically as she moved in a wide circle. The celebrants began to chant, ebba, ebba, ebba, complementing her dancing. This clear, high melody invited the bride and groom to lead the dancing. Many started shaking sietelens—hollow bones with rounded bones within that sounded a skody-bok-bok-bok, skody-bok-bok-bok.

Asel moved toward the woman and then felt Yosha taking her hand. They moved briskly with the lively syncopated music, their hands clasping and unclasping. She was in her element with her quick, shaking movements, her feet beating on the rocky shelf like sounds of ardeddd in the distance. She loved to dance, and Yosha's handclasp reminded her that he would soon desire more than the light touch of her fingers.

—— Bride Scents ——

Long after the first dance, Yosha could not seem to locate her. A time or two he caught the sound of her voice among the revelers. The afternoon wore on, and he began to wonder if she had made any of the traditional preparations. He grew weary of the singing and the sounds of children and their silly songs. He had been proclaimed king of all Tarn, but his emotions at the moment were a mixture of desire and apprehension.

The next time he heard her voice, he moved quickly toward her. Since they were to disappear without notice, he did not want to speak aloud. As he got close to Asel, he noticed that already the bride scent was gone and that it was therefore past time to leave. He reached out for her arm and felt it stiffen slightly. "Varial," he said in Yette on her wrist, "it is drawing toward sierent." She did not reply but came with him to the outskirts of the camp.

Asel then led Yosha to a trail to the south. It descended for some time, becoming not much more than a narrow path. Then she led him off the trail. Yosha concluded she had made this trek before since she was moving swiftly and surely.

She stopped, knelt to check a marker she must have left previously, then struck out upon a narrow ledge cut into the face of a cliff. After climbing uphill for a time, she said, "Wait a moment." She touched his shoulder, motioning him to pass by her. Then she dragged a boulder to the trail's edge and balanced it precariously.

"Let me help," he said.

"I know just how to place it," she said. "If anyone happens to use this trail behind us, it will make a racket as it crashes down."

"You have found a remarkably secret and secure place," Yosha said.

"Every bride is supposed to," she said without humor, moving past him again. She led him further up and, behind a trickle of waterfall, indicated a cave behind it. As they dodged the thin cascade, Yosha said, "After sierent, that waterfall will completely block the entrance—at least till midday."

She said simply, "I am told that's desirable."

She led him past three forks in the tunnel and finally up to a broad basin within the cavern. As they stopped before it, he caught scents he had never experienced before, aromatic spices in the soft leathers and furs that made up the bed before them.

Each Askirit woman chose her own fragrances, keeping them secret, that they might work their magic only on her wedding night, and these were having their desired effect. Yosha bent down and touched the edges and corners of the soft bower, noticing sea grasses and down which must have been brought from a village below. He thought of a saying among the Laij: "The Askirit are a thin-blooded, scabrous people. The only thing one might envy them for is their wedding feasts." He wondered if this were not what Laij soldiers really envied, for he doubted their brides made such secret and personal preparations.

He stood again and realized Varial was standing beside him, not busily gathering or directing something or making a point. He wondered if she had resolutely made all these preparations with the same call to duty she applied to everything else. He could imagine her words to the Enre as she gathered spices and fragrances and soft coverings for the bridal bed: "The marriage must be consummated. It is an affair of state."

He turned toward her. With the bride's and groom's fragrances now long gone, the time had come for their own personal scents. He heard her pull something from a small pouch, two narrow strips of soft material called vela. She had lightly applied to them the personal bride's scent she had chosen, and the aroma spread quickly to his nostrils. She put the two strips into his hand.

He reached over and touched her cheek, then found the ringlet of hair over her ear and began tying the thin fabric to it. The strip was very narrow, and his fingers felt thick and clumsy. He completed the task, then reached for her chin, turning her head so he could reach the ringlet on the other side. As he reached for it, he felt even more clumsy. The memory of Jemm's laughter suddenly chilled him, and he stopped. The only woman who had ever touched him provocatively, the only girl who had touched him with affection at all, had cruelly laughed at him.

Varial turned her body so that the ringlet was closer to him. "You hesitate," she said. "Is something wrong?"

"I am clumsy," he said. "I was afraid you would laugh."

She drew a short breath with pursed lips, meaning she heard and understood. She touched his arm, which was still raised toward her. "I will not laugh," she said, promising.

He finished tying the second vela, then drew from his pouch a tiny bag of the scent he had chosen and handed it to her. She opened it, removed the little bubble, squeezed it between her fingers, then dabbed faint touches behind his ears and on his throat. He then turned to her and caressed her face, following its contours. Her skin seemed both soft and alive, like the surface of a quiet pool. Her nose was an exquisite sculpture beneath eyes alive with lashes and movement. His every touch of her eyebrows, or the dangling hairlocks, or the little hills and valleys of her cheeks, or the bones beneath her skin brought nuances of texture, shape, and life. "There is a saying that the most erotic part of a woman is her face," he said. "Your face is more beautiful than all the songs." He brushed his lips past hers, in that same gesture of growing affection she had formally given him.

Asel stepped back from him, and he heard her reach down to her belt. He thought of another saying about the women of Tarn: that the most sensual moment for an Askirit man on his wedding night is when the woman removes her daggers, for then she is vulnerable to him. He heard Varial remove the blades on each side of her belt, then bend to the Enre malc on her calf.

"Now you are Asel," he said. "The time of sacrifice has come. But am I truly such a duty to you?"

She took his face in her hands. "Don't you know what your barest touch has done?" she asked. Then her lips once more grazed his in that light touch of affection, which he returned with a kiss that said far more.

Part Three

Before the worlds,
instantly,
all was light....

... hurtling light,
exploding light....

Who can imagine
such dazzling force
making the worlds?

—FROM THE ASKIRIT RITUAL

Chapter 9.

—— War ——

"Can a speck remain in the eye of a king?" Asel asked wryly. She addressed the question to no one in particular, and for a moment no one responded.

"What do you mean?" Yosha asked.

"She's heard that from the spies," Solket explained. "They say it's on the lips of all the Laij soldiers."

"We are the speck!" Asel announced with satisfaction. "It infuriates their king that he's taken all the coast—every city and village—but we still hold the crags."

Solket gripped his keitr belt with the shoulder of his missing arm; with his remaining hand—his left—he was checking each pouch for loosening threads. "Rumors are the Laij are so obsessed with taking the Skull," he said, "that they're gathering half the men in Aliare to storm it."

"All of Aris is abuzz with rumors and movement," Kark said. "They could attack any time."

"And that presents our chance," Yosha said. "As the Laij attack Hrusc at the Skull, we take back Aris."

Bralin whistled. "Every day, new Askirit join us," he said, wonder in his voice. "There must be twenty thousand now!"

"We have the force and the strategy to take both city and temple," Yosha said. "Let Hrusc battle them on the Skull. With Aris in our hands, we can bind the nation!" Yosha tossed a bag of crackly acei to Mosen, saying in high spirits, "Put it behind you and lean on it. We'll hear every twitch of your muscles. We've placed thousands of bags on the trails and ridges in strategic positions. Very noisy! Very effective!"

Maachah kicked at one of the bags of brittle fish bones so that it crackled loudly. "But we must be aware," he said gravely, "that if we control Aris, the Laij will return in a fury. And when they come, we will be like sand in the path of ute."

Asel had been sharpening the blades she always wore, and at Maachah's comment she stopped her work. "Yes, you are right," she said. "But the Laij took our cities through terror. They will never have that advantage again. We have planned thoroughly to take Aris. Our plans are just as thorough on how to keep it!"

There is a time before dawn when even near the sea, one can maneuver against the force of sierent outside a shelter. The aerated, sucking waters make footing precarious, and fingers can be torn from their grips. But the skilled who are prepared to risk much can make slow headway.

Yosha plunged into these sucking winds, grasping a long skin rolled on two poles. The night before, he and scores of other men had camped very close to the outskirts of Aris, where their spies had told them the Laij filled many of the small caves. The wind struck his back and shoved him along. Yosha cautiously let himself be pushed forward, scrambling down a gorge, awkward with the poles in his hands.

When he arrived at one of the caves, he sensed from the stinging spray pummeling his face that he and his men were early enough. He lowered his knees into the shallow water rushing by and started unrolling the skin against the cliff wall. As he loaded a keitr onto his launcher, he felt another man's hand on the top of his pole. Soon four sets of hands were on the poles, two at the top, two at the bottom.

Several men fired keitr into the cave. Instantly, Yosha and the others rolled the skin over its mouth, pressing it tightly against the rock walls. As he pushed his body against the skin, holding its edges from flapping in the strong wind, he listened for sounds from within.

He heard a man's scream. In response, Yosha's body spasmed slightly as he continued pressing his weight with that of the others against the covering. The pole was tight against his left shoulder, ready for a panicked Laij soldier to crash into the skin. The keitrs, finding no escape from the cave, would be infuriated, biting again and again anything that moved, Laij or merret.

The screams finally subsided, but they kept tightly braced. After waiting as long as he dared, Yosha blew a shrill bone whistle. Hundreds of Askirit who were braced against nearby cave apertures heard the signal and fell flat at the same time Yosha did, with the skins falling upon them. The keitr immediately sensed the unblocked entrances and flew off.

Yosha lay under the skin as the weakening gusts of sierent lifted its edges. Then they bounded up and stepped into the cave. They located the bodies of men and merrets and groped for the vials of scent the Laij used for protection. Quickly, they cut the cords tying them to the Laij wrists, slipped them into pockets, and in great haste dragged the bodies of the men and small beasts into the final swirls of sierent, which sucked them into the sea. Before the dawn had fully broken or the aurets announced it, Yosha and his men were gone.

Asel ran just ahead of some Enre and Askirit warriors who were dumping sacks of acei on the trails. Shortly before, she had led several thousand Askirit in an attack on Aris. As soon as the Laij and their conscripts had counterattacked, Asel and her forces had fallen back, luring them on to their traps in the crags. With the scent on their feet, they had no fear of the merrets, but they had retreated as rapidly as possible. It was a considerable distance to the crags free of aceyn where they had been able to set their traps. Asel hoped that a great Laij army was pursuing her, but she heard no reverberations behind her; under Laij discipline, the barbarians moved silently.

She had set the traps on more than three hundred paths and trails, covering every possible approach. High chasms flanked the area so that the Laij could not approach from the side. Asel crouched behind a boulder the shape of a massive thighbone. It was twice her size, balanced carefully, and snugged tight with ropes. She grasped a stout pole with a block at the end, as did three other Enre with her; each stood in a strategic position, well-poised to thrust their poles.

Silence. Asel hoped their enemy had not turned back to Aris. Down below the trails, on the plains below, she knew there might be thousands of Laij, or there might be none.

Silence. Every time a breeze rustled the acei on the trail, her hand tightened on the pole.

Silence. Each bird scratching in the acei tensed them. If the Laij had returned to Aris, she knew Yosha might be trapped in a pincers-movement as he attacked the city.

Then it came, the stark crackling of acei close below them, which had to be from a man's foot. She forced herself to wait until the sound was very close. She hissed, "Elt!" jabbing forward with the pole, her partner jabbing with her. She heard the cries of two men falling to the plains below even as she and her partner rolled to the side so the two Enre behind them could position themselves. She had practiced these movements thousands of times in the Askirit defenses against invasion, and it seemed exhilarating yet frightening to be using the classic strategy.

Before she was back in position behind the second team, the others had pushed more men off the little shelf. She knew that in these attacks, the Laij would force a rapid flow of men up the trail. They would flatten their backs against the walls, swinging their blades like axes. That's why it took four Enre at each post, for eventually a man would hit the Enre pole just right and break through.

"Elt!" Lunge and thrust!

"Elt!" Lunge and thrust!
"Elt!" Lunge and thrust!

The moment Asel's partner felt her pole struck by a blade and then grabbed, she let it go, yelling, "Aest!" Asel jabbed where she thought the man was and hit nothing. "Raikaa!" she shouted, and slashed at the ropes on the boulder as the other Enre fled. Another hard slash, and the boulder grated on the rocks beneath it. It slid down, releasing an avalanche, slabs of rock formations thundering down. At the same time, avalanches above the other trails were being released.

As the sounds reverberated around her, she tried to determine if the enemy who had struck the pole had made it to the top. She waited quietly, listening to the continuing roar of the avalanches, and then to the echoes of the falling debris far off in the distance. She could not afford to wait long, yet prudence required she assume the man was just below. Her advantage was she knew this little space as if she could see it. She gripped the pole, positioned herself, and swung it hard in an arc that would sweep the only area in which he could be hiding. She struck only air.

Slowly she crept backward, still cautious, wondering if the boulders had indeed devastated the army that had pursued them. She hurried to the knotted ropes that would let her down to other trails leading back to Aris.

The Askirit had the advantage in their attack on Aris. They knew not only their own capital city but had knowledge of every enemy cavern used as a barracks, every area used for maneuvers, every command station. When they had reached the outskirts of the city, they had blown shrill whistles. Every Askirit in Aris knew the whistles meant they must instantly flee to their dwellings and leave all work grottoes, public places, and the trails. But when Yosha's enemies heard the sound, they took it as an attack command.

Yosha's troops had moved swiftly to hundreds of selected caverns and had shot keitr into them. With half the defending forces chasing Asel, and most Askirit conscripts defecting to their dwellings, Yosha's superior numbers soon began to tell. The Laij sent their merrets in all directions, but the scent on the feet of the Askirit was the same as that of the Laij forces. Yosha was grateful most of the dwellings were not in the fighting, for the Laij did not protect the general Askirit population with the scent, only those conscripted for battle.

As he approached the temple, Yosha assumed that defenders lay thick at the entrances. He and his men crouched in positions under overhanging rock formations and fired a volley of keitr. The expected screams from the temple mixed with the sounds of men hurling spears at them. Hundreds of the thin, needle-like projectiles struck and clattered around them, many finding their marks. Yosha shifted the weight of the two extra keitr belts he carried, loaded one of the little assassins into his launcher, then ordered another volley, then another.

They crept forward against the lessening number of spears, long blades ready. Near the entrances, Yosha's foot touched a body. He stepped over it and soon felt another. As his men positioned themselves at each of the entrances, he concluded that any remaining defenders had fled into the temple itself. That meant they were trapped within, but it also meant they could hide in many places to ambush advancing troops. The temple was far too large to shoot keitr into it indiscriminately.

He listened intently as he placed his left hand at the edge of the entrance and sidled his way in. He guessed their defenders would not be hanging around the entrances to fight superior forces, but he moved as if they were. He listened for the slightest sound, his hand on the wall tracing the nearly flat arc of the great worship center. As his fingers moved along the wall, they sensed something strange. The carved faces and wings were altered.

He stopped and explored one of the faces, starting with the throat and the chin. A slash cut through the cheek and forehead. He moved his hand further along the wall. Here was a face nearly chopped away; next to it, wings and a face with deep gouges.

Despite the danger of enemies nearby, he impulsively

sheathed his blade and felt the wall with both hands. Desecration everywhere! He thought of the unfathomable hours spent by the artisans of hope and light, their work hacked at and defaced. He now knew why the Laij, after Aris's fall, had allowed no Askirit within the temple. He moved along the wall, feeling it with both hands, then turned away and ground his teeth. "Where are all the promises about the temple!" he agonized. "Where, now, is the hope of Aliare?"

He pulled the blade back out of its sheath and moved forward. Then he noticed something in front of him, a flicker of light at the temple's center. Could it be a firefly? No, it was not the season. Certainly no one would be striking flint. He stared into the darkness, moving forward, and then saw it again. He kept moving toward it, holding a keitr in its launcher. His foot touched an obstruction. He explored it with his toes and found it a waist-high wall on what had once been a perfectly flat floor where thousands of worshipers stood. The obstruction was made of cut stone, with a polished top like a work station. He pulled himself up; its inner edge was wet. It encloses a vast pool! he thought with horror. Those are phosphorescent fish and eels in the center of Eshtel's temple!

"Varial, the attack goes well," a captain reported. "Few of the forces that pursued you survived." They stood at their prearranged site, a promontory overlooking the north edge of Aris where most of the Askirit lived. "The avalanches were so loud they were heard here. I'm sure they put fear into the Laij and their wretched conscripts."

She acknowledged his news and immediately moved with her Enre into the city, tapping instructions in Yette on an Enre's palm. The strategy for hundreds of Enre was to enter Askirit dwellings, stealthily locate any Laij within and dispatch them. Every other shelter and work station in Aris would be attacked without warning by Yosha's warriors.

A tricky business, Asel thought, as she stood with two other Enre outside a cave. We must alert the Askirit within that we are allies but not alert an enemy. She hoped the Askirit within responded to the signals they had been taught from infancy.

She stepped on a clicker that imitated the chirp of a common insect. Trilp, trilp, trilp. The Askirit knew the insect always sounded four times; three trilps was unnatural and signaled friendly forces advancing. The instructions were: If alone, call out; if the enemy holds you, cough loudly. Very loudly!

Trilp, trilp, trilp. She signaled repeatedly, with no response. Might the enemy be holding people, gagging them? They would have to take that chance. She and the others stepped within and cautiously explored the wide tunnel with many sleeping areas. No one was there.

They moved on to another cave and repeated the procedure. This time they heard instant calls from both men and women. Still, they advanced cautiously, in case the Laij had broken the code. They found only Askirit within and immediately applied the protective scent to their feet. She and her partners secured four more caves and were heading for another when an Enre came running toward them. "Varial!" she was calling. "Varial!"

"What?"

The young woman stopped breathless before them. "They are shooting keitr at us!"

Asel gripped her shoulder firmly. "Who is shooting keitr at us?"

"We can't tell. Hundreds, maybe thousands shooting into us, advancing through Aris."

"But Yosha is sweeping east to west. It is not possible."

"They have killed Arsia and Quette and many more. Keitr, not spears!"

Yosha was well within the temple, hunting Laij defenders in the scores of rooms and halls, when he heard the shouts from the temple's entrances. He moved quickly toward the sounds, grimacing as he ran his fingers along the defaced wall of the sanctuary. He never reached the entrances. "Yosha!" one of his captains was calling, "Yosha!"

"Here," he called back.

"We've been ambushed by Hrusc! After we lost thousands taking the city, they've come at our backs, firing volleys of keitr at us before we knew they were enemies!"

Like a spitting beast, Yosha rammed air and moisture through his teeth. "Can we regroup?" he asked, moving closer to the entrances and hearing the chaos outside.

"Not enough people. I have only ten here—that's all!"

Yosha heard the movements of hundreds of men coming up toward the entrances. He thought ruefully of how his dire situation now was exactly the same as that of the Laij defenders he had trapped here such a short time earlier. In Yette, he touched his captain's arm, instructing him to have all his men fire three volleys at the entrances, then to follow him.

They fired the volleys in quick succession, then silently followed Yosha toward the stairs. He had them fire random shots across the sanctuary, then began racing up the long ascent. These ten at least would make it to fight Hrusc again, he vowed bitterly. He made the level of the priests' rooms, then went down the corridor to start the long climb to the Tolas far above. He had escaped once before this way, but from the Laij. This time he fled from his own countrymen. How could it be, he wondered, that Hrusc would attack them and leave the Skull unprotected?

As Hrusc's troops moved against them, Asel had been forced to give the order to flee the city. But the ways were blocked by the Stuugkt, who were making a tight, disciplined advance. Separated from the others, she found herself being pressed down a steep decline toward the sea's edge. Suddenly the feet of men just above and behind her pounded in a precise pattern down the very slope she had just come over. Asel ran even more quickly.

The sound of her movements alerted them to her position. She heard a launcher fire a keitr and she instantly bolted forward like a gust of sierent's winds, ignoring all risks of crashing into obstructions. She heard the projectile strike the rocks not far from her feet and then the scream of the keitr.

She moved her legs faster than she thought possible, running at full speed at the cliff's edge above the sea. Her legs were pumping as her body went into the air and plunged toward the water. But the keitr can fly faster than I can fall, she thought as she plummeted, tensing her body for the fatal bite. But she hit the water unscathed and let herself sink deep, then swam underwater toward the open sea.

She had taken less than a hundred strokes when something struck her body. The thing started dragging her backward and down into the water. It took her several moments to realize it was a fishing net of the type the Laij had introduced to the bay. Despite her struggles, her head kept getting dragged under, and she became entangled in the thick ropes. She felt herself being pulled with the motion of the net and fought to regain the surface.

She struggled to get a blade into her hand and succeeded. She tried to slash through the rope and finally freed her left shoulder. Grabbing the net, she pulled herself up and gulped some air, but immediately the net submerged her again. The blade was gone. She twisted to draw another, but it was torn from her hand by the moving ropes of the net. She tried to lunge up again for more air but was too tangled in the moving net. She lost consciousness before the net was raised and hauled into a Laij boat, which was in the process of evacuating the city.

—— Kelabreen ——

Asel walked in a thoroughfare of the great Laij city of Kelabreen, nervously awaiting an Askirit contact. She felt safer moving with streams of people than meeting outside the city. She passed the contact point again, her feet probing for the uniquely carved knobs that marked locations. She kept moving, matching the pace of the Laij crowd.

For two years she had been a slave of the Laij. In the bay of Aris, they had hauled her, barely alive, onto their great boat, which was hastily departing. When she regained consciousness, her condition helped her disguise her identity. She pretended she was still unconscious, but listened intently. No insignias were on her simple clothes and her blades had been lost. When she finally spoke to them, she told them her name was Ocia and she feigned stupidity, acting servile and awed. After regaining strength, she also feigned clumsiness. When a Laij soldier finally said sarcastically, "She can barely find her way to the wall," she grinned in satisfaction.

The Laij had taken her on the long sea voyage to Kelabreen, stopping every night on an island to ride out sierent. She had been put to work washing and cutting food, which she did obediently. When they had finally arrived in Kelabreen, she had been sold in the central market to a woman of wealth.

Laij cities were complex networks, descending as many as ten levels. The top stories were natural caves or simple excavations. But the deeper the rooms, the more finished and the more important. Asel had lived on the second level, beneath storage and equipment. Beneath her had been the eating and food preparation areas, with carved walls and polished floors.

Only once had she been allowed into the rooms directly below her. She had felt the elaborate cameos and intaglios depicting a vista of hunters, sailors, and threatening seas. She exclaimed to her mistress in child-like awe, "The animals feel alive. It's a wonder!" She used the empty prattle she had perfected of praising every Laij skill, though she knew well what the nimble fingers of Askirit artisans could do.

In response, the Laij woman said, "You should experience the vaults and pools of worship far beneath us!" Asel begged obsequiously to do so. "But no Askirit may enter," the woman said, not unkindly but in the same way an Askirit might explain to the most boorish barbarian why she could not enter the temple.

Laij women, who took no martial training whatever, were appalled at Askirit women's involvement in fishing and the military. Asel remembered the word used to describe all the Askirit women being sold in Kelabreen's slave market: "Sura," they called them, a word pejorative in the extreme, connoting coarse speech, loose sexual conduct, and masculine attributes.

Asel was in Kelabreen only a short time before she learned Rycal was in the city. Suddenly all the rage and bitterness she had felt about the loss of Aris and her freedom—of the promises wondrously fulfilled and then brutally shattered—all fused into one obsession. She became convinced she had been brought to Kelabreen to carry Rycal back to justice in Tarn. From that moment on she determined that every instant of every day in Kelabreen she would be working toward capturing Rycal and somehow taking him alive back to the devastated kingdom he had betrayed.

It had taken her nearly two years to make her escape. After she had slipped away from her mistress in the city, the Laij had begun looking for a stupid, clumsy young woman. She now assumed the identity of a free Laij, walking among them, saying very little lest her speech betray her. She was always ready with a short, plausible answer. Yet she knew she could make a small mistake; as she walked on the left side with the orderly flow of people, her fingers and left foot grazing the wall, she thought of many near misses since she had escaped.

Suddenly the sound of tiny bells sweeping around the corner right in front of her made her leap to the center of the street. She had been so alert for other sounds that the little bells had not alarmed her—until she realized they were close enough to touch. Her body was trembling as the bells passed her along the wall, the parlec walking slowly by, the tinkling sounds warning her of his parasitic disease. She wondered if the parlec's body was a mass of ulcerated sores. She shuddered, thinking of how close she had come to touching him, how defiled she would have felt if she had.

She resumed walking along the wall, more nervous than before. "This meeting could be a set-up!" she thought angrily, once more passing the contact point. She had searched for a long time for Askirit spies—spies she hoped were loyal to Yosha and Varial. She thought she had located one who was to meet her here, but worried that maybe she had misunderstood.

She was beginning to wonder if she should give it up when fingers on her shoulder raced a short way down her arm, saying in Yette, "Walk three more markers, then into the small opening on your left." She had not heard his footsteps, which gave her confidence in his skills.

Asel easily found the entrance and walked far into the narrow tunnel. Deep within, she once again felt his fingers on her shoulder.

They spoke entirely in Yette, standing side by side against the wall, listening for danger. She learned his name was Teloc. "I've heard Rycal is here," she said.

"Everyone knows that," the man responded, tapping sharply on her palm as if irritated at her obvious statement.

"I plan to capture him—very soon," she said, running her fingers over his wrist like an attacking soldier's feet. "All I need is help to get him back to Tarn." She felt his fingers tighten on her skin. She added, "Every Askirit dreams of bringing Rycal back. It is a necessity. I am determined to do it."

"What do you know about Rycal?" Teloc asked. "His location, his circumstances?"

"Too little," she said. "That is why I sought you out. Is it true he is often at the great pools?"

"Yes. But the pools are a vast network. It is the center of the city, the wonder of Kelabreen. They are heavily guarded. Haven't you listened to the tales? They sing of divers going to the depths and rising with more exuberance than the bubbles that dance beside them. What sights are brought to be seen there! Before Rycal, no Askirit was ever admitted—no wonder he goes there so much. But you cannot get at him. The pools are for Laij only— and, of course, the King of the Askirit." At the word "king," Teloc derisively ripped the word with the back of his fingernail across her hand.

"The water must flow in or out somewhere that a swimmer could enter."

"Yes, but it's deep. Very deep, with no guarantee of air, and who knows what protections. Perhaps grates. You would drown trying to get in."

"Perhaps," she said.

Teloc patted her in a fatherly way, sliding the edge of his palm across her shoulder, a warning against foolishness. Then he said, "Did you know that the sights you can see in the pools are also called the Beautiful Death? The Laij bring many of these wonders from the deepest seas. The men who dive for them experience the ecstasy of seeing what they bring up, but afterward, they often lie writhing in pain until they die."

Asel had not heard that before. "The Beautiful Death," she repeated. "Well, Rycal's death will not be so beautiful!" she snapped out on his palm. She went on to ask every question she thought might lead to information about the pools and about Rycal's habits and how he might be found alone.

Teloc's information was limited, but she probed exhaustively before trying to learn if he were Hrusc's man or Yosha's. Finally she asked, "What news do you have of the kingdom?"

He didn't hesitate, perhaps because she was no threat to him, and perhaps because she had partially declared herself with the word "kingdom." "Hrusc still commands the Skull," he said, "yet he is barely holding Aris. Yosha is building strength, but not quickly. You know he lost the queen in the battle for Aris?"

"Yes, I knew."

"And now there is a new Varial."

Asel's fingers floated away from the man's hand. Of course, she thought, if the Enre had not been able to find her, they would eventually have presumed her dead and have named a new Varial. She had not thought of it because she had been very much alive and plotting to return. She digested with difficulty this new fact that she was no longer Varial and, in fact, had not been Varial for some time.

She forced her fingers back to the man's palm and tried to keep them steady as she asked, "Will Yosha marry the new Varial?"

The man responded with a light flourish of his fingertips, as if the question were inconsequential. "Am I the king's courtier?"

For the first time since hearing Rycal was in Kelabreen, she found it hard to concentrate on her single goal of capturing him.

—— Stalking Rycal ——

Asel found it far from impossible to penetrate the great pools of Kelabreen. Shortly before sierent, when the rivers from the heights were a small fraction of their morning force, she plunged into a narrow, deep channel Teloc had indicated should lead to the pools. With one hand she pulled a pack, and with the other she probed ahead with a long, heavy blade. She knew that it was possible she would be blocked by something or that she might run out of air. But she counted on the lower depth of the river to give her adequate space above.

At one point the current quickened, and she was dragged

rapidly far beneath the surface, but then the water calmed long before her air gave out, and she found herself surfacing in a quiet, still pool.

She kicked forward, and as she swam, tried to orient herself. She thought she saw a long, wavy, shimmering creature, but it was gone so quickly that she was not sure she had seen anything at all. Her blade scraped against something. Sheathing the knife and approaching it, she found a flat ledge barely above the water's level. She pulled herself up, trying not to add to the gentle swish of water as she dragged in the pack.

Is anyone near? she wondered, searching silently to find a cavern in which to stash the pack. She moved for a long distance without success, so finally she stuffed the pack into a crevice.

The perimeters of the pools seemed to have no end. The one in which she had surfaced led to another, and then to another, in a maze of pools of all sizes. At one point she heard far-off voices that sounded as if they were engaged in casual conversation. Silently slipping into the water, she backed away in the opposite direction. As she did so, she saw in the water a flash of light—colored light—then another, far to her left.

With her left hand on the edge, she kept swimming from one interconnecting pool to another, stroking quietly under water, slowly surfacing and going down again. Frequently, she saw various shapes of light escaping in the distance, rippling, darting strands of blues and magentas and yellows, teasing her eyes. She was drifting into a small pool when she finally saw something close up. Many large circles of blue with feathery red tentacles fluttered in the gentle current nearby. Her amazement at being near such wonders was so great that she almost forgot to rise for air.

When she had surfaced and gulped, she quickly descended to stare again. She stayed with the diffuse light of the creatures a long time, watching their elegant movements, hypnotic in the shifting waters, wanting somehow to draw their beauty deep into her body and soul.

For days Asel explored, listening for voices, determining the places people could be heard around the perimeters and staring at the magnificent array of luminous wonders. Apparently many Laij came here to stare into the waters.

She found an underwater passageway leading deep into caverns that even during the low waters could not be reached except for a long swim without air. This is what she had been looking for. She returned to retrieve her pack and take it to the most sequestered pool.

Halfway back, swimming with her pack trailing behind her, she saw before her a wavering stream of many colors, a feast of luminescence—rows of white lights with long, waving fins of gold and aqua lace. She stopped, once more so amazed that all her purpose was forgotten. Yes, she thought, she could see how a man might take any risk to dive to the Beautiful Death. To see such things—such light and colors as she had always sung about and desired—was worth any price. How ironic that the Laij were the ones who had found these creatures and captured them for their culture . . . the Laij who were destroying the Askirit who longed for the light.

Asel continued her explorations, determined to learn every little pool and interconnection, every hiding place, every escape route. Eventually she moved her pack yet again to a cavern even more remote. She was relieved that she never sensed another person swimming. She hoped it was because the pools were in one sense holy to the Laij, not because there might be lethal creatures in them.

The large pools where people congregated were shallow, allowing them to see from above what swam at their feet. Always when she listened to them talk, she tried to detect an Askirit accent. She did not know Rycal's voice, but if he were the only Askirit at the pools, his inflections would give him away.

Floating on the water one day, listening to male voices, she heard one she suspected was Askirit. As she listened, she realized the discussion he was involved in was more wide-ranging and learned than anything in Tarn. They discussed Laij antiquity, cosmology, and scientific theories with an array of facts and insights to which she had never been previously exposed.

She returned the next day and decided that the voice was clearly Askirit. Here was Rycal casually talking just a few strokes from her! The men with him were not the same as the day before. In fact, for the next several days, Rycal came to the same place, but each time with different men, whom it became clear were specialists in various fields of knowledge. Rycal would ask many questions, and his companions never lacked for answers.

Once Asel caught an unpleasant scrap of conversation. She heard one of the Laij scholars say, "With all due respect, the Askirit is a coarse, adolescent culture."

Rycal's response made her furious. "Yes," he said. "Their range of knowledge is very limited. The people live for tales and visions in the night."

"And with such an impoverished understanding," the Laij scholar added, "we feel it is hopeless to civilize them. But," and here the Laij scholar laughed, "it must be possible. We have civilized you, King Rycal." At that, all the men laughed with him, and Asel had to restrain herself from assassinating Rycal immediately.

The men finally left, talking as they went, and Asel began to despair of her chances. There is no way I can get at him, she thought. He is always with others, talking their erudite foolishness! She started coming earlier to the place they met, and she realized one morning that someone was already there. Might it be Rycal? When the other men came, she heard that it was.

Early next morning, she again heard someone appear alone. She hoisted herself from the water and silently crept very close behind the man. She had to be sure it was he, so she lowered her voice and said, "King Rycal?"

He did not get out even a complete word. She recognized his

voice and instantly gripped the back of his neck with one hand and rammed her other hand against his mouth. She used a pressure point to render him unconscious, then silently eased his body into the water. Good, she thought, as she began towing him slowly across the pool. They will not know where he disappeared. They will search, but they may not feel they have to search so thoroughly in the pools.

As she pulled Rycal toward her hideout, she saw coming at her shimmering shapes, a school of large creatures, brightly phosphorescent, orange and purple, trailing whips of luminous green. They swam directly at her, then passed by—or through her, it seemed. She turned her head to look, but they were already gone.

—— A King's Mind ——

Asel hid in the remote pool during the inevitable search for Rycal. She had securely bound his hands and feet in the Enre manner, leaving him flat on the stones. "Cry out," she warned him, "and I will be forced to kill you. That's my only choice." She didn't want a gag in his mouth, for she wanted to taunt him and hear his responses. "You know that among your people your name has become a synonym for 'traitor.'"

Rycal's cheek was pressed against the wet rock floor. When he spoke, his voice sounded flat, like a shallow wave washing over her feet. "They know nothing of what happened," the bound man said. "For months, the Laij diplomats and I were working out peace arrangements—"

Asel bolted to her feet. "You were talking to the Laij for months? You knew this whole thing was coming? Who else did?"

"No one. I spoke with their diplomats, who insisted on rigid secrecy."

"Of course!" she exclaimed. "Why didn't *you* insist on something?" Her voice was filled with bitterness.

Rycal's voice from the floor was still flat and tremulous, but a little more confident. "The Laij are a cultured and powerful people, and I was trying to save Tarn from a terrible war," he said, as if explaining to a reluctant learner. "I nearly saved my people."

His tone infuriated her. "The Laij are cultured and learned, yet they use merrets?" she asked. "They're terrorists!"

Rycal snorted, then coughed. "You cannot rule without lethal force," he retorted. "And the Laij think that, from Aliare's beginnings, *we* have been the world's terrorists. They also know the Askirit to be considerably less advanced, not only in the sciences, but in philosophy and religion—"

Asel interrupted harshly: "Why didn't you send the order to evacuate Aris?" she demanded. "You knew it was crucial—that every moment counted. Yet the order to evacuate never came!"

Rycal shifted his bound feet and awkwardly moved his position. "The council didn't know I was meeting with the Laij. Those hotheads would have spoiled it. When the attack came, I knew everyone would blame me. So I needed just that one day to get out."

"Just one day?" Asel said. "Just one day to get out? That's the ultimate treachery. To lose a whole nation to save your own skin! And you ran to the Laij, who had betrayed you—you who are descended from generations of kings!" Asel was shaking with fury.

She waited for his response, but all she heard was her own loud breathing as she clenched her fists and ground her heel on the rocks. Finally he said in a weak voice, "I had a pact with the Laij that everyone would have applauded. I negotiated—"

But Asel didn't let him complete his sentence. Instead she demanded, "Sing me the song of the pit!"

"What?"

"Sing me the song of the pit! You know it. Everyone knows it. Think about our journey back to Tarn as you sing me the song of the pit!"

Rycal did not respond. Asel grabbed him roughly by the hair and said, "Sing, or your head's under the water—forever!"

Rycal coughed, attempting to clear his throat. He began singing in a quavery, uncertain voice:

> *Who is prey for the pit?*
> *Is it you?*
> *Traitor. Pagan.*
> *Are you prey?*
>
> *You fall forever in the pit.*
> *You fall to the abyss that longs for you,*
> *that waits for you. . . .*
>
> *Are you prey?*
> *Is it you?*
> *Traitor. Pagan.*
> *Are you prey?*

When he had finished, Asel forced him to sing it again, louder. Then, when his quaking voice had finished again, she taunted, "When traitors are given to the abyss, why can't we hear their bodies hit? The scream, you know, goes on and on and on and on . . ." She put her bare foot on his neck and pressed down. "If anyone in our history deserves the pit, Rycal, it is you."

The exiled king was silent for a very long time, but finally he said, "The Laij describe the Askirit as a barbaric race. I see why."

"Barbaric?" Asel said. "Tarn takes the light to all who will seek it. No one is thrown into the pit who seeks the light."

Rycal exploded in laughter and said, "Are you truly that naive?"

"And are you Askirit?" she retorted. "And are you therefore barbaric?"

"Contrasted with the Laij, perhaps. They, too, love the light, but not these light fables—"

"Blasphemy!" Asel exclaimed. "Is Eshtel a fable? You were once king of Tarn!"

"Yes, and there is much truth in all we were taught. But the Laij have studied far more broadly. They have learned from all of Aliare, and they bring the creatures of light to the pools, to nourish eyes and spirit, to nourish the light common to all of us."

"Rycal, your itching ears have brought diseases of the soul!"

"But the Laij clearly know much more than we ever did. Every Askirit memorizes the same rituals, the identical sayings from the ancients. But the Laij have not only scholars who have memorized their own history and poets—and mystics—but they also have thousands of other scholars who specialize, building up their knowledge. They probe every question, solving the most perplexing difficulties, passing the knowledge on to the next generations."

Asel slammed her fist against her palm. "Including such edifying topics as how to train vicious rodents to rip people's throats out!" she said, biting off and spitting out her words like darts.

"Ah, venom and teeth," he said expansively. "Where in Aliare don't you find them? They appear to be a crude necessity—the Maker's work, right? And, aren't those rather sharp teeth in your own jaws?"

"Sharp teeth and strong fingers," she said. "So you and the Laij have found truth?" she asked sarcastically.

"The Laij have broadened me. They have leeched superstitions from their souls. They've looked beneath the foulest rocks and unraveled mysteries." He coughed, then tried to laugh. "I took great risks," he said, "trying to bring the best of Askirit and Laij together, trying to shape a new world, to avoid the corruptions in both cultures."

She had argued his every point, but some of what he said seemed more plausible than she wanted to admit. She felt herself being carried along with his lines of reasoning, and almost in self defense, she said, "Rycal, you have conveniently come to many conclusions. You've heard and seen innumerable wonders—but your brilliance has destroyed you!"

"And you," Rycal said evenly, "hear nothing I say because of your provincial anger. You remind me of what the Laij say about bitterness: 'It is like claw marks of the keitr,' they say, 'not fatal like its bite, but sending fevers to the soul.'"

Just before sierent, long after she had first entered the pools, Asel said, "Rycal, now is the moment we leave."

The man rolled to a sitting position, straining against the bonds. "How?" he asked.

"Try swimming. It is late in the day; the currents are weakening. You can make it if you do everything I say. Or you can drown, trying to escape me."

"What keeps me from simply swimming to the other pools?"

"My blade. You have been trussed up here, and you have no strength to escape or to fight me. But I admit this—if you wish to escape the pit by dying now, you will have your chance in the water."

As they left the pools, Rycal did not attempt to escape her. They swam into the widest outflow that she had reconnoitered, and soon they were submerged and rushing through the swift narrows. As they finally surfaced, Asel pulled his head above water and was relieved to hear him breathing. She found the water's edge and dragged him to a bank of loose gravel. She was ready to strike if Rycal cried out, but he did not, and she walked with him as quickly as she could for the prearranged rendezvous.

Teloc was waiting deep within the cavern, and soon he and Asel were conversing in Yette, making plans for the long sea voyage. Rycal lay trussed at their feet. They pulled him upright and started dressing him in Askirit slave clothing, then attached a new identity pendant to his wrists, tossing the royal intaglios he had been wearing down the tunnel. Teloc rapped jubilantly into Asel's palm, "Rycal! In my hands! If you were not determined to take him back, I would strangle him right now."

"I wanted to do that myself in the pools and feed him to the fish," Asel said.

"Yosha and all Tarn will be amazed," he said with a brisk flick of his small finger. "Rycal taken from the heart of the Laij!" Teloc knew his own prestige would be greatly enhanced by this, if he could only stay alive in this chancy venture. Asel for an instant thought perhaps she should tell him she was Yosha's queen. But she stifled the urge, knowing he might divulge the knowledge under Laij persuasion.

They were able to move Rycal to another cavern, then in two days to a third, near the bays of Kelabreen. The docks were heavily patrolled by Laij troops, and their risks considerably escalated. Here they gagged Rycal, lest he call out to the frequent movements of men outside. More than once, Asel would tap out on Teloc's hand, "Don't move!"

The last time she did so, her fingers were still in motion on his palm when she felt something strike Teloc's legs, knocking him down and causing him to cry out for an instant as he fell to the floor. Rycal! she thought. Rycal had kicked Teloc so he'd cry out!

A voice from the cavern entrance demanded, "Who's there!"

They sat silent, Asel's hand on the back of Rycal's neck. "Who's there?" the voice demanded again, and they heard the sound of many feet running toward them. "Speak now, or we will send in our little friends."

The memory of a hundred shrieks passed like jagged points through Asel's spine. She was furious at Rycal for alerting them. In one motion, she released his neck and raised her right arm parallel to his face. Then with the full force of her anger, she drove the heel of her hand up into his nose to shatter cartilage into his brain. Rycal sagged bloody and limp; she ripped the gag off his mouth and the bonds from his feet, tossing them as far as she could. Then she called out, "We are here. We are simply finding shelter."

—— The Condemned ——

The Laij soldiers demanded identification. Teloc held out his wrists with the pendants. "This is false," the man said immediately. "You are Teloc; we have been searching long and hard for you." Teloc remained silent. The soldier reached for Asel's wrists. "I suspect these also are false. Who is the man on the ground? A friend? An enemy?"

Asel did not want them to think Rycal was her enemy. She hoped he was dead. She regretted now that she had hit him so hastily and off balance. To ensure a fatal blow, she should have turned and struck more forcefully. "He is Askirit," she said testily.

The man reached his hand to her face and explored it slowly, in a familiar and suggestive way. "So are you," he said. The man knelt and explored Rycal's face. "Yes, he is Askirit, by the bottom half, anyway. The rest of his face is a mess. What happened to him?"

"The Laij got to him," Asel said impatiently.

"Then that settles his fate, and probably yours," the man replied harshly. He left the cavern and soon returned with another soldier. This man knelt and ran his fingers over her left calf, then took her right hand and inspected her thumb. Finally he felt the nape of her neck, where she had a thick welt from the nets in Aris Bay. As soon as he felt it, the man said, "Ocia. Escaped slave."

The soldier observed, "He has memorized every mark of every felon in Kelabreen. Now he has one less to keep in mind."

The soldiers took her and bound her back-to-back with Teloc. "What will be done with us?" she asked, as they fastened the thongs on her wrists.

"You know as well as I. Escaped slaves are always executed."

Asel clucked her tongue and said sarcastically, "I thought the Laij were enlightened and the Askirit barbaric."

"Bringing felons to justice is not barbaric," he said. "You also know we dislike public executions. The condemned in Kelabreen are taken to Ibala."

At the word "Ibala," she had felt Teloc's shoulder jerk slightly against hers. The soldier gave a dirty little laugh. "As a woman," he explained, "you will surely wish it had been a more simple execution."

During her years in Kelabreen, she had heard as many horror tales of the islands of Ibala as she had heard glorious descriptions of the city's pools. She clenched her teeth and determined she would survive the place, even if she lost half her limbs and her sanity.

The solders began roughly pushing Teloc and Asel toward the entrance so that they were forced to stumble in their bonds like two crippled spiders. "Drag along that half-dead Askirit," the soldier said. "His identity is as false as theirs."

They were taken to a dock close by and pushed onto the floor of a boat. They fell, legs sprawling, heads painfully striking against each other and the deck. New soldiers got in and sat with their feet next to Asel's and Teloc's faces, with Rycal lying in a heap behind them. Sailors shoved off and paddled slowly with the currents, which soon grabbed the boat and sped it forward.

"What is Ibala?" Asel asked, finding it difficult to speak with her face flat on the deck.

The sailor nearest her laughed and said, "You will soon know far more about it than I."

"I am Askirit," she said. "I know nothing about Ibala." She longed for any scrap of information that might help her survive.

"Only the condemned and those diseased with parlec are lowered into Ibala. But it was not always so. Once they were productive islands. But an epidemic of parlec infected so many people, they had to find a place to put them."

Asel remembered the parlec she had nearly touched in Kelabreen. Commonly thought to be highly contagious, the disease attacked the face and throat, grotesquely twisting, then slowly disintegrating everything above the shoulders. Ulcerated, bleeding nodules started to grow and never stopped until death. A parlec could never touch another person; anything he or she contacted was defiled; a parlec was considered already dead.

"Left without the normal constraints of civilization," the sailor was saying, "Ibala became a grisly place. They preyed on each other so much that eventually it became a convenient dumping ground for condemned felons."

"But do you throw the parlecs in with the condemned?" Asel asked. "They are innocent."

"Yes, but innocently deadly to the rest of us," the sailor said. "Most of the parlecs commit suicide as soon as they learn they have it. Clearly the decent thing to do. And Ibala is a powerful inducement to get on with it." He chuckled. "None of us, after all, want to touch them and take them out there on these little boats."

"But why was Ibala chosen in the first place?"

"Because once in, you can never get out," the sailor said, obviously relishing his opportunity to taunt her.

They were on a wide bay approaching the thundering sounds of a great waterfall. "Get too close, and we all go over," he said. "We drop you into the waterfall, till you hit a huge ledge. That's Ibala—means gash. It's like a giant's mouth behind the waterfall, extending deep into the formation—a vast lake with many islands. You can't escape. Ibala is huge, but there's no tunnel through its jaws. You can't climb up against the waterfall; go down it and you'd be battered on the rocks below."

Asel's cheekbone felt numb against the hard bottom of the boat, but she forced herself to ask, "How can you know so much if no one ever gets back?"

"Before the parlecs were dumped there, people came and went by ropes and ladders. As I said, it was a wonderful, productive place then, full of hunters and fishermen. But no one lowers ladders now, only more felons and parlecs. Yet the Laij of Kelabreen have a fascination about Ibala. Sometimes they'll paddle boats out here above the gash and listen for screams and wails."

Asel thought, More evidence of an advanced civilization! But she said aloud, "Why did you say I have the most to fear?" Instead of words, he moved his bare foot to her face and zigzagged his toes across it in the Laij version of Yette, indicating violent assault. Then he pressed her head down tight against the deck under his heel.

"Then give me a knife," she said.

The sailor laughed.

"Give me a knife," she repeated, trying to sound both persuasive and desperate. As she pleaded, the irony was not lost on her that her face was as flat as Rycal's had been, and her words as painfully uttered as when she had taunted him with the song of the pit. "You have my knife," she said. "It's a cheap Askirit blade. What will it matter to you?"

A voice from the other side of the boat said, "Give her the knife. I like that idea. We can listen to the felons getting a little surprise!" The sailor agreed with him, and then the men laughed.

Madness

Not until they had put Asel in a net did the sailor place the blade in her hand. "You'll also have the rope by which you are lowered. You can use it to hang the brigands," he said, and laughed again.

As the boat came dangerously near the edge of the waterfall, they lowered her into the water. She was swept over the edge and into the waterfall, sliding in a cage of ropes down the vertical surface. She ducked her head, trying to breathe, and swayed and twisted in the water's force. She hoped she would soon hit the ledge and wondered how the net was supposed to open above her.

She put her hand above her head and fingered the tight opening, wanting to be out very quickly when the rope went slack. She wondered if Teloc would land close by; perhaps they could defend themselves together. She had listened to the Laij placing Rycal in a net, and she thought he was likely dead by now, dangling somewhere near her. She was torn between the desire to escape whoever might attack her and wanting to make sure Rycal was no longer breathing.

A scream of agony rose from somewhere beneath her, then a shout of rage. The ropes continued their slow descent, the water pouring heavily over her so that she had difficulty breathing. The ropes were painfully abrasive. She heard a crazy sound below her, a bizarre voice laughing as if at some raucous joke. It sounded bird-like to her, but also dementedly human.

Her feet hit something solid. She reached up with both hands and tore at the opening, releasing the net while listening for someone near. The net fell at her feet, and she stepped cautiously but quickly away, in a defensive crouch, probing with her toes that she not go over the edge. "It's a lip out over nothing," the sailors had said. "Go the wrong direction, and you'll be swept away by the falls."

She thought Teloc had been lowered to her left. She probed

cautiously, thinking she had heard him touch down on the ledge. Tight, dagger in hand, ready to spring, she decided to chance a word. "Teloc," she called softly.

Footsteps came toward her, then his voice, barely audible. "Here."

She reached for his hand and in Yette said, "Stick close. We've a better chance together."

"Cut me some rope for a weapon," he tapped back. She followed him the few paces to where he had landed and cut a length.

"Rycal must be to the left," she said. "Let's make sure he's dead." They moved side by side, the sound of the water pounding the ledge. She felt the loose rope that must have been dropped to Rycal's net. She picked it up and followed it.

Only slightly discernible above the water's roar, she thought she heard a click of bone on stone. Then another. And another. Something was clicking and moving toward them. They stopped and waited, crouched, ready. The sounds kept moving toward the place she thought Rycal had been lowered. Click. Click. Then the noises stopped, and she heard an odd voice say, "Can you hear me?" Someone was talking to Rycal's body, then calling out, "Tegres. Alstek. Help me, please."

She heard feet moving from almost directly behind her, and she turned defensively. But the man went past her to the voice, and another man came from another direction. They converged and then struggled with something. "He's nearly dead," the strange voice said.

"I'll carry him," a man said, sounding strong and confident. "Tegres, you bring the net and the rope. Were there others?"

"Must have been," that first, odd voice said. "I'll keep looking for them." The click, click, pause began again, this time coming slowly toward Asel and Teloc. As it got closer, Asel thought it had to be a cripple. Did they throw those broken unfortunates into this place, too? Why would a cripple be searching for them?

When he was nearly upon them, she decided he posed no threat and demanded, "Why are you looking for us?"

"Because you are in a strange place, and you do not know the way," the voice said, high and quavery, but with a light-heartedness completely illogical in this place. "Do not fear because of the screams. They are just the madness of men who wish to taunt the Laij above. And do not shudder because of the tales of this place. We have murderers and brigands and parlecs. But isn't all of Aliare full of such people?"

—— Healing ——

On the third day Asel had been in Ibala, she was kneeling at midday with Tegres by the lake, opening clams. She struck one hard against a rock and pried it open. "But what of all the tales of the Gash, this horror at which all Kelabreen winces?"

"They did well to wince," Tegres said. "I was here in the grisly days. We watched for the Laij to lower someone, and I won't tell you all we did to them. Just believe the tales. The parlecs we chased into the water—most of them drowned. Any time was a good time to beat each other brainless! But then Auret came."

"But he's just a cripple."

"Yes. And on some he had no power at all. You can still get murdered in Ibala. But to those of us who were desperate, he was a powerful fragrance of hope. I can't explain, but it's unmistakable when he's near."

Asel said, "His laugh unnerves me sometimes."

Tegres chuckled. "It must have unnerved the Laij. They don't throw cripples in here, but they don't allow the insane among the slaves, either. They called him a madman, and they lowered him to the ledge. And he is crazy. The more I know him, the more he scares me. He's full of riddles—like he's from another world. In fact, some say they've seen light from the wounds on his head. Not the wounds, actually, but the blood— the blood that keeps seeping from them. I won't say I've seen it, but then again, I won't say I haven't, either."

They finished the task. Asel offered to carry back the pile of clams, holding them before her in a small sack that someone had made from Laij rope. She was trying to remember what Yosha had told her about an odd cripple he had known in Aris. As she carried her little burden up the trail, she heard Auret's canes moving ahead of her, so she quickened her pace. Drawing abreast of him, she asked, "Have you been caring for the parlecs again?"

"Yes. They are the most in need. Except for Rycal."

"But how can you do that? Not only the smell, but taking the risk—"

"Excuse me a moment," he said, and found a rock on which to sit. "My body does not like all this climbing." He sat until his breathing was easier, then said, "It is far from certain that parlecs are contagious. But you asked how I can do that."

He paused, then said, "I almost couldn't. I was lowered with a parlec—just the two of us, the mad cripple and the diseased outcast. He had the stink of it exuding heavily, and when I had freed myself of the net and had gotten my canes in my hands, I was exhausted. But this man's face and entire head was greatly misshapen so that he could not breathe properly. He had landed on the ledge face down and was moaning and choking, with the water spraying on his back. I did not want to help him. I could handle no more weakness, and I did not want to touch his disease. I didn't want to grip his loathsome face in my weak fingers and turn it out of the water."

He stopped speaking. Asel shifted her little sack of food and said, "Yes, I understand. What did you do?"

"Such things were the very reason I had come," he said

simply. "I helped him." The cripple then rose, gripping his canes, and started walking again.

Asel, slowly matching his pace, said, "Why do the people call you Auret?

"You know the story."

"Of course. Auret, the DawnBreaker."

"They named me Ute. But my mother, Chaisdyl, wanted a nickname better than Kecha. So she called me Auret."

"Where is your mother?"

"Chaisdyl is dead. She died in Aris during the Laij attack."

"You mean her throat was ripped by a merret!" Asel said, bitterness rising.

"The body is of little consequence," Auret said. "Others must help me now." They reached the main camp, where those allied with Auret worked and ate. He sat down heavily, again out of breath, but as she started to move away, he asked, "How did Rycal come to be so seriously injured?"

She turned back toward him, hesitating. Then she said, "He was the worst sort of traitor." She did not wait for his response but moved off toward the others.

Ropes

Twenty-three days it took for Rycal to heal enough to be able to talk. He suffered continuous head pains and often felt nauseated. Auret tended him, feeding him carefully even when he pushed away the food.

It was thirty days before Asel spoke to Rycal. She did so only because she was bringing water to Auret as he dressed Rycal's wounds, winding the cloth over his eyes. As she leaned down to place the skin of water by him, Auret asked Rycal, "Do you forgive the woman?"

Rycal gave a little moan, but Asel felt a deep inner one. What was this cripple doing? Rycal gave no answer, so she did. "Who is Rycal to forgive me?" she asked angrily. "He betrayed his people. He betrayed Eshtel himself with unspeakable coward-ice! He deserves to be executed."

Auret took the quick breath that signaled that he understood fully. He spoke slowly, emphatically. "All that is true. But Rycal cannot be forgiven unless he first forgives you."

Asel forced air through her teeth in an angry whistle. "Who wants him forgiven?" she said. "I want him for the pit! Do you believe in justice? What of all those who died because of him—Chaisdyl and a thousand others? What of the loss of the Askirit kingdom?" She could not believe this bizarre man recommended forgiveness for Tarn's worst traitor.

"It is good that justice is not always given," Auret said cryptically. "In Aliare, many treasures lie waiting in the darkness. But they can be found only in the wreckage."

"What are you talking about?" she demanded, her voice becoming more shrill than she realized. "Yosha told me about you—that you are probably crazed from your battered head. You bring a strange peace to a strange place—but don't make us all lose our minds!"

A hundred days after they had been lowered into the Gash, Rycal sought Asel out, finding her at the water's edge making darts from the bones of fish. He said to her, "I have forgiven you."

"So?" she said. "All that means is you'll die with another strange resolution clouding your mind. Forgiving me does nothing. Don't expect pardon from any Askirit but the crazed cripple!"

Rycal said, "Yes," as if he had expected her words. "I am not looking for pardon. I have been a reptile—all leather and teeth, rooting about on my belly. I had to be shattered. I had to be dropped like a chewed bone into this place before I could find the longing. But it's in me now." He spoke descriptively, not trying to persuade her but simply informing her of an event.

She stalked away from him, determined not to allow his words to affect her. And even days later, when Rycal started helping Auret care for the parlecs, she plotted how she should make him pay for his unspeakable crimes.

Only one thought repeatedly disturbed her about Rycal. She kept remembering how she had taunted him as he lay trussed on the floor, face flat against the wet rock, making him sing about the pit into which he would be cast. The image kept merging in her mind with the sadism of the Sledge of the Dead taunting the children, and with the taunts of the Laij guard who had so recently told her with relish all that awaited her in the Gash.

Asel was washing Auret's wounds, patting the tender ridges by his eyes. They were oozing blood and, if anything, seemed to be getting worse. "Is the pain greater?" she asked him.

"A little," he replied. "How is your project with the ropes?"

"I knotted one long enough to reach Tarn," she said lightly. "Everyone says I will die in the attempt. But if I cannot reach bottom on it, I will swim with the fish."

"The chasm is straight down," he said, "and all the water rushes into one long chute with great boulders. The water, they say, will rip the rope from your hands, or it will entangle you like a deadly net."

She couldn't tell if his words were a warning or a challenge. "I must return to Tarn," Asel said. "You say the body means little. So be it. I must take the chance."

As she stepped back from dressing his wounds, he patted her forearm in thanks. "And I will go with you," he said. "Sometimes we are called to disaster." He said this last with a sort of reckless joy, his croaking voice carrying an edge of exhilaration.

Asel was stunned; he couldn't be serious. If she were unlikely to succeed, how was he to climb down that endless rope and survive the chasm? Yet he insisted, despite her objections.

"Why must you go to Tarn?" she asked.

"To help the children," he said. "You keep telling me about the children you brought out of Dorte. Remember—you were the one who said the voices still speak to them."

It was not difficult for Asel to grasp the knotted rope and face the long descent. It was not overwhelming to have Auret tied on her back like some dead insect weighing her down—he was small, and she found him surprisingly light. What she found almost impossible was leaving Rycal working among the parlecs and welcoming the new wretches lowered in nets—leaving a Rycal at peace. He deserves no peace! she thought in frustration and anger. Yet she could no more go over to Rycal and put a blade between his ribs than cast Auret over the ledge and into the chasm. Somehow, either act seemed the same when she was near the crippled one.

They would have to get all the way down and find shelter before sierent, so they were forced to leave at mid-afternoon when the waters still rushed forcefully past the ledge. She adjusted her thick gloves she had made from the skins of small animals. She knew she could not slide rapidly, for the friction would burn her hands, and the gloves themselves might bind up and be pulled off.

Knot by knot, they made their way down. Asel's feet probed for ledges that might give her occasional respite. The further she descended and the waters blew and whipped at her, the more she wondered, Why am I swaying here, suspended with this crazy cripple tied to my back? The rope was soaked and slippery, and the extra weight made her keep sliding, sometimes rapidly over several knots before she could slow it down by wrapping her rope-burned legs around it.

She felt a ledge at her toes and tried to balance herself

forward to stand on it. She missed it, and the effort left her shaking.

She continued their descent, the wind buffeting them, until her feet came to rest on a wide ledge. She stood, resting her arms, rubbing one hand at a time on each side. She stayed just long enough to relieve the trembling of her limbs, then kicked off again, descending knot by knot. She heard the increasing roar of the chasm below, where all the water from the falls converged. As she neared it, she realized she was a bit off to one side. Good, she thought, her feet trying to find boulders on its edge.

She felt them being sucked into churning waters and her hands being pulled from the knots. Drenched, shaking, she knew she could not hold on for long. Auret was just shifting his weight on her back when the pressure suddenly lessened, and the waters now were rushing past on the sides, giving them air to breathe. She rested a moment, clinging motionless on the knots.

When she resumed moving down, she soon felt her feet come to rest a massive boulder free of the water. She rested on it for a time, then rappelled farther down, the water now completely to the sides. She did not know if this boulder was in the center of the cascade or at its edge. As they descended, eventually she felt rock beneath her feet. She edged onto it, then turned away from the water's sound and began crawling carefully onto what was either a ledge above nothing or a way of escape.

She slashed the bindings that held Auret to her back. "We have made it to solid rock," she said. "Hopefully, the way ahead leads to something beyond cliffs and precipices. We must find shelter quickly."

They moved up and down across the fissures and humps of the rockscape as rapidly as possible, Auret's arm over Asel's shoulders as she supported him. She wished she could simply carry him for greater speed, but she had not the strength. She sensed their search up and down boulders could be endless; how easily they could get caught by sierent! She kept putting Auret down to explore formations that might have shelters, but she found none.

The winds began to rise. On and on they limped, moving faster than was safe on this precarious, unknown way. The winds began to tear at them, and she didn't know whether to stop and search again for shelter or to keep moving. At one point, she thought the ridges on a narrow width between boulders indicated a trail. It ascended, which was a good sign, so she followed it.

Sierent now was beating at them, tearing at her fingers. She held tightly to Auret's shoulders as the water's pressure began flattening them against the rocks. Her hand grasped a crack, and she pulled up, hoping they would find a cave. But she felt only boulders.

Now, not only the winds of sierent tore at them, but the waters as well. The full force of sierent began to roar all around them, deafening, drenching, tearing her fingers and feet from their holds and finally lifting their bodies into the aerated, whirling waters. Asel and Auret spun like chips in the froth, up, up, up into the powerful winds and sea.

Asel awoke and immediately felt deep bruises all over her body. She felt the most pain on her leg, and reached down to feel ridges of coagulated blood from a deep gash.

Not far away, she heard something moving toward her. "Are you awake?" Auret's hoarse voice asked, sounding stranger than ever in its great weariness.

"How can we be alive?" she asked. She thought they surely must have entered some other world.

"A shelter was mercifully near," Auret replied.

"But we were sucked into sierent!"

"Yes," Auret said, "sierent is fatal. So is the chasm. But you forget that I have gone through sierent and a greater chasm long ago."

Chapter 10.

Enre Suspicions

As Asel sat down as a guest in an old Enre's small dwelling, she let out a very deep sigh, as if in one exhalation she would expel all the days and nights she could not take an unguarded breath. For nearly a year their arduous journey had kept her always on edge, listening for the Laij, listening for suspicious sounds. When they had to move quickly, she carried Auret, who seemed unconcerned about dangers. Within earshot of the Laij, on boats and in villages, he would move slowly forward with crudely fashioned sticks, tapping out the shaky pattern she had come to know so well.

"I have a little kek," the woman said, "and some grel roots, freshly dug and washed."

Asel took the skin bottle from her hand and asked, "Have the Laij ever been here?"

"This far from the cities? We are a world away! And they wouldn't come with our men and Enre patrolling the crags. They're too busy trying to retake Aris."

"I've been gone a very long time. When I was taken by the Laij, Hrusc was attacking our forces."

"Hrusc!" She said the word with a violent expulsion of air through her teeth. "He's clever—more clever than Yosha and Varial combined. Why does Eshtel always make of the nastiest one the military genius? He should have made Hrusc stupid as a slug!"

"Maybe," Auret said, "Eshtel made him to long for the light, and to use his cleverness to find it."

"Hrumph! A priest's answer," the woman said. "Hrusc was a priest, remember? And now a self-proclaimed king and high priest both."

"When did he do that?" Asel asked.

"After he took Aris. He let Yosha and Varial take the city first, then crushed them. Oh, Hrusc's clever. He had left only a token force at the Skull. When the Laij invasion began to ascend the cliffs, Hrusc's men fired some shots, then disappeared. They let the Laij take the Skull. But while they were securing it against counterattack, Hrusc's men were placing nets below them. Then they released plenty of female chibdys. The keitr raged out of their caves and slaughtered countless numbers of Laij troops. Those who fled toward Hrusc's men hit the nets, which were full of tangled keitr. Laij escaped into empty caves, but then keitr soon flew back to their homes to spend the night. Nice companions! By the time the Laij regrouped, Hrusc had control of Aris. With the capital city, the temple, and even the King's House, he could have proclaimed himself anything!"

Asel felt greatly mixed emotions as she listened to the details of the Laij defeat, which thrilled her, and Hrusc's victories, which had crushed her own hopes. "And what about Yosha and Varial?" she asked. "What happened to them?"

"Yosha regrouped his forces, but Varial was lost. No one found her body. We waited a full year before naming a new Varial. She is Nesca, you know."

Asel bit down on the root and chewed, breathing deeply. Nesca, the Enre who'd always had her own ambitions. "I know her, but I didn't know she had been made the new Varial," Asel said. She took a long, slow drink. "So, is there a new queen?" she asked. "Did Yosha marry Varial?"

"Hrumph! Not yet!" she said with disgust. "Now that the other Varial let her urges control her brain, Nesca is probably concocting wedding scents right now." The woman made lascivious smacking sounds with her lips. "Never a Varial married in millennia, and now it's queen and consort!"

Asel grimaced and took another bite of the root. She chewed in silence, then said, "We need supplies, and we must evade the Laij. How can we make contact with Enre in the crags?"

After getting the supplies, Asel thanked the old woman and rose to leave. She was unable, however, to resist a parting shot. "Varial the queen married Yosha out of duty," she said. "It was an affair of state, to give hope to the nation."

At this pronouncement, made quietly but with conviction, the old Enre stopped fastening the pack she had filled for them. "Oh?" she said. "Did she now? Strictly for the Enre, eh? And I suppose she never did warm up to it."

Asel took the pack, said her thanks, and left with Auret for the crags.

—— Tears ——

As he moved with his men toward the camp, Yosha held in his left hand a zeskret with a broken wing. The bird lay motionless and warm, trapped by Yosha's fingers, straining against them only when he took a misstep and jerked his arm to regain his balance. Someone had heard it flapping across the trail and had brought it to Yosha, knowing his nickname and his love for the bird.

He enjoyed the distraction, thinking back to his boyhood when he would listen to their calls above his village. He disliked thinking of the choices before him, simply because he was not at all sure what the best plan might be. Hrusc was going to lose Aris—that much was clear. The Laij loss of both Aris and legions of men at the Skull had merely spurred them to begin building another massive army.

Yosha saw no way Hrusc could defend Aris, nor how he could strengthen his own meager forces. Wearily, he moved toward the camp, the broken zeskret in his hand, wishing for the old intensity and clarity that had given him the bird's name.

Bralin's voice greeted him as he entered the camp. The bird moved, and Bralin asked what he was holding. "A zeskret," he said. "Hurt somehow."

Bralin grunted sympathetically. "May it soon regain its wings."

"Sooner than us," Yosha said. "We trailed Hrusc's troops toward the sea. Probably a village raid. Any news here?"

"Varial is in the camp." Yosha detected something unusual in Bralin's voice, as if something were afoot. "She's in the cleft and wants to talk to you privately."

Asel was sitting alone when she recognized Yosha's characteristic gait, the swish of his soles warily testing the trail. But what had once been an impetuous pace was now subdued, even hesitant. As his footsteps began the last, short ascent, she heard a quick, nearly inaudible sigh. He comes to meet Nesca, she thought. A sigh can mean many things. She wondered why she felt so awkward, even timid. How was that possible when they had so often shared the waters of pleasant coves, the aromas of spicy foods, the passions of their bodies, and the threats of their enemies?

He was nearly in front of her. "Welcome, Varial," he said, "What news?"

She swung her foot over pebbles, making a scraping sound. His voice was courteous and warm, no more, no less. She hesitated another moment, then said, quiet as the breath of a sleeping child: "Yosha."

She heard him take a quick breath. He seemed to step back

from her. Did she imagine that? "I have escaped from Kela-breen," she said. "I've touched wonders, spoken their language, probed their mysteries. But always I planned my escape. Nothing could keep me from Tarn."

Once, Yosha had been standing on a dock when a huge wave had crested and unexpectedly struck him waist high, the warm water knocking him down and drenching him. Yosha now felt similarly jolted. Asel! It had to be Asel!

He could say nothing. Nothing at all. He found he had actually stepped back, and now he forced himself to step toward her. He moved cautiously, as in a strange dream, the zeskret in his left hand, his right hand outstretched toward her.

His fingers touched the side of her face, and as he felt the contours of her features, he gently flattened his palm against them, moving it over the ridges and valleys of her eyes and cheeks. Touching her skin was like touching moments of their past, touching flesh he had so often longed for, grieved for, but now—inexplicably—he found that flesh still alive. "How incred-ible and wonderful!" he said.

Asel grasped the hand on her face and led it to her lips. She kissed his fingers even as she reached out with her other hand to caress his cheek. For long moments they explored the soft wonders of their faces, fingers spreading the lotion of their tears. Then they kissed, standing together tight as a stone.

"We must not crush the bird," Yosha said apologetically. "It's a zeskret with a broken wing."

Asel reached down to touch it and felt the quick pulse at its throat. "It will fly again," she promised. "Swift and invincible!"

"You're the invincible," he said. "It appears the Enre erred in naming a new Varial."

"They did not err. I was gone too long."

"She is Nesca, you know."

"Yes. I have spoken to her, and I have blessed her." She made a wry whistling sound. "I'm told you've been less hasty. I've heard of no new queen."

He put both hands to her face. He pushed his nose playfully against hers, then kissed her hard, his hand outstretched on the back of her head, fingertips rubbing rhythmically over the strands of her long, thick hair.

—— Auret ——

Yosha sat stroking the wings of the zeskret, Asel beside him. Neither participated much in the heated strategy discussion around them. Asel had been greeted ecstatically by Maachah, Mosen, and Kark. Breea, who had come from working with the children, had rushed up to her and had pressed her pencray medallion against Asel's cheek in the Askirit gesture of filial love.

But the exuberance and amazement had quickly turned to the urgencies of war. "Aris may be invaded tomorrow," Solket said. "Hrusc will commit most of his forces to defend the city— and we could attack the Skull!"

Maachah objected, "I'll fight Hrusc's abominable Stuugkt, but we've never attacked another Askirit unprovoked. If we're to unite all Tarn under Yosha and Asel, we want the men who served Hrusc to remember that."

The discussion stormed on. Yosha's silence belied his inner exuberance. He kept tapping out personal messages in Yette to Asel, unable to get enough of her story.

The men presented arguments for various strategies: capturing villages, capturing Hrusc, positioning themselves between Aris and the Skull to split Hrusc's forces. Yosha finally sided with the latter idea—they would try to divide his forces and then attack both halves. They were discussing the plan's implementation when Asel said, "I hear Auret coming."

The sound of his canes was even slower and weaker than

Yosha remembered. Beside the cripple walked another man with heavy steps. Yosha wondered how he should thank Auret for saving Asel from sierent and probable rape on Ibala. Strangely, he found himself resenting the man; Auret had also healed and freed Rycal, and he had confounded holy worship in the Tolas.

As the two men made their slow way toward the group, the discussion ceased. Mosen tapped out on Yosha's wrist, "A remarkable thing: Belstin has suddenly started using Yette so hard my wrist hurts! I've not sensed him so forceful since he was caged!"

"Maybe it's Asel's return," Yosha signaled back, thinking of his own astonishment.

"He noticed her no more or less than Kark or Maachah. This agitation is different. My Holy Wreck is exclaiming, 'Light! Light! Light! Hope is here!' He rushes through psalms about light and power and grace, rippling over my hand, digging into it on the accents."

"Why?"

"It must be Auret," Mosen tapped out. "He's exulting that Auret is coming toward us."

The two men were closer now, a clatter of canes and accompanying heavy steps. Asel called out to him, "Auret!"

The strained, high voice of Auret said, "I have with me a captain who has been serving Hrusc. But his soul is troubled, and he yearns for the light. He wants to join you."

Asel said, "If you vouch for him, Auret, we will embrace him!"

Yosha was not nearly so sure, but since Asel had spoken, he did not contradict her. Mosen was tapping out on Yosha's wrist, "Belstin is shaking; his fingers are dancing across my arm like the voices of the singers in the Tolas. He says, 'Glory surrounds! Glory above! The dark falls away! Glory! Glory! Glory!'"

Belstin suddenly leaped up and ran to Auret, then knelt to clasp his legs, nearly toppling the spindly cripple. The trembling maniac said not a word, but Auret laughed and awkwardly got both of them settled and seated. Belstin kept hanging on to the cripple's legs, and Auret said to him, "My body has been bludgeoned by ute and sierent, and your body has been devastated by darkness. I tremble on my sticks; you tremble within. Belstin, I have laughed at the darkness, and you have ridiculed it. What more is asked than to be faithful in devastation? To glory in the shatterings?"

Yosha stood, and the zeskret fluttered a little in his hand. He walked to them and said the ancient phrase: "Glory out of wreckage!"

Auret produced a wry whistle. "Mosen's Holy Wreck has been freed into silence."

Yosha did not understand what he meant.

"What is in your hand?" Auret said.

"A zeskret. It's hurt."

"I sensed that," Auret said. Yosha felt his crabbed hand touching his and lifting the bird. "May I have him for a time?"

"If you wish."

Far below, Asel could hear aurets rising from the coasts, announcing the dawn. She said to Delin and Nen, "His name is 'Auret.' As a little child, Auret lived through sierent. Battered and crippled, his wounds are as painful as his words. But he is like his name; he brings the dawn."

Delin walked away. Breea said, "Delin longs for the 'freedom' of Dorte. He resents the military training and memorization. On Dorte he was an impish urchin, free to roam. He complains he was forced to leave."

Asel made a hissing sound connoting incredulity. "He followed us, looking for trouble and food!"

"Cold currents run in Delin," Breea said. "Cold as the voices taunting him. He says he must take Nen back—that his people are looking for him."

This time Asel hissed loudly and made a warning sound. "Keep him away from the boy," she said.

"They're inseparable," Breea said.

Asel sensed the pain in her voice, for once Nen and Breea had been inseparable, but now she was Enre and Delin could whisper adventures in the smaller boy's ears as they explored caves and coves. "Nen is still close as a burr to you," Asel said.

"But I'm like a mother," Breea said. "He's always trying to break away."

Auret was moving toward Nen and asked, "May I see?"

Asel wondered if Nen would be able to understand Auret's broken voice. She walked toward them and heard the little boy moving something, then noticed a tiny glow. She leaned closer to Nen. "What is it?" she asked.

Breea answered, "Carrion beetle."

Asel tightened her nostrils and lips; carrion beetles lived in decay; some were luminous, but the Askirit never fed their eyes on their light. Breea said, "Nen loves playing with them. Delin finds them for him."

Asel stared at the little glow moving slowly in the blackness, disappearing into a fold of clothing, then reappearing and moving in a curving line, searching in a circuitous route to nowhere. "The beetle is death," Asel said quietly, absently, as she stared at its movements.

"But light is unchanged by death," Auret said. He put his hand next to Nen's and let the beetle crawl onto his finger and across his palm.

—— Scents ——

Yosha noticed that Asel's voice was a splendid thing. It had the depth of one who has lived at the sharpest edges, yet it was kind, often rippling with an undercurrent of laughter and double meanings. She seemed to be wonderfully at peace with Breea, Auret, and the children—candid and full of energy and purpose.

Yet he was puzzled. During the day before, they had embraced and shared experiences and been inseparable. But then, as night drew close, she had left him abruptly. He had been talking to Mosen; Asel had touched him lightly on the wrist with a signal—the flip of two fingers on the bone. It meant "see you in the morning," a signal they'd often used years before. When he had turned, she had been gone.

It was mid-morning before Asel finally came to him. She announced, "We have a journey to make."

"What do you mean?"

She walked him out of earshot of the others and said, "Did you wonder why I did not come to you last night?" She touched his cheek and then said in Yette on his palm, "I was not going to get cheated by fast groping in a scentless troop camp!" She said it with a flourish of her fingers, and with high spirits placed a small pack into his hands. "Our trysting cave is not so far that we cannot make it well before sierent."

She raced her thumb and forefinger over his cheek in a provocative message, and he responded with a playful race of his knuckles over her neck. "It's traditional for the bride to lead," he said.

As they made their way across the terrain, Asel carried a much larger pack than Yosha's. "Let me carry it for you," he said.

"A slave of the Laij knows how to carry a far heavier pack than this," she said. By mid-afternoon, they had covered a considerable distance, and she stopped at a pool at the base of a waterfall. "I have fresh clothing in the pack," she said, and they washed and swam. The water refreshed Yosha; when Asel splashed water at him, he tried to catch her, but she bounded from the water and handed him the clothing she had brought.

They were soon at the narrow ledge he well remembered from their wedding night. Asel set the boulder precariously, as she had the first time, then led him to the falls and ducked behind them, pulling him in after her. They walked deep into the cave.

Then she kneeled and pulled the furs from her large pack, spreading them out on the floor. From his pack she removed several little bags that smelled of dried meats and spicy herbs. "I made many meals for my Laij masters," she said, "most of which you would hate. But I discovered some of their foods you may like."

She set the meal between them, and as they partook, he found the mixture of the new foods with familiar ones delicious and satisfying. He complimented her numerous times, and she said in good humor, "Remember, it is traditional for the bride to prepare for the groom."

"But when did you make all these preparations? And what if you had found me married to the new Varial?"

"Then I would have cast it all into the sea!" She paused and added, "Then again, perhaps I would have fought very hard for you!" Then she broke open her personal bridal scent, saying, "You know the custom. You experience this scent only in this place."

The perfume reached his nostrils and he said, "I do not have the groom's scent."

"Nor did I bring it for you, which means we must come back here very soon." She laughed softly, her slightly broken laugh that Yosha loved. It was both conspiratorial and sensual, an invitation echoing off the cave walls.

He wondered, having heard all she had been through, how she could still have such a laugh. He leaned to her and sniffed at the bridal scent on her skin. He raced his fingers over her arm, saying in Yette, "The bride is fulfilling all the customs—and more."

"But this time," she said, "it is no obligation."

Yosha awakened first to the loud roaring of the waterfall at the entrance. Reaching over, he drew his wife's hand to his face.

He unfolded her fingers and kissed them slowly, one by one, sliding his nose and lips against the slight moisture in the creases. She was curled up tightly, her knees blocking him from her. He sat up beside her. She luxuriously uncurled and began to stretch, so he nuzzled her middle, knowing her body's warmth created a pungent sleep scent he found pleasant.

She patted his cheeks and ruffled his hair. They lay listening to the waterfall and talking for a long time about many things. They talked about Kelabreen and Rycal and the Laij culture. They spoke of the enigmatic Auret. "He gave the zeskret back to me this morning," Yosha said.

"Was it better?"

"It flew from my hand," he said.

Asel drew a quick breath, meaning she had expected it would. "Auret takes a great deal of getting used to," she said. "But listen to him carefully. Even his strangest statements are true in ways you would never suspect."

They spoke, too, of Hrusc and the coming invasion, their words becoming grimly serious.

But at one point Yosha told a silly joke. Asel giggled. She was surprised at the sound that bubbled out of her and realized that for a moment, at least, she felt safe enough in this cave to act like a little girl.

"You are not supposed to giggle!" Yosha teased. "You are too important a personage."

"That's my first giggle in decades," she protested. "And just what will you do to me if I giggle again?" she said, taunting. "I am about to. Will it be worth it?"

He wrestled with her, and they both fell laughing onto the furs.

The force of the waterfall had considerably lessened by the time she asked, "Did you not crave a woman's body all these years? In men's eyes, you have been free. Even a king on the run still gets his pick of the beautiful young women."

"I craved both you and your body," he said.

"But the raids—I know about them. Many young Askirit women were brought here to wed the soldiers. I would think it was a considerable temptation."

"I touched none of them," Yosha said.

"You don't have to lie," she said, "and you do not have to tell me. I bring this up only to say I will never fault you for what may have happened."

"I touched none of them!" he insisted. "I cannot say I believed you were alive. I cannot say I was noble. But I was so stricken with grief at losing both Aris and you, that my passion has been only to keep the hope alive."

The Absurdity

Asel listened to Nen's little feet running across the encampment toward the sounds of Auret's sticks. She knew Delin felt jealous, for in the past Nen had always run to him. "He's my littlest brother," Delin would say, a pronouncement of dubious validity.

She listened to Nen enthusiastically chattering, feeling very grown-up because Auret let him swab his wounds. Asel wondered if Nen's efforts were really helpful, but Auret assured the little boy he wanted his help.

Then she heard Delin trying to get Nen to come away with him. Nen declined. Delin tried to cajole him. Nen showed some temper and fiercely insisted on helping the cripple.

Delin said, "Someone else will wash his wounds. You know Asel or Breea will do it." The younger boy ignored him, so Delin added, "Soon we will return to Dorte, all of us, and there you will have beetles enough to light the whole camp! We'll run free! We won't have to do all this memorizing and chanting and practicing and making food for everyone else!"

The little boy did not respond but busied himself with the cloths.

Auret said, "Delin, do you want to go back to Dorte? Then we must go together, for two are needed where the darkness is greatest."

Delin angrily retorted, "I don't need a guide! I know the place much better than you!"

"Perhaps." Auret then turned from him and started talking to Nen, thanking him for his care as the little boy wrapped his beetle in the damp rags he had been using to wipe Auret's face. Then he turned back to Delin and said to him, "When Asel and the others came to Dorte, what did the voices say to you?"

Asel waited with great interest to hear the boy's answer, but he did not give one.

Auret stood and awkwardly got his sticks under him. "What the voices say now is no better," Auret said, balancing himself carefully. "But when you hear a voice that says you should help your little brother, listen with an eager ear." He started walking away, but called back, "Don't worry, Delin. We won't steal Nen from you."

Asel listened as Auret moved up the main trail, calling out for Maachah. Then she heard them talking in the distance.

Not long after, Maachah sought her out and said, "We will soon be making crucial decisions. But I need you to support me on something even more important." That's all he said, and then he hurried away.

She walked with Breea to the meeting place. It was a wide bowl of flat sandstone, littered with boulders of all sizes. Asel hopped up on one shaped like a set of shoulders. She always felt comfortable on this one and listened as the men and Enre gathered.

Bralin began by describing the situation in Aris. "The Laij have massive armies north and south of Aris, ready to attack," he said. "Hrusc has prepared well, with new, nasty surprises and ambush techniques. Yet his men still expect to be overwhelmed; a thousand ships will invade the bay."

"Now's the time to move," Solket said. "The Skull is cut off and without supplies. We could take it from Hrusc a notch at a time—the lower caves right before sierent, before they can counterattack." The discussion heated up, with contrasting plans and charges of foolishness or timidity or recklessness.

Maachah spoke up. "I have a matter of considerable urgency to discuss," he said.

"What is it?" Yosha asked.

"At this moment, one factor is most important of all," he said. "It is this: We must be at our worship and our prayers."

The statement drew only silence. It was an awkward silence, coming after so much heated talk. Solket finally spoke up and said, "That's fine, but we did our duty by that just before taking up these positions. What's urgent is to decide how to attack—before it's decided for us!"

Maachah chuckled, as if someone had just whispered a joke in his ear. "Solket, were you so long gone from Tarn that you forget the Absurdity?"

Asel knew well what Maachah was referring to and repeated in her mind the saying from the liturgy. "The cosmos turns on this absurdity: your little prayers."

"Pray all you wish on the run, priest," Solket retorted. "But sierent is not far off. If we do not act, we will all be absurdly dead."

Auret asked, "Is prayer, then, mere fog rising?" It was the first time Asel had heard his voice in a gathering. "I have seen a battered remnant subdue a world through it," he stated.

Someone grunted, an odd sound that was perhaps derision. Asel said clearly, "Let us be at our worship and prayers!" and slid off her boulder, landing with a little thump.

Everyone waited for Yosha's voice, and he said, "Maachah, you are the one with the urgency. Waste no time at it."

Maachah led them in a ritual, selecting portions of the liturgy relating to the power of light in battle. "The illusions of evil will be disrobed," he said. "Light will penetrate every crevice, and evil will be trapped in the abyss."

After everyone had participated in the worship, he concluded by saying, "Praise is a feast beyond the spears of enemies."

The Liturgy of Hope always ended with the singing of one word over and over again: "Kelerai, kelerai, kelerai." Kelerai— the magnificent reversal, when the waters blasted out of Aliare on their way to the planet's surface, roaring out of darkness with unsurpassed power. Their singing began halfheartedly, but as the words lifted the triumphant melody, their voices grew stronger and more militant. "Kelerai, kelerai, kelerai," they sang, stretching out the word at one moment, and then singing it fast the next.

Asel stood next to Auret, hearing his strange voice nearly veer off into that bizarre laugh—almost, she thought, as if he had in his mind already joined kelerai and was triumphantly being propelled up through Aliare's darkness to the light.

When the singing was over, Auret touched Asel's forearm and in Yette said to her, "What was the greatest danger this day? Hrusc? The Laij? No. The greatest danger was that we might have been kept from this moment."

Chapter 11.

——— Spears ———

"Asel, have you ever feared the light?" Breea asked quietly. "They say the unworthy person shudders beneath it or writhes like a salted worm!" They and several other Enre were repairing their weapons and clothing in a shelter high in the crags. Breea swished her open fingers across each other, making the warning sounds of distress. "The ritual says if you're unworthy, the light destroys what you most love."

"Yes," Asel replied. "And it also says, 'Under light, the contaminated shrivel. They turn to dust.'"

"But we're all unworthy!" Breea said. "How, then, can we go through death to face the light?"

Asel reached over and clasped Breea's fingers, stopping their swishing sound. "I've always longed for the light; I never thought to fear it," she said. "Yet I have often felt unworthy. Perhaps when the light comes—"

A shout in the distance interrupted her. "Spears!" Enre sentries were shouting. "Thousands of men and spears!"

Asel and Breea raced down the trail, beginning to hear the clattering of spears below. How could the Laij have gotten so high into the crags so quickly? The sounds advanced steadily upward, striking fear even in the Enre.

"Melse!" Asel called out. It was the command for a maneuver only the Enre knew existed. They practiced it often against imaginary foes; now they moved downward toward live foes, hugging depressions and crawling through gullies to avoid the spears striking around them. Soon they were nearly at the Laij front lines.

Asel huddled far into a deep cavity that she hoped would not be detected by sweating, climbing spearmen. Around her clattered spears, spears, spears! Then the clattering was gone, replaced by the sounds of feet pounding past. She let a score of them by her, then blended in with their march, making an insect sound to alert other Enre that she was now moving with the Laij. Sounds of various insects and birds pinpointed the forty Enre as they moved among the wide ranks of men with spears and atlatals.

She threw high into the air a handful of small, heavy, serrated wheels. They fell nearly straight down and landed where she had aimed, among a thick knot of Laij soldiers. The impact wounded several and caused others to lash out against each other with their short swords.

An Enre threw over Laij heads a muck that, when it struck a rock near a precipice, made an ugly, moaning sound. It also gave off a stench that, though not poisonous, seemed dangerous; men escaping it crashed into comrades on the precipice, who fell from it.

Another Enre deftly tripped an enemy so that he struck another Laij with his sword, then was struck by someone else in turn.

Asel picked up spears from fallen Laij and cast them across to parallel ranks; volleys of spears came back. Beneath a sheer wall, packed tightly among the enemy, she quietly struck with her deadly hands, always throwing her foe against another to increase confusion, then fading away.

The Enre kept moving with the enemy, sowing fear and chaos. "Wraiths of the pit!" men shouted, but Laij officers, loudness masking their own uncertainty, yelled, "No! Mere Askirit enemies!" Ranks broke in numerous places and some Laij conscripts fled. Yet most kept climbing and casting spears, retrieving them as they gained ground ahead. They seemed to be sweeping toward the Skull, untold thousands moving as steadily as the sea. Asel knew it would take more than forty Enre to stop these thousands.

Ahead of her, a man screamed and clawed at his chest. Keitr! Someone was loosing keitr at the spearmen. Screams from hundreds of men getting hit rushed like violent waves through the ranks. Could this be Yosha attacking the Laij? Or Hrusc's men? Either way, she and the other Enre were now in the wrong place. She signaled loudly, hoping she was heard over the chaos of screams and panicked commands.

In the distance, she heard avalanches begin their gathering roars, accelerating as they crashed into masses of balanced boulders. She wondered if the ones she and Yosha had set to protect the Spider was one of them; the others must have been set by the Stuugkt.

She found a ridge that veered to the right, then steeply down. Sounds of spears and keitr assaulted her ears as she dropped down a sheer rock chute into a narrow entrance to a tunnel.

Within, she found several Enre already there and soon more than twenty, Breea among them. The others must find their own way, she thought, for she was determined to rendezvous with Yosha.

They set out at a brisk pace toward other passageways. At intersections, they split up, and soon it was Breea and Asel rushing together through turns and angles they had often traversed before.

Where five passageways came together, they paused briefly. Asel took the usual precaution of yelping and Breea hurriedly cast stones into the intersection. But men lying in ambush had concealed themselves cleverly, and as Asel and Breea passed, they leaped out and struck the women heavily from behind, throwing them down hard upon the wet stone floor.

* * *

Yosha, facing great numbers of climbing Laij, heard a keitr hit a man behind him; the man's scream mixed ominously with the sounds of spears clattering below. They were trapped between the Stuugkt above and the Laij below.

"We're caught like gnats between two hands," Maachah said, slapping his palms together.

"The spears sound like ardeddd drumming on all the crags of Tarn," Mosen said, his voice sounding odd coming from his position deep down in a crevice. "Releasing the avalanche will be like throwing a rock into the sea."

Nevertheless, Yosha braced his shoulder under the precariously balanced boulder and heaved upward. He felt it move easily, as if it were a great, hollow drum; it turned a little, then crashed heavily into the next set of boulders and began the great avalanche that they had set along the many entrances to the Spider.

They did not wait to listen; Yosha followed his companions into a slit of an opening that led into the caverns. They raced through the passageways toward a rendezvous point, with Yosha hoping Asel would meet them there. Kark was close behind him saying, "Reports are that Hrusc abandoned Aris; he's massing all his forces to protect the Skull and has thousands of traps set for the Laij as they climb."

"Then why is he attacking us, so far from the Skull?" Yosha asked.

Maachah said from behind them, "Maybe Hrusc knows he has us trapped. He could easily penetrate these caverns and kill us, or seal us in and take us later."

"But why is Hrusc fooling with us?" Kark demanded as they arrived at the body of the Spider. "It's the Laij who will swallow him and the last of the Askirit nation!"

Greetings from their men drowned out Yosha's muttered

response: "Does Hrusc care? How can someone so brilliant throw away everything that matters?"

—— Dreams ——

Asel lay hobbled and her hands bound before her. Stuugkt guards stood thick around her, alert for any sudden movements by this legendary Varial. But she was unaware of them. She was dragging herself from sleep, like a choi struggling to pull itself from the mouth of a predator. A strange mixture of alarm, wonder, terror and awe pumped through her. In the night, dreams had invaded her mind, but she was remembering only fragments of them. She recalled beings of light shimmering and alive; dark creatures gasping in rage; Dorte in ferment. She felt some awful momentum had begun, something wondrous yet dreadful, something beyond spears and keitr, Laij and Stuugkt.

She managed to sit up, and, heedless of the guards, loudly cried out to the light. She began interceding for the world, defiantly ramming her hands against the rock wall.

Oblivious to her bonds, she demanded the powers of light invade her body and Aliare. "Stop this suffocation!" she cried out. "Open! Illumine us!" Her hands rubbed against the bonds with Enre skill and suddenly they broke free. She stood slowly, still praying fervently, her hands grasping at the walls, then pushing against them mightily, her voice assaulting the stone and echoing down the corridors.

Stretching up, she felt two stalagmites projecting up; she reached out and gripped them like two horns. She twisted them, wrenching and lifting the great horns of the world up and up, demanding the light invade, refusing to accept the clammy, inevitable chaos soaking her spirit.

With the strength of her arms, she pulled herself up, then let her body hang from the projections, demanding in a loud voice, "Invade! Release! Free us!"

Suddenly she was aware of a blade's point against her arm. She regained her footing, becoming aware of the guards standing around her in a tight half circle, blades poised at her. She sank to a sitting position and then said to them, "Stop your shaking. I was not praying to escape from you." And she allowed them to refasten the bonds on her hands.

"We're trapped here in these tunnels," Kark said. "Every time we send out a sortie, no matter how distant the exit, the men run into Laij or Stuugkt." They were moving along a little used passageway that angled down from the heights.

"When the men do go out, they bring back terrible stories," Yosha said, "bizarre tales of a new plague."

"What tales?" Mosen asked.

"They say that suddenly, like the coming of sierent, the plague is everywhere entering men's bodies."

"But what is so bizarre?"

"Men start shaking," Kark said, "and soon they make an alien sound. It is said it sounds like a stone humming."

"*That's* bizarre," Mosen said.

They were descending a narrow ledge, and Yosha reached over to steady Maachah.

"Watch it here," Kark said. "Crumbles easily."

Yosha touched Mosen's side and said, "Single file. Careful with Belstin."

"A plague victim makes strange noises and starts breathing fast and deep," Kark said. "It sounds as if his guts are churning, making weird rumbling sounds. Suddenly, the man will rush to someone else and grab him, holding him as tight as a vise, smothering the poor wretch. When it's all over, both are dead. And when you pry the bodies apart, the odors are nauseating."

Solket made a rumbling sound of disgust from deep in his throat. "I've concluded it's all wartime hysteria," he said.

"But the reports are all the same!" Kark retorted.

"Of course they are!" Solket said. "Some crazed soldier tells the story, and it spreads everywhere. That's what happens when men are dying and terrified."

"But they also say," Kark added, "that the dead lie about like gutted fish ... that the plague is striking everyone, Laij and Askirit, priest and soldier!"

Maachah declared loudly, "Furies exploding out of Dorte! That's what they are!" He asked them to slow the pace a little, then put his hand on Yosha's shoulder and said, "The plague's unnatural! Can't you tell how thick the air is?"

"Belstin always said they were coming," Yosha said, trying to inject a touch of humor. But Kark agreed with Maachah, saying, "It's the old prophecy. The furies have been let loose to enter the worst among us so that they can smother the best!"

"Let's not cry furies yet," Solket objected. "Aliare's full of voracious parasites with odd feeding habits. Remember—the furies were blamed for the Laij merrets."

When they reached the vault of the Spider, they found three Stuugkt prisoners being interrogated. Their hands were tied tightly behind their backs; the guards had pulled one out from the others and were asking about Hrusc's troop deployment and the avalanches and traps they had set. He refused to speak.

"Why did Hrusc leave Aris so quickly?" Yosha demanded. "Does he think he can hold the Skull when the Laij are taking the rest of Tarn?" He asked the soldier where Hrusc had set his first line of defense and how many of the Stuugkt were this far forward.

The man responded to none of his questions or dire threats. Yosha was about to ask Kark to persuade him when he heard a strange sound in front of him, a sound alien to Aliare, dull yet menacing.

"He's got the plague!" Kark shouted. "Put more ropes on

him!" Yosha heard the guards grabbing at something and now could hear rumblings in the man's guts. A guard cursed in a terrified voice and cried out, "He's gotten his arms in front of him!"

Kark ran toward them, shouting, "Get a telc on him!" But as Yosha heard Kark running forward, he realized the prisoner was moving toward him. Yosha dropped to the floor and brought his knees to his chin, ready to kick him away. As he hit the position, he heard Belstin scrambling forward and breaking his silence, shouting as he had so often in the past, "Fiends! Gheials in his guts!" He heard Belstin's body collide with the prisoner's and both crashed on the hard surface.

"Belstin!" he heard Mosen cry.

With the others, Yosha rushed to the sounds of the scuffling. A leg swung hard against him and nearly knocked him down. He grabbed at it and yanked. Mosen was pleading, "Get them apart! Get them apart!" As Yosha clawed for a grip between the prisoner and Belstin, he felt other hands grabbing at the jerking bodies. He pried with all the strength of his fingers and arms, but in a surprisingly short time, both bodies were still.

"Get them apart!" Mosen was still yelling. "Get them apart!" It took them long moments to pry Belstin off, and when they did, they heard the splitting of skin and a stench filled the air. The prisoner's intestines laced through the shredded skin.

"Like gheial eels," Yosha said. "The creatures in our village were well named."

They hauled the body of Belstin away from the stench, moving silently, numbly. Mosen said, "The gheials go for the best of us."

"Yes," Yosha said. "But now Belstin is freed! He was always seeing the fiends, but now he is seeing the light."

"Yes, seeing the light!" Mosen repeated, his voice lightening a little. He stopped to rest and everyone stopped with him. "Yes," he said, "Belstin is right now—right now!—seeing the light."

Asel was lying bound among other prisoners. When the guards had dragged Auret in, she had cried out, "Don't handle him like that! Are the Stuugkt so brutal? The man's a cripple!" They had complied; he very slowly humped his way near her and sat beside her in silence.

For some reason she did not understand, she, too, kept silent, wondering at her troubled emotions brought by the dreams. She did not know what she wanted to say to him; with everything flying apart, his nearness steadied her.

An Enre nearby had been conjecturing about the plague rumors. When the woman turned to talk to someone else, Asel said to Auret, "What's happening? Plague. Tarn's annihilation. Terrible things are afoot!"

"Yes, and glorious things," Auret said. "Your prayers are now descending on Aliare with unthinkable judgments."

"What prayers?" she demanded. "Do prayers return as spears and keitr and plague?" She told him of her awakening from her dreams, remembering only shimmering lights and raging creatures. "I wanted desperately to know my dream, but I felt only awe and dread."

"Did you dream of Dorte?" he asked. "Did you dream of sledges atop the great butte?"

As Auret asked questions, she began remembering. The sledges awaited rituals. In the valley below, masses of the damned moved slowly toward them.

"And you were standing at the foot of the butte," Auret said.

Yes, she recalled, in her dreams she had stood waiting as thousands walked toward her, soundless except for their ominous breathing. She had wanted to flee, but they had pressed in from every side. She had turned and touched the sheer butte, fingers scraping against shards of shattered boulders that sloped down and were impossible to climb. She had turned to face them again, her back pressed against the shards.

But as the crowd in the dreams began crushing her against them, one woman jammed against her began singing softly.

Singing! Shimmering images of light appeared. A man sang also, and another woman, and then several more. The voices began to spread in little pockets throughout the vast crowd. Thousands began joining in, singing loudly and militantly—yes, militantly!

Even the Tremblers sang, then lifted boulders, smashed off the shards, and then climbed the butte—right to the very top—where they broke the effigies of hook-beaked birds and alien beasts. They cast the sledges down to the rocks below.

"It was a wondrous dream!" she exclaimed to Auret. "But is it true?"

"Did you think your visit to Dorte worthless?" he asked. "A spark can set off a conflagration."

"But why, then, do I feel catastrophe near? Why do I feel this terrible mixture of joy and gloom?"

"Dorte has vomited its decay," Auret said. "Evil has not burst out—it has been thrust out. And by the Tremblers!" He laughed then, as loudly as Asel had ever heard him laugh. "The Tremblers!" he said again, chuckling. "Ah, how little the fiends expected that!"

Asel tried to join in his laughter but ended with a rattle that died in her throat.

"You have often heard the saying," Auret said, " 'The furies' macabre dance leads to the pit, where they will find worse than themselves.' "

Asel's hands were clenched as tightly as when they had gripped the stone horns. "But what comes of all this?" she said, imploring. "Where is the light? How can you laugh in the time of war and plague?"

"Perhaps we should break out," Kark said. They were in the body of the Spider, placing nets in strategic positions as protection against keitr.

"But I don't trust any of our escape routes," Bralin said. "We don't know what's going on out there—our men who do get out don't come back."

"We know the Stuugkt and Laij are still fighting," Yosha said. "Let's break out in force through the far exits before one or the other gains control and comes after us." He was kneeling next to Maachah, twisting a net's edge into a crevice, when he heard running footsteps surging toward them from two of the escape routes.

Instantly, the men scattered in many directions, each to pre-selected tunnels. Yet as Maachah and Yosha darted into theirs, they had not gone a hundred paces before they heard sounds of advancing troops coming up their escape route.

They turned to race back and select another way, but by the time they were back in the main vault, Hrusc's troops were already about to storm it. They poured in and then spread out into disciplined ranks against the walls, sealing off all escape. Silently, Yosha sprung up on a high ledge and scooted into a shallow depression. What to do? Attacking was futile, but maybe dying that way was preferable to becoming Hrusc's prisoner.

Many hundreds of troops were now in the cave, advancing in the classic maneuver to penetrate every corner of a cavern, long blades making quick, unexpected yet methodical slashes every-where a man might be crouching. Now was the time for Yosha to call for his men to attack. He felt desperately torn. He would gladly die rushing Hrusc's troops, but was charging into certain death a denial of hope? What would Maachah, who rested just a hand's breadth below, say they should do?

Hrusc's voice suddenly boomed into the great cavern. "You men are all prisoners," he said triumphantly. "You may die here, or face Askirit justice."

Yosha retorted bitterly, "It is you who have turned Tarn's justice into mockeries!"

Hrusc laughed. "So say all traitors in all generations. Your many defeats prove your heresies."

Yosha spat at him. "Evil always argues its own purity," he said. "Yet the plague has devastated your troops."

"Not devastated," Hrusc said, his voice less expansive, but just as assured. "The Laij have suffered equally." Then he added with satisfaction, "And in other ways, they suffer far more."

"But how did you get your forces to the crags so quickly?" Yosha burst out. "You were in Aris—"

Hrusc spit and made a loud whistling sound. "Your spies were well informed ... except for what I—and I alone—had planned. Aris was hopeless. Just before sierent, I moved all our troops out, to caves above Aris. The Laij invaded an empty city, full of deadly traps. Then they stormed up the crags, but we devastated them with ambushes. Their numbers are beyond counting, and still they're assaulting the crags. But despite all that, they will fail!"

Yosha then heard Bles proclaim, "And we will regain Aris! We left surprises for them in their shelters, hidden keitrs wrapped and hanging from water clocks. They will release at sierent's peak. The keitr will be rudely dropped, and the Laij can stay with them or run into sierent!" Bles chortled, then added, "Yosha, you have always been on the wrong side of things."

Hrusc said heartily, "And now we no longer have a rebellion to worry about." He was clearly enjoying himself. "We now have many Rycals who will walk the bridge."

Yosha felt rough hands on his legs, jerking him down from his perch. Bonds were tightly affixed to his wrists. He was shoved forward and got his right leg under him just quickly enough to keep himself from falling. They pushed him into a line of prisoners.

Many times Yosha fell as he was rushed over the trails and past many checkpoints on their way to the Skull. He could hear the sounds of battle, but the Stuugkt seemed confident as they hurried the prisoners along. It was almost impossible to navigate the trails with bound hands, but they were shoved and dragged ahead anyway. Blood ran over his right eye from one fall, and his entire body felt bruised. He thought of what Laij soldiers said among themselves: "Never surrender to the Askirit. They will take you to the pit at the end of the world, where begin all the nightmares ever dreamed in Aliare."

When they reached one of the large openings that made up the Skull's eyes, Yosha was shoved forward into a narrow tunnel. It rose steeply, then leveled out as they emerged in the huge cavern. He knew the interior was an erratic series of outcroppings and ridges running around the vast, irregular chasm.

A guard singled him out and started walking him down a narrow ledge, pressing a long, sharp blade against his back. Yosha could try nothing against him here, for the slightest push would surely pitch him off and into the chasm.

The narrow ledge rose a bit, then the guard said, "Stop here." He was told to find a thick pole at his feet. Yosha touched it with his toes, exploring its round surface. "Walk it," the guard ordered.

"It's smooth and slippery!" Yosha protested, knowing that it extended over the pit.

"Then crawl it," the guard said, and pressed the blade against the small of his back. Yosha grasped the pole with both hands and stretched his body out on it, moving forward like a humping worm. Sweat made his hands slippery, and he kept thinking of how his body might slide around the pole and how impossible with these slippery hands it would be to get back on the top of it. He pushed forward mostly with his legs and steadied himself with his wet palms and fingers.

"Move!" the guard ordered. Yosha pushed forward more energetically with his legs, finally touching rock in front of him. He crawled ahead, the solid rock under his chest now, the pole fitted into a slot beneath him. He had hunched himself completely past the pole before the guard demanded, "Are you there yet?"

Yosha tried to work up some spit in his dry mouth and finally swallowed. "Yes," he called out. He heard the pole twist in its slot behind him, then slide away.

With great caution, he began exploring with his fingers the margins of the slabs around him. A small rock skittered away from his foot and then was gone without a sound. He knew that centuries before, the Askirit had chiseled cells into the face of the formations, narrow shelves, barely wide enough for a man to lie down on. Some were so small a prisoner's feet dangled over the edge.

The only way off the cell was by the pole or by falling into the abyss. Prisoners were reminded that even the largest boulder tipped over the edge would never be heard striking bottom. Most of those trapped in the cells tried not to sleep at all, lest they roll off. Yet many fell in the night or soon went mad. Strange sounds from below entered their nightmares with vividly imagined creatures reaching up to suck them from their ledges.

Yosha adjusted his body on the little shelf. He was thankful his legs did not dangle over. Some pebbles under the heel of his hand dug into it, and he reached over with his other hand and pushed them away. They fell off the ledge and began plummeting endlessly.

Yosha heard footsteps approaching on the ledge he had been forced to walk. As they came closer, he realized he was hearing the sounds of Auret's sticks, echoing eerily and disappearing in the massive cavern.

Auret! What did they want to bring that harmless cripple in here for? The clicking sounds kept coming toward him, slowly, grotesquely, growing louder and louder. Finally he heard the guard say, "Stop here." He extended a wide plank across the abyss, then Yosha heard Auret positioning himself in front of it. Finally the guard said firmly, "Move!"

He heard the sticks tapping on the plank as the cripple in his erratic pattern crossed the abyss. When Yosha heard Auret trying to stand in the cell as the plank slid away, he clapped his open palms to his cheeks and clenched his teeth. "I now know," he said aloud, "that the Askirit are as cruel as any barbarian."

The quavery voice in the next cell said simply, "All men are cruel."

Auret began scraping around and positioning his body. "I'm sorry," Yosha said. "I've destroyed you and all the others. I lost Aris, and when I could have taken this accursed Skull, I held back and lost everything." Auret did not respond, and Yosha added, "All the promises! I've believed all the promises! And I burned with seeking that holy light! But again and again, it's been ripped away from me. 'The good man dies, and the cruel man laughs.'"

He waited for Auret to say something, but the cripple was still silent.

Yosha mused, "A child teases another by holding out a firefly, saying, 'Touch it. Go ahead.' Then when the hand goes out, whoosh—the firefly is whisked away, leaving only darkness. Does Eshtel taunt us with light like that, whisking it away?" He shifted his weight and stretched out one leg, but felt it extend over the precipice and drew it back again. "I sought all the holy promises, as intensely as the zeskret rushes after the clestra," he said bitterly. "But our holy war has ended in the pit."

He heard the sound of legs moving in the other cell. Then Auret said, "Every war is a holy war."

Yosha waited for an explanation. When none came, he said, "Shouldn't Eshtel reign over all of Aliare?"

Auret replied, "He already does."

Yosha was about to object vehemently to that declaration when Auret said, "Every day the Holy is pouring down judgment and love, judgment and love, judgment and love. Every day, judgment and love—as surely as every day sierent cleans each crevice in the crags, as surely as sierent bears away the rancid scraps of the village."

Yosha swallowed, shaking his head. He remembered strange things this man had said at other times, and he forced air through tight lips. "How can you say that?" he demanded. "When have you seen judgment and love? The agonies of all Aliare grind our flesh and our souls!"

"We all feel dread," Auret said. "My body screams its messages of fear at me, even now. But the light—"

"The light!" Yosha exclaimed. "I believed in the light! I've truly believed! But where is it?" Yosha's legs were cramping. He put his right palm flat against the wall behind him and slowly stood, pushing his shoulders back against the rock so he would not lean forward. "Judgment and love?" he said. "Then how can you, a cripple, be stuck here, one slip from plummeting into the abyss?"

"I am here," Auret said, "because all through this night on the ledge, I will be praying for you."

Yosha's mind was on the abyss so close to his feet. He could not position himself securely. He kept thinking of creatures that might be coming up to drag him from the ledge.

He fought sleep, dozed off, awoke in a start, then fell asleep again.

He thought he heard something familiar, a voice from very long ago. The voice stirred up deep feelings, yet he was confused by it.

Then he heard clearly, and he understood. His father! It was his father! His voice mixed with the cries of birds rising in the crags; Yosha sensed the smells of hunting. Was that his father's rough arm that had just rubbed over his cheek?

"Yosha!" his father said. "I have always been with you. I have watched what they've done to you."

He tried to speak to his father, but he couldn't. "Yosha, we've got to do something together. Yes, together, you and I. It's Bles. We have him here now. We both know what he did to you, and to me. Bles always hated you. He desecrated my memory! But we have him now. Think of it, Yosha. Now we have Bles."

"Father," Yosha said, longing for him.

"Come down here with me," his father said. "Bles can be damned forever. But we must do it, both of us. Come, Yosha, say it with me. 'Damn you forever, Bles. Damn you forever. Forever. Forever.'"

Yosha called out again, "Father!" But he could get no more words out of his throat. The memories of Bles and his recent encounter with him ignited his outrage, and he envisioned his old enemy tumbling into the abyss.

"Come down here with me," his father commanded. "I have always loved you, Yosha. Now we must curse Bles, for he has always hated us. Damn him forever. Say it, Yosha. 'Damn your soul, Bles. Damn your soul forever.' Come down with me, Yosha. Come down with me."

Yosha found his right leg moving forward, and he felt his father's voice like a wondrous bittersweet memory that would flee away for all time if he did not obey. But his yearning for the light and his father's voice were like two streams of a waterfall, two forces plunging beneath him in a chaos of spumes and spray. "Move forward, Yosha. Come here with me," his father said. "Damn Bles forever—for me. For my memory. Say, 'Damn you, Bles, forever, forever.'"

Yosha moved his lips and opened his mouth, but it was dry, and he could not speak. He coughed and ran his tongue over his lips, tasting salt from his tears. He forced himself to speak. "Bless you, Bles," his voice came out, weak and thick. "Bless you, Bles, forever and forever and forever."

He wearily sank down, his legs splayed out before him, heels of his hands rammed into the pebbles. He kept mouthing the words over his dry lips. "Bless you, Bles," he said again and again, until they blended with another voice close by: "Bless you, Yosha, bless you forever and forever."

It was Auret's voice, weak though full of determination. Yosha then heard him pray, "May we each gather strength, and may we each resist the evils of tomorrow."

—— The Bridge ——

Asel felt the sharp edge of the guard's blade in the small of her back as she stumbled forward. Her hands were bound, but she evaluated her chances should she spin and strike him with her foot. But they had just emerged from the ledge leading away from the cells, and she was still shaky. Her spirit was drenched with the ignominy of the pit. She also knew they were walking along the precipice, and she was not oriented enough to position herself safely.

She heard others moving forward, and then the guard told her to stop. By the echoes and the crowds around her, she realized she was standing on the great lip at the pit's edge. Somewhere close by, the Bridge jutted far out, then extended in a semicircle to reach the farthest edge of the extended lip.

She stood waiting, the blade at her back, until she heard those to her left letting someone through. Hrusc's voice rang out not far from her. "The purity of the Askirit must always be tested," he announced in a loud voice. "Those who say they believe in the light are often traitors who subvert Tarn." With great emotion, he began to describe the evil that had brought the Askirit nation to devastation. "All the prophecies have been fulfilled," he asserted with a booming, nearly weeping voice. "Tarn has fallen to her enemies because of her impurities. But the Bridge has stood for centuries to test those who claim they are righteous. We have today many who make that claim!"

Asel felt a hand on her face, caressing it suggestively. Hrusc chuckled and said with heavy sarcasm, "Varial the Pure." Then in a loud voice he announced, "This so-called Varial has subverted the nation again and again! She has destroyed millennia of tradition by throwing away the purity of Varial and *marrying* . . . marrying a traitor! But she claims purity! So let her prove it by walking the Bridge."

The guard's blade pressed against her back. She thought of

the missing section of the Bridge and wondered how she might cling to its edge.

But as she was being forced to take a step forward, she heard Auret's odd voice, somewhere in the mass of people, calling out, "Hrusc! Hrusc!"

Then she heard the sound of Auret's canes as he moved toward them. "Hrusc, you cannot test Varial first. You must start with the least."

"She is Varial no longer," Hrusc said angrily.

"Perhaps," Auret replied. "But I am surely the least."

At that, Hrusc laughed, a hearty laughter full of snorts and expelled air. "Yes," he said, "you are surely the least in this band of scruffy heretics. Perhaps you also think you are pure enough to walk the Bridge."

Auret said nothing more. Then Asel heard the canes clicking toward her and the sounds of his laboring body, which seemed to her a shambles of suffering limbs. She moved aside, against the constant pressure of the blade at her back.

Auret passed her, and she felt she should object, that she should say something, but no words came. He stood in front of her on the narrow Bridge of stone, no wider than the width of a man's hand. How could the cripple even negotiate the first steps of that narrow rock?

The clicking stopped, and Hrusc said, "Do you need some help?" The clicking sound resumed. It progressed slowly in the pattern she knew so well. Click, pause, click, click, pause, click, click, pause, click, click, moving farther and farther out over the abyss. She had no idea where the missing section was, but as she listened to his laborious progress, she sensed the moment he had passed the angle where the Bridge started to bear back toward the farther edge. The clicks continued, steady, click, pause, click, click.

Then she heard Auret's laugh. It was a crazy, bizarre laugh, otherworldly and inappropriate to this place—high and loud and echoing all through the cavern, pealing back on them in waves as he kept laughing, drowning out the clicks of his canes. Guards and prisoners alike were moving toward the other end of the Bridge, hearing the laughter and straining to hear the clicks.

The guard's blade was tight against her back as she moved toward the laughter, which had suddenly stopped but was now echoing on and out the top of the Skull and up to the roof of Aliare. She heard the clicking again, the same pattern, click, pause, click, click, coming up to the lip where they all stood.

Auret stopped where the Bridge connected with the edge. "Hrusc," the thick, strained voice said, very softly so that Asel could barely hear it, "Hrusc, you, too, are a groping child." He said it not stoically or even sadly, but with such earnest love for the man who hated him that Asel thought, No, it is not possible; he is truly from a different order of things.

But Hrusc spat at him and said, "You used the sticks! Somehow you used the sticks!"

Auret snorted loudly. "All those scraps of integrity you once had," he said, this time with a great sadness in his voice. "But now you are such a rag of a man!"

"The sticks are blasphemous!" Hrusc shouted, and with his heavy staff swung hard, whacking Auret's canes into the air. Asel heard Auret gasp and heard his body turn, then fall onto the Bridge. She heard him scratching and clinging to it with his hands and arms, but then he screamed. His scream plunged with him and went down and down into the bowels of Aliare.

She heard Hrusc move to the edge of the Bridge, and the guard behind her pressed the point of his blade more sharply into her back. Auret's scream kept echoing, growing more and more faint, pulling her senses, it seemed, down with it.

Before the scream had fully faded away, there came a deafening sound above them, as suddenly as a dart hitting the throat—an ear-splitting crack, sharp as a blade, reverberating through the Skull and shaking the foundations under their feet. For an instant, the entire ceiling of their world shuddered in serpentine undulations. Instantaneous with the sound came something alien invading the Skull, something sharp and penetrating, a thin shaft of brilliant white light, which sheared the air and shocked the eyes, illumining the dark figures on the ledge, striking the Bridge, and plunging into the pit.

Screams and shouts rose in a chaos of terrified guards and prisoners rushing away from the light. Asel was knocked flat by them; someone stumbled over her as he ran from the precipice. She looked at the shaft of light from above, bright white against the shadows of black figures fleeing away from the chasm. She stood fully upright and shouted in exultation, "The Light! The Light! Enre! Askirit! The Light! Now is the time!"

But as she called out, she heard only fleeing feet and a great howling confusion. She blinked her eyes and looked not directly at the light, but at the entrance to the Skull, and saw vaguely the running figures fleeing into the darkness . . . people, she thought, whose eyes had strained for light all their lives.

Hrusc started cursing at his men. "Stuugkt!" he shouted, "The light is for us!" But the whine of fear in his voice betrayed him. Asel sensed even the guards next to him were backing away.

"This is our moment," Hrusc declared, his voice a parody of a bold commander. "Do not fear the light!" He stepped unsurely toward it and the pit's edge. Squinting, Asel could see his dark figure standing bent and diffuse against the brilliance. Tremors started again beneath their feet. As she watched, Hrusc collapsed onto his knees, making a loud pleading sound just as new tremors shook them. Asel was flung forward. Hrusc disappeared from where he had been standing. She heard his horrified cry for just a moment, and then it was gone into the depths.

Yosha barely saw the great shaft of light before he was knocked down in the melee. Gripping the floor, he turned to look again, his eyes mere slits against the intolerable brightness. He shielded his eyes and looked around but saw only wild motions of dark figures.

He had always sought and loved the light; but what was this penetrating force jarring his senses? What brought about that terrible crack through the roof of his world, exposing him to this alien brightness? Always that roof had been as ageless a reality as the crags and sierent and the birds in flight. Always he had sung of the light and longed for it, thinking it would come like the scents of the feasts, lifting, energizing, filling him with power and purity. Now, his view of the world had been shattered.

He tried again to look at it. Why did he feel so helpless? Was he still disoriented from his sleepless night on the ledge? He had heard Asel's shout, full of confidence, full of joy. How could she rejoice at this searing brilliance?

He forced himself to move forward toward it. What would it be like to touch it? Would it sear his hand? He crawled, not trusting himself to stand so close to the precipice. He reached the Bridge where the shaft of light descended stark and dominant, hurting his eyes. He trembled as he slowly moved his hand, palm up, toward this living blade of light that sliced its way through the blackness to the depths of the abyss.

His fingertips touched it. He felt nothing, but he saw flesh-colored nimbuses of light, diffused images of his fingers as he moved them further into the rays. He thrust his hand fully in and saw its fuzzy, lighted shape. He lifted his hand high into it and looked beneath to see the darkness of the shadow cast below his hand.

"Yosha!" Someone was shouting his name. He turned and called back, recognizing Maachah's voice. "Shot through with light!" Maachah shouted exuberantly. "All Aliare shot through with it! The light exposes all. Furies and Stuugkt are wriggling shadows. The light is here!"

Yosha moved his fingers in the bright rays, squinting against the terrible brightness, turning his hand and saying, "It has split the world! It came upon us like ute."

Maachah knelt beside him. "And it destroyed Hrusc!" he said. "The prophecies came true! Hrusc was a salted slug!"

Maachah boldly plunged his arm into the light, then touched Yosha's fingers, moving his own back and forth, bobbing them up and down, making shadows.

The old priest sensed Yosha's quietness. "Did you think light would be like scented balm?" he asked. "Light is astringent! It uncovers. It purifies. It cauterizes the soul!" He stood, brushed pebbles from his hand, euphorically called out to someone, and walked away.

Yosha again shielded his eyes from the brilliance and tried to decipher the shapes and movements around him. He noticed a very small figure moving toward the precipice and the shaft of light. The figure was obscure, but he decided it must be the child, Nen.

He saw him move closer to the edge, and, alarmed, Yosha quickly moved on all fours toward the boy. He was almost at its edge when Yosha caught him by the leg and pulled him back. The child gave a cry of annoyance and tried to twist away. "Nen, I don't want you to fall. You can put your hand into the light— but you are right at the edge."

The boy settled against him and thrust his hand forward. A little burp-like laugh erupted from the child as he twisted his hand around and up and down. Then he thrust both hands in.

As he watched the boy's hands playing in the light, the simplicity of his movements and his sense of wonder brought Yosha his own joy. Something deep within urged him to trust what he saw and felt. All of it was true! The promises were being fulfilled. The light, and all it stood for, was more than imagination.

The boy and the man lay squinting at the pit's edge for long moments, their four hands bending and arching and playing in the phenomenon they had always dreamed of.

But then Yosha noticed that the light seemed to be getting dimmer. Or was the shaft more narrow? He held out both his hands and saw that it now cut a swathe across his palms instead of lighting his entire hand and arm. The shaft was clearly narrowing.

Nen moved his fingers under the light, held securely by Yosha and seemingly content to sit entranced forever. But then the light narrowed to a line the width of a child's finger until, slowly, it became only a hair's breadth, which then disappeared like the cry of a bird in the wind.

Yosha sat staring at the place on his hand where the line had been. His world was back to the way it had been all his life, yet it was not at all the same. As he stared, trance-like, he felt Nen moving under his arm, as if he were struggling with something.

The boy held out an object before him, and as the little arm moved out of the way, Yosha saw a small glow. He was holding the carrion beetle; it was nestled in the rags he had always used to wash Auret's head wounds, and Yosha thought he saw in those rags an expansion of the beetle's glow. Perhaps, he thought, it was the effect of the blinding light on his eyes.

"We must go to the light," Nen said as they stared at the glow.

"Yes," Yosha agreed. "We must always be seeking the light. And now we have seen it."

"He has told me the way," the boy said.

"Who has told you the way?"

"Auret. He told me the way to the light above."

Yosha chuckled kindly and stroked the child's arm. "And where did he say the way might be found?"

"Through the pit."

Chapter 12.

───── Above ─────

Asel sat beside Yosha, a stream rushing over her feet. She said, "This stream can't be fed by sierent. We've been following it upward for days, and it's stayed the same size. It must come from above."

"And it's cold," Yosha said, "colder than any stream in Aliare. We must be very near the light."

They had taken all who would join them, former Stuugkt guards and children, Enre and priests, all who so greatly desired the light they were willing to brave the descent into the abyss. "The ultimate absurdity," Asel mused: "all of us led into the devouring pit by a child."

"I expected every ledge to crumble under our feet," Yosha said. "It seemed a slithering decay was always reaching for us. I can still smell it."

"But we lost no one!" Asel exclaimed. "And now we're so far above the abyss, so far even above Tarn, the light cannot be far. If we could swim upstream like fish," she said, "we could reach the light today!" She jiggled her feet rapidly in the stream; droplets sprayed on his legs.

"Can you imagine those who were born in the light?" Yosha asked. "How they must stop in wonder all the time? How can they do anything but stand and stare all the day?"

Asel clucked her tongue rapidly, making the sign for good things just ahead. "Out of the wreckage, hope," she quoted.

"With the changes we are feeling in the air, it cannot be too much higher."

Asel saw them first. She was just ahead of Yosha, pulling herself up a slippery place edged with dirt. In the blackness, the phenomena pulsed like sparks from flint, a little swathe of them in the opening above her. She fixed her eyes hungrily on them, exclaiming, "Light!" and started pulling herself eagerly up. Her foot slipped in the dirt, and she fell back a little on Yosha, who pushed her forward, then boosted her rapidly up through the opening. Their companions were close behind them.

They looked up to millions of diffused pinpricks of light against blackness, bright ones, pulsating ones, and millions so tiny they created vast clouds of light spread across the heavens. They stared, on hands and knees, until Yosha turned and rolled over on his back, looking up at the universe above them studded with lights. They seemed alive, coruscating, shifting. Yosha moved his eyes from one horizon slowly across the great expanse to the other side, and then around the vast perimeter. It was as if the entire roof of the world was alive with stars and light, all magnificently, benevolently shining down at him.

Asel rolled beside him, seeing bright stars standing out in unfamiliar but intriguing patterns. All the childhood stories of the light came back to her in a rush, and she lifted her arms to receive this wondrous universe above her. A fuzzy half-circle of yellow light hung among the stars, an arc that seemed a pendant for the shapes of white in the blackness. "Yosha, it's like thousands of flints, but shining down on us, steady, not dying out in an instant but glorious—more glorious than all the stories we have ever heard."

They lay on their backs, close together, staring, drawing in the light for their eyes and souls, others passing them as they also climbed out and drank in their own visions of these wonders. The air was dry and full of strange scents, teasing their nostrils, but they thought little of that as they looked at the stars, majestic, brilliant, exultant.

A little breeze sprang up and became for a moment a brisk wind. "Sierent," Yosha said. "It's good we're near the place we came out."

"Yes," said Asel, shivering a little as they stood, Yosha's hand on her shoulder. "But some say there is no sierent here."

"We've also heard we won't need to walk with our hands outstretched, groping," Yosha said. The light outlined the black branches of a large tree. As they started walking toward it, staring at its thick branches and the thin arcs of smaller ones above, they both felt a vague spatial disorientation. The branches were etched flat against the sky, and suddenly Yosha's foot struck the tree's trunk. They stood there awkwardly. They looked again at the night sky; the horizon was oddly curved, with faint wavy lines rising from it.

They sat down and tried to orient themselves. The branches and bushes against the lighted sky were distorted and flat, but they could not understand nor describe why their exultant feelings were being invaded by a sense of dismay.

He thought of the ancient imponderable used in the initiation of priests: "Can a bird swim in the depths of the sea? Can you who have lived in darkness walk in the light above?" He began to wonder if they belonged here.

Something like a ghostly afterimage moved on the periphery of his vision. He turned his head and squinted at a dark form barely visible nearby. He stood, but was afraid to approach it without putting out his hand, so he stepped forward, fingers outstretched.

A voice greeted him, familiar yet completely changed. "You need not grope in the light," the voice said. It was Auret.

Asel leaped to her feet. "Auret!" she said, and moved toward him. She reached out to touch his face, moving her fingers slowly over his eyes and across the faint traces of the old wounds. "Auret!"

"You will find the light far better than being Varial or queen," he said. "But here, you will face fire and ice."

Without so much as a limp, he led them to a knoll where they sat down. Yosha said, "The tale was right. You really are the son who slid into ute."

Asel was holding Auret's arm, feeling the strength of it. "You fell from the Bridge," she said, "with screams of death echoing, it seemed, forever...."

"The way was always through sacrifice," he said. "But death is not forever."

They sat on the knoll and spoke of Aliare and light. Yosha declared that the stars had made him see for the first time. "The light nourishes my eyes and my soul as if I were newborn!"

"Though you kept your eyes alive with the sparks," Auret said, "you are not yet ready for the light of the day. It would be a terror to you, as it was in the Skull. You would see but not see, for you have known only the night."

He reached over to both of them and placed his hands on their eyes. "You must be ready to see clearly how dawn splits the oceans of darkness." He held his hands on their eyes for a moment, then moved them down their faces in the gentle, wave-like motion the Askirit use to signal the deepest love. "You must be ready for the dawn. But it will take new eyes." He put his hand under Yosha's chin and lifted it heavenward, and then did the same to Asel.

They looked up to see the once soft and diffused constellations standing out boldly now. The brightest stars were sharply defined against the black, and thousands of additional stars had miraculously appeared. The clouds of distant suns were whiter, and the golden half-orb a clear yellow pendant, lightly shadowed.

"What of the others who came with us?" Asel asked, "Breea and Mosen, Maachah and the children.... They, too, must be made to see."

"I will find every one of them," Auret said, "and touch their eyes—if they are willing."

* * *

Asel and Yosha lay on their backs staring at the heavens. Out of the corner of his eye, Yosha was startled by a flare of light nearby. He turned his head and saw an orange flame brighter than anything in the blackness above. It cast shadows on the hands of Auret, who was holding a branch into it. The flame grew, rising from the ground and spreading into many flames. Yosha touched Asel's cheek and she turned her head toward him. Flared by the wind, the flames leaped into the air, like fingers rushing up, then separating and falling away.

"Fire can warm, or destroy," Auret said. He poked the fire, lofting showers of sparks into the night. Asel was entranced by the flames, as if they were living souls enacting a drama before them; she wanted to compose a song or make up a tale. Yosha started to reach out and touch them, but Auret warned him so that they simply held their hands close, marveling at the fire's warmth and how welcome it would have been in the darkness and chill of Aliare.

Asel caught a whiff of a familiar fragrance in the smoke and commented on it. "Wood from a fruit tree," Auret said. "Fire casts a fragrance as it consumes."

Yosha was absently-mindedly moving his fingers back and forth in front of the flames; the motion reminded him of the times he had sat like this with his fingers exploring the carved faces of his parents. He longed to have his most precious possession with him now, so that he could actually see their faces and compare their illumined features with the images in his mind. "How I wish I could have brought to the light the carving of my mother and father," he said.

"You will not need it here," Auret said kindly. "Your children would cherish it; your children's children would venerate it; and their children might be tempted to worship it."

Thinking of his parents had filled Yosha's eyes with tears.

His voice was edged with uncertainty as he said, "My father believed in the light. He would never have asked me to curse another."

Auret threw another branch into the fire. It flared up, and he said, "Look into the flames, Yosha."

He stared at them, shapes of brilliant, living light. A figure seemed to be running. It was a man, yet not a man, a being of firm substance, yet full of a flashing glory. A large bird glided past his shoulder, then flapped away. The man ran forward again and leaped upon an animal that reared back, then pranced away with a spirited whinny. The animal began racing upward into the height of the flames, turning as it did so toward Yosha. The man was turning his face toward him, looking intently into Yosha's eyes with both yearning and joy so that Yosha thought, Surely this is my father!

"You will join him some day in the light," Auret said. "You will touch his face, and the face of your mother. You will speak of many things. Together, you will hear the cries of birds, and you will know the joy of speed and wind and flight. But not yet. Some day you will be changed, as your eyes were changed."

"Soon?" Yosha asked.

"You have much to do here," Auret said.

Asel forced herself to ask, "And Rycal? Will he be changed?"

"Have you forgiven him?" Auret asked.

She flushed and said, "Only you can answer that."

Asel watched Auret's smile widen as he said, "*You* are answering it now, deep within yourself."

She nodded. She wondered whether to announce now to Yosha the secret she had been harboring. "I am with child," she said. "The past is a different world."

The man from the light reached both his hands to her belly and blessed her and the infant she carried. "Many births are coming," he promised. "The birth of your child. The birth of new wonders."

Asel, full of awe, placed her own hands on the life within her and said, "Already the child moving within fills me with wonder and hope."

Auret's hands, once crabbed and shaking, reached over and joined themselves powerfully with hers, resting them on the baby. "Birth and wonders come with fears and blood and pain," he said. "But your faith will lead to the greater birth . . . your own birth into a new body and another world."

Yosha was smiling. The fire had burned down to pulsing red embers. He stirred them, lofting more sparks, and asked, "What will happen now in Tarn?"

"And in Dorte?" Asel added.

"Unexpected marvels," Auret replied. He chuckled and said, "I will ask Delin if he wants to return to Dorte." Asel thought she could see in the dim light smile lines on his face as he said, "Remember, I promised him I would take him back—if he wanted to go."

"Perhaps we should all be carrying fire and light down to Aliare," Yosha said.

"But they would not believe us," Asel said. "Unless we can bring the lights of the heavens with us, they will laugh at our tales."

"As most always have," Auret said. "But not all. Not all. . . ."

Yosha put on additional branches to coax new flames. They stared into the growing fire until it lessened and once again died down to embers. Then they rolled on their backs again to look at the lights above, entranced by the limitless expanse of bright white against black. Never once through all the long night did either feel the slightest sleepiness.

"Yosha," Asel said, gently turning his head with her hand. "What is the little glow?" They looked at the black horizon and saw a light they had not noticed before.

It grew, spreading rays of colored light into the sky. It was red and yellow, but it grew brighter and brighter and suddenly became at its core a white light with many colors flooding from it. It quickly grew too bright to look at, and as they turned their heads, they saw the stars fading, overpowered by color spreading from that radiance.

They squinted against the brightness, not knowing how to describe to each other the wonders. The sky was becoming blue, many shades of blue, with vermilion and gold spreading across it through patches of white edged with gray. The gray contrasted with the vermilion and gold, making them richer, more vivid. Rays of red light shot from the hot center, slicing into the sky, arcing above them to the opposite horizon.

The stars were gone, replaced by a sky constantly changing. White clouds, banked in ridges, marched from the sun, floating on a sea of vivid red. Above them, clouds with rich, dark blues— great swaths of them—floated like lambent islands. Then, moments later, there were pastels. Pinks and light blues against the far horizon. The sky was like a living thing to Asel and Yosha.

"Auret," Yosha said, "how could we have imagined the dawn? It is thousands of dawnbreakers in flight, made of brightness and color." But when he reached over to touch his friend, Auret was not there.

They felt the air warming. They lowered their eyes from the heavens and saw hills in the distance and the greens of grasses and trees, all in depth and clarity.

Auret had been with them, and now he was gone. For a moment his departure felt like bereavement to Asel. But soon there flowed into her such a sense of praise for Auret and his love for them that she lifted her body and spun into a graceful Askirit dance, her feet lightly springing from the grass, her arms high above her head. She danced to the Maker of light, her spirit full of praises for all he had made: trees thick with leaves and trees slender and young, mountains white in the distance and hills close at hand, birds in flight and birds darting past, all in colors she could never have imagined. She felt a remarkable lightness and energy, dancing exuberantly, leaping like a child and spinning with abandon down a little hill by a creek.

Yosha's eyes were on her, full of the wonder of her body, the body he had often held but never perceived like this. Her beauty in the dance seemed as wonderful to him as the brilliance of the dawn. She spun on one foot in a full circle, then leaped across the stream, landing and then running in a burst that took her to the top of a little hill, where she raised her arms wide to her new world, light glinting off highlights in her hair.

He touched the petals of a bright purple flower, then ran his fingers down its stiff, thorny stem. He sniffed its fragrance, and felt a wave of nostalgia and recognition. In Aliare such fragrances came from bits in the sea. He closed his eyes and breathed its fragrance deeply, then looked down at the magical petals rippling in the breeze.

Asel felt the texture of the deep-green grass. An insect climbed aboard her forearm and began clambering over the tiny hairs. It was all sharp angles, a triangle head balanced atop high, ungainly legs. Its black body contrasted with bold red slashes down its back, with a bright green check on top of its head.

A flash of color darted past Yosha with a bold call. His eyes followed the bird to the stream's edge, where it flitted to a thin branch to pick at a white berry, then down again to the water, and finally off toward the hills as if on urgent business.

Asel sat beside Yosha, looking into his face, seeing clearly his eyes, his cheeks, his lips. She had brought the insect to him, and when he saw it tumble from the little hairs of her forearm onto its back, its legs rotating and turning frantically, Yosha's face turned into a huge smile. The smile lit up his features, stunning Asel. Previously, in the darkness of Aliare, her fingers had felt the creases of a smile on Yosha's face, the lifting of the cheeks, the lips raised and stretched slightly over the teeth, the little creases near his mouth. But looking into his smiling face, she felt like a different dawn had come, as if all the blossoms of the flowers she had been sniffing had opened and come to life, awakening in her a deep sense of joy and awe.

Yosha's eyes had turned from the struggling insect to Asel's eyes. She was looking deeply into his, and he sensed their power. He felt as if he were looking into her depths in a way he never could have before—that within those wondrous, living eyes of rich brown and minute flecks of gold was a creature alien from him but also a creature at one with him, inviting him to partake of mysteries. No wonder, he thought, that in the darkness we have sung about the eyes and touched them only as holy things, containing the very essence of life. He leaned toward her and grazed her lips lightly with his. She smiled, her face alight. "I cannot stop looking into your eyes," he said. "They open a path between us."

They looked up as a cloud blocked the light, its dark underside contrasted against the white and blue. "The light is more a living thing than the rituals could ever tell us," Asel said.

"Look at the way it plays on the ripples over the rocks," Yosha said, "hundreds of sparkles rushing like birds, with the brook nudging the reeds at the edge. The light seems to search out every cranny, every stone, and transform it, sometimes with a sparkle, sometimes with a color so rich—"

"Yosha," Asel interrupted, "could we have imagined so many colors and so many varieties of the same colors, dark and light, soft and brilliant, lustrous and shadowy? It fills me with new yearnings. I want to leap across those hills, to reach up to the birds, to grab the soft colors floating in the sky and pull them down. I yearn to be like the sky—alive with light and color and Eshtel's glory."

"Look over there," Yosha said, "our friends—Maachah and Breea and Bralin and Kark. Come on. I want to see their faces; I want to look into their eyes."

They walked briskly toward them, anxious to join their friends. "They're all there," Asel said, "I see Mosen and Solket and Delin and Nen—up where the light strikes the butte and casts a shadow."